THE GOLDEN WOOD

OTHER TITLES BY WILLIAM D. BURT

The King of the Trees
Torsils in Time
The Greenstones
The Downs
Kyleah's Mirrors
The Birthing Tree

The Lake Lights
The Vikings of Loch Morar

THE GOLDEN WOOD

BOOK THREE

The King of the Trees series

By

WILLIAM D. BURT

Author of the King of the Trees
and Creation Seekers series

~Published by Creation Way Books~
An imprint of KOT Books, LLC
13058 Donald Rd NE
Aurora, OR 97002

First edition 2002
Second edition 2023

Published by: Creation Way Books, an imprint of KOT Books, LLC
13058 Donald Rd NE, Aurora, OR 97002

Printed in the United States of America.

Cover by Terri L. Lahr
Illustrated by Terri L. Lahr and Rebecca J. Burt.

The author is solely responsible for the design, content and editorial accuracy of this work.

ISBN-13—978-0-9983079-5-4

"... and it came about, that if a serpent bit any man, when he looked to the bronze serpent, he lived."

Numbers 21:9 (NASB)

For my beloved wife, Johnnie,
who made room in her life for Lucambra.

CONTENTS

MAP OF BEECHTOWN AND ITS ENVIRONS
As Seen From a Griffin's Point of View

MAP OF NORTHERN LUCAMBRA
During the Reign of King Rolin and Queen Marlis

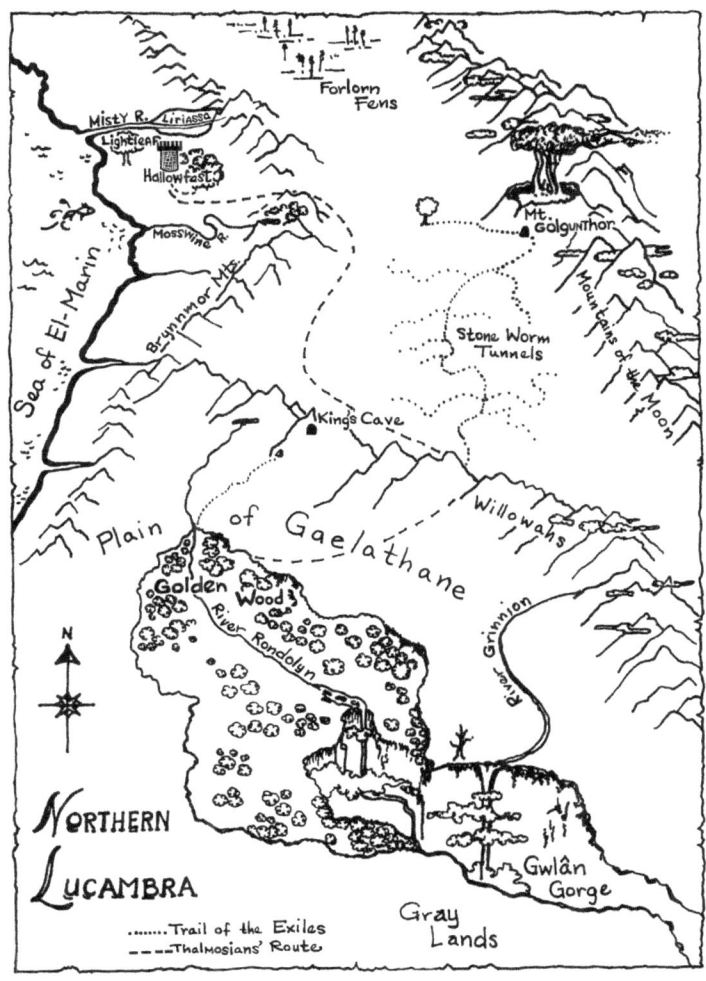

PROLOGUE: THE VISION

Bathed in sweat, Rolin son of Gannon jerked awake. Was it a dream, or had the King of the Trees just left him a message? Shakily, he slipped out of bed and went to the table by the open window. Sure enough, sixteen lines of spidery script gleamed on the polished tabletop, as if engraved by moonbeams. Before the fiery, flowing words could fade away, Rolin copied them onto a parchment sheet. Then he spread his hands over the table in hopes to preserve the writing until Queen Marlis could see it. At his touch, the letters blazed up, searing themselves into his mind. Rolin staggered backward as a long, shuddering *BOOM* shook his soul and splintered his senses. The disquieting sound disturbed his dreams for nights afterwards.

THE GOLDEN WOOD
PART I
FARMER GANNSON

CHAPTER 1
The Shattered Spasel

P apa, I'm bored," fussed Meghan, playing with the buttons on her father's green tunic. "It's raining and the griffins are too sick to fly." Her innocent gaze wandered around the Hallowfast's throne room before coming to rest on a bank of tall cupboards. Her eyes brightening, she asked, "May we look at some of your spasels?" She dimpled at Rolin and batted her eyelids.

Seated on his throne, the king laughed. His daughter's pixie moods never failed to pluck his heartstrings. "Of course we may, *cariad*," he replied. After Meghan hopped off his lap, he unlocked and opened one of the cupboards and searched among its crate-crammed shelves until he found a box labeled *THALMOS*.

"Here we are," he said, setting the box on the floor. "Now that the torsils are leafing out, maybe we'll see something of Beechtown in one of these." He smiled at Meghan. "Go ahead, open it."

Meghan lifted the lid off the box. Inside it, twelve glassy balls of assorted shades and sizes nestled in separate niches like so many dragon's eggs. Meghan's mouth made a breathless "O" as she leaned over the box, her flaxen hair spilling into it. Removing the darkest of the polished balls, she held it up in a sunbeam, where it glowed like liquid amber. She selected another of the spheres and frowned at its misshapen, flattened bottom.

"Why isn't this one round, Papa?" she asked, her sea-green eyes and pert mouth pouting.

King Rolin chuckled. "I haven't turned these spasels for several months and some of them have 'melted' a little."

"Melted?"

"Why, yes. They may feel as solid as glass, but the torsil sap they're made of still flows slowly, even in this cool room."

"Like that candle I left on my shelf?"

"Just like the candle," Rolin agreed. A few months earlier, Meghan had molded a crude candle out of beeswax. Now it was drooping like a snow-burdened fir.

A shadow passed across Meghan's face. "How can we unmelt them? I want to see what Grandfather Gannon is doing on the other side. Maybe he's lonely and missing me."

Her father tossed the lopsided sap ball into the air and deftly caught it. "Where is it written in all the lore of Lucambra that spasels must be round?" he said archly. "They're only more compact that way and the images are truer. I think it's high time I taught you the finer points of spasel care." Holding the ball with its bottom facing Meghan, he pointed to the flat underside.

"If Bembor and I didn't turn these spasels every so often, they'd all look like this. Once they've 'puddled out,' it's well-nigh impossible to restore them to their original shapes. That's why we give each one a quarter turn when it's starting to settle, like this." Rolin returned the ball to its compartment, flat side facing left. "Now you try it."

After turning several of the spasels, Meghan pounced on a reddish, potato-sized specimen. "Which one is this?" she asked.

"If I'm not mistaken, that is one of Lightleaf's. It should give us a good view of the valley below." Rolin felt a twinge of homesickness as he recalled his many happy hours spent combing Beechtown's hills and vales for herbs and mushrooms.

Meghan put the ball to her eye. "I don't see anything."

Her father smiled. "Of course not. You have to warm it first."

With puffed cheeks, Meghan lustily blew on the spasel. Gradually, a creamy fog curdled in its center, giving way to bright, swirling colors like wind-spun showers of autumn leaves.

Anxious to view what new scenes the spring's first spasel-warming might reveal, Rolin peered over his daughter's shoulder. "What do you see?" he asked her.

Meghan's nose wrinkled. "Just a big, shiny snake. I don't like snakes, Papa, 'specially big ones."

"Neither do I," said Rolin, staring into the spasel. Sure enough, a silvery serpent was winding through it, flanked by familiar landmarks. The "snake" was at least a mile long.

Lucambra's king rubbed his eyes and looked again. Recoiling in shock, he accidentally knocked the spasel out of Meghan's hands, sending it to shatter on the floor in a hail of shards.

"Oh, no!" Meghan wailed. "It's broken!" Her face shrank into a tearful mask of misery.

"I'm sorry," said her father as he swept up the fragments. "Don't worry, my sweet. We have lots more Thalmos spasels. Now run along and play with your brother and sister." He pulled on a long, gold cord dangling beside his throne. Somewhere in the Hallowfast's bowels, a deep-voiced gong sounded, and footsteps clattered up the tower stairs. Then two green-cloaked men burst through the door.

"Hail, Gemmio and Opio," Rolin greeted the brothers, who were among his most trusted advisors. "Is all well in my kingdom?"

"All is well, sire," said Gemmio, the taller of the two.

"I hope you've summoned us here on urgent business," grumbled Opio, panting heavily. "It's a long climb up those steep stairs, and you interrupted a fine game of chess."

"One that you were winning," Gemmio dryly reminded him.

"The exercise will strengthen your lungs for flute-playing, Opio," Rolin retorted. "Now, I'd like you both to go to Beechtown at once."

"The torsils are scarcely in leaf yet, and the spring market is still weeks away!" Opio protested.

"I realize that," Rolin growled. "I'm not sending you to Thalmos for sewing needles or cooking pots! Meghan and I just had a look-see into one of Lightleaf's spasels. There's trouble brewing in Beechtown." Then he described the sap ball's images.

The brothers blanched. "What would you have us do?"

"I need your eyes and ears there. After you find out who is stirring things up, bring me back a report. In the meantime, try to stay out of mischief. I've bailed you out of enough scrapes already!" The brothers nodded, their hoods flouncing like jack-in-the-pulpit blossoms.

"Very good," said Rolin. "By the way, if you see my father, give him my love and tell him to stay out of Beechtown until all this has blown over. He'll be safe with his bees up in the hills."

Once Opio and Gemmio had departed, Rolin returned to the box of spasels. With shaking hands, he lifted out another sap ball and warmed it gently with his breath.

CHAPTER 2
King Mardoc

Make way for the king! Make way! Make way!"
Timothy son of Garth shrank back into the crowds of
townspeople gawking at the endless, snakelike procession
of mail-clad men-at-arms. Sunlight glinted off their armor, shields
and spearheads. After a dreary winter, Timothy had been longing for
some excitement, but this was more than he had bargained for.

"Make way, I tell you!" A burly guard jabbed the butt of his spear
into Timothy's ribs, shoving him back into his father.

"There's no call for that—" Garth began, when the soldier expertly
reversed his spear and thrust its point against Garth's chest.

"No call for *what*, peasant?" sneered the man. When Timothy's
father courteously lowered his head, the surly guard moved on, poking
and prodding his way south along Beechtown's East River Road.

Timothy groaned and held his sore side. "What did I do to upset
that fellow, anyway?" he wondered aloud.

"Thugs don't need an excuse for throwing their weight around,"
his father replied, pulling him away from the cobbled street. "If this is
how King Mardoc treats his subjects, he'll find a chilly reception here!
Let's go home. I've seen enough."

"I haven't!" Timothy searched his father's stern, craggy face. A
tinker in the winter and a river raftsman the rest of the year, Garth
rarely raised his voice—or his hand—in anger. Now his jaw knotted
with a simmering fury at the guard's callous cruelty, but his honest
eyes spoke only of fear.

That April morning had begun much like any other until twelve
blaring trumpet blasts had rudely awakened the town. People
streamed out of their shops and houses to goggle at the soldiers
marching by, clinking and clanking in their bulky armor.

Timothy tugged on his father's tunic. "I'll stay off the main streets, I promise!" he declared. "These men must be bound for the square, and if I take some shortcuts there, I'll have my pick of the best spots. Don't you want to find out what's happening?"

Garth rubbed his stubbly face. "Very well, but keep out of sight! Those soldiers are spoiling for a fight."

Timothy bobbed his head as he darted down an alley. Ordinarily, he would be in mortal terror of running into Baglot son of Baldwyn, a hulking, shaggy-haired bully with close-set eyes who took delight in bloodying Timothy's nose—when he could catch him. Happily, today Baglot had bigger fish to fry; Timothy had spied his nemesis picking the pockets of unwary onlookers.

His buttonless tunic flapping in the wind, Timothy veered onto Baker's Street, arriving at the town square to find it bristling with spear-toting soldiers and curious townspeople. In hopes of gaining a better view, he shinnied up a maple tree near the gushing yeg fountain in the middle of the square.

Mayor Bigglesworth had erected this garish monstrosity as a memorial to the brief but bloody Battle of Beechtown, when many brave citizens had lost their homes and some their lives. His Excellency the mayor had lost neither. Now he stood hatless in the morning sun as a horse-drawn, red-and-gold carriage clattered up to the fountain. A sword-wielding soldier threw open the carriage door and reedily announced, "His Majesty, King Mardoc!"

Out of the carriage popped a rotund, dazzling figure. Timothy counted three ample chins wobbling beneath the king's soft mouth. A gleaming gold crown sat on his hoary head, matching his gilded robes. Bigglesworth blanched.

"Bow before His Majesty, King Mardoc!" snarled one of the burly men-at-arms, shoving the mayor to his knees.

"Whom are we addressing?" rumbled the king, waving his pudgy hand at the trembling dignitary.

"My name is Bigglesworth. I'm the mayor of this fair city."

"I've seen fairer pig sties," sniffed the king. His guards elbowed one another and guffawed.

The mayor's lips tightened. "For what purpose has His Majesty honored Beechtown with his august presence today?"

Mardoc's fat-rimmed eyes glittered. "We are not obliged to answer our subjects' impertinent questions. However, since this is our first meeting, we will tell you that the crown is here to collect the tribute due it from your backward hamlet."

The mayor's face crumpled. "Tribute? What tribute?"

The king snapped his fingers and a reedy servant with a hooked nose and black tunic unfolded from the carriage. Unrolling a crisp parchment, he read through his nose, "In the annals of His Majesty Mardoc, King of Nebo, Knight of the Square Table, Monarch of the Tartellans and of all lands hereabouts, Sovereign of all he surveys—" The reader paused for a breath. "The backwater municipality known as 'Beechtown' is in arrears in the amount of seven thousand, three hundred gilders."

The mayor scrambled to his feet and sputtered, "Seven—*seven* thousand . . . three hundred . . . gilders! That's a king's ransom!"

"Or in this case, a mayor's," the king smoothly replied with a meaningful arch of a plucked eyebrow. "The crown has received no tribute from you in more than forty years."

A string of broken words tumbled out of Bigglesworth's mouth. "Nobody knew—we've never heard—I'd never imagined—why, it's completely unreasonable to expect—"

"You are refusing to pay, then?" the king said in a silky voice. The mayor wilted under his glowering gaze.

"It's not a matter of refusal, Your Highness. It's only that we are unable to afford such a large sum all at once without depleting the town treasury. We recently exhausted our funds to rebuild after a dragon burned Beechtown to the ground."

A sly smile creased the king's oily face. "Ah, yes. The dragon. News of his rampage has reached our ears. You are to be commended for vanquishing the vile worm." The mayor drew himself up, and the yeg sprayed the back of his bald head.

Mardoc's eyes roved over the mayor's lavish residence, a towered mansion sprawling beside the square. "We are also pleased to see how quickly you have recovered from this disaster. T'would be a pity if all your work went up in smoke again." The king's finger twitched and a mounted torchbearer clop-clopped across the cobbles to set the mayor's front door afire.

—

Bigglesworth sagged against the pool ringing the fountain. "What do you want from me?" he whimpered, his face mottled white and red.

The king daintily waved a lace-trimmed kerchief at the torch-bearer, who doused the blaze with a bucket of water. "I believe that we understand each other now," said Mardoc. "It is in our mutual interest to clear up this matter as quickly as possible. I am referring to the hoard, of course." He looked very hard at Mayor Bigglesworth, whose fleshy face went positively blank.

"Hoard?" he squeaked. "What hoard?"

King Mardoc's squat neck flushed a rosy pink. "You know, gold, jewels, coins, that sort of thing. After a dragon's death it is customary to plunder the dragon's hoard."

A crafty gleam lit the mayor's eye. "We only drove off the dragon. Even if we had killed him, there's no telling where his hoard might lie." The king's servants glanced worriedly up at the sky, as if the dragon might drop in unannounced.

Mardoc swelled up like a frightened toad. "Nonetheless, don't tell us you rebuilt this town with potato paste and straw! Even your gold-plated fountain here bespeaks great riches. Either you discovered the serpent's stash or you know who did. If you're holding out on us, we'll have you thrown into the royal dungeons, where the royal rats will whittle you down to size!"

Timothy grinned to himself. The king's shrewd guess had come perilously close to the mark. Pricked to his core, Mayor Bigglesworth deflated like a ruptured jellyfish. "Perhaps we should talk about this matter someplace, er, more *private*, don't you think, Your Highness?" he croaked, wringing his hands.

The king nodded, greed glinting in his eyes. "That we shall, that we shall. First, however, we must arrange a proper welcome from our beloved subjects. Herald, see to it."

A barrel-chested servant decked in scarlet stepped forward and bellowed, "May all present within the hearing of my voice heed these words. At the sound of my trumpet, let every man and woman, youth and child bow down before His Magnificence, King Mardoc, Lord of Nebo, or know the sting of his displeasure." With that, the herald put a brass trumpet to his lips and blew a blaring note. The mayor jammed his fingers in his ears.

From his tree perch, Timothy watched a multitude of torsos bend toward the ground like poppy pods swaying in the wind. All but two. In that great sea of spectators, a pair of green-clad figures remained upright. The king's men were quick to point them out. Four of the king's finest fetched them.

Roughly dragged before the livid monarch, the two stood silent and unbowed. One man was tall and lean, the other broad-shouldered and paunchy. Timothy stared. Why would these lone Greencloaks risk arousing the king's wrath?

"Uncover before the king, knaves!" roared the herald. The two men pulled back their hoods to reveal shocks of curly brown hair flecked with gray. The king's face contorted with rage.

"What are your names?" he demanded.

"Opio and Gemmio, the sons of Nolan, Your Grace," one of the men politely replied.

Mardoc studied them through slitted eyes. "If you wish to save your skins, sons of Nolan, you will bow before us when the trumpet sounds again. Bow and live or stand and die."

"We mean you no disrespect, O king," said the taller of the two. "However, we may not bow, for we worship but one King, Ruler and Creator of all the earth."

Mardoc's eyes bulged. "What? Impossible! Who is this pretender that dares usurp our rightful throne?"

"His name is Gaelathane the Everlasting One," the shorter brother replied. "He is King of kings and Lord of lords. As His servants, we must obey Him rather than you."

"We'll see about that!" hissed the portly monarch, balling up his pudgy fists. "When my men put their swords to your necks, will your king save you then?"

"Whether He does or not, we still shall not bow before you," the Greencloaks calmly replied.

Mardoc's face purpled. "Guards! Behead these blackguards in the fountain! When the water runs red with their blood, let it be a lesson to the rest of their craven kind."

The king's men muscled Opio and Gemmio up to the fountain and forced their heads over the sparkling pool. Two broadswords flashed in the pale morning sun.

Then the mayor cleared his throat. "Excuse me, King Mardoc, but before we do anything rash, may I have a word with you?"

The king glared at him. Then he nodded curtly at the executioners, who lowered their swords. Stepping away from the fountain, Mardoc and the mayor stopped directly beneath Timothy's tree. He held his breath and stayed perfectly still.

"I should have your own head for this effrontery!" growled the king through clenched teeth. "Now, what is it?"

Knotting his fingers nervously, the mayor replied, "Only this. I am no great friend of the Greencloaks, but—"

"Greencloaks?" interrupted the king in a fierce whisper.

"That's what we call these vagabonds. They're partial to green cloaks and hoods. Anyway, if you're looking for dragons' hoards, only the Greencloaks can help you. It was their king who routed the dragon and their gold that rebuilt this town. Unfortunately, we've spent every gilder they gave us. I swear it."

Timothy smirked. He knew better.

Mardoc stroked his chins. "Gold, you say? Enough gold to raise a ruined town from the ashes?"

The mayor nodded, jowls quivering. "We made a new start."

"Where might these 'Greencloaks' make their home?"

"That is a mystery," said the mayor, biting a fingernail. "Nobody knows where they live. Very sly and slippery, the Greencloaks are. They come and go as they please and keep to themselves. Most often we see them at the spring and fall markets. I haven't any idea why these two were in town today, but I assure you they're harmless."

The king licked his lips. "You have done well in giving me this counsel. Tell me, do you have a secure jail or prison here?"

"We do." The mayor mopped sweat off his face with a kerchief. "It's on the east side. No one has ever escaped from it."

"Very good. Have our two tramps locked up there. Then you and I will speak further of these Greencloaks and their king."

Mardoc returned to the fountain, where he spoke in the herald's ear. Out came the trumpet for another piercing blast. Throwing back his shoulders, the trumpeter then loudly proclaimed, "The king is in a merciful mood today! For the time being, he is sparing the lives of these two miscreants. They shall be confined in the town jail."

The onlookers clapped and nodded approvingly. Spilling blood would spoil the first day of the king's visit.

Once the Greencloaks had been led away, Mardoc invited himself and his retinue to the mayor's house, leaving the square to Timothy and a few gawking busybodies. Timothy had just climbed down and was heading up Fishmonger's Street when a hand grabbed his collar and yanked him into a filthy alley.

"Timmy boy! Whatcher doin' here?" With a sigh, Timothy looked into the mocking eyes of Baglot son of Baldwyn.

—

CHAPTER 3
Bullies and Beggar Boys

Thought you'd get away from me this time, didn't you, shrimp?" crowed the bully, who was twice Timothy's size. "Ha! I've had my eye on you all day." He backed Timothy against the alley wall and twisted his nose.

"Ow! Let go!" Timothy squealed. He tried to pull away, but Baglot planted a beefy hand on his chest and held him fast.

"Not till you tell me what you was doin' up in that tree, sittin' pretty as a jay." Baglot offered him a gap-toothed grin, the memento of several brawling fistfights.

Timothy wriggled under Baglot's grasp like a worm on a fishhook. "I just wanted to get a better view. Honest!"

The bully's lip curled. "Eh, I'll bet you did. You had a regular front row seat. Mardoc and the mayor was standin' right under your tree." He thrust his face into Timothy's, his breath thick with hate and raw onions. "What did them two tubs o' lard say?"

Timothy swallowed a mouthful of chalk. "I—I didn't overhear much. I wasn't eavesdropping, really I wasn't. Mostly they argued over whether to lock up the Greencloaks or behead them."

Baglot gave him a hard look. "You sure that's all you heard?"

"Y-yes," said Timothy. The bully released him.

"I hope you're telling th' truth, Timmy boy. Sometimes the mayor hires me for special jobs, so I don't like sneaks spying on him. Got it? Now beat it, shrimp." Taking his cue, Timothy sped home as fast as his spindly legs could carry him.

As he burst through the door of the ramshackle shanty his father had built on the Foamwater's banks, his mother, Nora, looked up from her spinning wheel. "Goodness gracious, boy, what's your hurry? Did that bully chase you home again?"

Timothy didn't answer. Rushing into his room, he flopped down on his narrow bed and let the tears flow. When it came to fighting, he was no match for Baglot. Nursing his wounded nose, he listened to the soothing, rhythmic *clicketty-clack* of his mother's spinning wheel. Nora murmured a few words and then Garth's voice rose angrily.

"It's time Timothy stood up to Baglot," he growled. "If he doesn't, I'll give that bully the trouncing of his life!"

Timothy hastily dried his tears. He couldn't face his father with a swollen nose. Garth might rush out and make matters worse. After bracing a stick against the door for privacy, Timothy reached under his bed and dragged out the leather satchel he'd found hanging in a torsil tree. Pawing through the papers inside, he removed a thickish book emblazoned with the words, *Torsils in Time*.

Flipping through the pages, he came across the names, "Opio" and "Gemmio." So the sons of Nolan *were* friends of Rolin and Marlis! That clinched it. He had to help the brothers escape or at least keep their heads on their shoulders until King Mardoc's wrath cooled.

He could stage a jail breakout, but such a bold undertaking would require a workable plan and some trusty accomplices. He had neither. Summoning help from Lucambra was likewise out of the question, since his "satchel torsil" was a time torsil. Climbing it could create more problems than it solved. He would have to go it alone.

After returning the precious book and satchel to their hiding place, Timothy stayed on his knees to beg the favor of Gaelathane, the Greencloaks' king. Then he crawled out his window and took to the trail that led to Beechtown's bustling river district.

Keeping to alleys and skirting the square to avoid Baglot's prying eyes, he approached the mayor's magnificent, three-story mansion from behind. During the Battle of Beechtown, a couple of petrified yegs had smashed through its tile roof, breaking their wings. Those stone batwolves now flanked the front entrance, their snouts forever snarling. Timothy squared his shoulders and knocked on the charred door. *Thump! Thump!* The sound echoed dully across the square.

A hunched, hatchet-faced woman poked out her bun-topped head and barked, "Visitors by appointment only! Oh, a beggar-boy, is it? Shoo! Get on wi' you before I call the constable."

Timothy whipped off his cap. "I'm not a beggar, Ma'am."

"What is it you want, then?" While awaiting Timothy's answer, the gray-haired matron rewound her bun, pulling it so tightly that her eyes slanted and her wrinkles squeaked.

Timothy's tongue swelled in his mouth. "I, ah—"

"Out with it, boy. I've got work to do, or the king will have my head." The matron's bony fingers absently caressed her neck. "He threatened as much three times today already."

"I'm offering my services as an errand boy, Ma'am. Now that King Mardoc is here, you must have some chores I could do."

A gleam of interest sparked in the matron's eyes, and she dragged Timothy inside. "Chores we have a-plenty! I'll speak to the mayor about you. What's your name, boy?"

"Timothy," he said, leaving off "son of Garth." The mere mention of his father's name might send the mayor into a frothing fit.

Timothy fidgeted in the foyer as the matron strode to the end of the hall and rapped on a door. Sticking her head inside, she exchanged a few short words with someone. Then she returned.

"His Excellency will see you now," she droned, looking down her nose at Timothy. "Try not to gawk."

Timothy reluctantly shuffled down the corridor and knocked on the door. The mayor's voice warbled from inside, "Don't be shy, boy. Come in, come in. We're all friends here."

Evidently the mayor and his royal guest had become very good friends indeed. Rosy-cheeked with wine, they slouched comfortably before a crackling fire. The mayor belched loudly, jarring his eyes out of focus. He shoved an empty goblet at Timothy. "Timothy, ish it? Fetch ush shum more wine." Timothy did as he was told.

From that day on, he fetched wine, meat, bread, beer, pastries and assorted other delicacies for the two dignitaries, who spent most of their time lounging by the fire in the Badgers' Den, as Timothy called it. On his fourth day in the mayor's service, he was carrying a stack of meat pies into the den when he tripped over a wine bottle and dropped the pies. As he scraped pie innards and outards off the floor, he felt a hand on his shoulder.

"Never mind the pies," the mayor said. "Myrtle will clean them up. Just have a seat over there by the fire, if you please. The king and I wish to have a word with you."

26

Bigglesworth slowly sipped his wine before coming to the point. "Our esteemed guest wishes to learn more about these 'Greencloak' vagrants. Rumor has it that a boy named Timothy is no stranger to their ways. Are you *that* Timothy?"

Timothy gulped and squeezed his fingers until the knuckles cracked. "You m-must have m-mistaken me for someone else," he stuttered. "I know precious little about those fellows."

The mayor snapped his fingers, and a bulky figure stepped out from behind a curtain. King Mardoc watched Timothy closely.

"Hullo, Timmy boy," said Baglot. "How's yer nose to-day?"

CHAPTER 4
Mardoc's Plot

Timothy felt the blood drain from his face. "Baglot! What are you doing here?"

The swaggering bully roughly tousled Timothy's hair. "Didn't I tell you that the mayor calls on me when he's got a special job? I seen you talking with Greencloaks in town before. You seemed to get on with them real friendly-like."

Timothy shook his head. Was Baglot blackmailing him into doing Bigglesworth's bidding? Or had he already told the "two tubs o' lard" that Timothy had eavesdropped on them?

The king coughed politely. "We wished to speak with you, young man, not only because you might possess some knowledge of these Greencloaks, but also because of your, ah, *special skills.*"

Timothy stared blankly at Mardoc. He couldn't imagine what the king was getting at. Oh, he could catch fish with a basket woven of willow wands, spear frogs or patch a thatched roof, but he gathered those weren't the sorts of skills Mardoc had in mind.

"Our Lordship is referring to your remarkable powers of evasion," the mayor put in dryly. "Baglot here recommended you. He said your wits are as quick as your feet."

Baglot brushed some strands of greasy hair out of his face. "Just doin' a friend a favor," he said, smirking at Timothy.

"Since the Greencloaks are also notorious for their elusiveness," the mayor went on, "we're asking your opinion as to how we might find their kingdom." Seeing Timothy's horrified expression, the mayor hastened to add, "Oh, we mean them no harm, despite what was said about heads rolling in the fountain and all."

"Hear, hear," said Mardoc. "Fine chaps all, those Greencloaks."

"Then why lock them up?" asked Timothy in bewilderment.

"Heh! Heh!" Mayor Bigglesworth brayed through his nose. "It's all part of the 'Trumpet Test,' as we call it." He glanced anxiously at the king like an actor who has forgotten his lines. Mardoc nodded back at him. "I was in on it from the beginning. We were looking for men of honor and valor who are unafraid to stand on their principles. Men like Opo and Gemmo."

"Opio and Gemmio," Timothy corrected him. Seeing the mayor frown, he quickly added, "What do you want them for?"

"To serve in the king's army, dolt!" Baglot retorted.

The mayor said, "King Mardoc needs reliable types as men-at-arms and courtiers. He was hoping the Greencloaks' leader—this *Gaelathane* fellow—might part with a few more stalwarts like Opio and Gemmio. Since those two are as closemouthed as a couple of river clams, we're in a bit of a bind. That's where you come in, my lad."

Timothy felt sick. He was being asked to betray Lucambra! His daring plan was unraveling like an old sock.

King Mardoc fixed him with a stony stare. "Well?"

Stalling for time, Timothy asked, "Didn't those two Greencloaks say anything about Luc-, I mean, about their king?"

Tapping a slippered foot, Mardoc said, "They did tell us that 'True riches are found only in Gaelathane.' I take that to mean he's wealthier than most." Greed burned in the king's eyes like hot pitch.

Timothy settled back in his seat, his thoughts chasing shadows around the vaulted ceiling. "I think the Greencloaks won't talk to you because they don't trust you or anyone else in this town."

King Mardoc rubbed his chins. "Then whom will they trust?"

"Only each other."

"Naturally," Baglot guffawed. "They're brothers!"

"Quiet! Let him finish," the mayor snapped. Baglot sulked.

"What I mean is that if you really want to know more about the Greencloaks, you should listen in when they think no one else is around." He didn't mention that Opio and Gemmio might speak the Lucambrian language with each other in private.

"Eavesdrop, you mean?" said Baglot with a conspiratorial wink.

"Shut up, Baglot," said the mayor, cuffing him behind the ear.

Just then, a knock came softly at the door, and Myrtle the matron minced into the room to stoke the fire. When she had left, King

Mardoc asked, "Just how are we supposed to 'listen in,' as you put it, without their knowledge?"

Timothy feigned a yawn. "It's really very simple, Sire. Station your eavesdropper in the cell next to theirs. If he places a tin cup against the wall, he'll hear all the better."

"Brilliant, absolutely brilliant," murmured the mayor, nodding. "Why didn't we think of it ourselves? An eavesdropper!"

"You did well in bringing this young man to our attention," King Mardoc told Baglot. "I'll wager he's solved our problem. As a reward for your services, we hereby appoint you the Royal Eavesdropper." Timothy stifled a laugh as Baglot's jaw dropped.

"What?! You want me to sit in a jail cell all day with my ear against the wall? Why can't Timothy—?"

"Oh, we're quite sure you're the man for this special job," said the king archly. "Unless, of course, you wish to refuse." Mardoc's manner left no room for argument.

"All we need now is a trumped-up charge," mused the mayor. He jerked open the door and called, "Myrtle, will you come in here—oh." Ears red and face flaming, Myrtle stood in the doorway, caught in the act of eavesdropping herself.

"I want this ruffian thrown into a jail cell right next to those two Greencloaks," Bigglesworth gruffly told her. "Immediately."

With a scowl to split her bun-tightened face, Myrtle took in both Timothy and Baglot. "Yes, of course, but *which* ruffian?"

Jabbing an accusing finger at Baglot, King Mardoc thundered, "That one. He's a traitor to the crown! If it weren't so late in the day, we'd have him hanged here and now."

Myrtle stiffly bowed. "Very well. It will be done." As if eager to set the noose herself, the matron wolfishly eyed Baglot's neck. Glancing out the window, she said, "Your Highness, there's still enough daylight to prepare the gallows. Shall I summon the hangman?"

"Nooo!" screamed Baglot, bolting for the door. "You can't do this to me!" Bigglesworth stuck out his foot and tripped the bully as he flew past. Then a couple of the mayor's hovering servants pounced on the hapless boy and dragged him away.

Cries of, "I'm innocent, I tell you, innocent!" wafted down the hall until the mayor shut the door.

"Very good, Baglot," he chuckled. "That's quite a convincing act. No one will suspect the real reason we've sent you to jail."

The king puffed out his ample cheeks. "Let's just hope the rascal doesn't forget why he's there. He may need reminding."

"That he may," Bigglesworth sighed. "He's a headstrong lad and swine-lazy to boot. Now, fetch us more wine, Timothy. The red this time, not the white. Tell Myrtle to bring us some nuts, too."

That night, Timothy slept better than he had in months.

CHAPTER 5
The Marked Loaf

What is it?" Answering Timothy's knock, the mayor's voice cut through the door of the Badgers' Den.

"It's me, Timothy. May I come in?" A week had passed since Baglot had been hauled kicking and screaming off to jail. No one had heard a word from him since. Now Timothy was worried the town bully might make some real mischief. Somehow, he had to warn Opio and Gemmio of their peril.

Entering the den, Timothy found the mayor feeding a stack of parchments into the fire. The fat man's face darkened with guilt and suspicion. "What do you want?" he demanded.

"I'm sorry for disturbing you this morning, Mayor," Timothy said. "I thought I'd visit the jail to see how Baglot is faring. Maybe he's picked up some gossip from the Greencloaks."

"Oh, yes. Baglot. He completely slipped my mind. I have some more important matters to attend to now. Run along, then."

"Here, let me help you first," Timothy offered. He swept a paper off the stack, crumpled it and tossed it onto the fire. In no time at all, he had finished the job.

"Thank you, boy," said the mayor, mopping his brow. Timothy smiled to himself. He'd had a good look at several of the parchments, which were lined with large figures and sums under the heading, "Tribute Tax." He'd even slipped one into his tunic while the mayor wasn't looking. Evidently, His Honor had been ignoring the crown's tribute notices all along. No wonder he was so anxious to get his hands on another windfall of Lucambrian gold!

Mayor Bigglesworth broke in on his thoughts. "Stop by the kitchen on your way out and pick up some bread for your friend. He won't work if he's hungry. Oh, and don't let the cook ruin the roast. Mardoc will have my head on a pike if he's served burnt pork again." Under his breath, the mayor added, "If that meddler doesn't leave soon, he'll ruin us all, tribute or no tribute."

On his way out of the room, Timothy scooped up a dying cinder that had popped out of the fireplace. Once in the hallway, he tore a scrap off the parchment he'd rescued from the fire and scrawled on it with the piece of charcoal. Then he scuttled down the gloomy passage to the mansion's cavernous kitchen, where he dutifully passed the mayor's message along to Tribble, the cook.

"By the time supper arrives, those two fatbags will be so soused they wouldn't know a roast from a head of cabbage," Tribble groused as he stuffed and trussed a haunch of pork.

Timothy laughed. "Be careful where you say that, if you value your own head. Soused or not, the king has excellent hearing."

The cook grimaced. "As if Bigglesworth wasn't bad enough, we've got an uppity house guest with the manners of a troll. Very well, I'll mind the roast. Was there anything else?"

Timothy's gaze darted around the kitchen. "Actually, the mayor asked me to filch a loaf or two for the servants."

"Bread's not baked yet," said Tribble. He waved at a long table where glistening mounds of dough bloated like beached sea serpents. "Dough's just risen. It's not quite ready for the ovens."

All the better! thought Timothy. "That's all right. If I help you with the baking, could I have a pinch of dough? I'm starved."

The cook brightened. "Of course! Help yourself, lad. When you're done nibbling, knead the dough out a time or two and we'll make loaves of it. See that you wash your hands first."

After rinsing up in a basin of water, Timothy attacked one of the "sea serpents." Nipping bits off a flabby snout here, an oozing belly there, he popped the sweet dough into his mouth. When the cook's back was turned, he kneaded his parchment scrap into the remaining lump, making a loaf that he marked with an "X."

Later, he helped Tribble slide the fragrant, steaming loaves out of the ovens with long wooden paddles. He deftly pocketed the last two loaves, including the one with the "X."

"Those'll burn holes in your breeches," the cook warned him. "You might want to wait till they've cooled off a bit."

"But they'll keep me warm!" Timothy shot back as he scurried out the door. Minutes later, he was trotting up Gaol Way, a muddy, rutted road scarred by the passage of gang-wagons bearing drunks and thieves, pickpockets and murderers to and from the jail. Occasionally, those passengers ended their miserable lives on the triple gallows that stood outside the stark brick building.

Timothy shivered as he passed the ghastly scaffolding, thankful that hangings were rare in town. Steeling himself, he trudged up the jailhouse steps and knocked on the iron door. After explaining his business to the squinty-eyed jailer, he was ushered through a second door into a dingy chamber with four barred cells. Only the two middle ones were occupied. *Clang!* The jailer slammed the door behind him, leaving Timothy alone.

"Timmy boy!" Baglot's rasping voice echoed harshly off the brick walls. Hurling himself against his cell door, the bully thrust both arms through the iron bars. Timothy jumped back.

"You've got to get me out of here!" Baglot pleaded. "I'm sick of moldy potato soup and—" He kicked at something brown and furry. "Rats! This place is crawling with them!"

Noting Baglot's grimy face and hollow cheeks, Timothy dropped the unmarked loaf into his tormentor's flailing hands. The boy tore the bread apart and wolfed it down, all the while kicking away the rats that swarmed over the crumbs at his feet.

"The mayor sends his regards," Timothy said lamely.

"Bless 'im," muttered Baglot as he wiped his mouth. "I thought he'd forgotten all about me. When is he letting me out?"

"I'm not sure. He wants to know if you've heard anything."

Baglot motioned Timothy closer. Then the brawny bully's arms shot out like tentacles and seized him, slamming him painfully against the cold cell bars. "You tell that old snake I ain't doin' his dirty work no more!" hissed the prisoner. "Either he lets me out of here, or I tell the jailer all about the—"

Whang! From out of nowhere, a cudgel rang through the rungs, knocking Baglot to the floor. A gnarled, greasy hand grabbed Timothy by the collar and pulled him back from the bars.

"Don't ivver turn yer back on these vermin," growled the jailer. He spat into the cell and asked, "Are ye all right, boy?"

Timothy nodded, though his cheekbones stung from being smashed against the bars. "Thank you, sir. I . . . I need to talk with the other prisoners, too, if I may. Just for a moment, that is."

Shouldering his club, the jailer shrugged as he made for the door. "Suit yerself. Jest keep yer distance from them bars!"

Timothy peeked into Baglot's cell, where the bully lay crumpled on the filthy stones. A lump was sprouting from his bloodied head. When he groaned, Timothy ducked out of sight.

"If it isn't our young tree-climber from the square," a deep voice declared. Timothy whirled to find Opio and Gemmio watching him from their cell with green-eyed amusement.

"You . . . you saw me that day?" Timothy gasped.

"You were hard to miss!" said the taller man, a smile wreathing his haggard face. "That red jerkin of yours stuck out like a cardinal in a snow patch. My name's Gemmio, by the way."

"I'm Opio," put in the shorter brother. Timothy shook their hands through the bars, dismayed at how gaunt Gemmio had grown on his skimpy jail rations.

"I doubt anyone else noticed you in that maple," Opio said with a wry grin. "Most Thal—, I mean, most people don't look up unless they're hunting birds or squirrels."

Or unless they're the town bully looking to pick on someone, thought Timothy ruefully.

"Do you wish to be known as 'Climber,' or have you a real name?" asked Gemmio, arching his dark eyebrows.

Blushing, Timothy introduced himself. Then he announced, "I brought a little something for your breakfast." After handing the marked loaf to Gemmio, he motioned for him to break it in half. "The bread's still hot in the *middle*," he said with a broad wink.

Gemmio retreated to the back of the cell, where he tore the loaf in two while his brother kept a wary eye on the jailer's door. When Opio signaled that the coast was clear, Gemmio tossed one of the halves to him. Biting into the bread, the Greencloaks cautiously chewed while Timothy held his breath.

All at once, a peculiar look came over Opio's face. Probing his mouth with thumb and forefinger, he fished out a yellowish wad. At Timothy's impatient nod, he unraveled the sodden parchment and showed it to Gemmio, whose lips moved silently as he read the smeared black lettering: *Please be careful! A spy in the cell next to yours is eavesdropping. Speak softly. A friend in Gaelathane.*

The brothers looked up at Timothy wonderingly. "Thank you for the bread, *friend*," said Opio. "However, our neighbor has overheard nothing. Between demanding to be let out and griping about the plain food, the hard bed, the cockroaches and rats, and the disreputable company, he has had no time to eavesdrop. Why did you—" Another groan sounded from Baglot's cell.

The jailer's head poked inside. "Ye'd better leave before that 'un comes to," he said, pointing at Baglot. "I can't wait to watch 'im hang. He's been a real pest. I'd steer clear o' them two as well, unless ye want to swing with 'em on th' wrong end of a rope."

After casting a parting wave at Opio and Gemmio, Timothy chased after the jailer. "Swing with them? What do you mean?"

The surly jailer threw open the outer door and grunted, "Ask *him*."

Then Timothy saw a man standing on a ladder set on the gallows platform. He was tying a noosed rope around a crossbeam fixed above the scaffolding. Two more ropes lay loosely on the wooden beam.

"What are you doing?" Timothy called up to him.

"What's it look like? There's to be hangin's tomorrey."

An invisible hand squeezed Timothy's throat. "Who?"

"Them three that's in the jail now," came the reply.

"No! That can't be. You must be mistaken. They're—"

The hangman scowled down at him and spat. "Don't argey wi' me, guttersnipe! Th' mayor jest sent word that I'm supposed to stretch them varmints' necks at dawn. 'Spies,' he called 'em. I jest do as I'm told. I knot the nooses and set 'em. Eh, yes, I spring the trapdoors, too." He chuckled as he pulled an imaginary lever.

Leaving the hangman to his ropes, Timothy raced down Gaol Way toward the mayor's house. He had the servants' entrance in sight when he tripped over a brick and sprawled into a mud puddle. Before he could gather his wits about him, a pair of powerful hands picked him up and set him back on his feet, dripping and dirty.

"Take a tumble?" asked the man, who wore the baggy, homespun breeches and loose leather jerkin of a Thalmosian peasant. A floppy, broad-brimmed hat shadowed his face.

"I should watch where I'm going," Timothy muttered.

The stranger clucked his tongue sympathetically. "It's been a wet winter and a muddy one, too. Are you hurt?"

When Timothy shook his head, the man asked, "You haven't by chance seen a pair of those ne'er-do-well *Greencloaks* skulking about, have you? I have been looking for them."

"That depends on who's asking," Timothy warily replied. After some thirteen years of living on the seedy side of Beechtown, he had learned to distrust strangers.

The man touched his hat brim. "Pardon me. We haven't met. Gannson is the name. Farmer Gannson. And you are—?"

Timothy looked the shabby fellow over. Something in the farmer's shadowy eyes told him he had nothing to fear. Still, trust had to be earned. "Timothy son of Garth. My father is a raftsman."

"An honest trade," allowed Farmer Gannson with a courteous nod. "I've been trying to find a couple of acquaintances. They arrived here a week or so ago. I don't know where they're staying."

"What are their names?"

Gannson weighed his words. "Two brothers, the sons of Nolan."

"Opio and Gemmio?"

"You know them?" The farmer hovered over Timothy.

"I do. They're in the town jail, until tomorrow."

Farmer Gannson sagged like a sack of potatoes. "Do you mean they're to be released then?"

Hot tears welled in Timothy son of Garth's eyes and a sob rose in his throat. "N-no. Tomorrow they're to be hanged!"

CHAPTER 6
The Hangings

Gannson reeled backward as if struck by lightning. "Hanged?" he said hoarsely. "Whatever for?"

Feeling lower by the minute, Timothy detailed the plight of the two brothers. "I'm afraid you'll never see your friends again," he sighed. The gallows loomed large in his mind.

Farmer Gannson's eyes burned into Timothy's. "Perhaps, and then again, perhaps not. 'Until the noose is set, there's room for hope yet.' We can't give up on those two just when they need us the most."

With a reassuring wink, Gannson melted into the market square crowds, leaving Timothy to ponder why a Thalmosian farmer would take such an interest in a couple of "ne'er-do-well Greencloaks," and what he had meant by "we" and "us."

Limping the rest of the way to the mayor's mansion, Timothy threw open the door of the servants' entrance, sending Myrtle and a bowl of soup flying. He found the mayor and his bothersome guest in the Badgers' Den munching walnuts by the fire. The two men looked up with mild annoyance. King Mardoc frowned disapprovingly at Timothy's mud-stained clothing.

"It's customary to knock before entering," growled the mayor. "What is it this time, young man?"

"The Greencloaks . . . Baglot . . . hanged tomorrow . . . but why?"

Mardoc chuckled. "You must have spoken with the hangman. So far as he knows, our three jailbirds will be treading air at dawn. See to it that no one thinks otherwise, unless you wish to share their fate." The king's threat hung in the air like a sword.

Timothy collapsed into an armchair. "I don't understand. I thought Baglot was supposed to eavesdrop on Opio and Gemmio. Now you want to put them all to death?"

"Our plans have changed," said the mayor, gleefully rubbing his plump hands together. "Baglot is about to lead us to the Greencloaks' kingdom while we flush out their king."

Timothy's head spun. "Flush him out?"

"Indeed," replied King Mardoc, picking his teeth with a piece of walnut shell. "This is how we'll do it . . ."

When Mardoc had finished, Timothy sat in stunned silence. How could he forewarn the king of the Greencloaks against this ambush? If only he could free Opio and Gemmio before the trap was sprung!

That night, pebbles rattled on Timothy's window, saving him from a dream in which he was smothering in a mountain of Baglot-faced bread dough. Outside, Farmer Gannson's floppy hat bobbed above the sill. Hurriedly dressing, Timothy squeezed through the window and dropped to the ground.

Outside, a weeping willow cast slinky shadows in the moonlight. A hand beckoned to him through the tree's drooping boughs. When Timothy approached, the hand drew him inside the green canopy, bringing him face to face with Gannson. The farmer's homespun hat was pulled low over his eyes, shrouding his features in gloom.

Timothy shivered. Maybe the fellow wore the hat to hide some hideous disfigurement. Fear coursed through his veins. "How did you find me?" he demanded in a fierce whisper.

Gannson peered out through the leafy curtain. "Finding you was easy. Even the birds know where Timothy son of Garth lives."

The birds? "What are you doing here?"

Gannson's shadow loomed over him. "I need your help."

"What kind of help?" Timothy wished he had armed himself with a rock or a stick, just in case.

"Why, help in freeing Opio and Gemmio, of course," said the farmer, as if he were discussing the current price of potatoes.

"What can I do?" Timothy said. "I don't own a sword, and I'm just a boy. Anyway, so many of the king's men are prowling about that we'd need an army to break those two out of jail."

Gannson sighed. "When I was your age, I learned that any boy makes an army when he's willing to obey Gaelathane."

"You know Gaelathane?" Never before had Timothy met any Thalmosian who acknowledged the King of the Trees.

"I do indeed. Are you also one of His servants?"

Timothy shrugged. "I suppose so. I've never met Him."

"Then perhaps you can explain the message you passed to our two jailbirds today in a loaf of bread," said the farmer dryly.

Timothy's mind raced. "You knew? But how?"

"I just had a little chat with Gemmio and Opio," Gannson replied. "You were very kind to visit them, by the way. They've been rather lonely. Greencloaks have few enough friends as it is in these parts. They asked me to thank you again for bringing them that bread." He coughed delicately. "Let us hope it was not their last meal."

"How did you get into the jail to see them?"

"I have my ways. Now, why did you risk your life to help a couple of strangers, and Greencloaks at that? Also, how did you know the other prisoner was eavesdropping on them?"

After Timothy poured out the details of Mardoc's plot, Gannson whistled softly. "So it's the king of the Greencloaks they're after, is it? He might just turn the tables on them."

"Sir, if you can, please warn the king, won't you? I'd feel dreadful if something happened to him."

A low chuckle rumbled in Gannson's throat. "You can rest assured I will. I know him well. Meantime, a hangman's dawn waits for no man. If you're game, here's the plan . . ."

Before daybreak, Timothy arrived at the jail to find King Mardoc's carriage and horses already standing in front of the gallows platform. A restless crowd was gathering around the scaffolding. Below each noose stood a black-hooded figure guarded by two men-at-arms.

Scores of gray-mantled men mingled with the spectators, jingling and jangling when they moved. The trap was set; any Lucambrians who took the bait would fall into a deadly net. Timothy prayed that the Greencloaks' king was too canny to play into Mardoc's hands.

At a trumpet blast, knotted nooses were set around the prisoners' necks. Standing with King Mardoc on the gallows platform, the mayor raised his ceremonial staff. "Friends," he began, "we are assembled here to witness the justice due these miscreants: Opio and Gemmio, wretched sons of Nolan; and Baglot the worthless son of Baldwyn."

"Get on with it, Mayor! Hang 'em high!" screeched Myrtle's voice from the jostling throng.

"In King Mardoc's realm, the penalty for treason is death," the mayor droned on. "His Majesty, King Mardoc, has the sole honor of sending these traitors to their just rewards. May all of his foes likewise perish!" The trumpet blared again, and with a dramatic flourish, King Mardoc yanked the trapdoors' lever. *Clunk.* The three hooded figures dropped out of sight, and their ropes went taut.

As the hushed crowd surged forward to catch a closer glimpse of the grisly scene, Timothy casually made his way through the press of bodies toward the jail. He had just ducked inside the door when a burly arm blocked his way.

"Watch'er doin' here now, boy?" sneered the jailer. "Yer friends already took the long drop. Looks like ye missed th' show!" As the jailer guffawed, a lanky figure carrying a beeswax-scented bag over his shoulder lurched up the jail steps. The jailer's bulbous nose twitched at the strong smell of ale.

"Ah'm shposhed t' shleep here fer a few daysh," mumbled the stranger, whose hair hung in greasy ropes over his eyes.

"I'll give you a few days," growled the jailer, aiming a kick at the drunk. "Take this, you—"

Clonggg. The beeswax bag caught the jailer in the side of the head. He flew backward through the doorway and into the jailhouse. The disturbance raised scarcely a ripple in the sea of spectators.

"We must hurry," muttered the drunk, whom Timothy recognized as Gannson. The farmer pulled Timothy inside and closed the door. Then he rummaged through a corner closet, finding a couple of staffs and a pair of bone-handled knives. "The sons of Nolan will be glad to see these again!" he said.

After pocketing the jailer's keys, Timothy followed Gannson to Baglot's cell. The other boy was waiting impatiently.

"What kept you?" he grumbled. "That lazy lout of a jailer was s'pposed to leave me his keys. Where is he, anyway?"

"There's been a change in plans," said Timothy, dangling the keys just out of Baglot's reach.

"What sort of change?" grunted Baglot suspiciously. "Say, who's this drunk with you? I want to see the jailer—now!"

"All in good time," said Gannson amiably. Taking the keys from Timothy, he unlocked Baglot's cell and stepped inside.

"Hey! What do you think you're doing?" cried Baglot. "Stop that! Hands off me! Leave me alone, or I'll—mmph." Before you could say 'tunics and trousers,' Baglot lay bound and gagged on the floor, clad only in his undergarments. Trading his own clothes for the bully's, Timothy flung his glaring enemy a parting gibe.

"I'm sure someone will find you soon," he said. "Otherwise, you may have to wait for the rats to gnaw your ropes off!"

Meanwhile, the farmer was throwing off his rags. Underneath, he wore a chain-mail hauberk and a gray cloak. He was pulling a freshly-dented metal helmet out of his sack when Opio and Gemmio appeared with the jailer's limp, trussed-up body. Like Gannson, they were now disguised as men-at-arms.

After Gemmio and Opio left the jailer on the cell floor with Baglot, Gannson locked the door and tossed the keys inside. "That poor fellow never knew what hit him," he said wryly. "By the time he wakes up, we'll be long gone. Timothy, you go first, and we'll follow. You're our decoy, remember. We'll make Mardoc and his puppet mayor rue the day they jailed Nolan's sons."

"Wait! What about me?" cried Baglot, spitting out his gag. "Don't leave me here; I'll be hanged for sure!"

"It's too late," Timothy told him. "You've been hanged already!"

As planned, Mardoc's men had captured three deserters of about the right build to stand in for the "spies." Thanks to the executioner's hoods, no one had been the wiser.

Wraithlike, Timothy slipped out of the jail and into the warm April sunshine. Most of the gawkers had drifted off, though a few still lingered near the gallows. Having shed their thin disguises, the king's men lounged about, leaning on spears or polishing helmets. Eight stood guard around Mardoc's carriage.

As Timothy passed the carriage, one of the men stared narrowly at him and nudged his neighbor. With four other guards, they moved toward Timothy. Two more made for the jail.

According to Mardoc's cunning plan, if the Greencloaks' king didn't fall for the staged hangings, the jailer was to "accidentally" drop his keys into Baglot's cell. Baglot would then unlock his and the Greencloaks' doors, giving him the perfect excuse to escape with Opio and Gemmio and learn Lucambra's secrets.

His heart thudding painfully, Timothy resisted the urge to run. As far as his pursuers knew, he was Baglot son of Baldwyn, following the freed Greencloaks to their hideout. Veering off North River Road, he plunged into a willow thicket.

Behind him, crashes and curses mingled with the clinking and clanking of armor. Doubling back, he rejoined the road where it met Bridge Street. Stony-eyed yegs mocked him from the parapets as he strode along the bridge. Then shouts rang out.

"He's on the bridge! Catch him! Catch the spy!"

Breaking into a run, Timothy nimbly dodged several rough-hewn characters who tried to cut him off. "Not so fast, laddie!" growled a thickset soldier blocking the bridge. Clad in a skirt-like, chain-mail hauberk, he wielded a huge sword in a two-fisted grip. Grinning, he raised the sword over his head.

Suddenly, rumbling thunder struck the bridge. With a panicked look, the swordsman dropped his weapon and pressed himself back against the parapet. The stones shook as a four-horse team pulling red-and-gold lightning clattered up onto the bridge at breakneck speed. The colorful royal carriage slowed, and a hand reached down from the carriage to Timothy.

"Need a ride?" Gemmio asked with a smile.

CHAPTER 7
The King Revealed

Taking Gemmio's hand, Timothy hopped up on the running board. Beside him, a white face briefly appeared at the window. Perched on the driver's seat with the sons of Nolan, Farmer Gannson tipped his floppy hat to Timothy, twitched the horses' reins and hollered, "Giddyap!" The coach lurched forward.

"Thank you for rescuing me!" shouted Timothy, hanging onto a stanchion for dear life. He had never ridden anything faster than a river barge before, and as the rocks and trees whizzed by, he wondered how Gannson managed to keep his hat on.

"I've always wanted to leave this town in style," the farmer replied with a wave and a grin.

"Where are we going?" asked Timothy.

"Down the road apiece," Gannson answered. He crammed his hat over his ears and snapped the reins to coax more speed out of the horses. Timothy's stomach turned over.

Gemmio glanced back at the road behind them and gave Gannson the thumbs-up sign. The farmer eased the sweating horses down to a trot, and Timothy felt his heart and stomach return to their proper places, although his heart was still pounding.

"You up there! Stop this carriage at once and let us out!"

Timothy looked back to see Mardoc's ring-studded hand waving out the carriage window. His crownless head followed. Opio removed the horses' water bucket from its hook and tossed its contents through the window. Indignant sputtering noises sounded from inside.

After another three miles or so, Gannson brought the carriage to a halt, and everyone hopped down. As far as Timothy could tell, they were alone on the dusty road. Brushing himself off, Gannson pulled open the carriage door.

Inside, two raccoons blinked back at Timothy and his friends. Dirt had covered Mardoc and the mayor from head to toe, leaving only their eyes clear. Water dripped off the king's head, streaking his face and stringy hair with mud. Stiffly, the two dignitaries climbed out and stood beside the carriage in dusty splendor.

"What is the meaning of this—this outrage?!" screeched the king. "Who are you? Speak! I demand to know your names!"

Opio and Gemmio bowed. "Your Highness, we are your humble and obedient servants." As the brothers doubled over with mirth, Mardoc's face purpled under its mask of mud.

"How dare you! How dare you!" the red-faced monarch roared. "Deserters! Renegades! You are a disgrace to your station and to the crown! Mock us while you may, but I'll wager you'll sing a different tune wearing the hangman's necklace."

The mayor spat out a mouthful of dust. "Shut up, you fool! Do you want them to kill us both?" Turning to Gannson, he said, "What are your demands? Better pay? More ale? Promotions? I think you will find us reasonable men."

Farmer Gannson made no reply. Instead, he began to strip. Off came the cloak, the hauberk, the trousers. Underneath, he was wearing a long green robe embroidered with trees and vines. A broadsword was strapped about his waist.

Last of all he removed his broad-brimmed hat. Shaking his head like a proud warhorse prancing into battle, he let loose a thick chestnut mane. The man Timothy had taken for an aging tiller of the soil now appeared as a young warrior in the prime of life.

"You have badly misjudged us," Gannson said with a menacing glint in his eye. "You wished to meet the king of the Greencloaks. Well, here I am. What do you have to say for yourselves?"

Mardoc and the mayor went whiter than chalk.

Throwing off their gray cloaks, Gemmio and Opio lowered their borrowed swords on the two dignitaries' necks. "Kneel before the king, knaves!" growled Gemmio. "Kneel and live or stand and die."

The dust-men knelt.

"I never should have listened to you in the first place," Mardoc hissed at Bigglesworth through clenched teeth. "If I'd beheaded these rogues in the square, none of this would have happened!"

Timothy knelt, too. "You're King Rolin, aren't you?" he breathed, taking in the man's auburn hair, green eyes and royal bearing.

Gannson let out a warm, welcoming laugh that thrilled Timothy to the very core. "Indeed I am—Rolin son of Gannon. How did you know my name?"

"Rolin son of Gannon," Timothy repeated to himself. Gannon's son. *Gannson.* So that's why his name had sounded so familiar! "I—I read about you in a book I found," he said, feeling flustered.

Lucambra's king raised Timothy to his feet. "I apologize for the deception, but as you can see, I cannot openly show myself in these parts without endangering myself and my people."

He turned to his cowering captives. "In what possible way have we 'Greencloaks' injured Beechtown or the crown that you should repay us so unjustly? Tell me, and I will make it right."

When neither man answered, Rolin said, "My men and I intend no harm to your persons or property, nor do we demand your silver or gold in ransom. We ask only to be left in peace, to trade freely with the good folk of Beechtown and to come and go as we please. You will find no worldly wealth among us; we are a simple people with simple needs. Break faith with us or spy on us, and we shall withdraw our protection from this town, and should another vicious dragon catch you napping, you will not escape his wrath. Now go, and may Gaelathane have mercy on you."

Listening to King Rolin, Timothy had been leaning against one of the carriage's metal-rimmed wheels. How often he had watched his father mend such a wheel! Examining the hub, he noticed that the lynchpin was loose. That would never do.

Minutes later, Timothy was wiping off his hands when he saw a cloud of dust rising above the road behind him. Racing around the carriage, he found Bigglesworth and Mardoc climbing inside. The Greencloaks stood talking with heads together.

"Someone's coming!" Timothy cried.

"Yes, my men are coming," said King Mardoc with a smirk. "Run while you can! When they catch you, you'll be drawn and quartered. Hanging is too good for the likes of you brigands."

Gemmio cast a worried glance northward up the road. "Speaking of brigands, isn't that Bartholomew the Bold coming our way?"

Looking in that direction, Timothy saw another dust-cloud. A band of black-clad horsemen armed to the teeth emerged from the cloud, furiously spurring their galloping mounts.

King Mardoc chuckled. "Surely you don't expect us to fall for that old trick. Face it—your goose is cooked!"

Opio yanked the portly king halfway through the carriage window and pointed his head up the road. "Now who's the goose?" he said and dropped Mardoc back into his seat.

Sweat beaded the king's brow. "Who are those men?" he asked, nervously playing with his rings. "Friends of yours?"

"We're no friends of robbers," said Rolin grimly. "Bartholomew the Bold is an infamous highwayman who lives with his men north of here in the Forest of Fellglade. They prey upon lone merchants and other travelers along this road."

Gemmio shaded his eyes. "I'd say they'll be here in about three minutes. By the time Mardoc's men arrive, it will be too late."

"Too late?" squealed the king. "What do you mean?"

Rolin jerked his thumb at the advancing horsemen. "Those riders are ruthless. They would sooner lop heads as take hostages for ransom. Don't worry; they'll just want your finery, your crown, your rings and your horses. I doubt they'd have any use for this coach."

Mardoc's entire body quivered like jelly. "Help! Do something! I command you to protect us from those bandits!"

"Sorry, but we've got to leave now," said Rolin. "We don't fancy having our throats slit, not to mention being drawn and quartered." To Timothy's amazement, the Greencloak king sauntered off toward the woods with Opio and Gemmio.

Mardoc screamed after them, "I'll give you anything you want, up to half my kingdom! Just don't leave us here!"

"Please?" said the mayor hoarsely. Hoofbeats drummed and the robbers' swords flashed in the sunlight.

With a wink at Timothy, Rolin said, "Did you hear that, men? He said 'please'! I suppose we can't refuse now." Leaping onto the driver's narrow perch, Rolin began backing the horses while Gemmio and Opio helped swing the coach around. Once the carriage was pointed toward Beechtown, Rolin lashed the reins, and the horses dashed off at a mad canter.

"Head for the woods, boys!" he hollered. The three "renegades" dove into the trees and climbed through the forest until they were high enough to look down on the road. Rolin was fighting for control of the team as the carriage careened around a corner on two wheels. The gang of brigands was closing in from behind, while the king's men rapidly narrowed the gap in front. Coming into a straight stretch, Rolin jumped off and rolled to the side of the road, hat in hand.

"May Gaelathane protect him!" breathed Gemmio.

Mardoc and the mayor were only seconds from rescue when the wheels of their driverless carriage began to wobble. Suddenly, all four wheels flew off, dropping the carriage onto the road with a grinding *crash*. Still harnessed to their burden, the spooked horses dragged it along willy-nilly, while the loose wheels bounded ahead and smashed through the ranks of Mardoc's mounted soldiers. Men and horses scattered as the coach followed, plowing a gouge in the dirt road. Even from a distance, Timothy could hear the shouts and screams.

The wheel-less carriage continued jolting down the road, flying apart as it went. Finally, its two terrified passengers were left clinging to little more than a horse-drawn, upholstered sled.

Soldiers and highwaymen alike stared after the wrecked carriage before it disappeared in a cloud of dust and splintered wood. Then Mardoc's horsemen bestirred themselves and raced away after their master. Scratching their heads, the bandits reined their horses around and rode back the way they had come.

Opio and Gemmio were still speechless with shock when King Rolin rejoined them. He appeared none the worse for his escapade, although he was quite out of breath from laughing.

"You should have seen the look on Mardoc's face when the wheels fell off his carriage!" he howled, holding his sides. "He and the mayor won't soon forget that ride."

"If they survive the ride at all," Gemmio remarked.

"They're both too fat to break any bones," Opio snorted.

"Are you sure about that?" asked the king pointedly. "Anyway, I don't understand how all four wheels fell off. One or even two might come loose, but four? I'd say someone tampered with them."

The three men turned eyes on Timothy. "You wouldn't happen to know anything about those wheels, would you?" Rolin asked him.

Timothy was all innocence. "Why look at me? I don't know a thing about carriages. I'm just the decoy, remember?"

Rolin smiled. "If I'm any judge of character, you know more than you're letting on. My Beechtown friends tell me that your father is one of the finest wheelwrights in these parts. Come now—the truth."

Timothy could see there was no use denying it. He removed four iron pins from one of Baglot's breeches pockets. "The lynchpins were loose," he said lamely. "I was going to replace them, honest I was."

King Rolin folded his arms and regarded Timothy with a severe look. Then he and the sons of Nolan burst out laughing. Gemmio and Opio slapped their knees with glee.

"He pulled the lynchpins! He pulled the lynchpins!" Opio kept saying, as though he wished he'd thought of it himself.

Grinning, Rolin tousled Timothy's hair. "You have more mettle than we ever imagined, son of Garth! Next time, though, ask me first before pulling any more stunts like that, all right?"

Timothy nodded, sensing there was more to come.

"You won't dare show your face around Beechtown again until this unpleasant business has blown over," the king continued. "The entire town will be clamoring for your head. I suggest you find a place to hole up for a while until things cool off east of the Foamwater."

Timothy stuck out his chin. He wasn't about to hide like a hunted rabbit, dreading the day when Baglot and his gang dragged him off to the gallows. "Take me with you," he said.

The men stiffened in guarded surprise. "We would if we could, Timothy—but we can't," King Rolin said gently. "You don't know what you are asking. Our laws would not allow it."

"I do know what I am asking. I want to climb a torsil tree and see Lucambra and fly on a griffin's back. *The Tree lives!*"

"How could you know about such things?" Gemmio gasped.

"Oh, I have my ways," said Timothy with a sly wink at Rolin.

The men looked helplessly at one another. "We can't leave him here," said Rolin. "The Thalms might catch him. Let's take him up to the cabin. He'll be safe there until we can decide what to do with him."

"Agreed," said the sons of Nolan. With that, they headed north through the woods with Timothy. Wherever they were taking him, Timothy hoped he would find a hot meal and a soft bed.

CHAPTER 8
Bart and Wiggin

That evening, Timothy enjoyed a scrumptious oatcakes-and-honey supper, courtesy of Rolin's red-bearded father. Pointing his batter-caked spoon at Timothy, Gannon remarked, "For such a little sprout, he can surely put away the 'cakes. He reminds me of you, Rolin, when you were a lad. Where did you find him, anyway?"

"Down in Beechtown," Rolin replied. "His father is a raftsman. I thought you might be able to fatten him up. I could use another stack of those oatcakes myself, if you please."

BANG! The door flew open and in flounced a plump, fiery-haired woman with blue eyes and several missing teeth.

King Rolin choked on a bite of oatcake. "Hullo, Aunt Glenna," he said, managing a sickly smile.

"Nephew!" Glenna smothered him in her embrace. "You're a sight for sore eyes. Where have you been? Are you home for good? Your boy needs more meat on his bones." She pinched Timothy's cheek.

Rolin introduced Timothy, Gemmio and Opio, passing off the men as a couple of the king's friendlier guards. "They're out in these woods looking for deserters and ne'er-do-wells," he explained.

Glenna looked the brothers over. "You two fellows ought to marry a couple of our local girls and settle down in town. There's plenty of work on the river. My brother would do well to take a page from that book." Rolin and Gannon rolled their eyes.

Rolin's aunt prattled on about the weather, her rheumatism, the scarcity of ale since King Mardoc had come to town and the hazards of hill life. Then she glanced out the window at the gathering dusk. "Goodness gracious, it's late! I must be going. There's a curfew now, and the streets are swarming with soldiers." When the door finally closed behind her, everyone breathed again.

"I apologize for my sister," Gannon said with a sigh. "She means well, but she takes some getting used to." He added under his breath, "A lot of getting used to."

"Is she always like that?" Gemmio asked.

Rolin laughed ruefully. "I'm afraid so. It's usually best just to listen and agree with her. If Mardoc's men are out in force as she says, though, it can't bode well for us—or for Timothy."

Timothy stopped chewing mid-bite as all eyes turned on him.

"For better or worse, you've thrown in your lot with us, dear boy," said Rolin. "Our enemies are your enemies, and our friends are your friends. Now we must find somewhere to hide you, and I can't think of a better place than right here in—"

Thump! Thump! The door rattled under a heavy-handed knock. The Greencloaks groaned and Gannon winced.

"Glenna must have forgotten something," sighed Rolin. "She's grown more absent-minded of late. I'll try to keep her out on the porch." His hand was on the door latch when the *clump-clump* of heavy boots drummed through the door. Rolin froze.

Before Timothy could think, Gannon had whisked him into a back bedroom. A ladder stood in one corner, its upper end disappearing through a dark hole between the unfinished ceiling beams. "Up the ladder, and be quick about it," whispered the beekeeper.

Timothy flew up the ladder and into the attic. Saws and coiled ropes hung from the cobwebbed rafters, while broken beehives, sacks of beeswax, boxes of punkwood and beekeeping tools littered the patchwork floor. At the far end, a dirt-streaked window let in some dying evening light. Muffled voices rose from below.

Timothy peered through a knothole in the floor. Two roughneck soldiers in plain tunics stood in the doorway talking with Rolin. Their eyes darted about the room. Gannon sat by the stove toasting his feet. The sons of Nolan were nowhere to be seen.

"Ye're sure th' little rapscallion didn't come through here today?" the taller one was asking.

Rolin shook his head. "Nobody's been this way in a coon's age. Most folks don't like our bees and our backwoods ways."

"I'd keep a lookout for him, if I were you," said the other man. "He's wanted fer treason an' kidnapping. When we catch 'im, he'll swing from th' tallest gallows in town, along with anyone that helps him. There's a reward fer turnin' in th' scamp, mind ye."

Timothy strangled a throaty gasp. With a price on his head, where could he safely hide now?

Rolin eased the two men out the door and closed it. Then he sat down heavily at the table. Following the sound of voices, Timothy was creeping across the floor when his knee brushed against something crackly, and lantern light burst into the attic. He had dislodged a loosely-bound booklet from a gap between two boards. Shoving the grimy papers into his pocket, he pressed his ear against the crack. *Now I really am eavesdropping!* he told himself with a guilty pang.

". . . I'd welcome the company, and I could use his help with the bees," Gannon was saying. "Believe me, I won't let him out of my sight. It will be like having you home again."

"Then it's settled," said Rolin with a resigned sigh. "Timothy's to remain here with you until Mardoc has left town. The king won't stick around long once he empties the treasury and the mayor's wine cellar! Until then, these woods will be crawling with his men. We'd better head back to Lucambra first thing tomorrow."

In the loft, Timothy sat up so suddenly that he cracked his head on a rafter. Stay with Gannon and tend bees? He'd be placing Rolin's father in mortal danger! Besides, his heart was set on Lucambra. If he sneaked out of the cabin now, maybe he could trail the Greencloaks to their torsil in the morning.

Taking down a coil of rope, Timothy tied one end around a post and fed the other through the opened window. Then he eased himself out the window. To his horror, he heard voices approaching.

"Blimey, Bart," whispered one. "Are ye sure he's in there? I didn't see nobody 'cept fer them two beekeepers. Maybe we should have asked to stay the night. It's cold out here."

"Pipe down, Wiggin!" growled another voice. "Them fellers ain't fools. If they figger out we're deserters, th' game's up! They could turn us in fer a reward, and ye know what General Gorn does to deserters! Anyway, when we was inside, I saw th' table was set with five plates, not two, and cushions was piled on one of the chairs. That's where our runty rebel was sitting. I'll stake a month's wages on it. Now here's what we'll do . . ."

Clinging to his sweat-slick rope, Timothy inwardly groaned as he listened to Wiggin and Bart discussing their plans. Just when he couldn't hold on any longer, the rope went slack. The knot had failed! Grabbing air, Timothy fell on the men's heads.

Bart and Wiggin collapsed beneath him, breaking his fall. After picking himself up, Timothy sped off into the darkness.

"Great flaming balls o' thunder! Me bleedin' head's busted," groaned Bart as he staggered to his feet.

"They're onto us, Bart!" howled Wiggin. "They dropped a rock on us. Let's get out of here!"

"You ninny!" Bart growled. "That was no rock. The boy fell on us from that window. There he goes! After him! The reward's ours!"

Glancing back, Timothy saw the men were following right on his heels. Bart lit a tall torch, and its light flooded the forest, sending the darkness scurrying for cover. Menacing, many-fingered shadows leapt out of the trees, reaching for Timothy. Blindly, he ran on.

Splash! Timothy gasped as he slid into a chilly creek. Grasping some branches, he hauled himself up the opposite bank and pressed on. A string of oaths curdled the air as the two men plunged into the water after him. Without their armor, they bore down on him like a couple of ravening wolves, though the water doused their torch.

When Timothy stopped to catch his breath, he noticed a white light bobbing through the forest. As it moved away from him, the noises of pursuit faded. Soon, the woods had fallen silent again, save for the occasional *whoo-whoo* of a horned owl.

At last Timothy came across a well-trodden trail. Water gurgled nearby. Had the creek swung round to meet him? Still on the lookout for pursuers, he followed the path uphill through whispering poplars, their gray trunks pale under the moon.

He turned aside at a grassy glade, where the moonlight silvered the trees' new leaves. Hungry, cold and forlorn, he found a soft spot under a dainty, small-leafed tree and sat cradling his head in his arms. Up in the loft, his escape plans had seemed quite clever. Now he was lost and friendless, far from finding a Lucambra torsil in the trackless woods.

Lying down, he drew himself into a ball. Hot tears worked their way from under his eyelids as a heady, sweet fragrance stole into his nostrils. Ears roaring, he whirled into a troubled sleep.

CHAPTER 9
Touch the Top, Then Drop

These tree-killing two-legs!" rumbled someone. "Why can't they leave us be? I hear a whole pack of them thrashing and crashing about down the hill. It's giving me the timber shivers. I wish I lived by the river. It's safer down there."

Timothy woke straight out of a dead sleep and shrank back into some streamside bushes. From the sound of it, one of the king's men was lurking behind a maple not ten feet away!

"They've made a burning, too," moaned another voice. "If it gets away, we're doomed! Where's Silvertip when we need him?"

A third boomed, "Don't make such a fuss! Our wood's too wet for burning, and those two-legs will pull up roots soon enough. 'Men of pride will come and go, but trees abide to live and grow.'"

Rumbly grumped, "That may be, but before these two-legs go, they could still wreak havoc. I say, let's spread the Word!"

Biting his lip until he tasted blood, Timothy huddled in hiding like a cornered rabbit. A band of deserters must have surrounded him! What on earth were they talking about, and why couldn't he see them? "Gaelathane, please help me!" he cried.

"Why, here's another one," Moaner said. "A tad small for a two-legs, and his bark is too loose on him. He looks awfully—"

"Didn't you hear him?" broke in Rumbly. "He spoke the Name! We've got to help him, two-legs or no. I'm sending out the Word." A sigh rustled through the woods, though the wind was still.

That did it. Convinced the game was up, Timothy bolted from the bushes and sped down the trail, only to run smack into King Rolin, who was garbed again as Farmer Gannson.

"Here you are!" said the king, holding onto his floppy hat. "What's the hurry? Are those polecats after you again?"

Timothy's head was spinning. "Polecats? What polecats?"

"I was speaking of the two-legged variety. You're lucky that pair didn't hog-tie you and drag you back to Mardoc. They would have wrung Lucambra out of you for sure. I had my hands full as it was luring them away from you with my lightstaff."

"I found more deserters just up the trail!" Timothy declared as he clung to Rolin. "You've got to chase them away!"

"Hold on, now," Rolin said. He held Timothy at arm's length. "You say they're hiding upstream? How do you know?"

"I heard them talking about 'wreaking havoc' and 'spreading the word' and 'Silvertip'!" Timothy wailed. "Who is Silvertip, anyway?"

Rolin gave him an odd look and started up the path with Timothy following. As they neared the glade, Timothy whispered, "Those men are all around us. They're probably armed, too."

"I don't see anyone," said the king with a half-smile. "Not an eye or a nose or a hand or a helmet."

"That runty two-legs is back," observed Moaner.

"Say, the other one looks like Rosewand's friend," said Boomer.

"Any friend of Rosewand's is a friend of mine," Rumbly said.

"There! Don't you hear them?" Timothy cried.

"I do indeed," Rolin replied. He was smiling from ear to ear. "Let me introduce you to Bigbole, Dryroot and Dripleaf."

Timothy's head swam as the truth niggled at the fringes of his mind. "What funny names!" he said.

"That's because we're trees!" Rumbly retorted.

"Trees?" Timothy said, bewildered. "But how—?"

Rolin slapped him on the back. "You've gotten the Gift, my boy, that's how! You're one of us now."

"Gift? What gift?"

Leading Timothy to the pink-blossomed tree that had sheltered him during the night, Rolin said, "Meet Rosewand the amenthil, my sythan-ar. Rosewand, this is my friend Timothy."

"I am pleased to make your acquaintance," said Rosewand in a sweet voice like the sound of pure water trickling over smooth stones. "May you be blessed of the Tree. I trust you slept well last night."

All the air left Timothy's lungs. "How can this be?" he gasped. "I thought only Lucambrians understood tree-speech."

Rolin waggled his finger. "Not exactly. The Gift is no respecter of persons. It's a blessing Gaelathane freely offers to all through the scent of amenthil blossoms. That's why we call it a gift."

Timothy's mind churned. He'd read of the amenthils but had never hoped to see one. Now he could converse with the trees and other forest creatures, just like the Greencloaks!

Suddenly, a branch snapped. No sooner had Rolin drawn Timothy behind Rosewand than a pair of green-hooded heads came bobbing up the path. It was Gemmio and Opio.

"Drat that boy!" wheezed Opio. "If it weren't for him, I'd be home eating chestnut cakes with quince marmalade."

"And I'd be lounging in a hot spring," said Gemmio wistfully.

"If it weren't for Timothy, you'd still be rotting in the Beechtown jail—or worse," Rolin reminded the two as he and Timothy stepped out of hiding. The brothers reddened.

"We were all very worried about you!" Opio scolded Timothy. "What made you run off like that?"

Shamefaced, Timothy told the three men how Bart and Wiggin had clumsily foiled his hasty plan to shadow the Lucambrians to their torsil. *I'll never see Lucambra now,* he thought.

"I doubt those two will be giving us any further trouble," said King Rolin with a knowing look.

"Maybe they won't, but their friends will," said Gemmio darkly. "They're advancing up this hill in a line, beating the brush like fox hunters. Some of them are even setting fires trying to smoke us out." Timothy noticed an acrid gray haze drifting through the trees.

"We'll be long gone before any fires reach us," said Rolin.

"What about your father?" Timothy asked. He hated to think what would happen if fire reached the quaint log cabin.

"He'll be safe enough," the king replied. "If the flames come too close, he can flood the ground around his home from Cottonwood Creek. Now come along. It's high time we climbed Scarlimb." He set off toward the creek, but Opio and Gemmio stayed put.

"Aren't you coming?" Rolin asked them in a puzzled tone.

Avoiding the king's gaze, the brothers glanced at each other and then at Timothy. "Yes, but where will the boy go? You're not planning to leave him here for the Thalms to find, are you?"

"He's coming with us," Rolin firmly replied. "We can't very well send him back to the cabin with all those soldiers about. Besides, he's gotten the Gift! Now we must hurry." He beckoned to Timothy.

Exchanging wondering looks, Gemmio and Opio followed their king across the creek. Timothy joined them, wading through the frigid mountain waters to the far bank. A late afternoon mist was gathering as they made off through the woods. Plunging through a salal thicket and up a ferny hillside, they came at length to a shiny-leafed tree with deeply furrowed bark. With a leap, Rolin caught a stout, scarred limb and climbed up.

After Gemmio and Opio hoisted Timothy into the torsil, they clambered up themselves. The three had settled on a branch to rest when a chorus of shrieks, squawks and growls broke the woodland stillness. Two men were charging through the trees with a grizzly bear in hot pursuit. Its shaggy coat rippled with each loping stride.

"Great gallows and gargoyles!" howled one of the men, whom Timothy recognized as Bart. "He's a-comin' fer us, Wiggin!"

"Why did I leave off me armor?" Wiggin groaned. "It's up this tree fer me!" As the grizzly galloped toward him, Wiggin scuttled up the torsil's trunk like a big, hairy crab. "Get up here quick, Bart!" he yelled to his companion, reaching down an arm.

Bart made a running leap for Wiggin's hand—and missed. *Thud.* Timothy felt the tree shudder as Bart plastered himself against the trunk. *Snap.* The bear's jaws closed around Bart's boot. With a yelp, he shot up the tree minus his footwear.

After chewing the boot to bits, the grizzly shook himself, reared on his hind legs, embraced the trunk, and climbed. "We're goners, sure as there's a sun in th' sky!" wailed Wiggin. The tree whiplashed as the grizzly clawed its way up the trunk.

Sitting above the other climbers, Rolin scowled down at the two deserters. "I hadn't planned on this," he said. "To the top, everyone!" He climbed higher, then higher still. As Timothy and the Greencloaks followed, the tree's crown swayed alarmingly.

"Touch the top, then drop," Gemmio whispered.

When the three Greencloaks had disappeared in turn, Timothy slid down after them. Stomach churning and toes tingling, he laughed with pure delight as Bart, Wiggin and the bear faded from sight.

———

CHAPTER 10
Lucambra

"Will the bear eat Bart and Wiggin?" Timothy anxiously asked. The torsil was still shaking with the movements of its unseen climbers.

The king chuckled. "Silvertip wouldn't hurt a flea. He just doesn't like two-legs trespassing on his territory."

"You know him?" asked Timothy in surprise. He had made up pet names for some of the herons and ospreys that regularly fished in the Foamwater, but he couldn't imagine speaking of a grizzly bear in such familiar terms, much less predicting what it would do.

As if reading Timothy's mind, Rolin said, "Silvertip and I have a friendly understanding. He keeps the woodcutters out of the forest on the other side, and I protect him from hunters."

What does bear-speech sound like? wondered Timothy as he took in his new surroundings. Thalmos's dark, fir-mantled hills had given way to stately ranks of silver-skinned beeches that thrust their green fingers skyward. The cool air bore a sharp, clean sea scent. Glowing with a dewy freshness as if newly created that day, Lucambra was all Timothy had hoped for, and more.

"I don't like the looks of this," said Opio with a worried frown. "See how Scarlimb is wobbling? Those potato eaters will make passage if they climb any higher. A pox on that bear!"

Rolin's eyes pierced the shadows under his hat. "Then we must prepare them a proper Lucambrian welcome, mustn't we!"

"What sort of welcome did you have in mind?" Opio was asking when a commotion broke out in the torsil's top. Bart and Wiggin were bouncing from branch to branch, pinball fashion. Rebounding off some lower limbs, they belly-flopped onto the ground with grunts. Timothy ran over and helped them up.

Rolin waved his arms at the befuddled deserters. "Quick! That bear is coming down the tree after you. Flee for your lives!"

"Flee? Which way?" they croaked, glancing wildly about.

"There." Beyond the king's pointing finger, gray beeches marched down gentle hills to a grassy plain, where a stony spear stabbed the brooding, cloud-heavy sky. "You'll find food and lodging in that tower," Rolin told the two. "However, you must run swiftly, for the bear will not rest until it has tasted man-flesh. My men will accompany you to ensure your safety."

"I told ye from th' start that desertin' was a bad business," Bart said to Wiggin as they hobbled into the woods after Opio and Gemmio. "Drat that bear fer pullin' me boot off!"

"Better yer boot than yer head!" Wiggin retorted.

By now, Rolin was laughing until the tears streamed down his face. Timothy frowned. "Why did you send them to the Hallowfast? Aren't you afraid they'll spy on you?"

Rolin stopped laughing, though a smile still played at the corners of his mouth. "How did you know about the Hallowfast?"

Timothy shrugged. "I read about it in my book."

The king's face tensed. "What else have you read in that book of yours? Did you find it 'by mistake'?"

Before Timothy could reply, a tall, hooded figure emerged from the bushes. Broad of shoulder and heavily muscled, the man bore a bow and arrows and a long staff.

"Who are you and what are you doing here?" the grim woodsman demanded. His flinty gaze settled on Timothy, who suddenly realized that his brown eyes were trumpeting, *I'm a Thalmosian.*

King Rolin deliberately lifted his head and tipped back his hat. "Satisfied, Sigarth?" he said with a mischievous grin.

The scout winced. "Forgive me. I didn't recognize you in that getup." His eyes strayed pointedly back to Timothy.

"This is my friend Timothy son of Garth," Rolin said. "Timothy, may I introduce Sigarth son of Sigwyn. He and his brother Skoglund are the royal huntsmen, at least when they're not keeping me in line." Glowering, Sigarth touched two fingers to his hood.

Rolin told the huntsman, "Gemmio and Opio are 'escorting' two lost Thalms to the tower as we speak, under the pretense of protecting them from a bear. You must arrive first and continue the deception. Give them a royal reception, complete with our finest wines and meats. I want their stay with us to be as pleasant as possible."

Sigarth's face sagged in shocked bewilderment. "But why? What if they should escape? We can't have them running around loose. Let me lock them up in the dungeon instead."

Rolin sighed. "What would that accomplish? Entertain them, and they'll happily remain our guests."

"Guests?" Sigarth groaned, with a look that would curdle milk. "I'd rather ship them home or exile them to some out-of-the-way torsil world where they can't get into any trouble."

The king cleared his throat. "If you'll recall, the council once tried to exile *me*. Gaelathane doesn't let in otherworlders without good cause. Since these two are already on our doorstep, we might as well treat them hospitably. 'Better to make a friend of an enemy than an enemy of a friend,' Bembor always says." He patted Sigarth's shoulder.

"I know this goes against the grain. Just do your best, and keep our potato eaters locked in the banquet hall so they can't guess where they really are. Now, you'd best be off if you're going to catch those two."

With a curt nod to Rolin—and a scowl for Timothy—Sigarth son of Sigwyn disappeared into the forest.

"You'll have to forgive him," said Rolin. "He cannot abide any Thalmosians or their ways. Years ago, Thalmosian hunters mistakenly killed his parents as they were climbing a torsil. Now he is a hardened, bitter man, though absolutely trustworthy."

"I fear we have more two-legged company," a deep voice broke in. It was Scarlimb.

"What do they look like?" King Rolin asked the tree.

"Most of them are shiny skinned and carry long choppers. You won't let them cut me down, will you?"

"I suspect that's the last thing on their minds," Rolin answered. He told Timothy, "Some of Mardoc's men must have observed Bart and Wiggin making passage. We'd better leave before they decide to do some climbing themselves."

"Aren't you going to stop them from getting into Lucambra?" Timothy asked. He was sure the soldiers would spare no tree—or tower—in their quest for the Greencloaks' fabled gold.

Rolin grimaced. "What would you have me do? Chop down poor Scarlimb? I'm sure he wouldn't like that. Besides, we can sorely afford to lose another torsil between here and Beechtown."

"Why not send some griffins over to scare the men off?"

"As it happens, the royal sorcs are ill and unable to fly, much less fight. Now, we'd better hurry if we're to reach the tower in time to play the part of gracious hosts."

"But they have a half-hour's head start!" Timothy protested.

"Then we'll have to leg it, won't we?" With a crooked grin, Rolin loped into the watchful woods. When Timothy caught up to him, the king was climbing another torsil.

"I thought we were going to the Hallowfast!" Timothy said.

"We are," Rolin called down. "This is no ordinary torsil, you see." Timothy didn't, though he was too polite to say so.

Following Lucambra's king to the top of the tree, Timothy climbed down to make passage. After shaking off the tingling and dizziness of torsil travel, he dropped to the ground. He was surprised to see the Hallowfast looming through a gray mist.

"We're still in Lucambra?" he said. "I thought torsils—"

Rolin laughed. "Not all trees of passage lead from one world to another. If you split a torsil nut in half and plant each half in a different spot, you'll have yourself two *tara-torsils*. When the trees grow large enough, you can travel between them—in the same world. Just now, we covered two miles in an eyeblink."

As Rolin was speaking, Timothy saw two ragged figures staggering up to the tower with Gemmio and Opio. Glancing fearfully behind them, the deserters beat on the door and yelled hoarsely. When the door opened, the pair fell over each other getting inside.

Timothy laughed. "Those two still think there's a bear—"

"I smell two-legged spoor," a growly voice broke in. Then a hoary eagle's head and neck emerged from some tall clumps of wild catnip, followed by a winged lion's body. Most of the bedraggled beast's fur and feathers had fallen out in patches.

Timothy jumped back. "It's—it's a real talking griffin!"

The peevish creature cocked a bloodshot eye at him. "What were you expecting—a stuffed one?" To Rolin, the sorc growled, "Was he dropped on his head when he was a two-leggling?"

———

"I'll explain later, Ironwing," said Rolin. "Scarlimb the torsil has reported the makings of a nasty Thalmos-breach. I'd like you to dash over there and keep an eye on him in case something's brewing."

With a woeful groan, Ironwing collapsed, legs splayed out and neck as limp as a dead eel. His mournful expression gave Timothy the giggles until the sorc glared at him.

"I know you're not feeling well," said Rolin sympathetically. "I wouldn't have asked if it weren't important. If you like, I'll have a fat goose waiting for your supper."

Sighing, the sorc heaved himself off the ground. "Oh, very well, if you insist. Just remember: If I don't return by morning's light, you must send my remains back to the Willowahs."

"Go on with you, silly old sorc!" said Rolin. Still grousing under his breath, Ironwing sulked into the woods, his black-tipped tail twitching an insolent good-bye.

"As solid a sorc as you'll find, except when he's into the catnip," Rolin said, setting off for the Hallowfast with Timothy in tow. "These days, he's 'nip-tipsy most of the time. I wish I knew what was ailing him. He and Windsong simply won't discuss it."

THE GOLDEN WOOD
PART II
IN WINONA'S FOOTSTEPS

CHAPTER 11
The Breaching of Scarlimb

Are we there yet?" Timothy groaned as he forced his leaden legs up the Hallowfast's endless flight of spiraling stairs. Didn't Greencloaks ever rest?

"Yes, we are!" Rolin said, throwing open a door on his left. Inside, Timothy expected to find a bevy of shackled skeletons grinning from dank stone walls. Instead, rich tapestries hung beside stained-glass windows depicting woodsy landscapes and rampant griffins. Polished tables filled the floor.

"It's about time you arrived!" Sigarth barked. He stood beside a table groaning under trenchers of meat, fish and cheese; pots of sweet pudding and porridge; baskets of bread; pans of pastries; boxes and boxes of apples and pears; and flagons of mead and wine. Bart and Wiggin sat opposite each other, contentedly puffing away on briar pipes. They had all but emptied the flagons and many of the platters as well. Timothy's mouth watered.

"To yer health, good sirs!" burbled Bart, raising his mug of mead to Sigarth and Rolin. His watery eyes rolled like a pair of loose gilders, and he reeked of alcohol.

"Long live th' Greencloaks!" chimed in Wiggin thickly. The man upended an empty flagon. "Ah, the wine's gave out. Breakfast's no good without wine, nor shupper, either." Prattling on, he finally nosed into a bread basket and began to snore. Not to be outdone, Bart planted his face in a mince pie.

"What happened to Opio and Gemmio?" Rolin asked Sigarth. A sour look pinched the huntsman's thin features.

"They went looking for 'a hot spring' and 'chestnut cakes.'"

"In that case, I'll leave our trenchermen in your capable hands," said Rolin with a grin. "Have the servants lay them out on a couple of tables for the night after taking the leftover food up to the throne room for our meeting. Once you've cleared this mess away, meet me up there with the others. Oh, and while you're at it, ask the cook to send along a hot meal, too. These provisions are growing cold."

"As you wish," Sigarth sighed. He collected the empty flagons and disappeared down the stairs. After rescuing the mangled bread basket and mince pie from the snoring deserters, Rolin headed for the door. Grabbing an apple, Timothy followed him.

The king led Timothy higher along the winding, torch-lit staircase. They had passed three or four landings when the steps ended at an arched door. Pulling out a key, Rolin unlocked it.

"We'll have a cozy chat in here before our supper arrives," he told Timothy. "That lone apple won't hold you until breakfast." Timothy blushed and tried not to look as famished as he felt.

Though also adorned with tapestries, this room was plainer than the last. A narrow window let in some soft, cloud-dampened light that fell upon two thrones sitting side by side on a dais. Ornate cupboards ranged along the right side, opposite a fireplace that could have taken off the chill if a fire had been lit. A smattering of sturdy wooden stools completed the furnishings.

Rolin expertly sent his hat sailing onto a wall hook. Then he shed the rest of his Gannson disguise and plopped down on the leftmost throne. "It's good to be home again," he sighed.

"I don't understand why you brought me here," said Timothy. "I'm a Thalmosian, you know. What if I betrayed you?"

"Betray Lucambra? After you risked your life to save Opio and Gemmio? I think not. If I'd had any doubts about you, I would not have taken you into my confidence in the first place. By all accounts, you've proven yourself a true Tree Friend."

"What's a Tree Friend?" While Timothy didn't dislike trees, he had never thought of them as friends, either. Then again, he'd spent many a drowsy summer's day lazing under his weeping willow, sharing with it secrets only trees can keep.

"A Tree Friend is anyone who serves the Tree King and Lucambra. You've more than earned the title. Without you, we couldn't have pulled off Opio and Gemmio's escape." Rolin smiled. "On their behalf, Farmer Gannson and Lucambra's king thank you."

—

Kerr-aack! Lightning flared through the window and splashed the room with garish light. Thunder growled like prowling bears. Then the door swung open and dozens of rangy Greencloaks filed in, each doffing his dripping cloak and bowing to the king. Their deep-set eyes settled on Timothy, who studiously avoided their gazes. A low, excited murmur filled the chamber.

Everyone fell silent as an erect, white-haired Lucambrian clad in an emerald robe and a silver-striped cloak entered carrying a staff. Right behind him, a green-gowned, bright-eyed woman swept into the room. On her head sat a circlet as golden as her silky tresses. Timothy and the others made way for the pair as they mounted the dais.

"Hail, my queen," cried Rolin. He kissed her hand and escorted her to the throne beside his. Then he embraced the old man. "Bembor son of Brenthor, welcome! May your years roll down like the green waves that gladden the Sea of El-marin."

With a bow, Bembor replied, "And may your youth be renewed as the eagle's, O King!" Leaning on his staff, he cried, "All rise! *Cyngor Llwcymru*, the Lucambrian Council, is herewith convened. May Gaelathane's wisdom and love guide us in these proceedings, and may our lives reflect the glory of the One Tree."

"Mae'r Goeden yn fyw!" all echoed as one. Then the king and queen seated themselves on their thrones. Hoping to escape further notice, Timothy stole off to a stool in the corner.

King Rolin cleared his throat. "Our first order of business is to bring before you a true *Coeden Ffrind*, a Tree Friend, and the first Thalmosian to set foot in this hallowed hall in many a year. Please come up here with us, Timothy son of Garth."

Necks craned and voices muttered as Timothy ascended the dais. He nearly tripped over Baglot's baggy trousers.

"On this solemn occasion, our beloved land is once more in peril," Rolin went on. "As I speak, King Mardoc of Thalmos is overrunning Beechtown with his army like a plague of locusts. He aims to discover and plunder the country of the Greencloaks, and I fear he may well succeed if we do not find a way to stop him."

"Plunder us of what, pray tell?" growled a scout standing beside Sigarth. Though slighter in build than his neighbor, the man wore Sigarth's unruly hair, surprised eyebrows and fiery expression.

"*Heddwch!* Peace, Skoglund," said Rolin wearily. "I've already dealt with your brother once too often today. The Thalms are after the riches they mistakenly believe we possess." The council rumbled its displeasure, and the king raised his hand for silence. "We have long since given away what wealth Mt. Golgunthor yielded us, though it may prove difficult to convince King Mardoc otherwise."

"We'll convince him at the point of a spear!" shouted Sigarth. The other Greencloaks clashed their staffs in approval.

"We'll ambush his army through the torsils and send the whole lot of them packing!" another Lucambrian cried.

"We may be the ones sent packing," said Rolin heavily. "Two of Mardoc's men have made passage into Lucambra, and more are sure to follow. The torsil Scarlimb has been breached."

With a rafter-shaking roar, the councilmen leapt to their feet and shook their fists at Timothy and Rolin. "Away with the Thalmosians!" some cried. "Treason!" others bellowed. The enraged crowd surged toward the dais. Cringing, Timothy clung to Rolin's throne.

Thump! Thump! Thump! Bembor stamped his staff roundly on the dais. "Does any man here dare challenge the High Chancellor's staff?" he thundered, his face a chiseled mask of wrath. The younger council members silently slunk back to their stools.

"By the laws of Lucambra and by the eternal grace of Gaelathane," Bembor growled, "Rolin son of Gannon is sovereign over this land. Though he be Thalmosian by birth, no Lucambrian of truer heart has ever lived. Should any man dispute his claim to the crown, let that scoundrel prove it upon my body in mortal combat."

His face filled with remorse, Sigarth bowed to Rolin. "Forgive me, sire. And you as well, Bembor Brenthor's son. A hot heart ever begets hot words. My clansmen and I intended your majesty no dishonor."

"None was taken," Rolin replied. "Besides, I care less for my honor than for Gaelathane's. Next time, my dear friend, let your heart cool before you pour it out. Hot words burn both in the speaking and the eating." Laughter rippled through the room.

"This boy risked capture and death to save the sons of Nolan," the king continued. "Were it not for his bravery, Opio and Gemmio might even now be hanging lifeless on a Thalmosian gibbet. I cannot let such a selfless deed go unrewarded. Bembor, my staff, please."

Bembor came forward and handed Rolin his rod. Resembling a crystalline tree limb, it shone with an inner light. "Kneel, Timothy Garth's son," Rolin commanded. Trembling, Timothy obeyed.

"I dub thee *Timotheus,* Tree Friend," said Rolin, touching him on the head and shoulders with the staff. "May you walk before the King in the light of His Tree all your days, and may your life be long and satisfying. *Mae'r Goeden yn fyw!*"

"Mae'r Goeden yn fyw!" repeated Marlis and the council.

"Rise, Tree Friend," said King Rolin, helping Timothy to his feet. "Emmer, please set this young man's seat up here." At this request, a grizzled Greencloak placed the stool beside the two thrones. Sitting on it, Timothy entwined his feet in its legs and tried not to look at anyone.

"Our next matter may also concern Timothy son of Garth," the king announced. "A fortnight ago, Gaelathane left the queen and me a message." At these words, an expectant hush fell over the council.

A ffy rhag cleddyf fflam dan gêl,
I guddio mewn ystorfa fêl,
A ddysg gyfrinach ple pob caeth
A gwobr fawr o'r diwedd wêl.

Ar hap a damwain daw o hyd
I'r llyfr sy'n ganllaw doethion byd;
Ac a ddarlleno golud mawr
A gaiff, lle erys glwth yn fud.

Ymaith â chi, nac ofnwch draw
Y ffon na'r bwa cam pan ddaw,
Y sawl sy'n glynu wrth y gwir
Gaiff elli aur yn y pendraw.

Ar frathiad dwfn Mangyl ddeint,
Pan gwymp pob dyn o'i chwerw haint,
A fyddo'n rhydd, wele'r Pren,
Pob coll yng ngolau hwn gaiff fraint.

"I don't see where Timothy comes into that rhyme," said Emmer.

"Nor do I," grumped Timothy, who hadn't understood a word.

"My pardon," said the king, patting Timothy's head. "I had almost forgotten you are not yet versed in *Llwcymraeg*. My queen, will you give our young friend here the sense in the Common Tongue?"

Rising to her feet, Queen Marlis fixed her gaze upon a distant spot beyond the tower's walls and recited,

The one who flees from flaming sword,
Who hides himself in honeyed hoard,
Will seize the key to captives' plea,
And in the end, a great reward.

He'll find the book but by mistake,
Whose words the wise will not forsake;
Its pages lead to wealth indeed,
Where greedy hearts will not awake.

Depart at once but do not fear
The bended bow or the smiting spear;
A grove of trees with golden leaves
Awaits for those who persevere.

When mangles' fangs have bitten deep,
And men shall fall from bitter sleep,
Who would be free, behold the Tree,
For in its light the lost will leap.

"From the second stanza," said Skoglund, "it seems we're looking for a book that leads to a hidden treasure."

"One that puts people to sleep," hazarded Marlis. "How odd!"

Timothy was worried about the last stanza. Whatever 'mangles' were, he didn't want to meet one on a dark night!

"I say it's all pure nonsense," a gangly Greencloak snorted.

King Rolin slowly nodded. "I would agree with you, Larkin son of Gaflin, except for the fact that Timothy recently hid from a couple of Mardoc's men in my father's attic, which contains some of the hoarded tools of my family's beekeeping trade."

"The 'honeyed hoard'!" Marlis exclaimed.

Wondering whispers buzzed through the council while several servants entered the hall to light the wall-torches and kindle a fire on the hearth. The flickering firelight cast swooping, bat-like shadows among the men's restless forms.

Next, other attendants appeared with tureens of chestnut soup and platters of leftover bread and meat. Gemmio and Opio quietly slipped in behind them, famished looks on their faces. Timothy was slurping up his soup when a Greencloak and two sopping griffins slouched through the door. The scout's ready smile, pert nose and impish green eyes vaguely reminded Timothy of Queen Marlis.

"Welcome, Chief Deputy Scanlon and our faithful sorcs," said Rolin cheerily. "We wondered what had become of you three. Dry yourselves off and have some supper."

"I'd like that fat goose now, please, and one for Windsong as well," growled Ironwing, his tail leaving a muddy trail. He was looking even more bedraggled than when Timothy had first met him.

"And a spot by a nice, warm fire," sighed Windsong. He padded over to the hearth and stretched out, purring his delight.

"You shall have both," the king laughed. "But first, dear friends, please tell us what kept you out in such weather."

"Spying on the Thalmosians!" grunted Scanlon. "There must be hundreds of them, and more are climbing down Scarlimb. They are fell and well-armed; it was nip-and-tuck outrunning their arrows." He glanced about. "What's to eat? I'm starving."

"You're always starving," quipped Marlis.

"I'll be glad when my feathers grow in again," sighed Ironwing. "It galls me to run away from danger instead of flying into it. Ah, dinner is served." With a casual flick of his paw, he snagged a slab of venison off one of the servants' platters.

"Ironwing seems downright cheerful compared to his usual testy self," Marlis remarked.

"Perhaps he smells a major conflict afoot," Bembor said. "Griffins are at their best just before a battle. And may I remind your majesties that we must either send these troublesome Thalmosians back the way they came—or exile every last man of them?" He winked at Timothy. "Present company excluded, of course."

"Routing the potato eaters may prove very difficult, particularly without the sorcs' wings," observed Scanlon. "Perhaps we should ring Elgathel's bell to summon some of Whitewing's—"

All at once, a great shout shook the tower's stones. The king and queen half-rose from their thrones. "What in Elgathel's name was that?" Rolin exclaimed. Again the roar burst upon the Hallowfast like mighty waves crashing against sea-cliffs.

While the others gathered beneath one of the room's few deep-set windows, Scanlon and Emmer hurriedly propped a flimsy wooden ladder against the wall below it. After testing the ladder's bottom rungs, the two backed away, shaking their heads. Green-eyed glances roved about the room before settling on Timothy.

"It looks as if you're the climber of the hour," said Scanlon with a tight grin. "I'll hold the ladder for you, if that helps."

Fervently wishing for some extra feet on his wiry frame, Timothy pushed his way through the crowd to mount the swaying ladder. Upon reaching the window, he looked out on a forest of flickering, torch-like lights under a star-studded sky. Metal flashed redly.

"I see many men surrounding the tower," he called down. "And every one of them is holding a flaming sword." It was only then that he realized the "torch" Bart had lit while chasing him had actually been a sword.

CHAPTER 12
Sorcs and Scorbies

King Rolin groaned and covered his face. "I should have known that's what the riddle meant. Thalmosian warriors often smear their swords with pitch and set them ablaze at night to frighten their enemies. It makes a daunting spectacle."

"It's a pity the storm has passed," said Larkin. "All that iron would have drawn the lightning like a carcass does flies." Other Greencloaks wept or prayed aloud for the safety of loved ones.

Grim-faced, Rolin thumped his staff on the dais to restore order. "Our worst fear has befallen us," he said. "The Hallowfast is besieged. There isn't a moment to lose. Scanlon, double-bar the downstairs door. The rest of you prepare the tower's defenses."

Now the throne room hummed with activity. The men brought out longbows and arrows, blowpipes and darts, while some women came in to cover the windows with an arrow-proof mesh woven of honeysuckle vines. Timothy helped Gemmio and Opio wrap the blunt ends of their blowpipe darts with cattail fluff to make them fly.

After tufting his pile of darts, Timothy tried to strike up a friendly conversation with Windsong. Smelling strongly of damp fur, the sorc lay curled up asleep in front of the fire.

"Hello, my name is Timothy," he said, scratching the griffin's head. "I'm a Thalmosian from Beechtown."

A bloodshot eye opened and the griffin croaked, "Pleased to meet you, I'm sure. My name is Windsong, the royal scribe, the royal steed, et cetera, et cetera. I'm also royally tired. Too much running around and all that. Don't ask me for a ride, either. I can't fly, and I don't know when I shall again." Then the eye closed and the sorc started snoring.

Timothy was trying to rouse Windsong when Bembor reconvened the council. The old Lucambrian bowed to Rolin, giving him the floor.

"Thank you, Bembor," said the king. "I am sure all present will agree that we must settle on a plan of action before our 'visitors' invite themselves to dinner. And speaking of dinner: Scanlon, please leave some food for the rest of us!" Caught in the act of wolfing down his third helping of venison, Scanlon turned red and waved his hand. Laughter trickled through the council, clearing tension from the air.

Sigarth was the next to speak. "Why can't we simply cut down Scarlimb? That way, no more Thalmosians could get in. And they might not find another Lucambra torsil for weeks."

Scanlon shook his head. "They've evidently already thought of that possibility. Scarlimb is surrounded by armed guards."

"Then let's ring Elgathel's bell to call for sorc reinforcements, as Scanlon suggested earlier," declared Larkin. "The least they could do is fly us all out of harm's way."

"Nay, dear friend," said Rolin. "The last I heard, King Whitewing was busy quelling a sorc-rebellion down south. Still—" He glanced at the griffins. "What say you, Windsong? Would your relatives come to our aid if we rang Elgathel's bell?"

Opening his eyes, the sorc stretched out until he resembled a moth-eaten fur rug. "Our kin would come if they could," he said. "For all we know, though, they are as ill as Ironwing and I."

Stroking his white beard, Bembor said, "If you would tell us what is afflicting you, we might be able to help."

"We are beyond help," snarled Ironwing.

"I am afraid Ironwing is right," Windsong sighed. "Few sorcs ever recover from the *scorbies*, as we call it. Every few generations it sweeps through our dens, leaving misery in its wake."

"Is it fatal?" asked Rolin with a worried frown.

"In time, yes," the griffin grunted. "Scorbies is a wasting disease that causes most of our fur and feathers to fall out, which is worse than death for a sorc. If we can't fly, we can't hunt. If we can't hunt, we starve. It's a depressing state of affairs."

"What brings on the illness?" Queen Marlis asked.

Windsong feebly chittered. "Nobody knows. Some sorcs say that scorbies is spread by foxes or deer. Others blame it on bad water or eating too many squirrels or not enough greens. Personally, I think it comes of eating too much cooked meat."

"Surely in all your delvings into griffanic lore you must have come across a remedy for this dreadful disease," Rolin said. "Name the cure, and if it is within my power, I will obtain it."

The griffin ruffled his tattered wings. "I once heard that in bygone days, ailing sorcs found relief by eating certain wild berries. However, Ironwing and I have consumed all sorts of berries and other fruits, to no avail. Water sprinkled with gold dust was also supposed to help."

The king and queen traded disappointed glances. "Alas, the largest cache of gold in Lucambra now lies beneath Mt. Golgunthor," said Rolin. "I could grind up my crown if it came to that, but since it was a gift from Whitewing, I am loath to do so."

"Nor would we sorcs expect you to part with so great a treasure on our account," Ironwing said, dipping his eagle's head.

Recalling what he'd already read in *Torsils in Time*, Timothy asked, "Would drinking Glymmerin water help cure the scorbies?"

"It would, if contrary currents hadn't pushed that healing flow far out to sea," said Bembor gloomily.

"Then we're stuck here," concluded Skoglund in disgust.

"Perhaps our esteemed *Tree Friend* here can offer some helpful advice," sneered a councilman. "After all, the king's riddle promises that the boy 'Will seize the key to captives' plea,' does it not?"

"Since you bring up the riddle, my dear Hedwyn," said King Rolin coolly, "we might well consider the next stanza:

He'll find the book but by mistake,
Whose words the wise will not forsake;
Its pages lead to wealth indeed,
Where greedy hearts will not awake.

Rolin turned a shrewd look on Timothy. "You've spoken about finding a book about Lucambra; do you have it with you?"

Timothy hung his head. "No, it's still at home under my bed." If he had known earlier who "Gannson" really was, he would have handed over the manuscript to him in the first place. "Anyway, there's nothing in it that could help us now."

Rolin's face fell. "Maybe Gaelathane was referring to a book you have yet to find—or a different one you've already found."

Timothy's heart lurched. In all the excitement, he had forgotten the booklet he'd discovered while hiding in Gannon's attic. He patted Baglot's roomy breeches pocket. The book was still there. Pulling out the soiled pages, he said, "I did find this moldy old thing stuffed in a crack in the attic floor, but I can't see any use for it."

"Might I have a look?" Rolin asked. Taking the ragged book from Timothy, the king squinted at the spidery letters squiggling across its pages. "I've seen this before," he said. "After my dear mother and grandmother died, Father found it in a cupboard." He handed the book to Bembor with a resigned shrug. "I cannot read the old script, Grandfather. You'll have to tell us what it says."

As Bembor examined the yellowed pages by torchlight, his beard cast a bushy shadow on the wall. "This is written in High Llwcymraeg, the language of Elgathel's court," he marveled. "Few other vestiges of this ancient dialect have survived the Dark Years after his death. *But where are the missing pages*?!" Bembor's eyebrows bristled at Timothy.

"That's all of them, I swear!" Timothy squeaked.

"Peace, Grandfather," said Rolin soothingly. "I believe the boy is telling us the truth." He coughed apologetically. "Besides, I vaguely recollect Father's cramming some of those pages into cracks around our cabin windows to keep out the drafts. He must have used the rest to plug a gap in the ceiling. Anyway, I—"

Bembor's shriek cut him off. "*What*?! He tore out those pages for draft-stoppers? Didn't that dimwit realize what this was?"

Wincing, Rolin evenly replied, "Probably not. To him, it was just another musty old book with writing he couldn't read."

"The bumpkin!" Bembor raged. "If only he had known—"

"Grandfather!" flared Marlis. "You mustn't speak of Gannon so harshly. I'm sure he meant no harm."

Bembor's thunderclouds retreated just as actual lightning and thunder burst again upon the Hallowfast. "I'm sorry; you're right," he sighed. "Gannon had no way of knowing the value of his find." He lovingly brushed flecks of dirt and dust off the book's battered cover. "Timothy Garth's son, you have discovered a truly priceless treasure. This is the diary of Queen Winona, Elgathel's bride."

CHAPTER 13
The Queen's Tale

A great gasp went up from the Lucambrians. "That book is my grandmother's diary? Are you sure?" asked Rolin as he and Marlis looked over Bembor's shoulder.

"As sure as I'm a staff bearer," Bembor replied. "Although the writing has faded with time, it's clearly High Llwcymraeg, penned in Winona's hand. I have read other samples of her script."

"Read us the diary now, please!" begged the royal couple.

Bembor skimmed backward through the cracked, brittle pages, smoothing and straightening them as he went. "Here's as good a place to start as any," he muttered. "The writing at the top is smudged . . . ah, now it's clearer:

Ruin! Ruin! All is lost! Kith and kin, leaf and limb, all are gone, burnt to ash. Lucambra's end has come. If only we hadn't been so lax, perhaps the king would still be alive. Alas, he lies now in a cold stone casket, marred by the dragon's fire. How lonely the tower feels without him! At night, I can hear the yeggoroth flying at the windows, trying to break in. I pray the bars will hold.

Bembor moistened a finger with his tongue and rubbed a page. "Dratted dirt," he grumbled. "Now, where was I?"

Weep for the king! Weep for the amenthils, charred to skeletons! Weep for my people, scattered like sheep without a shepherd. The winged lions have also deserted me, save faithful Stoutheart, who brought me the king's body and his sword. May Gaelathane reward him and his descendants. Some of the sorcs were too sick to fly into battle, but most lacked the courage. Would that Elmar's men had returned in time! Would that I could flee to the Isle of Light, where the Tree reigns and death never sets its frosty foot. Alas, I lent Elmar my ring. I hope it served him well, though I fear he has already met his doom.

"Who was Elmar?" asked Timothy, fascinated with the queen's tale. He could feel her presence in the room as wind gusts whistled through the arrow barriers, extinguishing the guttering torches one by one and swaddling the place in shadows. Bembor, Rolin and Marlis raised their lightstaffs to drive back the darkness.

Bembor said, "I once came across a half-burnt scrap of parchment that mentioned a captain of the tower guard named Elmar. It seems he embarked with a band of stalwart scouts on a perilous mission from which no one ever returned. His party's fate was never known."

"But why would Winona loan Elmar her ring, and how could it have helped her reach Luralin?" asked Marlis.

"That I cannot answer. We do know that Elgathel gave Winona a wondrous ring fashioned by the finest sorc-smiths of that day, deep in their worm-delved dens. Wait—here is something interesting."

For days now, I have stayed as still as death, hoping the yeggoroth would give up and leave me to my grief. They have not. After another sleepless night, I hear footsteps trudging up the stairwell. Arming myself with my husband's broken sword, I prepare to defend the Hallowfast with my blood. Since the door's bolt is broken, I must throw myself on Gaelathane's mercy.

When the door opens, who should stumble through but Elmar son of Selwyn! The wild, hunted look in his eyes has haunted my dreams ever since. He is terribly wounded about the head and neck. The yegs must have found him. I cannot think how he entered the tower, since the outer door is locked.

He staggers into me. "Hear me well!" he whispers. "The ring is lost forever, beyond mortal reach." He utters but seven more words before falling to the floor: "Beware the Guardian of the Golden Wood." Ah! Merciful Gaelathane, but the man is dead! From where he lies, he will rise no more. I must close his eyes or they will drive me to madness.

"More smudges," Bembor remarked. "At least we know now what became of Elmar—and the queen's ring."

He read on. "Now Winona goes downstairs, only to find the door still tightly locked. Nonetheless, something appears amiss. Perhaps the bodies of the tower's fallen defenders unnerve her. Now she's gone back upstairs to the throne room. When she tries to move Elmar's body, an object falls out of his pocket. Let's see what it is . . .

Is this what we've waited for so long? Of such we have plenty and to spare. Another pocket holds a single leaf of burnished gold. It resembles a torsil's in shape, though torsil leaves turn scarlet in autumn. Elmar paid for these baubles with his life.

I must leave, for I sicken within the cold walls of this watchful prison. It reeks of death. I will seek a new life in the land of the tree-cutters, where I shall bear my slain husband his only child. Would that he had lived to see his heir! I shall find small comfort in passing on his legacy through these last few mellathel.

"Mellathel? What are those?" Timothy asked, his heart burning with the love of rich, melodious names.

"That is what we call fresh amenthil flowers," said King Rolin as he wiped his eyes. "Once dried, they can preserve one's words and thoughts until the right person revives the flowers and breathes their scent." Pausing, he added, "The queen placed those 'message-flowers' in a special box for safekeeping."

Bembor picked up the tale. "Then Winona's daughter, Janna, passed the box down to her son, Rolin. He found and opened it after his mother's death and revived the flowers. From Queen Winona's message, we learned that Rolin was to be Lucambra's next king. But that is another story. The next entry reads,

During my final night in the Hallowfast, Gaelathane appeared to me. "Take heart, child," He told me. "I will be with you wherever you go, and I shall deliver this land through your offspring." He also spoke of Lucambra's last days and gave me these verses that make up what I call The Ballad of the Ball.

THE BALLAD OF THE BALL
When breaks the ball from sudden fall,
And thunder splits the ground;
When coats are shed and hope is dead,
And enemies surround;

Though strong the arm that threatens harm,
Let fainting heart not fail;
Beneath the stair you'll find the pair
That shows the sheltered vale.

Then seek the queen amidst the green
Of vacant trees and tall;
Where flowers bloom beneath the moon
And none can scale the wall.

So count the cost to save the lost,
The twelve who still survive;
Release from gloom of leafy tomb
And wooden eyes revive.

At Gaelathane's request, I have laid Elmar and his possessions to rest where no yeg or gork will ever find them. 'Tis a fitting tomb, since Elmar's best gift was in coming through the stairs.

"*Through* the stairs?" said Opio. "Surely she must have meant *up* the stairs. Those steps were hewn out of solid rock."

Larkin made a face. "Up the stairs, through the stairs, in the door, through the floor—what does it matter how Elmar got in or where he's buried? Dead men's bones don't talk. Let us leave off this pointless riddle-picking and rout the Thalmosians."

"Seeing that we are too few to overthrow Mardoc's army," said Rolin quietly, "our lives may depend upon solving these two riddles. In fact, the first verse of Winona's ballad was fulfilled in this very room." He described the accidental breaking of Meghan's sap ball, quipping, "I haven't made such a mess since I destroyed Felgor's prize Gundul-spasel with my lightstaff!"

"The next verses also fit our plight as snugly as bark on a tree," Marlis remarked. "Now that the sorcs are ill and have 'shed' their 'coats,' our 'hope' of rescue is very nearly 'dead.'"

"Thanks to the 'enemies' that 'surround' us," spat Sigarth.

"A pox on beekeepers!" Bembor exclaimed.

Rolin blinked in confusion. "The queen wrote that?"

"No, no. More pages have been torn out. Ah, here's the next legible entry. Now that's peculiar."

"What's peculiar?" asked Timothy. He squeezed between Rolin and Marlis to have a better look at the diary.

"The color of the ink has changed," said Bembor. He held up the book. "See the difference? This later writing is lighter and more watery." He sniffed the page. "My guess is that Winona concocted her ink from the drippings of Inky-Cap mushrooms."

Scanlon wrinkled his nose. "Mushroom drippings? How crude! Surely the queen could have found better."

"Not where she sought refuge. Just listen to this:

An outcast, I write these words in the shelter of a kindly Thalmosian fir. Anguish has gripped me, for my time draws near. Gaelathane, my heart cannot carry its burden alone. Grant me the grace to survive in this bleak land and to raise the babe I will bear You.

"Poor Grandmother," Rolin sighed. "If only she had realized what was to come!"

"If only we knew how she escaped the tower under those yegs' very noses!" countered Bembor. "Here is her last entry:

Today I have brought a babe into this land of exile. Her name is Janna—"Daughter of Sorrow." I never thought I could feel such joy as thrills my heart this hour. No longer am I one, but two. With Gaelathane, we are three, and three will make us a family. While my daughter lives, I shall never be lonely again.

What should I say to her? 'Janna, I can give you only the love of my heart and the knowledge of the King. His love is far greater and deeper than mine. Whether you plant your sythan-ar here or on some lofty hill in the Land of Light, place your first and final trust in Him. He will never disappoint you. If I am gone by the time you read these words, do not forget the box. May Gaelathane go with you always. Your devoted mother, Winona.'

Closing the diary, Bembor said with breaking voice, "Neither of those brave women ever returned to Lucambra. They perished in Thalmos, and Gannon buried them in their beech wood. Now do you understand what sustained them in that foreign place?"

"The hope of going back to Lucambra?" Timothy ventured.

Bembor shook his head. "It was faith, lad, faith in Gaelathane. They trusted Him with their very lives. We must do the same, seeing that our land has fallen once more on evil times."

CHAPTER 14
The Siege of the Citadel

Q ueen Marlis?"

"Here."

"Bembor son of Brenthor?"

The chancellor lifted a finger. "Here."

Timothy had awakened that morning in a strange room. The last thing he remembered was lying against Windsong's deliciously warm side, listening to the councilors discuss Winona's diary. The next thing he knew, a red-headed boy about his age and size had shaken him out of a sound sleep on a comfortable bed and was offering him a fresh change of clothes. After Timothy had dressed, the stranger hurried him up the stairs to the crowded banquet hall. Perched atop a table, Scanlon was taking the tower's roll.

"Elwyn son of Rolin?" he called out.

Timothy's companion waved and whistled shrilly. With a shock, Timothy realized he had slept the night in a prince's bed!

"Gwynneth daughter of Marlis?"

"Over here." A lithe maiden in lavender robes had spoken. Artfully interwoven with white ribbons, her golden hair cascaded down her back like cloud-laced sunbeams. Timothy was smitten. If only she would look at him! Waiting and hoping, he finally caught her eye and received a shy smile for his efforts.

"Meghan daughter of Marlis?" Necks craned and heads turned, but no one answered.

"Meghan daughter of Marlis?" Scanlon repeated more forcefully. Silence echoed through the room.

"She's probably playing with her kittens under the tables," Elwyn declared. However, a hands-and-knees search of the room turned up only Windsong and Ironwing, who were scavenging for scraps.

Rolin wearily rubbed his face. "Elwyn, please check her room." Elwyn rushed out of the hall and clattered down the stairs.

"Emmer son of Fandol," Scanlon went on, his voice faltering.

Emmer raised his head and an eyebrow.

"Mycena daughter of Emmer."

A petite brunette with Marlis's delicate features smiled nervously at Rolin. "It seems we're both prisoners again," she said. "This time, though, I'm afraid I can't help you escape."

Rolin wanly smiled back. "That's all right. If we must be cooped up, better the Hallowfast than the dragon's mountain."

"Timothy son of Garth?"

"Here!" Timothy answered.

On went the roll call until everyone but Meghan was accounted for. (Bart and Wiggin had been locked in the wine cellar.) Still Elwyn had not reappeared. Instead, a burly, grim-faced Greencloak named Garreth filled the doorway. "I found one of the accursed potato eaters downstairs, Sire," he said gruffly. "I don't know how he managed to sneak inside. He wishes to parley with you."

"Very well. Send him in," King Rolin curtly replied.

The scout returned with a liveried Thalmosian bearing a white flag and a small scroll. "Which one's your king?" he demanded. Garreth pointed to Rolin, who was standing beside Marlis.

"That whelp's the king?" the envoy scoffed. At his words, swords rang in the hushed hall.

"Sheathe your weapons," Rolin ordered. "As the Tree once said, 'He who raises the sword must be prepared to die by the sword.'"

"A wise choice," sneered the envoy. "We could trounce this rabble before breakfast with our bare hands! And what puny defenses. Your front door wasn't even locked. That's how I got in."

The Lucambrians exchanged puzzled looks. "I know I barred that door last night," Scanlon muttered. "As far as I know, nobody has left the tower since then."

Arms akimbo, King Rolin told the Thalmosian, "If you and your forces have come in peace, you are welcome to visit our land. If not, state your purpose and be done with it."

The emissary's lip curled. "As you wish." Unrolling his scroll, he read, "General Gorn, commander of His Majesty King Mardoc's army, to the usurper styling himself 'King of the Greencloaks.' We hereby demand your immediate and unconditional surrender, whereupon this land and all its inhabitants will become subject to the king. An annual tariff of one million gilders will be levied upon your treasury. All gold, jewels and other valuables will also be forfeit to the crown. Finally, you will hand over the turncoat, Timothy Garth's son."

Timothy hid under a table. He wasn't eager to face Mardoc's men again, much less the hangman.

Angry murmurs rumbled through the hall as King Rolin gritted, "And if we do not agree to your terms?"

The envoy crisply rolled up the scroll and handed it to him. "We'll tear down this tower stone by stone and kill you all."

The murmurs turned ugly. "Hang this Thalmosian scoundrel from the ramparts!" cried the greasy-aproned royal cook.

"Give him his gilders—in cold steel!" growled the armorer.

"Throw him out the window!" hissed Ironwing, springing onto a tabletop. He thrust his snapping scimitar beak right in the horrified Thalmosian's face, sending him reeling backward.

Rolin held up his hand. "Peace! Since this man has come under my roof, anyone who harms him will answer to me." He turned a cold eye on the emissary. "Tell your General Gorn that we reject his terms. On the contrary, we demand that he depart immediately. If he and his forces do not leave our realm within three days, I cannot guarantee their safety. Now go."

The envoy opened his mouth and closed it again, astonishment spreading across his features. A gloating look followed. "In that case, I've another matter to discuss with you."

Just then, Elwyn burst through the door. "She's not here, Father," he panted. "She's not anywhere in the Hallowfast!"

The envoy smirked. "That's what I wanted to tell you, *sire*. We came upon your little daughter strolling through the forest. She is now enjoying King Mardoc's hospitality."

With a bellow, Rolin flew at his enemy, knocking him to the floor. Choking the emissary with both hands, he growled, "If any harm comes to Meghan, I'll—!"

Rushing forward, Scanlon restrained the king. "Rolin, you can't! You gave him your word of honor, remember?"

Still glowering, Rolin helped the envoy up. "Two of your men are in our custody. We will exchange them for Meghan."

"A bad bargain that would be," wheezed the man, fingering the red marks on his neck. "You've done us a favor by taking those laggards off our hands. They're not worth the clothes on their backs, let alone the ransom of a princess." With that, he turned on his heel and stalked off. Pausing by the door, he added, "Some of our fighting forces have withdrawn to make preparations for war. Do not be deceived. They shall soon return with engines of destruction that will quickly bring you to your knees."

CHAPTER 15
Derwin Son of Stolland

Hitching up her heavy green skirts, Meghan waded through the dew-spangled grass toward the beckoning woods. She had awakened before daybreak to find that the Thalmosians had left during the night. Supposing all danger had passed, she had taken a sack and a silver knife from the kitchen. Then she had crept down the winding stairs.

Finding the stone door double-barred, she wrestled the heavy wooden beams aside just far enough to push open the slab. Outside, a moist, wide world basked in the dawn's gray stillness.

It was all her fault. If she hadn't broken her father's spasel, the Thalmosians wouldn't have found their way into Lucambra. At least that was how she saw it. The only way to make amends was to present the king with a brand-new spasel.

Since Lightleaf was notoriously stingy with his sap, Meghan searched out Butterbark, a Thalmos torsil whose trunk was warted with thick lumps of solidified sap. She was prying off the ready-made spasels with her knife and dropping them into the sack when she heard a *Thack! Thack!* Dropping the knife and bag, she let her feet carry her into a clearing littered with felled trees, their cut ends still oozing.

Whack! Whack! Swinging a notched axe, a tall, hairy-armed man with sandy hair was hacking at a standing tree, which groaned at every blow. With a splintering screech, the tree toppled over and crashed to earth, its branches whiplashing.

Meghan ran up and pummeled the woodcutter's back with her fists. "Stop that! You stop chopping down our trees!"

"Hold on, Missy," the man said, turning to catch both her wrists in a meaty fist. His peasant's blouse and trousers were sprinkled with wood chips. "What's the matter? I ain't hurtin' nobody."

Meghan stamped her foot. "Yes, you are! You're cutting down our friends! My father will be very upset when he finds out what you've been doing. Now, let go of me."

The woodcutter released his hold. "All right, Missy. There ye are. Only ye must promise not to hurt me again." Meghan nodded. "Now, tell me: Who is yer daddy?"

Rubbing her wrists, Meghan sullenly replied, "He's King Rolin, and all these trees belong to him. And you sure talk funny."

The man eyed her thoughtfully. "If yer father's the king, I guess I'd better leave off. What's yer name, Missy?"

Meghan told him.

"A nice name, that," said the woodcutter with a gap-toothed grin. "Mine's Derwin. Friends?" He held out his hand.

Staring in horror at Derwin's hairy paw, Meghan took a step back. "You're a Thalmosian! Only potato eaters shake hands!" Before she could run, Derwin caught her around the middle and threw her over his shoulder like a sack of nuts. With great, loping strides he carried her kicking and yelling through the forest and into another clearing overflowing with varicolored tents.

Derwin stopped at a bright red one sporting a blue banner and pushed aside the flap. He poked Meghan's feet through the flap and then followed with the rest of her. Inside the shadowy tent, a grizzled warrior was sitting on a camp stool honing his spear. He looked up sharply from his work as Derwin set Meghan on her feet.

"Beggin' yer pardon, General Gorn," Derwin began with a bow. "I found this girl in the forest while I was a-cuttin' trees fer firewood. She's a feisty one. Says her father is the king."

The other man rose from his stool to tower over Meghan. "So you're Rolin's daughter, are you?" he rasped. Meghan didn't like the look on his craggy face, nor the bottomless black pits behind his eyes.

"Yes, I am," she replied. "Take me back to him now, or—"

"Or what, you impudent scamp?" said the general coldly as he hoisted Meghan off the ground by her hair. Wriggling in his grip like a speared fish, she stared into his hooded eyes.

"I am not accustomed to taking orders from little girls," he growled. "In this camp, I give the orders. Remember that, if you ever want to see your father again!" Then he released her.

***

Whump! Meghan landed on her back, knocking the wind out of her. She was still gasping when Derwin scooped her up.

"Ye needn't have dropped her, General," he said reproachfully. "She's only a girl. Let me find her something to eat and send her home. She'll only get under foot if we keep her here."

"Mind your tongue, peasant, or lose it," spat the general, running a finger along one edge of his spearhead. "Feed the brat some scraps if you will, but don't let her out of your sight. Her parents will no doubt pay a pretty price to have her back. And don't bring her in here again, as you hope to live. She favors her father all too well. Now leave me!"

"Come along, Missy," said Derwin, bowing backwards out of the tent. Taking his hand, Meghan followed her captor through crowds of swaggering soldiers, all armed to the teeth. A dreadful chorus of shouts, curses and boisterous laughter hammered at her ears. The camp reeked of wood smoke and roasting meat.

"Where are you taking me?" Meghan asked the woodcutter.

Derwin regarded her with kindly blue eyes. "Scraps ain't fit fer a princess," he declared. "I'm finding ye a decent meal. We have a tent kitchen not far from here, an' I'm on good terms with th' cook."

On the encampment's outskirts, they found a long line of men snaking through an open-air pavilion. Under its canvas top, soot-stained servants ladled out soup from bubbling cauldrons. Ducking under the side of the tent, Derwin reemerged moments later with two steaming bowls. He handed one to Meghan.

"One fer you and one fer me," he said, settling on a log. "Go on, try some." Meghan sat down beside him and began eating.

As the watery potato broth spread warmth through Meghan's limbs, her fears drained away. She even steeled herself to look into the rough, battle-hardened faces of passing soldiers. Some glanced at her curiously, wondering at her presence in their midst. Others smiled, perhaps recalling their own daughters.

"What are you going to do with me?" she asked Derwin after she had finished her soup.

The woodcutter wiped his mouth on his sleeve. "The general told me to keep an eye on ye, Missy, and that's just what I aim to do. Ye've given me a good excuse to rest my axe awhile."

Meghan fidgeted. "I mean . . . when can I go home?"

Derwin avoided her gaze. "That depends on yer father. If he agrees to the general's conditions, ye could go back to yer family today, I'll wager. And don't glare at me like that. It warn't my idea to come here, wherever we are."

"We're in Lucambra, and you potato eaters don't belong here," said Meghan matter-of-factly.

Derwin burst into laughter. "Is that what ye call us? And why don't we 'potato eaters' belong in Lucambra?"

Meghan resisted the urge to kick Derwin in the shins. "Because this land is ours, that's why! Gaelathane gave it to us."

As if reading Meghan's mind, Derwin propped his legs up on a stump out of harm's way. Then he pulled out a briar pipe, stuffed it with some pungent leaves, and lit it. Meghan watched in fascination as his mouth pumped out little puffs of blue smoke.

"Is that so. And who is this Gaelathane?"

"He's the King."

Derwin frowned. "Gaelathane is your father?"

Meghan rolled her eyes. Honestly, these Thalms could be as dense as stones sometimes! "No—I mean yes."

Derwin chewed on his pipe stem. "No or yes. Which is it?"

"My father is king of Lucambra, but Gaelathane is the King of kings. He made the world and us, too, so He's also my Father."

The pipe fell out of Derwin's mouth and he guffawed, "Made the world, did He? Out of what? Dirt?"

"No, silly. He made it out of love."

Derwin sternly pointed his pipe stem at her. "Now listen here, Missy. Nobody made this place. It just happened, like a . . . a tree that grows up from a seed."

"Then where did the seed come from?" Meghan was retorting when she spotted a wheeled contraption made of lashed-together logs rattling toward them. Resembling a peak-roofed, low-slung hut, its topmost timbers supported a free-swinging log. The whole engine was being pulled along by a team of muscular men-at-arms using ropes.

"What's that?" Meghan asked, pointing.

Derwin looked away. "A battering ram."

"What's it for?"

"It's used to knock down walls and gates and doors."

"Oh." Meghan had a horrible thought. "Like the Hallowfast's?"

"If that's what ye call yonder tower, then yes. If yer father refuses to surrender, our men will have to break down the door. They're very good at such things, mind ye."

Swinging her legs, Meghan stared at her feet. "If they do break in, then what? We haven't any potatoes inside. Father doesn't like them. He had to eat too many when he was a boy."

Derwin chuckled. "It's gold and gems that Mardoc wants, Missy, not 'taters, though I daresay he's got enough riches already."

The battering ram had just rumbled past when another ram not made with hands struck the earth like a mighty fist. Meghan's log heaved and bucked, catapulting her into the air like a rag doll. Earth and sky spun in a pinwheel of greens, blues and browns before strong arms caught and held her.

CHAPTER 16
Thunder Splits the Ground

When the shaking struck, the Hallowfast rocked and swayed like a storm-tossed tree. Timothy was knocked beneath a table, where he lay stunned and breathless as Elgathel's bell pealed madly in the sorcathel above.

After the throbbing thunder had died away, the cries and groans began. Some of the Lucambrians lay buried beneath fallen debris, while others were tangled in jumbled tables and benches. The sorcs had escaped harm by fluttering off the floor until the shaking stopped. Once the dust had settled, Marlis and her ladies-in-waiting ferreted out salves and bandages and then attended to the injured.

When the banquet hall was somewhat restored to order, Rolin took Elwyn and Timothy up to the throne room. There they found thrones and cupboards flung topsy-turvy. Sap balls rolled about on the floor like giant marbles. Scores had shattered.

Elwyn moaned, "We'll never replace all those broken spasels! I've not yet warmed most of them. Now we'll never know where they led."

"So much damage," Rolin murmured. "What new mischief has Gorn devised this time? We'd better have a look outside." With Elwyn's help, he pulled down a recessed ladder leading to a ceiling hatch. Timothy steadied its base while Rolin and Elwyn climbed up and threw open the trap door. Timothy followed.

"Welcome to the sorcathel!" Elwyn greeted him. "Keep your head down. The enemy has already shot some arrows up here." Timothy noted the barbed shafts littering the sorcathel's stones like oversized, feathered knitting needles.

Rolin stood gazing over the ramparts, his royal robes flapping in the wind and rain. "It wasn't the Thalmosians at all," he said, gesturing toward the ground. "See for yourselves."

Sidling up to the parapet, the boys looked down on a tormented land laced with deep rifts. In the distance, Mardoc's advancing army milled about in disorder like frightened ants.

"Those fissures will help slow down the enemy," Rolin observed. "Then again, we were banged up the worse for being in the tower. Thank Gaelathane it didn't collapse around our ears. As you can see, an earthquake favors neither side in battle."

"That was an earthquake?" Elwyn exclaimed. "Lucambra never has earthquakes. What could have caused it?"

"Mt. Golgunthor must be to blame," his father replied, pointing southeast. Seen through a gap in the Brynnmor Mountains, the range dividing Lucambra's seacoast from the inland plain, a shattered cone belched smoke, ash and flame. Even from afar, those ghastly fires splashed the tower's stones with blood.

Elwyn's eyes grew as round as spasels. "The dragon's mountain hasn't erupted in hundreds of years!"

"I know," said King Rolin, his face darkening. "If this continues, the Thalmosians will be the least of our worries. Come; we must break the news to the others."

Back in the banquet hall, the Lucambrians received Rolin's tidings with dismay. "This tower can't take another beating like the last," said Sigarth. "The next tremor may tear it to pieces."

"Taking us with it," remarked his long-faced brother. A muddy, muttering current ran through the crowd.

Rolin waved his lightstaff to restore order. "Dear friends, I regret to say it is no longer safe to remain here. Difficult though the parting may be, we must leave our beloved Hallowfast."

"It's no safer outside with those run-amok Thalms," growled Opio. "Better to die up here than to give Mardoc the satisfaction of seeing us all swing. It won't be his deserters he hangs this time, either."

Long-limbed and sunken-eyed, Larkin son of Gaflin spoke up. "Opio is right," he said. "Leaving the Hallowfast now would be sheer madness. We'd be walking straight into the enemy's arms. It would be better that we should perish together in the collapse of the Hallowfast than to hang separately on Mardoc's gallows."

"I disagree," said Ironwing. "Though we cannot fly, Windsong and I would rather meet death with the sun in our eyes and blood on our beaks. Let us fall upon the two-legs while they feast in their tents and make them pay dearly for their insolence!"

"Speak for yourself!" retorted Windsong. "If necessary, we can still run swiftly, even if it means putting our backs to the enemy. Sorcs have a saying from our dragon days, 'Burnt fur and feathers bring no glory when none survives to tell the story.' We do not fear death, yet neither should we seek it as an escape."

Bembor raised a hand wrapped in a bloody bandage. "Let us have no more talk of death," he said gruffly. "The king wishes to preserve our lives, not throw them away. If he deems it best for us to flee the Hallowfast, then flee we must."

"We can't just run off and leave Meghan to the Thalmosians!" Gwynneth protested.

"We won't, *cariad*," said her father. "For the time being, though, we must entrust her to Gaelathane and obey His words:

Depart at once but do not fear
The bended bow or the smiting spear—

BOOM! A stone-rattling rumble resounded through the tower. Thinking another quake had struck, Timothy dove for cover.

King Rolin held his head and groaned, "That terrible sound has haunted me ever since Gaelathane's last visit."

Emmer cautiously ascended the rickety ladder Timothy had climbed earlier and peered out the deep-set window. "The Thalms are using a battering ram to break down the door!" he exclaimed.

"It's a good thing we made the door secure after that lout of an emissary left," said Scanlon. "Let the enemy pound on it now!"

"No door is secure against the likes of this ram," Emmer declared. "Fell words and designs mark the iron head that caps it, and twenty men with ropes give it life and voice. The Thalmosians have even brought some horses, though I can't imagine how they got them up Scarlimb, much less down again."

By unspoken agreement, the king and queen knelt on the stone floor with the other Lucambrians in united prayer to Gaelathane for deliverance. Meghan's name crossed many lips.

"Mae'r Goeden yn fyw," Rolin finished.

"Mae'r Goeden yn fyw!" echoed his listeners.

"Mae'r Goeden yn fyw!" crowed Timothy. Then he covered his mouth. Was it proper for those words to pass a Thalm's lips?

BOOM! Again the battering ram demanded entry.

With steel in his eyes, Rolin raised his staff. "We must keep our heads if we're to outwit our enemies. As Queen Winona was trapped in this tower, so are we. As she was surrounded by enemies, so are we. As she escaped, so shall we, following the clues she left us in her diary. We must search the stairs!"

CHAPTER 17
Beneath the Stair

This place has six hundred and forty steps," protested Opio, who didn't care for climbing stairs. "I've counted them. How will we know where to look?" *BOOM!* The tower shuddered under another blow of the battering ram.

"Spread out along the staircase and test every step," Rolin ordered. "If that hidden entrance still exists, we will find it."

"Last one to the bottom is a dirty gork!" cried Elwyn. Racing out the banquet-hall door, Timothy, Elwyn and Gwynneth flew down the steep, spiral stairway. Timothy was leading when he lost his footing and bounced down the final few steps—"Oof! Oof! Oof!"

"Are you all right?" asked Gwynneth as she helped him up.

Timothy rubbed his scraped shins. "I think so," he said. "I guess this makes me the 'dirty gork,' though—" *Crash!* The battering ram shook the door, jarring Timothy from teeth to toes and splintering the topmost wooden barricade.

"We've got to find another beam to brace the door!" cried Elwyn.

Charging up the stairs, Timothy tripped again and banged his bleeding shins. Groaning, he collapsed on the offending step.

"You should watch where you put your feet," Elwyn told him.

"It's not Timothy's fault," Gwynneth flared. "That step is sticking out." Sure enough, the fourth tread from the bottom was askew. Elwyn tugged on it and the step silently swung out, leaving a rectangular hole. Stale, fetid air poured from the opening.

"Phew!" Elwyn sniffed. "It smells like something died down there. I'll bet it's been closed up for ages."

Just then, the grownups came clattering down the stairs. While a couple of men replaced the broken door-brace, Marlis shone her lightstaff into the hole, illumining some sloping steps.

"Amazing!" murmured Bembor. "A secret stairway, and it's right under our noses, too. Who would have guessed it? The quake must have dislodged this tread just enough for Timothy to trip over it. We owe you yet another debt of gratitude, my lad." Nursing his shins, Timothy thought he'd settle for some bandages instead.

WHOOMP! The battering ram struck again. Cracks spiderwebbed the weakening door and flakes split off its stone face. Bembor and Rolin traded worried glances. They looked down at the step-well and then at Timothy. Rolin handed him a lightstaff.

"You just want me to go first because I'm the smallest," Timothy grumbled. Because of his size, he was frequently called upon to sweep chimneys, chase birds and bats out of attics, unstop clogged wells and the like. He longed for Baglot's brawny build.

"Think of it as an honor," said Rolin with a sympathetic look.

Gripping the lightstaff, Timothy lowered himself through the yawning hole until his feet found the second set of stairs. His skin crawled as he pictured all manner of nasty creatures lurking in the darkness below. He shivered in the chill air.

A bat flittered into the pool of staff light and as Timothy recoiled, he bumped a stone block jutting from the wall on his left. With a grinding whir, the block retracted and an entire section of the top staircase slid back, widening the hole. Shouts of alarm rang down until Timothy assured his friends that all was well.

He crept down the steps, the battering ram's dull boom chasing him into the darkness, keeping time with his thudding heart. Soon, he felt the sure footing of a smooth stone floor. Holding the lightstaff overhead, he drove the shadows from a cavernous vault. At the far end, a decaying wooden door sagged ajar.

Then Timothy saw he was not alone. Lying on a stone table near the stairs, a skeleton greeted him with a toothy grin. Timothy touched a withered finger, and it crumbled to dust. "I'm so sorry!" he gasped before realizing the remains were past feeling pain.

Beside the slack-jawed skeleton lay an overturned clay pitcher and two cider-colored puddles. Timothy probed one of the puddles with his finger. The "cider" was as solid as his lightstaff.

"All clear!" he called up to his companions, and dancing shadows began descending the hidden stairs. Lightstaffs wove and bobbed like giant fireflies. Following the sorcs, Opio climbed down last with a bulging bag—and stuck fast. Sigarth and Skoglund each grabbed a hefty leg and pulled with a will. Cloth tore.

"Ugh!" Opio grunted as he popped through. "That was a tight fit! Why didn't those old Lucambrians leave us more room?"

"They were a sight skinnier than you are," retorted Sigarth.

"Close up the hole!" Bembor barked from below.

"How?" Opio called back. Then Timothy rushed up the stairs to find another stone block projecting from the wall just below the one that had retreated into its niche. When he pushed on the block, all the steps grated back into place—and none too soon.

With a roar, the door burst asunder. Every eye turned upward as booted feet drummed up the stairs. The griffins paced.

Hours passed before the muted shouting and footsteps finally died away. "They must have finished plundering the place," Gemmio grunted, sitting dejected with his head hanging between his knees.

His brother hefted the bag he had brought with him. "At least we had time to collect the royal crowns, a few weapons, some changes of clothes, and some provisions and water."

"Thank you!" said Marlis. "You didn't by chance remember to pack any soap, did you?" Opio shook his head ruefully.

"Scanlon, please call the roll again," said King Rolin. "There should be sixty-two of us, including Timothy and the sorcs."

While Scanlon counted heads, Timothy motioned Elwyn and Gwynneth over to the skeleton table. "Brrr!" said Gwynneth. "This poor fellow has been lying here a long time." She nudged Elwyn. "I can't help feeling that his eye-sockets are staring at me."

Elwyn shivered. "Me, too. What a horrible way to die, cooped up in the darkness without food or water! We'd better find a way out of here soon or we'll end up looking just like him."

"No, you won't," said Bembor, examining the skeleton. "Our friend didn't die in this crypt. Were he still alive, he had only to leave through yonder doorway. No, Winona dragged his body down here, where 'no yeg or gork' would ever find him."

"Elmar?" exclaimed Timothy. "This is Elmar?"

"Who else could it be?" Bembor said. "It certainly isn't Elgathel. The high king's body still lies in its casket."

"What are these odd puddles, then?" asked Elwyn. "They look as if someone knocked over the pitcher and left the spill."

Bembor flashed a smile at him. "Take a closer look."

Elwyn picked up the pitcher, which was chipped on the lip where it had struck the table. He shrugged. "It looks like an ordinary clay pitcher to me, Grandfather."

Timothy peered into the jug, which was half full of a watery-white substance with a black dimple in the center. When he poked the stuff, his fingernail left dents. "This is wax!" he said.

"Right you are," Bembor chortled. "Elwyn mistakenly assumed that something had spilled out of the pitcher. In truth, this is a 'candle-jug.' Back in Queen Winona's day, Lucambrians often lit their homes with wax-filled pitchers. She must have brought this one downstairs to light her way in the darkness."

"These puddles aren't wax," said Elwyn. "They're too hard."

"They're spasels, silly," Gwynneth said, tossing her head.

"I thought spasels were supposed to be round," said Timothy as he ran his fingers across their glassy surfaces.

"They are, if you don't leave them in one place too long," Rolin said. "Despite the chill in this chamber, these two have slowly lost their shape. Left in the sun, they would 'melt' much faster."

Bembor shone his lightstaff over the table. "These spasla must be the 'possessions' that Queen Winona placed with Elmar's body in this 'fitting tomb.' No wonder she was so disappointed! Our people had sap balls a-plenty in those days."

Timothy couldn't see the use of two spread-out, puddly spasels. Even if they still worked, what would they show? Flattened people? Flattened trees? At Bembor's direction, he and Elwyn gently pried both of the hardened pools of sap off the table. Then they breathed on the spasels, warming them.

A milk-white mist befogged Timothy's spasel. As the mist cleared, shimmering colors swirled across the sap sheet's glossy surface. Then the patterns faded, leaving the spasel dark.

"That's all?" Timothy said. At the very least, he had expected some wooded, castle-crowned hills or a dragon or two.

"Just wait," said Bembor. Collecting all the lightstaffs, he slid them into a space beneath the stairs. Darkness reigned.

"Dousing the light will bring out the images better," King Rolin explained. Timothy gasped as the spasel lit up with myriads of bright pinpricks, like stars dancing on a midnight pool.

"I don't recognize those constellations," said Marlis. "Let's see what the other spasel has to show us." As Elwyn finished warming the second "puddle," he produced a woodland scene where graceful trees glowed golden in the setting sun.

"How charming," said Scanlon sourly. "Elmar's 'Golden Wood' is just a sunset-gilded forest. What's to fear in that?"

Marlis sighed. "My dear brother, Elmar didn't say, 'Beware the Golden Wood,' but 'Beware the *Guardian* of the Golden Wood.'"

"At the moment," Emmer pointed out, "we've more to fear from the Thalmosians if they discover what that fourth step is concealing."

"Then we had better try the door," said Rolin. "Now, where did Bembor put my lightstaff?" He rummaged around under the stairs. Rocks rattled. "Coal? They kept their coal in here?"

Emmer ambled over to pick up a chunk. "This is fine, hard *glo*," he said, stuffing his pockets with some of the smaller pieces. "You never know when a few lumps might come in handy."

As Rolin handed out the lightstaffs, Gwynneth grabbed one and shone it on the skeleton. "Look!" she cried. "Here's something else!" She pointed to Elmar's neck bones, which were encircled with a leather thong that was attached to a small pouch.

The boys glanced at each other and then at Gwynneth. "Don't look at me!" she said, throwing up her hands. "I'm not going to touch him. One of you can take off that bag if you like."

"Oh, all right," grumbled Timothy. "I'll do it." Gingerly lifting Elmar's skull, he removed the strap and pouch. At his friends' urging, he opened the sack and shook it. Out dribbled a stream of yellow speckles that gleamed softly in the staff light.

"Gold dust!" Rolin exclaimed. "Where did Elmar get that?"

"Maybe he kept his golden leaves in this pouch, and they crumbled to dust," Bembor said. "Since he probably hid the sack under his tunic, Winona wouldn't have noticed it. After the corpse's clothes rotted off, the pouch was all that remained."

"Why don't we try giving some of that dust to the sorcs?" Elwyn suggested. "Windsong said it might cure the scorbies."

"There's a waste of perfectly good gold, if you ask me," muttered Larkin. Ironwing glared at him and flicked his tail.

After Opio filled the candle-jug with water, Timothy sprinkled some gold dust inside. Then the sorcs lapped up the mixture.

"How do you feel now?" Elwyn asked them.

"The same," Windsong sighed.

"No taste to it," said Ironwing. "Opio, you don't happen to have any conies in that sack of yours, do you?" He didn't.

Since nobody else wished to wear Elmar's pouch, Timothy looped the strap around his neck and stuffed the bag inside his shirt. When he looked up again, Rolin stood on the stairs, facing his subjects.

"The hour has come for us to part company," the king said, his voice hollow in the airless room. "We are too many to travel together, but too few for an army. Even if we could muster our scattered forces, we are no match for Mardoc's men—or his horses."

"We're not surrendering, are we?" his hearers asked.

"Hardly," Rolin replied. "However, there is a time to fight, and a time to lick our wounds. Even so, we are not slinking away like whipped curs with our tails between our legs. Let us leave this place with heads held high, for Gaelathane's deliverance is nigh and He will repay the Thalmosians for their misdeeds."

Marlis joined Rolin on the step. "Anyone who follows the crown hereafter will wander far from home and kin, a fugitive in his own land, with little reward for his loyalty but hardship, heartache and loss. For that reason, only those who freely drink the bitter cup of exile may join us in our journeys."

The room fell silent. Then Skoglund laid his sword next to Elmar's bones on the stone table. "I will follow my lord and lady wherever they fare, even unto the gallows," he said.

Metal sang as the others drew their swords and placed them beside Skoglund's. "Even unto the gallows!" they cried as one.

In the end, King Rolin and Queen Marlis chose ten companions to join them in exile: Prince Elwyn; Princess Gwynneth; Bembor son of Brenthor; Emmer son of Fandol; Scanlon and Mycena, son and daughter of Emmer; Opio and Gemmio, the sons of Nolan; and Sigarth and Skoglund, Sigwyn's sons. Windsong and Ironwing would serve both as scouts and as running mounts.

When Larkin objected to being left behind, the king told him, "In my absence, I am entrusting you with our people's welfare. Please take all who are fit to travel to the Valley of Liriassa. Bembor's brother, Marlon, will be there to help you."

"What about me?" Timothy cried. Surely the king wouldn't leave him in the tower or send him back to Thalmos! He hated to think what would happen if Mardoc's men caught him.

Rolin smiled thinly. "I haven't forgotten you. As the thirteenth two-legged member of our party, you will be 'the Bearer of the Relics.'"

"What's that?" Timothy asked.

"The one who carries Elmar's gold-dust pouch and spasels," Rolin explained. "Take care not to lose them!"

Timothy swelled with pride. Relic-Bearer! It was a high honor for one who was neither a Lucambrian nor even a gallant bowman of Beechtown. He wished Baglot could see him now.

Sigarth raised his hand. "Sire, do you think it wise to bring the boy along? Whatever else he may be, he's still a Thalmosian, and a very unlucky one at that. We've had nothing but trouble since he arrived here. I'd feel better sending him home and leaving our number at twelve instead of thirteen."

"Then perhaps you ought to stay behind yourself," Rolin returned. "You know very well the queen and I don't hold with superstitious fiddle-faddle. Gaelathane will see us through whatever lies ahead, whether we are thirteen in number or thirty. Besides, we all owe our freedom and our lives to Timothy. He deserves the same chance to earn his cloak and staff as any Lucambrian lad."

"Hear, hear!" Bembor cried, leading the other Greencloaks in a staff-stamping. Elwyn loudly clapped. Then Timothy's scalp prickled a warning. Glancing around, he caught Gwynneth gazing at him. She lowered her eyes and blushed.

Minutes later, Skoglund had torn down the rotten door, admitting a blast of cold, dank air from a lightless tunnel. Waiting with their chosen companions, the king and queen bade farewell to Larkin and the other refugees, who shuffled down the passage like condemned men trudging to their deaths. Then Rolin removed his and Marlis's crowns from Opio's bag and placed them on the skeleton table.

"We won't be needing these for a while," he remarked.

"I suppose not," said Marlis. Tears streaked her cheeks.

"There, there, my sweet trillium," the king said, embracing his queen. "We'll be back before you know it to reclaim our own. The Land of Light won't suffer long under Mardoc's thumb."

"It's only that I fear for our daughter," Marlis choked out. "Who knows what those barbarians will do to her?"

Rolin clasped Marlis's hands. "Gaelathane will watch over her and us as well," he said. Then he and the queen took up their lightstaffs and led their comrades-in-exile through the doorway.

CHAPTER 18
The Tower Falls

*C*RASH! Meghan winced as the battering ram struck home. A team of sweating soldiers swung the log back into position, only to release it again.

CRACK! Derwin cocked his head at the sound. "That door's about to bust," he said. "Fer yer sake, Missy, I hope yer father raises the white flag. He hasn't a prayer of holding out now. After that earthquake, he'll be glad to leave his tower."

WHOOMP! As Derwin had predicted, the stone door shattered. While Thalmosian troops poured into the tower and rushed up the stairs, tears trickled down Meghan's face. In her few short years, the Hallowfast's very name had been a refuge from the real and imagined dangers of the world. Now she wept with the incurable pain of hopes dashed and innocence lost.

After a few minutes, General Gorn peered inside and was nearly bowled over by a soldier. "It's empty!" he cried. "Nobody's in there!"

"What?!" roared the general. "Search this blasted tower from top to bottom. Keep an eye out for gold and gems, too. If we don't bring back some rich booty for Mardoc, heads will roll. Now get on with it!" Quailing before Gorn's wrath, the man bolted up the stairs.

Meghan trembled. What had happened to her friends and family? Surely they couldn't have escaped unnoticed. She tried to recall all of the Hallowfast's secret nooks and crannies where she had played hide-and-seek with Elwyn and Gwynneth. Most were too cramped for grownups. She wiped her eyes on her sleeve.

Derwin patted her head. "Don't fret, Missy. Yer family will be all right. Just between ye and me, I hope we don't find yer father. Better that he save his skin and leave his gold for Mardoc."

"We don't have any gold," Meghan retorted.

As the men-at-arms tossed the tower's contents outside, Meghan sadly relived her fondest memories of the place: Spasel-gazing in the throne room; rolling balls down the stairs (much to the annoyance of those below); flying kites from the sorcathel; golden summer sunsets that dissolved into fire; rain rolling in from the sea; and of course, the splendid parties and feasts.

By late afternoon, the Hallowfast was well and truly looted, but none of its residents had turned up. It appeared they had all vanished into the El-marin's gray mists. General Gorn was furious.

While he fretted and fumed, his greedy men pawed through the Lucambrians' belongings. Beds and dressers; tables and chairs; cups, saucers and spoons; jars and vats, clothing and mats; ropes and hooks; lanterns and books were all carelessly jumbled together outside the front door. One drunken soldier was admiring himself in Meghan's favorite mirror. Then he peevishly broke it over his neighbor's head. Sickened, Meghan looked away.

Leaving his comrades to quarrel over the spoils of war, Derwin led Meghan away. They were strolling among some shore pines when a magnificent, four-legged creature came proudly trotting toward them. Boasting a barrel-chested body, flowing tail, long neck and massive jaws, the pointy-eared beast looked bigger than a griffin, bigger than any animal Meghan had ever seen. A freckle-faced boy was riding it, holding some straps that ran through a harness around its head.

"Help!" Meghan cried, clinging to Derwin. "What is that thing?"

"Why, it's a horse," he replied. "It won't hurt ye. Haven't ye ever seen one before?"

Meghan shook her head. "Father has told me about them. We don't have any in Lucambra, 'cause they can't climb torsils."

"Climb what?" asked Derwin with a perplexed look.

"Torsils. You know, trees of passage. You climbed one to come here." She stared at the horse. "How did you get it up the tree?"

Derwin grinned. "Ropes and pulleys, Missy, ropes and pulleys!" He caught the horse's reins as it arrived in a cloud of dust.

"Hullo!" said the young rider. Leaning down, he shook hands with Derwin and then offered Meghan his hand. The deeply tanned boy looked to be twelve or thirteen. Hidden under an overgrown mop of dark hair, his eyes were all but invisible.

Meghan ignored the hand. "Who are you?" she asked.

"Name's Midge. I'm a stable boy. Maggie and I are just getting some exercise. Want to come along?"

"On that beast?" Meghan exclaimed. "Is it safe?"

"Of course it is," Derwin laughed. "Here, let me show you." Over Meghan's protests, the woodcutter grabbed her under the arms and hoisted her onto the horse's back behind Midge.

"Hold onto me and you'll be fine," Midge assured her. Clinging to Midge's middle, Meghan wasn't convinced. The horse smelled rank and sweaty and the ground looked very far away.

Midge urged Maggie into a walk, then a brisk canter. Meghan's teeth rattled in rhythm with the horse's gait. "Not so fast!" she squealed. Midge twitched the reins and Maggie slowed.

Midge and Meghan spent most of that day and the next riding Maggie around the Hallowfast and up and down the beach. Derwin often joined them on another horse named Plum. The second day, they were returning to the stables when—*RHOOM!*—earthquake thunder rippled again through the earth. Maggie leapt into the air as though stung by a thousand hornets. "Whoa, Maggie, whoa!" Midge shouted, but the horse had already lost her head. Her eyes rolling in terror, Maggie tore off at a full gallop.

"Keep your head down!" Midge shouted as some low-hanging branches flashed by. Onward they went, the horse's hooves pounding the ground and throwing up great clods of dirt. At last Maggie halted, her chest heaving and lips dripping foam.

"There, Maggie, there," crooned Midge. "You're all right, girl. Let's have a little rest now, shall we?"

But Maggie didn't want to rest. Sniffing the air, she neighed and charged off again, this time in a different direction.

"Whoa, Maggie!" Midge cried again, yanking on the reins. He might as well have tried to tether the wind. Jolting along on the horse's back, Meghan could scarcely hang on. With a joyful whinny, Maggie galloped up to a torsil where fifteen or twenty mail-clad Thalmosians and their mounts were assembled. To Meghan's surprise, Derwin and Plum were among them.

The soldiers' dark-haired, broad-beamed captain stared hard at Meghan. "Who's this?" he grunted suspiciously.

"Didn't you know?" said Midge. "She's our hostage. The king's daughter, or so they say. Ask Derwin if you don't believe me. We were riding for the stables when our horse bolted."

"A princess, eh?" sneered the stubbly-faced Thalmosian. He eyed Meghan narrowly. "Can she draw water?"

Still seated on Maggie, Meghan forced her aching body upright. "I can if you ask me nicely!" she huffed.

The Thalmosians broke into coarse laughter. In two strides, their captain had Meghan off the horse. "Is this nicely enough?" he spat with a spite-twisted sneer. Meghan squirmed in his ham-fisted grip. Really, hadn't these Thalms any manners?

"Put me down!" she squeaked.

"Do as she asks, Asper," said Derwin wearily.

Asper's eyes flashed fire. "Who are you to tell me what to do, woodcutter? Go chop your trees and leave the fighting to me."

Derwin's jaw tensed. "Meghan's my charge, Brother. That's Gorn's orders. Take it up with him. If ye want her help, be gentle!"

"Very well," snorted the captain. He set Meghan down and the other men gathered around in a forest of spears and legs.

Asper leaned over Meghan, his breath reeking of beer and sausage. "First off, we want to know why this tree doesn't work. Up we climb, down we climb, and we're still where we started. Maybe you know a spell to set things right. For your sake, I hope so."

"I don't know any spells," said Meghan. "Father says they're wicked." A torsil that wouldn't grant passage? How strange! Perhaps the tree was rotten inside, though it looked healthy enough.

"Maybe the tree's too old," she suggested.

"Or we are," the hard-bitten captain countered. He studied her with dark, flinty eyes. "Since you're a young one, you try it."

Knowing better than to refuse outright, Meghan studied the ground. What did the captain want with this solitary torsil? If she gave in to his demands, her people might be imperiled, although escape to the other side also lay that way. She sensed Asper's rage mounting like pent-up steam inside a kettle.

Suddenly, a stabbing pain under Meghan's chin forced her head up. The tip of Asper's razor-edged knife blade was pressing against her flesh. The captain's black eyebrows bristled.

"CLIMB!" he roared.

"Leave her be," said Derwin sternly. He loosened the cords on the axe strapped across his back and gripped its handle.

Asper wheeled on him. "You stay out of this, peasant!" Returning to Meghan, he said, "I have lost my patience with you, *princess*. Climb now or die."

CHAPTER 19
Torsil Rings

Ugh!" Timothy grunted. "What a nasty place! I'll bet nobody's been through here since Queen Winona left." Inside the black tunnel, water dripped down his neck and cobwebs plastered his face. The darkness seemed alive.

"Then we are treading on hallowed ground," Elwyn remarked. "Someday, we shall tell our children about this secret passage."

"If we live that long," said Timothy. As he brushed aside cobwebs and roots, dark shapes squeaked and fluttered into the shadows.

"Bats," said Elwyn casually, as if he ate them with eggs every day for breakfast. Windsong and Ironwing tried to catch some of the furry creatures with their paws, but the clever bats eluded them.

Without warning, the tunnel veered downward, plunging steeply through the slippery rock. After some distance, it gradually leveled out, and the rank air freshened with a salty sweetness. At last, filtered sunlight flooded the passage and a patch of blue-green water appeared at the end. A roaring sound echoed down the tunnel.

"It's the Sea of El-marin!" Elwyn whooped. "We're free!"

Pushing aside some mats of beach grass overhanging the tunnel's mouth, Timothy ducked outside to join his friends. He shielded his eyes against the coppery sun, which was riding its fiery cloud-chariot down a rippling aisle of crimson waves.

"We must hurry," said Rolin. "If the high tide catches us down here, we could be dashed against the rocks! No shouting or singing, either. The enemy has ears everywhere." On the cliffs above, a horse whinnied, and Timothy instinctively ducked.

"Better to face a thousand foes than to get this grit between our toes," Ironwing grumbled poetically. He and Windsong shook the sand off their paws with expressions of supreme sorc distaste.

After a half-hour's slogging through the sand, Timothy and his friends escaped the tide through a gap in the crumbling cliffs. On higher ground, they encountered a sea of hissing, waist-high saw grass that sliced ankles and calves like razors. The grass gave way to copses of contorted sea pines, where the going was easier. After nightfall, the company turned north, traipsing by staff light across the pine barrens.

Trailing at the lightless back of the line, Timothy stumbled over roots, fallen limbs and shin-splitting rocks. "First it's the stairs and now these dratted stones," he complained to Elwyn. "My legs will never be the same! Where are we going, anyway?"

"I guess Father wants to put as much distance between us and the Thalmosians as he can. If we keep heading north, we'll run into the Misty River, and beyond that, the Forlorn Fens."

"What are those?" Timothy asked, disliking the name.

"Peat bogs," Elwyn replied. "Miles and miles of them. Most people who go into them never come out again."

Timothy shivered. The exiles were trapped between the sea, the fens and the Thalmosians. Not for the first time, he wished he were back home in his snug cottage beside the Foamwater.

After spending the night in a sandy hollow, the fugitives awoke stiff and grumpy on their prickly pine-needle beds. A clammy, many-fingered fog had rolled in from the sea to spangle rocks, leaves and limbs with dew. The mist muffled the murmur of waves breaking on the shore and the cries of seabirds.

King Rolin turned his face eastward. "We must travel swiftly while the fog is with us," he said. "It will mute the noise of our passage through the forest and hide us from spying eyes."

"If we don't blunder into the enemy first," said Ironwing.

Noon found the exiles cresting a high hill overlooking the verdant plain. Southward, the Hallowfast loomed lonely and defiant, wreathed in smoke from the enemy's campfires. Elwyn pointed out the Valley of Liriassa nestled in the fog-bound foothills of the Brynnmors, and the Misty River flowing through it.

Bembor peered into the wispy haze clinging to the treetops. "It would seem the enemy has cut us off from the inner ring."

Inner ring? Timothy looked questioningly at Elwyn. The prince whispered, "Grandfather means a 'torsil ring.'"

"Oh, I see," Timothy replied, though he really didn't.

Bembor shot him a stern look from under his bushy eyebrows. "If you'll stop chattering, I'll explain," he said. "Some years ago, we Greencloaks planted three nested circles of tara-torsils around the Hallowfast. Torsils in the innermost ring connect with others up and down the seacoast; those in the middle ring lead to points east of the Brynnmors; and those in the outermost ring range north, south and east to the farthest reaches of Lucambra. Now we must find a middle- or outer-ring torsil before our enemies can find us!"

Timothy gazed over a sea of greenery. Where in all those trees might a torsil be hiding? With the others, he scrambled down the hill's southeast side, a dry, rubbly slope overgrown with scrub oak. At the bottom, they were back on moist ground, where firs and spruces spread their roots amongst lady ferns and bracken. The lush, sweet odor of growing things filled the air.

Zing! Something flew past Timothy's ear. *Zing! Zing!* More arrows sped by, their feathered shafts lent wings by Thalmosian bowstrings. "You there! Stop!" someone shouted.

Running blindly, Timothy tripped and sprawled in the dirt. Then a hand reached out and pulled him into a hollow behind a spruce. "Don't move!" Gwynneth hissed. Heavy boots clumped by the tree. Then all was quiet. Clutching her ankle, Gwynneth grimaced in pain. Timothy realized then that she had saved his life by tripping him with her foot. He nodded his thanks.

With a whisper of leaves, Skoglund's head popped out of the dense undergrowth. Motioning curtly to the pair, he said, "This way—and don't make a sound! The Thalms are everywhere."

Following Skoglund, Timothy and Gwynneth rejoined Elwyn and the grownups, who set off at a brisk trot. Hampered by her sprained ankle, Gwynneth was lagging until Timothy helped her lean on his shoulder. They were making good time when shouts rang out ahead, forcing the company to backtrack.

"They're driving us toward the Hallowfast," Scanlon moaned. "They seem to know these woods better than we do! I wish we had a map showing where all those tara-torsils stand."

Just then, Timothy spied tortoiseshell bark through the brush. Nudging Bembor and pointing, he said, "Isn't that a torsil over there?"

The chancellor stopped midstride and squinted. "I do believe you're right!" he exclaimed. "It's a good thing we brought you along on this trip." In a trice, everyone had gathered at the foot of the droopy torsil, whose name was Longlimb.

"This is a middle-ring torsil," Rolin said. "We must have passed through the outer ring already. It's Longlimb or nothing!"

Longlimb it was. Led by the sure-footed sorcs (who clawed their way up the tree), Timothy's cloaked companions quickly swarmed up the torsil. *Swish-thunk!* As Timothy began climbing, an arrow plunked into the trunk. More arrows whizzed by his head, twitching the leaves as they passed.

"Hurry up!" Elwyn hissed down at him. Timothy had just reached Longlimb's top when the tree shuddered. Losing his grip, he toppled backward. *How blue the sky is!* he thought before his head burst into stars pinwheeling in a perfect blackness.

CHAPTER 20
The Torsil Map

W ell?" Captain Asper demanded. "Are you going up this tree now or not?" He drew his knife blade lightly and stingingly across Meghan's throat, bringing tears to her eyes. Blood trickled warmly down her neck.

"Have ye gone an' lost yer senses?" Derwin cried. "Mardoc sent us here to find gold, not distress innocent maidens. Look at her! She's bleeding and scared out of her wits. Ye can always find another o' these bewitched trees if this one doesn't work."

Asper tossed his knife aside. "You fool!" he grated. "Nobody knows where the gold is hidden except for those dratted Greencloaks, and we just chased a pack of them up this tree. If it weren't for the earthquake, we'd have caught them, too."

"That's no excuse for hurting Meghan. Let her go."

"Not on your life!" Asper's fists clenched as he turned on his brother. "What do you understand of waging war? Cutting firewood is all you know, piling up wood chips for your bread and butter! You don't have to dodge arrows and darts the way we did earlier today.

"We surprised a company of the enemy headed north, and they fought back. I lost several men, and the whole lot got clean away. These people are like gremlins, and your imp is one of them; just when you think you've got 'em, they disappear."

"Meghan hasn't disappeared yet," Derwin pointed out.

Meghan clapped her hands over her ears. "Stop it! I'll climb the tree. Just please quit your arguing!"

"That's better," said Asper as he lifted her into the torsil tree's leafy embrace. "Now up you go—and no funny business, either!"

Grasping a skinny limb, Meghan wondered what Asper meant by, "funny business." She was in no position to escape, after all.

As she wormed her way up the tree, she found several fresh arrows sticking in the trunk and pulled them out. At the top, she whispered to the torsil, "Why didn't you let those men through?"

From root-deep in the earth, a rumbly voice replied, "King Rolin bade me deny all two-legs passage until further notice."

King Rolin? Meghan's father and the rest of her family must have climbed this tree to escape Mardoc's men! Then Rolin had "locked" the torsil gate to thwart pursuers, thereby also shutting out Meghan. "But I'm the king's daughter!" she wailed.

"I am sorry. Orders are orders, as you two-legs say in your word-bitten way. Only Gaelathane could make me change. We trees may not be as quick witted as you legged creatures, but we're constant. 'No truer friend you'll ever find than a trusty tree with a truthful mind.' That's a fact you can sink your roots into."

Meghan wanted to sink her teeth into Longlimb. "Truthful mind" or not, the tree had both raised and dashed her hopes of seeing her loved ones again. Still, she drew some small comfort from knowing which way the royal family had taken.

The torsil continued prattling away as Meghan sadly climbed down. On the ground, she found the men examining a glassy, platter-shaped object. "Can you tell us what this flatcake thing is?" said Asper. "We found it lying under the tree."

The cloudy "flatcake" reminded Meghan of a frozen mud puddle with tiny air bubbles trapped inside. As she stroked the puddle's sticky-smooth surface, a whorl of brilliant rainbow hues blossomed at its center, forming branches and twigs bearing burnished leaves the color of a summer's sunrise.

Then Meghan remembered her father's throne-room lecture. If spasels weren't turned, they'd end up with pancake bottoms. Was this such a spasel? She put it to her nose and smelled the familiar, musty-sweet odor of aged torsil sap.

"What's it doing?" Asper sharply asked her.

"I think it's showing us another place," Meghan replied.

"*What* other place?" The captain snatched the flattened, oblong spasel from Meghan's hands, and the woodland scene faded. "What's wrong with it?" he snapped. "Is this more Greencloak trickery? Make it work, or so help me—"

Meghan took the spasel back and rubbed it. "You have to keep it warm or the picture goes away," she said sullenly.

"So you *do* know what it is, then!" crowed the captain. He grinned triumphantly at his men.

"But what is it?" they asked.

Meghan's head whirled. How much could she tell the potato eaters without betraying her people? It was bad enough that her captors knew of the torsils. Still, she had nothing to gain by lying, and Asper would pry the truth out of her if she did.

"We call them 'spasels,'" she said. "They're made of tree sap. Most are round. That's why I didn't reco'nize this one."

Entranced, Asper stared into the platter's depths. "Tell me, little princess, does this place truly exist?"

Meghan bit her tongue. What could she say—that these sap balls revealed scenes in other worlds, worlds open to conquest through the torsils? "I—I don't know," she said.

Asper gasped and pointed. "It *is* a real wood. I can see the leaves moving!" He motioned Derwin over. "Look at this! Trees with leaves of gold. Thousands of them! We'll all be richer than kings!" The other men crowded in to gawk. Greed shone in their feverish eyes as their captain held the spasel over his head like a crown.

"Think of it, lads," he breathed. "With so much wealth, we could live as lords anywhere we wished! No more General Gorn. No more King Mardoc. Only one person stands in our way."

"Who's that?" the soldiers asked, eyeing one another.

Asper pointed at Meghan. "This girl's father! He and his crew aim to grab th' gold before we do. I'm sure of it." He shook his fist at her. "We must get there first! Who is with me?"

"Hai! Hai! Hai!" Asper's men shouted and banged swords and spears against their metal shields. "We go, we go to seize the gold!"

Asper spoke again. "Men, we must ride swiftly, for the enemy has a head start. We have the advantage of surprise and of our horses."

One of the soldiers glanced around. "Speaking of horses, where's that dratted boy and his broken-down nag?"

The captain cursed. "The brat's gone off to blab our plans to Gorn! Why wasn't someone watching him?" While the men traded stricken looks, Meghan caught Derwin in a smug, secret smile.

"No matter," Asper continued. "If we ride now, we can still beat them to the prize. We've got something they don't: The map someone so foolishly left behind." Asper's lips curled mockingly as he tapped the spasel. "This is a map, isn't it, princess?"

Meghan blinked back tears. She wouldn't help these cruel men—she couldn't! Still, if her parents had set out for the spasel's golden grove, the soldiers might take her straight to them.

"Well?" said the captain. His eyes bored into hers like hot iron spikes. Meghan squirmed. How could a spasel show the way? It wasn't inscribed with the points of the compass and showed no landmarks. Then she recalled what Bembor had once told her about the special kinship between spasla and their trees.

Asper and his men surrounded her, fists raised and faces grim. "Tell us how to read the magic map!" they demanded.

Meghan looked her captors in the eye. "It isn't magic, and it's not a map you *read*," she said. "It's a map you *watch*."

THE GOLDEN WOOD
PART III
GOLDEN FOREST GAIN

CHAPTER 21
A Stoneworm Snack

Timothy awoke to find himself lying on a makeshift stretcher that swayed like a ship's hammock. Windsong was licking his face with his raspy tongue. "Welcome back! We were worried about you," purred the sorc.

"So was I," Timothy groaned. A thousand knives stabbed his body when he tried to move.

"Oho, so our casualty has returned to the land of the living," said Skoglund, who was carrying the front end of the stretcher.

"It's about time, too," Sigarth grunted from the back. "For a boy his size, he's heavier than a sack of stones. My arms must be inches longer." As the other exiles gathered around, the sons of Sigwyn set their burden gently on the ground.

Wobbly-kneed, Timothy stood, steadying himself on Sigarth's shoulder. He held his spinning head. "What happened to me?"

"The earth shook just as you were making passage," Skoglund told him. "You fell right out of Longlimb."

"And landed on me," said Opio ruefully.

"He couldn't have picked a softer spot if he'd tried," said Bembor with a chuckle. "How are you feeling, my boy?"

After Timothy took a few deep breaths, the earth and sky righted themselves. "I'm fine; just a little dizzy—oh, no!" He patted his pockets until he found a hard, flat shape. Much to his relief, the sap sheet was unbroken. However, its twin was gone.

"The second spasel must have dropped out when I fell," he said miserably, his eyes fastened on the ground.

Gwynneth touched his arm. "We can manage without the other one," she told him with a sympathetic smile. "You mustn't blame yourself; you didn't lose it on purpose."

"It's a marvel you didn't lose your life in the bargain!" said Sigarth gruffly. "We were thankful you made passage as you fell; otherwise, we'd have had to drag you back up that torsil."

Rolin said. "It turns out that since Longlimb was a middle-ring torsil, we fell short of our goal. I had hoped to reach the Willowahs. In fact, we've been taken somewhat out of our way."

"Quite a bit out of our way, I'd say," said Sigarth. He jabbed his thumb toward a soot-streaked, smoking mountain squatting on the stony plain, its flanks veined red with fiery lava flows.

Timothy gasped. "Mt. Golgunthor! Aren't we awfully close?"

Marlis patted his shoulder. "Don't worry; we're perfectly safe here. The mountain is farther away than it appears."

"Then I hope we don't go any closer," said Timothy. He glanced at Mycena, who stood as if in a trance, staring at the peak with sunken, bloodshot eyes. "Is she all right?" he asked Marlis.

The queen put a finger to her lips. "Hush! She's remembering the years she spent in that mountain as Felgor's slave."

Rolin decided to pitch camp, since Timothy was still unsteady on his feet and Emmer, Gemmio and Scanlon were out searching for food and fuel. Darkness was falling when the three dragged into camp, grimy with gray ash. Scanlon and Emmer were carrying bundles of dead fir branches, while Gemmio bore several braces of fat grouse. "Thanks be to Gaelathane, we'll have meat for supper," Gemmio said. "Now, where's that brother of mine with his flint and steel? We'll need a fire to roast these dainties." Timothy's mouth watered.

"Did someone mention meat?" said Ironwing. He ambled over to sniff the birds. "Leave us some of the raw, will you? There's hardly a decent, plump coney left in this wasteland."

While Opio coaxed bright sparks into fire with his flint and steel, a warm, windless night muffled the stark landscape. Mt. Golgunthor rumbled and boomed under a sickle moon.

Soon the campfire was in full crackle, and Timothy and his friends were enjoying succulent roast grouse washed down with stream water. They were picking the bones when Windsong and Ironwing suddenly hissed, the hairs bristling on their backs.

"Something reeks of Gundul out there," chittered Windsong. "We just can't see what it is. The scorbies blinds us at night."

"It's yegs, or I'm not a sorc," Ironwing growled.

Just on the edge of hearing, Timothy caught a hideous, twittering howl, rising and falling like the wind. Fear tingled up his spine.

"There. On that hill." Ironwing's head and neck pointed like a compass needle. Curling over and around a nearby rise, a black tide poured across the plain to a chorus of yips and yowls.

"They're well out of bow or lightstaff range," Rolin groaned.

"They know it, too," said Emmer. "What are they waiting for? The bat-curs outnumber us. Why aren't they flying at us?"

Windsong's eyes glittered like diamonds. "They're half grown, that's why. Yearling yegs don't have fully-formed wings, just two humps where the wings will break out later."

"Then we're at an equal disadvantage, since we can't fly, either," growled Ironwing.

"Their eastern flank looks the thinnest, Sire," said Opio.

"Then east it is," the king said. "Weapons, everyone; to battle!" Timothy drew his knife as the Greencloaks readied their blowpipes, bows and staffs. Then they marched against the wingless yegs, whose red eyes glowed like coals in the dark. Bows twanged, arrows whistled and light beams lanced the night, sending batwolves fleeing into the sorcs' waiting claws and beaks. In minutes, the Lucambrians had smashed through the line.

"To the mountain!" cried King Rolin, and his followers broke into a tireless trot. Still limping, Gwynneth was forced to ride Ironwing. Timothy dropped back to the rear, where he spotted some moonlit yegs flanking the fugitives. Suddenly, six of them split off from their companions and streaked straight for him.

"Help!" he cried. As the words left his lips, three searing light-beams petrified the closest yegs. Arrows and blowpipe darts felled a few others. The rest broke off, keeping pace at a distance.

Onward Timothy ran, fearful of falling farther behind and being picked off like a straggling deer harried by wolves. Then he stumbled and fell. Instantly, Windsong was at his side.

"Climb on me!" said the griffin. As Timothy obeyed, a skulking batwolf wearing Baglot's face rose from the jagged stones and pounced. Windsong reared up to meet the challenger, unseating his rider. Timothy tumbled off but picked himself up again.

Dust flew as the two foes scuffled. Windsong was well on his way to trouncing his foe when he began flagging. Fatigue and the scorbies had taken their toll, and the yeg was young and strong.

Timothy tensely waited for his chance. There—the yeg had pinned Windsong to the ground. Seizing the opening, Timothy dove under the batwolf's belly and thrust his knife upward with all his might. With a strangled screech, the creature collapsed.

Windsong tottered to his feet and croaked, "Hurry—before we're waylaid again!" Knife in hand, Timothy jumped on the sorc's back.

Amidst the agonized grindings and groanings of its tortured stone, the smoking dragon's mountain spewed fiery fountains of molten rock. Lava ran down its sides and flowed in red-hot rivers across the ashen plain. Rolin and Emmer kept up the grueling pace as one by one, their pursuers dropped out of the hunt. Others took their place.

Mycena gasped and collapsed. "I can't go on," she sobbed. "Just leave me here. The yegs will overtake us all anyway."

"We'll have none of that," said Marlis. "Windsong will carry you." Timothy gladly gave up his place to the queen's sister.

All at once, the earth rolled and shimmied, throwing everyone but the griffins to the ground. Timothy was tossed about like a stranded fish flopping on dry land. Gritty ash filled his eyes and nose. The earth flexed its muscles once more and then fell still.

As the dazed batwolves milled about aimlessly, Timothy and his companions collected themselves and staggered onward, only to run up against a gaping chasm. "The earthquake must have created this," Rolin exclaimed, shaking his head in disbelief.

"It appears to stretch for a great distance, too," said Bembor. Hope wavered in his ageless eyes. "It's possible a crevasse like this one opened a new passage to Gundul. That would explain all these yearling yegs." The other Lucambrians shuddered.

Behind them, the batwolves had shaken off their confusion and were advancing again. "We're trapped," Skoglund moaned.

"Not while we have our staffs," Rolin said. He petrified several yegs before the others took the hint and backed away.

"Does anyone have some rope?" asked Gemmio. Nobody did.

"Then we must take our stand here," said Opio grimly. "We'll make those yegs rue the day they came after us!"

Timothy groaned. If only he had so much as a string to tie around a rock and throw into the bushes on the other side! Then he noticed a torn torsil clinging to the cliff's brink, and another standing on the opposite rim. He pointed them out to Scanlon.

The chief deputy whistled. "Will you look at that! The quake split this torsil clean in two. And there's the other half on the opposite side. I couldn't have done a neater job if I'd tried."

"How odd to find a torsil way out here!" Bembor observed. "It's as if Gaelathane Himself had planted the tree and then clove it in two."

"C'mon, Timothy," said Elwyn. "Let's have a look at our half! Maybe we'll find enough fresh sap in the split to make a spasel ball." Taking a staff for protection and light, the boys followed the fissure's rim to the torsil, whose leaves were already wilting.

"Poor thing," Timothy said. "What an awful way to die."

The tree rattled like a dying man gasping out his last breath. "I'm not . . . dead . . . yet."

"Oh, dear," said Elwyn, stroking the torsil's bark. "If only we could put you back together again!"

"No," said the tree sadly. "For this purpose Gaelathane planted me here. He warned me that one day my heart would be torn in twain for His sake, but I did not think it would come to this *splitting*. Of what use is half of Tenderleaf to anyone now?"

"Maybe of great use," Timothy returned. *If a divided torsil nut can create two tara-torsils*, he reasoned, *why couldn't a split tree do the same*? He wriggled up Tenderleaf's undamaged side.

"Be careful!" Elwyn told him. "Even if Tenderleaf can still grant passage, he could die and strand you on the other side—or in Limbo!"

"Any side would be better than this one!" Timothy shot back. Climbing into the torsil's wobbly top, he slithered back down. The world whirled about him, and he found himself in Tenderleaf's other half, looking across the chasm at Elwyn's lightstaff.

"Hi! I'm over here!" he shouted, waving his arms.

Soon, the others were climbing Tenderleaf's flimsy half-trunk. Last of all, Windsong and Ironwing scurried up the tree, just escaping the snapping jaws of a hundred hungry yegs. Tenderleaf bent down perilously low over the ravine with the sorcs' weight. "Hurry, oh, please hurry!" Timothy cried, hopping on one leg and then the other.

As Tenderleaf's top snapped upright across the chasm, the griffins appeared in Timothy's half-torsil and slid down. "Welcome to my side!" he greeted them.

"Thank you!" they replied, rubbing against him with rumbling purrs. Then the exiles crowded around to embrace him in the hearty Lucambrian manner. Gwynneth lightly kissed him on the cheek. "Well done," she whispered. Timothy's face burned.

"You saved our lives, Relic-Bearer!" Bembor boomed. "Since we Lucambrians are accustomed to *planting* our tara-torsils, we never would have seen Tenderleaf for what he was without your help. There's a good deal more to you than we ever suspected."

"Indeed there is," Windsong chimed in. "The boy saved my life by killing a yeg with his knife!"

"And just look at all of them!" Elwyn said. Thousands of batwolves crowded the opposite side, their long, pointed bats' ears standing erect like a forest of dark spears. Elwyn shook his fist at them and yelled, "We've beaten you this time, yegs!"

"Yes, this time," Bembor murmured. "However, we are still a long way from any safe haven. The closer those batwolves drive us toward the mountain, the greater our peril. If they give chase again, we'll need Golgunthor at our backs." Timothy stared eastward, where the fiery peak lent a lurid glow to the night sky.

"You mean *when* they give chase," said Scanlon. "Look there."

To the southeast, countless black shapes were gathering on the shadowy plain. Opio groaned. "Will we never be rid of these accursed creatures? This place is crawling with them!"

Staggering with fatigue, the exiles made off again for the looming mountain. As before, Timothy followed on foot with Windsong, who again bore Mycena on his back. Her eyes shuttered, the queen's sister reminded Timothy of a pallid lily with wilting petals.

Morning's light was flooding the dreary flatlands when the ragtag company reached Golgunthor's foothills. Weaving through a canyon, they looked up to see yegs blackening the rimrocks. Rolin had lent Timothy his lightstaff to guard the rear, and he picked off a stray yeg with it. The creature's petrified body tumbled down the cliff and smashed to pieces on the valley floor.

"Bravo!" cried Mycena, patting Timothy on the back.

"Keep moving! Keep moving!" Opio bellowed. Timothy picked up his pace, breathing with sharp, ragged gasps.

At last the ravine opened onto a foothill skirted with a wide apron of crumbling stone. The fugitives toiled up the slope and collapsed on the ground behind some giant boulders. Packs of batwolves slouched just beyond staff and bowshot range, their long tongues lolling from grinning jaws. The griffins sat in the open preening themselves, as if daring the yegs to disturb their ritual.

Having returned King Rolin's lightstaff to him, Timothy flung some stones at the yegs. "Go back to your dark lairs!" he cried. The beasts only leered at him with Baglot eyes.

"That won't do any good," said Elwyn, who was sharing a boulder with Timothy. "They'll hang around until we're too tired and hungry to fight. Then they'll finish us off, one by one."

"Not if I can help it," Timothy declared, standing. Digging his heels in behind the boulder, he pushed. The boulder didn't budge.

"What are you doing?" asked Elwyn. Then a grin spread across his face and he, too, planted his shoulder against the rock.

"One, two, three!" Timothy counted, and they pushed together. With a crunching noise, the boulder rocked forward and back. "Again!" Timothy grunted. This time, the massive rock rolled out of its place. Gathering speed, it bounded down the slope, mowing over fifteen or twenty yegs and scattering the rest.

"Hooray!" cheered the defenders. Taking Timothy's cue, they sent more boulders bouncing down the hill. Yipping and yapping in alarm, the surviving batwolves retreated into the canyon.

"They'll be back," said Bembor gruffly, but he couldn't hide a smile of triumph.

Unfortunately, by dislodging the biggest boulders, the exiles had sacrificed their only cover. "When the yegs return, where will we hide then?" Timothy asked Elwyn.

"We can always go down there," said the prince. He pointed to a four-foot hole in the ground where the first boulder had lain.

Timothy peered into the hole, which was the mouth of a shaft that slanted back into the hill. "What if this is a bear's den?" he asked.

"How would the bear get in and out with a boulder on top?" Elwyn asked him with a half-laugh.

Timothy had to admit Elwyn was right. But what beast could bore such a large tunnel and cover the mouth with a boulder?

Emmer and Rolin scrambled over the scree to join them. "So you've found a stoneworm burrow!" Emmer said. "Stoneworms often conceal their tunnel entrances with rocks. This 'worm must have been a young one, judging from the size of his hole. You don't often see them so far north; they prefer the Willowahs' softer limestones and sandstones to these tough granites."

"They must have strong jaws and teeth," Timothy marveled.

"Stoneworms don't have teeth," Emmer explained. "Their mouths are full of diamond-hard plates for crushing rock. They can tunnel through stone very rapidly if they're in a hurry."

"Speaking of hurrying, we had better take cover in this burrow," said Rolin. Raising his lightstaff, he petrified a prowling yeg with a blast of light. Then he whistled and waved to the others. "Time to leave! We're going underground before it's too late."

Timothy was aghast. "We can't go down there! What if we run into the stoneworm?" Any creature that could chew stone would easily make mincemeat out of two-legged trespassers.

"Stoneworms are harmless and slow-witted creatures," Emmer said. "Of course, we wouldn't want to frighten this one. It could bury us under tons of rubble just getting away." He tapped a finger on his lightstaff. "What this lonely old 'worm needs is a snack." While the others kept the yegs at bay, Emmer pounded his staff into the ground with a rock. Then he began rubbing a smooth stone across the rod's top, *scritch-scritch*.

"What in the name of Elgathel are you up to this time, Father?" Marlis demanded. "We need that staff to petrify yegs!"

"I'm sure Emmer knows what he is doing," said Rolin. However, Timothy could tell the king was worried, too.

As Emmer continued rhythmically stroking the staff, it hummed and thrummed in a mournful melody that reverberated through the earth. All at once, the ground trembled violently and a blunt, pale snout poked out of the burrow. Mycena shrieked and fainted, while Marlis blanched snowberry-white.

"Where did you learn to do that?" Bembor gasped. "I've never seen anyone call up a stoneworm before."

Emmer looked pleased with himself. "It's an old trick fishermen use for driving earthworms out of the ground. I've never tried it on stoneworms before. Apparently they don't care for the vibrations any more than nightcrawlers do."

The wrinkled beast emerged from its burrow, its white, hairless body rippling like an enormous caterpillar. Timothy couldn't see how the stoneworm had fit into the hole in the first place.

"Agh!" said Gwynneth. "What an ugly beast!"

"Ugly or not, it may be our only hope for survival," Emmer told her. He dug some lumps of coal out of his pocket and fed them to the blind, grublike creature. "Stoneworms love coal," he added with a quiet laugh. "They can smell it from miles away. It's a good thing I brought some from the Hallowfast. I never dreamed I'd be feeding it to a stoneworm!"

Emmer coaxed his newfound pet away from its burrow with more coal. Then he threw the rest among the waiting yegs. "There!" he said. "That should keep our friend busy long enough for us to borrow his burrow, and he'll slow up the yegs."

One after another, the exiles dove into the dark hole. Emmer yanked his lightstaff out of the ground before joining them. Timothy ventured in last, hoping the yegs wouldn't follow. He knew they liked caves and tunnels, as bats do.

Elwyn handed back a lightstaff to him. "Hold onto this," he said over his shoulder. "You're supposed to protect us with it."

"From what?"

Elwyn grinned in the staff light. "Just watch for red eyes."

CHAPTER 22
Sleepyeye

W e're coming closer!" Meghan told Derwin as they sat beside a roaring campfire. On her knees lay the misshapen spasel. Out of its depths, the mysterious golden trees reached up to her with lifelike limbs and leaves. Each passing day brought the sap sheet's scenes into sharper focus, proof that the party was traveling in the right direction.

For days, the Thalmosians had followed a noisy, snow-fed river through the moss-mantled Brynnmor Mountains. A cold rain had been falling, muddying the ground and sharpening tempers. On the fourth morning since leaving Longlimb, they had arisen to an early sun gleaming redly upon Mt. Golgunthor's lava-spattered shoulders. Ash clouds and molten rock blasted from its thundering summit. Around it stretched the broad plain cradled between the Brynnmors and the Mountains of the Moon.

"Where there's mountains, there's gold!" the men whooped as they spurred on their mounts.

Down they had jogged through fir-flanked foothills until a vast prairie of tall, waving grasses greeted them. Consulting the spasel, they rode south, their armor and weapons gleaming in the glaring sun. Once, Meghan glimpsed other bright figures following them. When she blinked, they vanished like a shimmering mirage.

After the riders had pitched camp that evening, Meghan lay back among the night-whispering grasses, listening to the music of their lilting green words. The stars spangled the limitless sky-prairie just as hemmonsil flowers had once carpeted Luralin. If only those twinkling beacons could tell her where to find her family!

"Have we far to go, do ye think?" Derwin asked her.

"Yes, is it far?" Asper chimed in, his eyes glazed with gold-lust.

Meghan wearily sighed. "I don't know. I haven't seen any golden trees here yet." The Thalmosians could "read" the spasel as well as she could. When Meghan could give them no satisfactory answer, they would mutter, "Maybe it's over the next hill."

But now the hills had melted into an endless, thirsty plain tufted with wiry grasses. A hissing wind cut through the numbing silence. Gazing up at the cold, glittering stars, Meghan slept.

Before dawn, the Thalmosians set off again. As usual, Meghan sat in front of her woodcutter on a sorrel horse named Gert. Savoring the wind and sun in her face, she fancied herself a brave young warrior-princess charging into battle. As they galloped beside her, the men sang out a full-throated war chant:

Riding, riding to the thunder
Of our horses' flying hooves,
We follow fiercely to the plunder
O'er the plains to gilded woods.

Spear and sword and speeding arrow,
Smite our foes that dare surround;
Split the bone and spill the marrow,
Let their blood besoak the ground!

Let us ravage, let us pillage
Every inch of conquered soil;
Bind the slaves and burn the village,
Hasten, men, to take the spoil!

Still the spasel led them southward, past the smoking dragon's mountain that rocked the earth in its wrath, across silt-milky rivers, ever closer to the Willowahs. Meghan watched the sky, hoping that some of Whitewing's sorcs would rescue her. Alas, only hawks and vultures lazily circled overhead. When Asper suspiciously asked what she was looking for, she replied, "Birds, just birds."

Then the ground plunged into moist valleys and climbed steep, pine-rich slopes, forcing the men to stop more often to rest their mounts. From horseback, Meghan stripped Juneberry bushes of their dry, purple fruits to fill her famished stomach. Though scant and seedy, their sweet, almondy flesh was nourishing.

When the Willowahs' jutting flanks blocked the way south, the Thalmosians turned east toward the snow-tipped Mountains of the Moon, searching for a way through the forbidding range. Even as they found a promising mountain pass, a distant dust cloud heralded the approach of a great host. Possessed by the promise of gold before him and by the threat of Mardoc's army behind, Asper drove his men and horses mercilessly.

Up into the pass they climbed, pushing through glittering groves of long-needled pines. Meghan's world shrank to a kaleidoscope of sweating, lathered horses, hunger, thirst and dust. Only the spasel's images kept her spirits from being trampled like the dirt beneath the horses' hooves. Then even that hope dulled as the spasel's crisp, golden leaves gradually turned fuzzy, their colors fading.

"What do you mean, we're going the wrong way?" hissed Captain Asper. "Does that pancake thing talk to you?" Exasperated, he slammed the flat of his sword against a tree trunk.

Meghan didn't answer. Instead, she focused on the ancient spasel's wavering images, dreading the day when they might vanish altogether, dashing all chances of ever finding her loved ones. She drank in the spasel-sky, always stacked high with the same crimson clouds. Did the sun never set in this golden world?

It was a grumpy band of soldiers that camped that night beside a fir-fringed lake. In the waning light, bug-hunting bats swooped over the still water. Meghan gnawed on a hard crust the captain had tossed her. Still hungry, she wolfed down Derwin's portion. "Don't worry, Missy; we'll find them," the woodcutter whispered.

"I hope so," Meghan replied, the words catching in her throat. As the gloom gathered beneath the sighing trees, she lay down beside her protector and snuggled under her skimpy cloak. Murmuring a plea to Gaelathane for her family's safety, she slept.

Later that night, Meghan awoke to screeching cries. Sitting up, she saw ghostly forms chasing bats over the moon-mirroring lake. Bat-eating sorcs? She'd never heard of such a thing. Certainly Windsong and Ironwing wouldn't eat flying mice! As weariness overcame her curiosity, Meghan drifted back to sleep.

After that, the high-flying sorcs began shadowing Meghan and her captors every evening. Asper's men shot arrows at them, but the winged beasts always soared out of range. Once, though, Meghan thought an arrow found its mark.

As the air grew cooler, the fragrant pines gave way to alpine firs. Then one day, white patches appeared among the scattered trees.

"Snow!" cried Meghan. To the men's amusement, she hopped off Gert and jumped into the nearest snow bank. After riding a sweaty horse all day, she found the cold, crusty snow marvelously refreshing. She even hit Derwin with a snowball or two.

Captain Asper was impatiently calling her when a mournful wail carried past her ears. *Hooooooooo!* Was it the wind? The sound came again, an anguished, animal cry of pain.

Ignoring the soldiers' shouts and curses, Meghan dashed into the trees. Following the eerie sound, she slipped and slid down a snow field and skidded into a fir thicket, where she fetched up against a tree. A knot of tawny shapes drew around her.

"*Whoooo* are you and what do you want?" one of the creatures challenged. "Haven't you done enough damage already? You are in our domain, so go away and—*hoo!*—leave us be."

Owl-headed sorcs! Nine pairs of saucer-sized, yellow eyes regarded her from dished-out, white-feathered faces. A tenth griffin lay on the snow with an arrow protruding from its flank. A Thalmosian arrow.

"My name is Meghan, and I only want to help," she said. At this, the owl sorcs turned away and *hoo-hooed* at one another. Then their neckless heads swiveled back to her.

"What could *youu* possibly know about *moonsorcs*?" they said.

"Enough to know that your friend is hurt," Meghan retorted. Gnashing their curved beaks, the sorcs made way for the girl.

The wounded griffin lay in a sheltered spot between two firs. His eyelids drooped at half-mast. "My name is 'Sleepyeye,'" said the sorc in a pain-filled rasp. "My eyes always look this way."

Meghan stroked his soft fur. "I am sorry you were shot," she said. "The men who did this are very cruel. Not all two-legs are like them. Now let me look at your arrow."

Fortunately, the shaft was not deeply embedded, and Meghan managed to wiggle it out. Sleepyeye groaned and closed his eyes.

The other sorcs crowded around and nuzzled their comrade. "What did you—*hoo!*—do to him?" they asked suspiciously.

"I just pulled out the arrow," Meghan answered. After cleaning the wound, she packed it with lichens. "Don't fly for a week or so," she told Sleepyeye. "And stay away from men with bows!"

"Thank you for—*hoo!*—helping us," said the moonsorcs, bowing to her. "May your fields abound in fat mice and your larders with grain. It is well you came when you did; if Sleepyeye had died, we would have fallen upon your party and killed you all!"

CHAPTER 23
Wormstickers

"ere they come!" Timothy muttered to himself. He had been scuttling down the burrow backward for fear the yegs would catch him unawares. Still, he was unprepared when a cluster of burning red eyes sprouted in the darkness, and batwolves rushed toward him. With a yell that came out as a yelp, Timothy aimed his lightstaff and let fly.

The leaders had time only for a surprised screech before they turned to stone. Those following piled over the top of their petrified companions, only to meet the same fate. Soon, a welter of yeg statuary had plugged the tunnel from floor to ceiling.

When no more live yegs showed themselves, Timothy made off down the passageway. He hadn't gone far when the tunnel divided. "Elwyn! Gwynneth! Rolin! Marlis!" he called. "Where are you? Those pesky batwolves won't be bothering us again!" The rocks merely mocked him with his own words.

After much head-scratching, he decided on the left-hand tunnel, since it angled down and the going would be easier. His friends were probably waiting for him around the next bend. He would sweep into their midst, holding his lightstaff aloft like a victory torch. How they would thank him for his yeg blockade! Gwynneth might even kiss him on the cheek again.

Instead, he found only a vacant passage as he wound his way down into the mountain's heart. His ears popped from the depth and his legs wobbled with fatigue. The rank, stifling air burned foul in his nostrils.

Pausing to rest, he noticed some black lumps crowding the tunnel walls. Smooth and hard to the touch, they smelled faintly mushroomy. However, even the smallest bumps resisted his efforts to pry them off the wall. Were they growing right out of the rock?

Then he came upon some oversized, wrinkled gray sacks lying on the ground. Stepping around them, he felt a sharp pain pierce his left foot, then his right. As he hopped from one foot to the other, several conical, needle-sharp spines rose through the floor. Others were also poking out of the walls and roof.

Timothy tried to weave among the spines, but more of them kept appearing out of countless holes in the rock, lengthening with each passing second. "Help!" he cried, but no one answered.

Now the cruel floor-spikes were lifting his pain-racked body off the ground, while the ceiling spines grew downward to meet him. In just moments, he would be skewered from all sides like a pincushion. Blood trickled down his arms and back.

"Gaelathane—" he croaked. Before he could finish his prayer, the mountain convulsed like a dying thing, tossing him about on his spiny bed. He closed his eyes and waited for the end. A cloud of gritty dust boiled through the tunnel, followed by a hot, choking wind. Gagging on the stench, Timothy wrenched open his eyes.

Molten rock was flowing toward him, burbling and spitting as it came. Golgunthor was erupting again, spewing its red-hot vomit through the stoneworm burrow. And Timothy was in its path.

Any spines that did not instantly shatter from the searing heat withdrew into their holes, dropping Timothy to the floor. Forgetting the pain, he staggered up the passage, sulfurous smoke searing his lungs. Behind him, fiery rock was filling the tunnel.

At last he reached the fork in the passage and entered the upward-sloping branch. Now he heard voices. Putting on his best speed, he sprinted up the tunnel with his lightstaff, spurred on by the dim glow of staff light ahead. There his friends all stood, waving at him! Beyond them, the passage abruptly ended in a pile of rock.

It turned out that the exiles had traveled some distance up the right-hand tunnel when Timothy was missed. Rolin had decided then and there to return for him. Elwyn ran up ahead of the others to the spot where Timothy had petrified the yeg-pack. Not finding him, he went back to rejoin his companions. They had nearly reached the fork in the tunnel when the earthquake collapsed the passage behind them, blocking it off. Now the men were digging through the rubble, trying to clear a large enough opening to crawl through.

All hopes of a hero's welcome dashed, Timothy tried to warn his friends of the peril oozing through the passages beneath them. His words came thickly, and he spoke with the hoarsened voice of a stranger. The others regarded him doubtfully.

"Where were you, anyway?" Elwyn asked him. Before Timothy could reply, a scarlet tongue of molten rock crackled into the tunnel with blast-furnace heat. Those exiles who stood closest to the flow reeled backward, and the sorcs' fur smoked.

"Dig!" cried Rolin. Now even the griffins pitched in to help clear the passage. It seemed that for every rock they worked loose, two more would take its place. Timothy's eyes watered in the swirling reek, and his wounds burned with a white-hot fire.

"We're through!" shouted Emmer, just as the scorching lava's breath licked at Timothy's heels. In a flash, everyone squeezed through the hole—except Timothy. He had just entered the opening when Mt. Golgunthor rumbled again and falling rocks pinned him inside. A roaring filled his ears and his flailing feet grew unbearably hot. Then hands grabbed his tunic collar and roughly pulled him out.

"His feet! His feet are on fire!" Opio shouted. Gemmio swatted his rolled-up cloak against Timothy's smoking shoe soles. When the greedy flames were quenched, the Lucambrians began piling rocks back into the tunnel, plugging it again. At the other end, an overheated boulder exploded with a bang.

King Rolin squatted beside Timothy. "Are you all right?"

Weakened by his injuries, Timothy wobbled to his feet. "I can manage," he wheezed through cracked, swollen lips. "Want . . . water." Then his head spun and darkness covered his eyes.

When Timothy awoke, Gwynneth was dribbling sips of water into his mouth. Her eyelashes were moist and matted with tears. "Don't talk," she whispered. "Just drink this and lie still."

Timothy couldn't have talked if he had tried. Wilting from the heat, the foul air and loss of blood, he squinted up at a circle of blurry faces. "Sometimes that boy's more trouble than he's worth," Sigarth was saying. "Let somebody else carry him this time!"

"'More trouble than he's worth'?" Elwyn retorted. "If it weren't for him, we'd all be yeg-bait by now!" Then the prince described finding the stopped-up passage filled with petrified yeg bodies.

Bembor stamped his staff. "Well done, son of Garth!"

Emmer gently prodded Timothy's arms and legs. "No broken bones. He seems to be bleeding, though. Let's see what's wrong . . . Great griffins! He's been shot!"

"Shot!" the others exclaimed. "With what? When? How? There's nobody down here except for us."

"Hold on," said Emmer, unbuttoning Timothy's tunic. Timothy winced as pain lanced his back. Then Emmer held up a four-inch, bloody spike. Mycena clucked her tongue. "The poor boy's riddled with holes! Who would do such a thing, anyway?"

"Who or *what*," said Bembor. "Let's hear what Timothy has to say for himself, and quickly. Our barrier won't hold for long."

Refreshed by the water and a couple of honey cakes, Timothy briefly recounted his harrowing experiences. When he had finished, Bembor examined the sharp, tapering shell Emmer had removed.

"If memory serves me, this is a *wormsticker* spine," he said and handed it to Timothy. "The creature that lives inside it started life as an egg tucked under a fat stoneworm's skin. After a wormsticker egg hatches, the 'stickling' sucks its host's blood until it has grown big enough to latch onto a tunnel wall, where it bores a burrow in the rock and makes this tough, pointed shell. When another stoneworm brushes by, out pops the shell, embedding itself in the stoneworm's hide. The wormsticker has a quick lunch and lays some eggs. Then the whole cycle begins again."

"Ugh!" said Gwynneth. "Those poor stoneworms!"

Bembor snorted. "To them, a few wormsticker prickings are like mosquito bites to us. Occasionally, large colonies build up in heavily traveled tunnels. Timothy must have run afoul of such a nest." He poked Timothy in the chest with his lightstaff. "You are fortunate Gaelathane was looking after you, my lad. If that eruption hadn't driven the wormstickers back into their holes, they would have sucked you dry." Recalling the "sacks" that he now realized were shriveled stoneworm skins, Timothy shuddered.

Just then, the rockfall began to sizzle and glow. "Let's go!" Rolin barked. He grabbed Timothy under the arms and deposited him on Windsong's back. Then he slapped the griffin's flank, and off they shot into the darkness.

CHAPTER 24
Terror in the Tunnels

Rock had always been and always would be. It was Timothy's whole world now—his pillow and his prayer, his strength and his despair—and it stank of sun-starved, stale air and dank dust. Rock crushed the heart and numbed the mind, stealing precious memories and leaving death in its wake. Beechtown itself, Baglot and Mardoc, Lucambra and Luralin, all were but other names for *rock*.

Grit caked Timothy's parched mouth and shriveled stomach. Fresh water and hot food were but a distant dream. The food in Opio's bag had run out, and the only water to be found trickled slimy and foul through cracks in the rock. Hemmed in by hollow shadows and sullen stone, Timothy felt struck blind. Only the light of Rolin's staff shining far ahead reminded him that eyes were for seeing.

"Where are we going, or do you know?" he asked Windsong.

"I believe we have left Golgunthor's roots and are approaching the Willowahs," the sorc replied. "If not, we might be traveling in circles. In their quest for food, stoneworms often follow coal seams, so their tunnels rarely make straight lines."

A blanket of gloom settled over Timothy. With only Windsong's padding steps to mark the plodding hours, he was sure weeks had passed since he and his friends had entered the stoneworm burrow.

Sensing Timothy's dejection, Windsong said, "Cheer up! In these untrodden tunnels, we may come upon some *gogoniants*."

"Are those like wormstickers?" Timothy asked the griffin.

"No, gogoniants are the rarest of gems, found only deep beneath the Willowahs," Windsong purred. "They are also called 'glory stones' for the way they capture the moon's light. It is said they were formed from the Tree's tears when evil first entered this world. Every griffling dreams of finding a gogoniant glowing in some dark cavern."

"Have you ever seen one?" Timothy asked.

"Not in nature. Only ten have come to light; nine of those are set in Whitewing's crown. The tenth was lost generations ago."

Timothy peered into the darkness. However, not once in many aching hours did he spot moonlight wrapped up in a rock.

Failing in that search, Timothy turned to his spasel for comfort. He discovered that breathing on the sap sheet every so often would keep it "awake" in the chill tunnels. When the stars pricked its depths more brightly, he guessed night had fallen in that far-off place; when the stars dimmed, morning had dawned.

Soon, he and his companions were following "spasel time." As soon as the platter darkened, Rolin would call a halt and everyone would bed down for the "night." Using the spasel as a pillow, Timothy would awaken when it brightened. With each passing "day," he pulled a thread from his tunic and tied it around his finger. So it was that the spasel became his sole lifeline to the worlds above and kept him from surrendering to despair.

During a rest stop, Opio grumbled, "I'm so hungry, I could eat a whole stoneworm!" He tightened his belt another notch.

Presently, Timothy came across more of the black, knobbly growths he had first found where the wormstickers had attacked him. "What are these things?" he asked Emmer, pointing them out.

"Stone fungi," Emmer replied. "The 'worms love these even better than they do coal. I suppose we could try cooking and eating some. It would be better than starving, if anyone's interested."

Elwyn wrinkled his nose. "No, thanks. I'd rather go without."

Timothy had tied five strings around his finger when at the spasel's next "dawn," the stoneworm tunnel forked. Ironwing and Windsong sniffed around the mouths of both passages. "I smell the upper world this way!" Ironwing chittered, speaking of the right-hand branch.

"Ironwing is right," said Windsong. "There's a current of fresh air flowing out of here. Even if this tunnel is only a ventilation shaft, it should still lead us to the surface."

After an hour's toiling upward through the passage, the company came upon bats hanging like brown kerchiefs from the roof, a sure sign the outside world was near. Soon, other passages began branching off, some of them breathing forth a faint piney scent.

Windsong flapped his useless wings and hopped on his hind legs. "I smell home! We must be near the main colony."

Ironwing nosed about, his beak quivering. "Where is everybody? We always post guards on the lower levels in case evil underworld creatures or other enemies creep up from below."

"Maybe they've all gone north to fight the Thalmosians," Timothy offered. He pictured hordes of ferocious griffins descending upon the terrified foot soldiers and driving them over the sea cliffs.

"Or they're off hunting," said Elwyn.

Scratching himself, Ironwing replied, "In any case, many she-sorcs and grifflings would remain behind. There is a stench about the place, too. Something is amiss."

Timothy and his companions shadowed the sorcs as they snooped into deserted cubbyholes, tunnels and caves. They found only fur and feathers lying thickly on dusty floors.

"They're all gone, dead, disappeared," Windsong wept. He yowled so loudly Timothy was sure the tunnel would collapse.

Gwynneth hugged the griffin's neck. "Don't give up, dear friend. I'm sure the others are here somewhere. We'll find them."

Windsong cocked his head. "I hear something. It sounds like—" Fur and feathers bristling, the sorcs sped off just as the screeching of ten thousand brawling alley cats roared down the tunnel.

"Now what?" muttered Opio.

After several bends, the tunnel opened onto the floor of a gigantic vertical shaft where a ghastly scene was playing out. Hundreds of sorcs were biting, scratching and clawing one another with bloodcurdling shrieks. The dead and dying sprawled on every hand, while feathers and fur choked the air.

One of the sorcs shot past the tunnel mouth, wings whipping and lion's claws poised to slash. As it banked, Timothy caught a glimpse of yellow eyes gleaming in a barn-owl's saucered white face. Then the beast pounced on Windsong.

"Help! What was that?" Elwyn gasped.

"Moonsorc," Ironwing tersely replied as he raced to Windsong's aid. After dispatching the squat-necked creature with a savage swipe of his paw, he looked wild-eyed back at Timothy and the Lucambrians and screeched, "Shoot them! Shoot them all!"

In a trice, the Greencloaks waded into the fray and sent a deadly volley of arrows and blowpipe darts up the shaft. Lifeless owl sorcs began dropping out of the darkness. Soon, the shaft was clear and the fighting tapered off, leaving heaps of twisted bodies.

"Hail, griffin friends!" cried a scrawny eagle sorc whose scruffy neck and back were bleeding in a dozen places. "Many thanks for your timely help. Your arrival narrowly averted disaster."

"Keeneye?" King Rolin gasped.

The griffin lowered his eagle's head. "Yes, Rolin son of Gannon, it is I, although I am surprised you recognized me. You and your friends are looking well." Then Keeneye nuzzled Windsong and Ironwing, who had escaped their run-in with the moonsorc almost unscathed.

Emmer asked, "Why the bad blood between you and these owl sorcs? I thought griffins always stuck together."

"Usually we do," said Keeneye. "We've had a falling out with our cousins. I can't explain it all now; let me take you to someone who can." Keeneye led the visitors through a bewildering maze of passages, stopping at a tall door flanked by stone griffins in rampant poses. Keeneye rapped on the door with his beak. There was no reply, but the door swung open of its own accord.

Inside the gloomy chamber, an ancient sorc lay listlessly draped over a bench. His snowy head bore a crown set with lustrous gems that shone like a circlet of stars, and he wore a *soros* around his neck.

"It is I, Sire," Keeneye announced. "We have successfully repulsed the moonsorcs, but with great loss of life. Our two-legged friends here helped rout the enemy. Now I must attend to my other duties."

"Welcome, strangers," said the sorc. "Forgive me for not rising, but illness has gravely indisposed me. I am Whitewing, king of the sorca. May I ask what business brings you to our lairs?"

"Hail, King Whitewing!" said Rolin. "My companions and I have journeyed through many perils to seek your aid. The Thalmosians have invaded Lucambra and the Hallowfast is taken!"

"You seek *our* help?" Whitewing said bitterly. "Surely you can see how hard-pressed we are from within and without. Our race is dying."

As Whitewing lifted his head, Timothy saw a white film clouding his blank eyes. The griffin king was blind.

CHAPTER 25
For Want of a Berry

The scorbies broke out here four years ago," Whitewing began, staring sightlessly. "First our feathers started falling out, then our fur. Now we can barely walk, let alone fly. Starvation stalks our steps like a dragon's shadow. The few conies and squirrels our youngsters catch cannot feed so many, and our numbers dwindle."

"What about the moonsorcs?" Timothy asked. Seeing Bembor's warning look, he covered his mouth. Whitewing turned toward him, a rumble rising in his throat.

"I was coming to that, two-leggling. For generations, our kin in the frosty Mountains of the Moon have coveted our sunny lairs. Biding their time until the scorbies left us weak and defenseless, they have fallen upon us like a plague of yegs. I doubt we can hold out against them much longer."

"I don't understand," said Marlis. "How is it that the moonsorcs can still fly? Don't they get the scorbies, too?"

"They do," Whitewing replied. "However, the moonsorcs also possess a hoarded secret that we sunsorcs have lost. They know where the *serenblod* grow."

Windsong stopped sharpening his beak on the back of a bench. "Serenblod!" he exclaimed. "I have read of those plants' healing virtues in the ancient annals of our race. In two-legged parlance, they are called 'starworts.' According to *The Complete Encyclopedic Griffanic Chronicles: Amenthil to Waganupa*, starworts have not grown in this land since the world was young."

"Ever the learned one, eh, Windsong?" Whitewing chuckled. "I must admit I have missed my royal bard these past months. Your depth of knowledge might prove useful in this present crisis. You are correct: Though starworts once grew abundantly in our isolated mountain valleys, overpicking and dragonfire reduced them to a few isolated pockets. Then those patches also died out. However, you are misinformed: Starworts do still survive in the Land of Light."

"Be that as it may, O King," said Windsong, "a rare plant cannot solve our dilemma. Even Ironwing and I suffer from the scorbies, and we are unable to fly. Our names no longer befit us."

"Then you are in good company," Whitewing said. "Yet here your learning falls short again, for these starworts are vital to our existence. Without their fruits, we will succumb to the scorbies. Even one berry a month will ward off the disease. Alas, we have long since consumed the fresh with the dried."

"Why don't you follow the moonsorcs to their secret starwort patches?" Timothy asked.

Whitewing wagged his head. "Time and again we have sent spies to trail our foes when they fly off to gather the 'starberries.' However, they always leave after dark, when their owl's night eyes and muffled wings help them to elude their pursuers."

"Without these starberries, how did you survive your other bouts with the scorbies?" Gemmio asked.

"The last outbreak took place in the reign of King Threeclaws," wheezed Whitewing. "Then, as now, we had used up our starberry stores. At that time, your King Elgathel sent his tower guard to help us find more berries. After they left us, we never saw them again, save Elmar son of Selwyn, their leader." The king fell to coughing again.

"Elmar!" Bembor said. "What became of him and his men?"

Whitewing paused to catch his breath. "A few months later, Elmar returned alone. The fellow was ragged, half-starved and had 'stared at the sun once too often,' as we sorcs say."

"He wasn't in his right mind," Windsong explained.

"This mad fellow ranted and raved about 'the Guardian of the Golden Wood' and other such drivel," Whitewing went on. "No one could make beak or feather out of his ramblings. Still, he did bring back a bag full of ripe starberries, for which we richly rewarded him.

"Sadly, those precious fruits arrived too late. As you know, we sorcs deserted Elgathel in his hour of need, and he lost his life. Our cowardice was largely to blame. However, many of our warriors were too weak and ill to fly or fight. Starberries would have turned the tide."

"No wonder Winona wished for Elmar's return," said Bembor. "'For want of a shoe, the horse was lost; for want of a horse, the rider was lost; for want of the rider, the battle was lost.'"

"What have horses to do with starworts?" Whitewing asked.

"I was quoting an old Thalmosian proverb. In this case, 'For want of a berry, the sorcs were sick; for want of the sorcs, the king was lost; for want of the king, the battle was lost.'"

"Aptly put," Whitewing grunted morosely.

Timothy squirmed on the hard wooden bench, and the spasel poked him in the ribs. *The spasel!*

"What do starworts look like?" he blurted out breathlessly.

"I have heard their flowers are cross-shaped and shine like stars in the darkness," said the griffin king.

"Look into my spasel!" Timothy cried. He held up his already-warm sap-platter for all except King Whitewing to see. In its depths, tiny bright crosses studded the blackness.

CHAPTER 26
The River Son

W hat do you all see?" Whitewing eagerly asked.

"I see little crosses shining like stars!" Timothy replied.

When Rolin described the spasel and its long history, tears flowed from the king's blinded eyes and he said, "Mad though he may have been at the end, Elmar still had the foresight to fashion a *wilith* as a signpost to the starworts' home. Can you find this place?"

Bembor stood. "The image should grow brighter as we approach the spasel's torsil-of-origin. Whether we can locate the starworts themselves is another matter."

"How can we be certain those aren't real stars?" said Sigarth.

"Because they don't twinkle as real stars do," Rolin said. "Also, they often appear to bend and sway, as if wind-blown."

"We should have noticed that before," said Skoglund glumly.

Whitewing feebly waved a ragged wing. "Forgive me; I must rest now. Keeneye will show you to the Starwort Room. If you scour the floor, you may find a few berries. Now go with Gaelathane." The king chirruped, and Keeneye appeared.

Leaving Ironwing and Windsong to visit with their friends and relatives, Timothy and the Greencloaks followed Keeneye through more labyrinthine passages until they came to an iron-bound, oaken door with a heavy padlock. "We must protect the berries from thieves," Keeneye explained apologetically. "Even the most noble sorc may resort to stealing rather than lose his powers of flight." Gripping a brass key in his beak, the griffin unlocked the door.

By staff light, the room appeared surprisingly small and dingy. A burned-out candle set in a wall-niche had evidently once illuminated the place. On a small table lay a yellowed ledger covered with names, dates and numbers, evidently a record of the sorcs' starberry rations.

A thorough search of the room turned up only a few mummified berries that made a disappointingly paltry pile. "I'm afraid we haven't helped you very much," Emmer told Keeneye.

"Do not be discouraged; it was to be expected," Keeneye replied. "Countless sorcs have combed this storeroom for starberries."

"What's this?" Gwynneth said. Using her mother's lightstaff, she was examining the room's back wall. Rows of shining symbols stood out against the gray stone.

"This is a find indeed!" breathed Bembor. His aged knees creaked as he knelt to pore over the writing. "These letters aren't inlaid in the stone," he said. "They were written right on it in the Common Tongue, though by what means I cannot tell. Rolin, could you read them for us? These old eyes aren't up to the task."

Taking the lightstaff from Gwynneth, the king read,

When comes the one,
The river son,
Whose people are not mine;
His name shall spell
The truth to tell
In riddle without rhyme.

"Hmph," grunted Gemmio. "That makes absolutely no sense."

Rolin waved his hand impatiently. "There's more: Cach-Cone-Cros-Pen-Plai-Glden-Orest-Ain-Gwln-Goge-Wor-Aven."

"More nonsense," growled Sigarth. "Someone's played a clever trick on us. The writer is probably laughing at us right now with his head under his wing, if you ask me."

"Nobody asked you," Opio retorted.

"Hush!" Rolin commanded. "Even sick sorcs have better eyes than we two-legs. Since the starberries ran out years ago, our friends should have noticed this writing long before now." He doused the staff's light with his cloak, and the letters disappeared.

Gwynneth gasped. "What happened to the words?"

"They're not showing, that's all," her father mysteriously replied. When he uncovered the staff, the writing again glowed a dull silver, like streaks of stardust smeared across the stone.

"Aha!" cried Bembor. "This is Gaelathane's work, or I don't know my beard from a barley loaf. *He* traced these words in such a way that they would appear only when staff light is shined upon them. He must have intended His riddle to remain hidden until a staff-holder came along. That much is plain."

"That's all that is plain," said Scanlon. "What does 'Cach-Cone' mean? Bury some cones in a 'cache,' the way squirrels do?"

Mycena pulled on his ear. "Stop joking; this is important! The sorcs are depending on us to help them solve their riddle."

Scanlon rubbed the side of his head. "Just because you're my baby sister doesn't mean you can lengthen my ears!"

The nonsensical words reminded Timothy of a game he often played by the river with his father. They called it "whirly-stick." One person would scratch a word in the sand with a stick, leaving out a letter. While the other player tried to guess the word, the "whirler" would erase it letter by letter by twirling his stick until the word was scratched out or his opponent correctly guessed it. Timothy usually won, since Garth was a poor speller.

"I think I can help," he spoke up. "Suppose each of those words is missing a letter. If we find the right letter for each word, we might solve the puzzle. For instance, 'Glden Orest' must be 'Golden Forest,' don't you think?"

"By the Tree, I believe the boy is right!" Bembor exclaimed.

Now the others joined in the guessing game. "'Plai' must mean 'Plain,'" Elwyn said, stabbing his finger against the stone.

"'Cross Open Plain,'" cried Marlis, who loved word games.

Keeneye poked his head into the huddle. "Pardon me, but mightn't 'Cach Cone' mean 'Catch Coney'?"

"What's a 'coney'?" Timothy whispered to Elwyn.

"It's a rabbit, silly," Elwyn shot back.

"'Catch Coney, Cross Open Plain,'" Rolin summed up. "'Golden Forest'—"

"'Gain'!" Gemmio put in.

Marlis said, "Gaelathane wrote something similar on our tabletop: 'A grove of trees with golden leaves.'"

"I still think it's poppycock," said Sigarth. "Besides, didn't Elmar warn Winona to 'Beware the Guardian of the Golden Wood'?"

"Pipe down, Brother," Skoglund growled. "I want to see where all this is leading."

"Let's go back to the first part," suggested Bembor, who had more experience than the others unraveling riddles and rhymes. "What could 'the river son' mean?"

"That must be Rolin," said Queen Marlis, smiling at the king.

"Our relic-bearer lives closer to the Foamwater than I did," Rolin countered. "I think he answers the description better."

"Any river-dweller could fit that riddle," Opio argued. "Besides, if the 'river son' is a real person, he's probably long dead."

"I disagree," said Bembor. "I believe these words point to a flesh-and-blood, present-day deliverer. Moreover, 'Whose people are not mine' might refer to the Thalmosians."

"A *Thalmosian* deliverer?" scoffed Sigarth. "I say, let Gaelathane deliver us *from* the Thalmosians!"

"'His name shall spell, the truth to tell,'" Rolin murmured. "Whose name, I wonder, and what does it spell?"

"Maybe we're looking at this all backward," Timothy suggested. "What if the key to the riddle is not what's right here in front of us, but what's missing?"

Bembor clapped a hand to his head. "By Elgathel, he's right again! What do the missing letters spell?"

"'Catch'—there's a 'T,'" said Gemmio, tracing the letter in the air.

"'Coney' makes a 'Y,'" said Opio.

"'Cross' gives us an 'S,'" added Marlis.

"And 'Open' was missing the 'O,'" Rolin said, sweeping his lightstaff in a circle.

"Don't forget the 'N' in 'Plain,'" said Bembor.

"'TYSON,'" said Emmer. "Is that someone's name?"

"Not a sorc's," Keeneye said, hanging his head.

"O-F-G doesn't spell anything, either," said Scanlon.

Gwynneth let out a shriek. "We've spaced the letters all wrong! They should say, 'TY—SON—OF—G—'"

"'TY' could be short for 'TIMOTHY'!" Elwyn exclaimed.

Bembor shook Timothy. "Quick, lad—your father's name again!"

"G-Garth," he answered through rattling teeth.

"That makes, 'Gwlan Gorge, Wort Haven,'" said Scanlon.

Rolin stared intently at the wall. "Then the entire riddle reads, 'Catch Coney, Cross Open Plain, Golden Forest Gain, Gwlan Gorge, Wort Haven.' These must be clues for finding the starworts!"

"It's certainly a 'riddle without rhyme,'" Mycena sighed.

"Except for 'Plain' and 'Gain,'" Skoglund said with a grin.

"More gibberish," muttered Sigarth.

Bembor thumped his staff. "Gibberish or no, those missing letters spell out the name, 'Timothy son of Garth'!"

CHAPTER 27
Tuft to the Rescue

"Get up!" Asper's bulk towered over Meghan in the blue twilight. She shuddered, recalling the withering tongue-lashing she'd received after her encounter with the moonsorcs. Derwin alone had believed her story of Sleepyeye and his arrow wound. The others had only laughed and called her hurtful names.

Asper roughly hauled Meghan to her feet. "Fetch us some decent firewood, and be quick about it," he barked. "We'll want a real blaze tonight. Don't run off the way you did yesterday, either. My men will be watching you—and I don't mean you, Derwin."

Happy to escape Asper's glowering looks, Meghan left the rocky hollow where the Thalmosian soldiers had pitched camp. The gloomy, wind-harried firs fringing the dell mirrored her own dark mood. If only the moonsorcs had taken her away, she might have escaped her dreadful captors! Still, she wasn't sure she could trust those savage, solemn griffins. Where did they live, and why hadn't Windsong and Ironwing mentioned owl-headed sorcs to her before?

Her stomach rumbled. As if stinging words weren't punishment enough, Asper had halved her bread ration. "You won't stray far on an empty belly," he had told her with a sneer.

Derwin tagged along with Meghan despite his brother's orders. "Here's a fir with plenty of dead wood in it," he offered, reaching high into the tree to break off some limbs Meghan couldn't reach.

As the two snapped brittle twigs and branches off the fir, a chill wind sprang up to whistle and moan among the rocks. Meghan couldn't help shivering. The dismal dell had a nasty smell to it that raised the hairs on the back of her neck. She worked faster, filling her arms with kindling. "We have enough to start a fire now," she told Derwin. "I'll come back for more later."

The woodcutter agreed, and they trotted back to the hollow, where Derwin tried to kindle a flame from a wad of dried moss with his flint and steel. "Tinder's too damp," he said. The other men grumbled about "raw meat" and "cold feet," so Derwin redoubled his efforts.

As her friend struck sparks from his flint, Meghan hunkered down against the evening chill. Clumps of black fur lay strewn about the trampled ground, recalling her recent visit with Rolin to a pasture down the hill from Grandfather Gannon's homestead. Burnt bones and singed fur lay scattered everywhere in the grass, and an evil smell lingered in the air. During her father's boyhood, he had joined some terrible battle in that field . . .

Greyson. Farmer Greyson. The field was his, and Meghan's father had spilled batwolf blood among its sheep-shorn grasses. However, the hair in this protected nook looked too fresh for creatures the king had hunted out of Lucambra years ago.

The firs hissed and roared as waves of wind-warriors marched through their tops. Yammering and screeching sounds echoed down from mountain peaks as a dark cloud fanned across the sky, sprouting long, curling fingers that reached for Meghan.

She screamed to shatter rock. *Yegs!* Where had they all come from? Though Meghan had never seen a live batwolf before, Beechtown's petrified ones were terrifying enough.

She screamed again. "Gaelathane!" A hail of Thalmosian arrows sprang up to greet the yeg-swarm, and a few of the creatures tumbled shrieking to earth. Too few. The sky turned black as diving batwolves thrashed the air to a thrumming roar.

Reeeeurrrk! With warbling screeches, gray ghosts swooped down. Hundreds of yegs began dropping out of the sky, while others fled in a panic. Flinging herself on the ground, Meghan blocked her eyes and ears against the horrible sights and sounds of mortal combat. A yeg fell beside her, its wings shredded to ribbons. Derwin beheaded the snarling beast with one stroke of his axe.

"Meg-*hoon!* Meg-*hoon!*"

Meghan rubbed her eyes and sat up. Beside a heap of slaughtered yegs, seven moonsorcs sat staring at her with owlish eyes. "It's all right; these are my friends," she told the rattled Thalmosians, who nervously clutched their bows, swords and spears.

A sorc with a great horned owl's erect ear tufts loped up to Meghan and laid a bloody yeg's head at her feet. "I am Tuft, chief of the—*hoo!*—moonsorcs in the *Dyggorech*, the Moon Mountains," he said. "We have heard how you saved Sleepyeye's life, and I present you this gift as a token of our gratitude."

Meghan avoided looking at the gory yeg's head as she thanked Tuft. Then she relayed his message to her captors in the Common Tongue. Sheepishly, Asper's men laid aside their weapons.

"Tell your friends they are—*hoo!*—fortunate to be alive," said Tuft. "Ever since the wolves-with-wings returned to these mountains, they have met in this—*hoo!*—spot to plot the overthrow of men and sorcs. Tonight, however, we were waiting for them. Now then, what errand brings you into our realm?"

When Meghan had repeated Tuft's words, Asper replied, "We seek a forest with trees of gold. Do you know of such a place?"

The moonsorcs put their heads together. After much hooting, they appeared to reach a consensus. Tuft again addressed his two-legged audience. "We have heard—*hoo!*—rumors that such a forest lies far to the south. However, many perils await travelers on that journey. You would be wise to abandon your quest and return the way you came."

As Meghan interpreted, Captain Asper's right eyelid began to twitch, though he still wore the same bland expression. "Thank you for your counsel," he said. "All the same, we will take our chances. We cannot return to our king empty-handed."

"Better to return empty-handed than not to return at all," sniffed one of the moonsorcs. Meghan pretended not to hear.

"Then I wish you luck," said Tuft. "I leave you with a final word of advice: If you—*hoo!*—value our friendship, do not treat with any of the sunsorcs, for they are our mortal enemies."

With sharp, guttural cries, the moonsorcs spread their downy owl's wings. "Wait!" cried Meghan. "Take me with—" But it was too late. The griffins had already silently vanished into the night.

"Break camp for a night march!" Asper bellowed. "We must put miles between us and this accursed place before dawn. I won't be caught napping by those wolf bats again." With many a groan and a grumble, the men packed up and set out.

Before she dozed off on Gert's swaying back, Meghan heard Asper and his brother talking quietly. "How do ye suppose she learned to talk with them flying critters?" Derwin remarked.

"More Greencloak sorcery, I'd say," Asper replied. "The next thing you know, she'll be turning us all into toads."

"Toads or no, it's a good thing we brought her along. We'd have been goners if she hadn't befriended them lion-owls."

"Maybe so, but I'll take a dumb beast to a talking one any day."

Meghan bit her tongue. She already knew what Asper's horse thought of her owner, and it would singe even a soldier's ears.

CHAPTER 28
Andil of the Wood

The sun was rising in the eastern sky when Meghan and the gold-hunters gained the lip of a saddle-shaped pass through the Willowahs. Descending the other side, they rode through stands of pine, trembling aspen and white-boled birch. Soon, the mountains and their shadowed foothills ended in a rippling sea of wind-worried, tasseled grasses that stretched to the horizon.

Stripe-winged killdeers skittered away at the two-legs' approach, crying mournfully, "Not so near! Not so near! Our eggs are here!" The air turned cool and sweet, as if unbreathed by man or beast since the creation of the world.

That night, Meghan gazed up at the whispering stars wheeling in their familiar constellations: Gaelathane the Guardian; Waganupa the Tree; Morved the Bear; Sonwen the Sorc; Heldamarr the Heron; Poldwyn the Elk; Ramaria, Queen of the Faeries; Mishmar the Bat; the High Cross and Draconia, the Dragon. *Trust the King, and He will help you,* they seemed to say. Then she slept.

"Ho there, sleepyhead! Rise and shine! The day's a-wasting."

Meghan opened her eyes to find Derwin standing over her, hands on hips. Asper joined him. Favoring her with a thin-lipped smile, the captain said, "Well, what's the map say today?"

The sun-warmed spasel now yielded images so bright and clear that Meghan felt sure the torsil they sought must be near. She settled on a southwesterly heading as the most promising.

For several days, the travelers plowed through silver-stippled grasses that waved higher than the horses' bridles. They rarely lacked for water, since many small streams meandered across the prairie. As they rode under a spring sun that shone in swallow-swooping skies, spirits soared and the men sang,

Gold! Gold! So smooth and soft, so wondrous bright;
A treasure worth the seeking, soon within our sight;
A forest ripe for picking, each leaf a gleaming thing;
A bushelful will make us every man a king!

Gold! Gold! The answer to our poverty;
Luscious gold! The only key to liberty;
Costly gold! We love her more than life or kin;
Precious gold! To have her, we would sell our skin!

Meghan's heart stirred with a different kind of music as she sang
a song of Lucambra she'd learned at her mother's knee:

When dawn came o'er the restless sea,
The very first day, the very first day;
The Land of Light was born of the Tree,
The very first day of Creation.

When evening lit the barren hills,
The very next day, the very next day,
Sweet waters ran in leaping rills,
To quench the thirst of Creation.

When Dayspring saw His leafless land,
The very next day, the very next day,
The King of kings stretched out His hand
And green then grew His Creation.

When light had spangled the dewy dawn,
The very next day, the very next day,
The Maker formed a long-necked swan,
The very first swan of Creation.

When all was done except for one,
The very last day, the very last day,
Then Man was made, of leaf-light spun,
The very last day of Creation.

When she had finished, Derwin said, "Missy, I've been thinking about yer Gaelathane. Mind ye, I ain't sayin' I believe in Him. I can't understand why He would care for the likes o' me. I'm jest a simple woodcutter, not royalty like ye."

"Gaelathane's a woodcutter, too," Meghan told him.

"What? Only commoners cut wood. Besides, if He's King of the trees, why would He want to chop them down?"

"He just cuts the bad ones," Meghan replied. "Anyway, He only appears as a woodcutter when He wants to. King Gaelathane cares for everybody because He made us and died for us."

Derwin leaned forward in the saddle. "Died for me? He doesn't even know me. And what good is a dead king, anyhow?"

"He knew you before you were born," Meghan said, recalling one of her mother's favorite sayings. "Anyway, He's not dead any more. After three days, He came back to life."

"Did He, now," Derwin murmured. "How does a young girl like ye know all this?"

"Because I asked Him into my heart when I was little," Meghan stoutly declared. "And He's still there!"

Four days later, the Thalmosians' rowdy songs had soured into curses and complaints. A blistering sun beat down; water and wild game were growing scarce. The talk was turning to the merits of horse meat when a thick mist settled over the prairie. When it finally lifted, a grove of linden trees had appeared, their fragrant shade beckoning like cool water to parched desert wanderers.

Riding into the grove, they came upon a long colonnade of stately lindens, their overarching branches forming a leafy, vaulted roof. To Meghan's ear, the trees murmured contentedly as bees droned among their ivory, nectar-rich blooms.

At the end of the green aisle stood a table laden with all sorts of meats, cheeses, wines, fruits and breads. Dismounting, the men were about to fall upon the feast when Asper stopped them. "This food must be enchanted! Do not touch any of it, lest you die."

"You will find only life abundant here," said a wizened little man who was standing at the head of the table. Wrapped in a hooded white cloak, he gestured to the untouched repast. "Please be my guests! This table has long been prepared for you."

When the suspicious soldiers made no move to eat, Meghan helped herself to some bread and cheese. After watching her carefully for signs of distress, the men eagerly stuffed themselves.

"Who are you? A hermit? A huntsman? A wayfarer?" Asper asked his host between mouthfuls of mutton.

The old man smiled and twirled his staff. "I've many names, I do. To you, Asper son of Stolland, I am Andil of the Wood."

"Andil of the Wood!" Asper gasped. He stared at the stranger. "I never knew—I thought you were—but how do you know my name?"

The little man returned Asper's stare. "Oh, I know a good deal about you and your men. Indeed, all about you."

"Then state your business with us," said Asper curtly.

Andil's deep-set blue eyes burned brightly beneath his hood. "Ah, yes. The gold won't wait, will it?"

"How did you know about the gold?" Derwin blurted out.

"The wood you seek belongs to me," Andil replied. "I'm rather particular about the folk that enter it and what they do there."

"Where do the gold trees lie?" asked Asper, his eyes agleam.

Andil pointed his staff behind him. "Two days' march from here, no more. You will find them easily. However, you all would be well advised to return whence you came, as Tuft warned you."

Asper drew his sword. "Are you threatening us, old man?" he snarled. "Do not hinder us or we shall hew you to pieces!"

Andil of the Wood threw back his hood and shot Asper a piercing look. Asper's sword fell from his hand. "You are free to pass or not, as you wish," said the hermit, whose hoary head bore many scars, as if raked by thorns. "Be warned that he who picks a leaf in the Goldwood will never pick another. Farewell, son of Stolland. We will meet again!"

"Wait!" the captain cried. But the old man had vanished.

"Who was that funny old fellow?" asked the gold-hunters.

"Andil of the Wood," Asper said in a distant voice. "My mother once met him in the Forest of Fellglade. Supposedly he rescued her from the jaws of a mountain lion."

"But *what* is he?" asked Meghan, already suspecting the truth.

The captain scratched his head. "That I don't rightly know. Legend has it he was a gnome or elf that inhabited the heart of the forest. Only certain kinds of people ever saw him."

"What kinds?" the other men asked.

Asper looked away. "'Those in need or those in greed,' my mother used to say."

"That fits us on both counts," Derwin observed.

"Whatever he is, he's harmless," Asper said. "Now let's be off. The food's spoiling, and this place gives me the shivers."

Refreshed by their meal, the men mounted their horses and rode out of the trees. When Meghan looked back, only grasses waved where the linden grove had stood.

CHAPTER 29
The Seekers of the Wood

A h, that's purrrrfect," murmured King Whitewing as Timothy brushed his belly fur. "For a two-legs, you have a sure touch. Where did you learn how to groom a griffin?"

While Timothy hated to see any sorc reduced to such a pitiable state, he enjoyed easing Whitewing's misery. The king was growing frailer by the day. "I've been practicing on Windsong and Ironwing," he said. "They're fussy—er, *particular* about their fur and feathers."

"As all sorcs are—especially when what little we have left is falling out! I shall be sorry to see you leave, 'river son,' but 'If the elders' wings are not spread, the children cannot be fed,' as we say. If you are to replenish our stock of starberries, you must go away for a time."

"I shall miss you, too," said Timothy. He had already spent many a pleasant hour in the blind king's company, listening to tales of the world when it was still fresh from the hand of Gaelathane.

With a throaty *skirrrr*, Whitewing nuzzled his balding head against Timothy's side. "Your ribs are sticking out," he said sadly. "I regret we cannot send you on your journey better fed."

"I'm not very hungry," Timothy lied. During the past three days, he and Elwyn had been trapping rabbits, squirrels and groundhogs for their hosts, with no thought of filling their own stomachs. Timothy was glad enough for the sun on his face and the clean, pine-scented air in his nostrils.

"Don't worry about me," he added. "I'm sure we'll find plenty to eat in the Golden Wood. Do you know the way there?"

Resting his head on his scraggly paws, Whitewing said, "Our old tales hint at such a place far to the south, beyond the Plain of Gaelathane. Your wilith may guide you to that forest. Perhaps you will even meet some of the Wood Folk there."

"Wood Folk? Don't you mean the People of the Tree?"

Whitewing snorted. "I may be old and sick, but my mind is still as sharp as my beak! The Wood Folk are the tree-people who lived here before any two-legs set foot in this land. They rarely appear nowadays, since they keep to themselves unless threatened." The king yawned. It was time for his afternoon nap.

Fearful that he might have few other chances to speak with Whitewing, Timothy said, "Windsong once mentioned that powdered gold mixed with water could cure the scorbies."

Whitewing waggled his gaunt head. "Not cure it, young one. Gold can only restore some strength to wasting muscles and ease the pain of the disease. I should know. I drink it every day."

On the eighth morning after the exiles' arrival, a great cloud of dust arose far to the north. As the day wore on, sunlight glinting off shields and helmets spelled the grim truth that Gorn and his army were still pursuing their prey. Whitewing and his councilors hurriedly conferred with their two-legged visitors.

"I had hoped you could stay with us longer as our honored guests," the king said. "Such a mighty host is hounding you that we must send you on your way, though not empty handed, as you two-legs say. It's a pity we have little to give you but our pure mountain water." Whitewing's attendants piled sloshing water skins at the exiles' feet.

King Rolin bowed. "We thank you for your hospitality, King Whitewing, especially in such trying times for all of sorcdom."

"We have yet another parting gift for you," said the king. At his piercing warble, seven pairs of proud-necked griffins trotted into the hall and lined up before Whitewing's throne.

"These are some of our youngest and fittest warriors," Whitewing said. "Though they can no longer soar, I am lending you their strong legs, beaks and backs, which will serve you well."

Greatly gladdened, the thirteen companions all stood and bowed, thanking the king for his generosity. Of the griffins who had aided Rolin and his friends on their Luralin-quest years before, there were Flamefeather, Spearwind and Sharpclaw, Windsong and Ironwing. Keeneye also had begged the king's leave to join the expedition. Sadly, Farsight and Longfeather were too ill to travel, while Snowfeather had recently perished of the scorbies.

Eight more stalwart sorcs rounded out the company: Grayneck, Sharptongue, Brighteye, Starwind, Longtail, Broadwing and Blacktail. There was also "Runt," a pint-sized, red-feathered afterthought who was tagging along to serve as Timothy's mount.

When Bembor protested that Runt made fourteen mounts, while only thirteen were needed, Keeneye explained that portly Opio would require two sorcs to carry him in turn. Opio sulked.

Whitewing concluded, "I bestow upon you all a new title: 'Seekers of the Wood.' May my faithful subjects bear you across the Plain of Gaelathane to the object of your quest—if it is more than a myth. Should you succeed in 'gaining' the Golden Wood, please send your mounts home, for if the legends have any feathers to them, that forest is no fit place for a sorc."

Whitewing paused to scratch himself. "I must warn you that on his return, Elmar told us, 'Pick no leaf from any tree in the Golden Wood!' Even in a madman's ravings there is often some truth. Now may Gaelathane speed your way to the starworts' haven!"

"And may your wings never falter!" his audience politely replied. As Timothy and his companions filed out, he wondered whether this parting blessing would ever ring true again for the sunsorcs.

"And catch a coney for me, too!" Whitewing called after them.

However, the Seekers of the Wood were in no position to catch conies—or anything else, for that matter. Heeding King Whitewing's advice, they returned to the stoneworm burrows, where they would lose their pursuers and also make better time than overland.

After the first hour, Timothy's feet were sore. Though Runt had plenty of spunk and spark for a sorc his size, he tired so easily that Timothy often had to get off and walk beside him.

"I'm very sorry," Runt said, his eyes half-lidded with fatigue. "I never dreamed a two-leggling could weigh so much! Drinking gold-dust water would boost my stamina, but when the daily ration comes around, the others push me out of the way."

"Why would they do that?" Timothy asked.

Runt's head drooped. "I am despised because of my size. Also, I am unlike my litter-mates, who are bigger and stronger than I. Even they won't share their food with me. They say I don't belong. You and everyone else would be better off without me."

"Nonsense," Timothy said. "I enjoy your company. Besides, I'm sort of a runt, too, for a two-legs." Stroking the sorc's silky gray fur, Timothy lowered his voice. "I'll tell you a secret. I have a little bag filled with gold dust, and it's all for you."

Runt brightened. "Thank you! When I feel better, I'll carry you and your baggage as far as you like."

Timothy patted the griffin's head. Despite having to walk, he had taken a liking to his mount, who had none of the airs and prickliness peculiar to his race. Timothy suspected, too, that if any danger came calling, Runt would give a good account of himself.

Again the sunless days and moonless nights melded into one dark, dreary blur as the Seekers of the Wood tramped under the Willowahs' roots. Water and food ran low, despite Whitewing's water skins and the venison strips Sigarth and Skoglund had dried during their stay in the griffins' mountain lair.

After a particularly long and tiresome march, Timothy was still chewing on his breakfast ration of venison jerky when a shout rang out ahead. "We've found water!"

Everyone rushed up in a helter-skelter of wings, legs and arms to find a cavern pool partially filling the burrow. Dripping stalactites hanging from the domed ceiling met their mirrored mates in the dark waters beneath. Ghostly-pale water lilies floated on the pond's surface amidst myriads of bobbing, balloon-like bladders attached to thick stalks. A cloying, sweet scent thickened the air.

"How can anything so lovely survive in this darkness?" Gwynneth murmured. She tried to touch the nearest lilies, but the flowers grew just out of reach. The griffins poked about and sniffed the water while Timothy and Elwyn tossed rocks into the pond.

"I've never seen water lilies like these before," Bembor remarked. "I wonder what those bladders are for."

"Maybe they help support the lilies," Timothy offered.

"We're fortunate it's not flood season," said Emmer. He pointed his staff at the high-water marks etched on the cavern walls.

"That we are," said Runt. "You know how sorcs hate to swim!"

Elwyn was cupping his hand to draw some water from the pool when Windsong said, "I wouldn't do that if I were you."

Elwyn withdrew his hand. "Why not?"

"The water has a bad smell about it," the sorc replied. "Besides, haven't you heard that you are only supposed to drink from streams and rivers? Running water renews itself, but still waters stagnate."

"The lilies seem to like it," Elwyn grumbled as he stared at the pool.

"My throat is so dry, I could drink a bucketful of water," said Gwynneth, using her reflection in the pond to arrange her hair.

"I could, too," Timothy chimed in.

"It's all that jerky that's making us thirsty," Scanlon said.

King Rolin held up his hand. "Let's stop here a bit. You all look worn out, and we'll cover more ground after a short rest."

"Well said," yawned Spearwind, curling up on the shore. "And I'm taking this spot. Wake me when you find the starberries."

The other griffins hunkered down beside him, snuggling closely together for warmth. Just looking at them made Timothy drowsy. "I wish I could sleep like that," he told Elwyn.

Eyelids drooping, the Lucambrians lay down next to their mounts, pillowing their heads on the griffins' bodies. "I don't know what's wrong with me," said Marlis with a huge yawn. "My eyelids won't stay open. I must have slept poorly last night."

Timothy found a vacant spot by the water and collapsed near Runt, who was already snoring. The last thing he remembered was the lily blossoms' sweet scent swirling into his brain.

Minutes or hours later, someone shook him awake. A white-winged figure was standing over him. Before Timothy's eyes could properly focus, the personage disappeared. *Such perfect wings!* he thought, accustomed as he was to the sorcs' bedraggled ones. He tried to roll over, but his head and body were floating apart. With a mighty effort, he turned his head toward the pool. Right at the waterline, his leather bag was sizzling and smoking.

"My water skin's on fire," he dreamily told himself. "How odd. Now I shan't have anything to drink, though I'm very thirsty. I'll just go back to sleep . . ." All at once, with a *pop*, the bag sank under the water and a searing pain jabbed Timothy's leg. He rolled away from the pool to find his trousers were smoking.

"Help! Fire!" he shouted, but his voice came out in a breathy croak. Feeling full of wool from head to toe, he poked and prodded his friends, who were all but dead to the world.

"Can't a body take a nap in peace?" muttered Skoglund.

Opio rolled over. "I'm fresh out of tinder, so we can't have a fire," he mumbled. "Rock won't burn. Now leave me alone."

Timothy wouldn't leave anyone alone. The water level was rising rapidly, completely covering the sloping shoreline in places. Soon the Seekers of the Wood would be trapped.

"Get up!" Timothy shouted, kicking Elwyn. "Get up! Get up!"

"Go away," Elwyn grumbled.

"What's all the fuss about?" Bembor growled, rubbing his eyes.

"The water—it's burning things!" Timothy announced.

Bembor squinted. "The water—? Why, it's coming closer, isn't it?" He flopped back on the ground and began snoring.

"GET UP!" Timothy screamed. Startled, Runt and the other sorcs scrambled out of harm's way, their wet fur smoking. Rolin sprang to his feet and stared wildly about. With Timothy's help, he dragged the protesting Lucambrians away from the creeping waterline. The effort seemed to clear the king's head.

"It's the water lilies that put us to sleep," he panted. "We should wade through the water to reach dry ground while there's still time."

"No, you mustn't!" cried Timothy. Using his knife, he clipped off part of a leather shoestring, which he dipped in the water. When he pulled it out, most of the string was gone, and the remainder sputtered and smoked like grease spattered on a hot stove.

Horrified, the Seekers backed away from the poisonous pool, which had already blocked their escape routes. Mycena cried out, "Gaelathane, if ever we needed Your help, it's now!"

"If only we could fly, we could reach the other side!" moaned the sorcs, uselessly flapping their weakened wings.

Scanlon scratched a mark on the shrinking shoreline with a stone. After water covered the mark, he scratched another. "It's still rising," he said grimly. "When Elwyn and Timothy threw those rocks into the pool, they must have set something off."

"That's it!" King Rolin exclaimed. "It's the bladders!"

"Bladders?" everyone asked, looking around. Many of the air sacs bobbing among the water lilies had disappeared.

Opio rolled his eyes. "So the water covered them, just as it's going to cover us if we don't find a way out of here."

"Don't you see?" Rolin said. "Those bladders aren't for buoyancy; they control the water level! Floating on top of the pond, they take up little space. When the lilies are disturbed, though, they retract their bladder stems, causing the water to rise."

Marlis nodded. "The same thing happens when you drop a large stone into a full barrel of water; it overflows."

"If we don't want to become lily food," Rolin went on, "we must trick these plants into lowering the water level."

Gemmio suggested, "Why not try throwing more rocks into the water?" Following his example, the Lucambrians hurled handfuls of pebbles and stones into the pool, which swallowed them whole. Still the water rose, lapping hungrily at the fugitives' feet.

Skoglund spat. "Apparently these lilies aren't easily fooled."

"That's because they don't eat rocks and the like," Rolin said. "They must feed on lost creatures that stray too close to the water and on small stoneworms that happen by. Now if we had some meat . . ."

"You're saying we should feed them?" Timothy asked, his eyes burning from the water's acrid fumes.

"We ate the last of the jerky for breakfast," Emmer said.

"There's always Runt," muttered Sharptongue.

"If only we had a bag of nuts or fruit . . ." said Gemmio.

Bag. Timothy thought back to his water bag dissolving in the acid pool. "Our water skins!" he cried. "They should work."

The others gaped at him. "What would we do for water without them?" Sigarth demanded. "Do you want us to die of thirst?"

"Better the water skins than our skins!" Rolin snapped. "Hurry—do as he says." However, the rising pool had cut off the Greencloaks from their baggage, which they had left farther back in the burrow. Only Timothy had brought his water skin, and the pond had eaten it.

Just then, a white-robed man suddenly appeared near the still-dry baggage. "Back! Get back! This pool isn't safe!" Waving, Timothy shouted to the stranger, who was standing ankle deep in water.

"Who's he talking to?" asked Scanlon, glancing around.

"The fumes must have addled his head," said Opio gloomily.

Timothy blinked his eyes, but the man was still there, beckoning to him. *Come over here.* Timothy jumped as the words rang out in his mind, although the visitor's lips hadn't moved.

I can't, he silently replied. *There is death in the pool!*

Do not be afraid. You must trust Me and walk this way through the water. Do not look down, but keep your eyes on Me.

At these unspoken commands, Timothy found himself wading into the pond. "Hey! What are you doing?" Elwyn called after him. "You'll burn up! Wait! Have you lost your mind?"

His gaze fixed on the stranger, Timothy hardly heard the shouts and cries behind him, nor did he feel the water's icy bite. In a few strides, he was chest-deep in the pool. When water lilies blocked his way, he pushed them aside. As if in a dream, he strode dripping from the pond, only to find himself alone.

A few paces down the dark burrow lay his friends' belongings. *The water sacks!* Rummaging through the baggage, he dragged out all the water skins he could find and flung them into the pond. *Sploosh! Splash!* The sacks fell among the lilies, raising frothy waterspouts. Bruised and broken blossoms gathered on the water's roiling surface.

Then the pond belched. Where the water bags had fallen in, huge bubbles boiled up and burst on the pool's surface, releasing clouds of stinking smoke. Inch by inch, the noxious water subsided.

"It worked!" the Seekers cheered. All except Opio, that is, who had gotten water in his boots and was hopping from one foot to the other. He had to take off the boots and wait until they stopped smoking.

After the water had receded further, the Lucambrians raced over to embrace Timothy and pump his hand. The griffins purred and rubbed against him in gratitude.

"Are you hurt?" Gwynneth asked, her eyes dark with dread.

"I don't think so," Timothy replied, feeling a bit dizzy with all the attention. Unconvinced, Rolin ordered him to roll up his trousers. Pink from their dousing in the pool's frigid water, Timothy's legs were as whole and healthy as ever.

Gemmio scratched his head. "That acid pond water should have stripped the flesh off his bones in seconds!"

"What really happened to you out there?" asked Marlis gently.

Timothy described how the winged personage had awakened him and how the second man's gaze had guided him through the deadly waters. His friends stared at him in amazement.

"The first was an angel, and the other was Gaelathane!" Rolin said.

"Then why couldn't the rest of us see them?" asked Spearwind.

"I could," said Runt in a small voice. Several of the other sorcs gnashed their beaks at him and flicked their tails.

"Liar!" Blacktail hissed.

"Not necessarily so," Bembor said. "Gaelathane often chooses to reveal Himself only to one or two in a crowd. Timothy, by obeying the King, you saved our lives. *Diolch yn fawr!* Thank you!"

Emmer glanced back at the pool. "We'd best collect our gear and be off before those lilies get wind of us again," he said. With a sharp look at the boys, he added, "And let's have no more rock-throwing until we're clear of these tunnels!"

Once more taking up the rear on Runt, Timothy was leaving the water-lily cavern when he heard musical tones. Looking back, he and Runt saw a towering, bright-winged being standing in the midst of the water lilies, singing in a strong, clear voice,

When the water rises and your hopes are growing dim,
Open up your heart and give your troubles all to Him;
Do not be discouraged when the tunnel seems so long;
Let my wings enfold you as you listen to my song.

Gaelathane upon His throne is worthy of our thanks;
He alone can help you when dark waters brim your banks;
He has paid the penalty to satisfy your debt;
In the darkness doubt Him not nor all His love forget.

When the tides have turned away with sacrifice of skins,
Thank Him for the blood that bought the pardon for your sins;
He will make a way for you when death would drag you down;
Give Him all your struggles; He will never let you drown.

Timothy murmured, "Many thanks for waking me and saving our lives, whoever you are." Then he and Runt followed their companions down the beckoning stoneworm burrow.

CHAPTER 30
Sleep Smitten

"Now we're in for it." Derwin pointed at the sky, where boiling black clouds blustered. Rumbling thunderheads sailed across the prairie like plundering sky-ships rigged with crackling lightning. Blotting out the setting sun, they trailed their ominous shadows behind them like dark nets set to snare unwary travelers. Garishly lightning-lit, the prairie grasses rippled in silken waves of greenish gold. Flames leapt where jagged lightning met earth, and the horses' eyes rolled in terror.

As the rain lashed down in torrents, Meghan hunched her head against a wet, hair-snapping gust. Leading their mounts on foot, the soldiers shouted to one another to avoid becoming separated. Feeling very small, Meghan clung to Derwin's hand.

All at once, the company halted on the lip of a great gash in the earth. Unable to proceed farther, the gold-hunters huddled on the canyon rim. Weary and soaked to the bone, Meghan curled up beside Derwin and fell fast asleep.

When Meghan awakened, the thunderstorm had passed and a hale morning sun was coaxing steam from the sodden soil. Lying on his stomach, one of the men was peering over the edge of the ravine. "We've found the golden trees!" he crowed.

Sure enough, far below the frowning cliffs gleamed a waving sea of gold. The wondrous wood flowed through the canyon southward until it vanished in a golden mist. To the north, the gorge gradually grew shallower.

"Never have I seen such wealth!" Asper exclaimed. "And to think we have it all to ourselves. Every last man of us will wear a gold crown and live in luxury. Down with King Mardoc!"

"Down with King Mardoc!" the men-at-arms roared.

Derwin muttered, "They'll sing a different tune when Gorn catches up to them, mark my words." He hoisted Meghan into Gert's saddle and swung up behind her as his countrymen leapt astride their own mounts and thundered north along the rimrocks. Where the steep canyon flattened out, they met a leaping river hurrying down from the surrounding plain. Following it through a ferny dale, they descended into the rocky ravine.

Riding south beside the river, they gained the outskirts of the Golden Wood. Overcome with awe, the Thalmosians reined in their horses and gazed upon the ranks of living gold.

As she rode up with Derwin, Meghan gasped. A tall, bright being wielding a whirling sword stood before the golden trees. *He must be an angel!* she realized. The horses whinnied in fear.

"Do not enter this forest or pick its leaves!" cried the angel. "Great peril awaits those who seek worldly wealth in this place. Return whence you came whilst you may." Then the angel disappeared, his flashing sword the last to vanish.

When Meghan told the men what she had seen, they scoffed. "Ye just don't want to share yer father's treasure with us," they sneered. "Well, we won't fall for yer childish tricks!"

"Are ye sure ye saw what ye saw, Missy?" asked Derwin.

Pulling down the corners of her mouth, Meghan nodded.

"How can you expect us to believe in something that none of the rest of us saw?" Asper said. "What is an 'angel,' anyway? Is it a kind of sprite or fairy? Mind you, I still think it's all rot."

"Angels are Gaelathane's messengers," Meghan sniffed. "And I did see one! He told us not to go into the forest or to pick any of its leaves. Then he said we should go home."

"Gaelathane's supposed to be th' high king in these parts," said Derwin with a glance at Meghan.

"*Another* king?" exclaimed the soldiers.

Meghan said, "He's not just the King of our land, but of every world. I call Him the 'Tree-Maker.' He created all the green, leafy things, the animals and us, too. He's always with me."

The men looked around with puzzled expressions. "We don't see anybody else here, king or otherwise," they said.

"That's because most times, you can't see Him," said Meghan.

"A king ye cain't see ain't no king at all," they guffawed.

With an exasperated bellow, Captain Asper drove his spear into the ground. "Enough of this poppycock! Angel or no, we're going into these woods to collect our gold. Miss Meghan, you may stay here or join us, as you wish. Derwin, I'm leaving you in charge of the horses."

Meghan winced as the greed-crazed Thalmosians brandished their weapons and roared, "The gold is ours!" Dismounting from their horses, they broke into a run and plunged into the wood.

Meghan was relieved to see them go, but she was also afraid. "I don't think we'll ever see them again," she told Derwin.

"Nonsense," he replied as he hitched the horses' bridles to some trees. "They'll beat around in the brush fer a few hours and then come back out. Ye'll see. We'll wait for them here."

Meghan hoped he was right, though she couldn't shake the feeling that something dreadful was about to happen. Hadn't Andil of the Wood and the angel both warned against picking any leaves? She lay down under a golden tree and looked up into its kindly canopy. How brightly the leaves gleamed! What harm could there be in taking just one? Her arm reached up and then wearily fell back. "Just one," she murmured. Then she slept.

Meghan awoke to shouts and shrill screams echoing through the forest. Derwin sat up beside her, rubbing his eyes. The sun hung low in the west, its rays burnishing the gilded leaves.

"What was that?" Meghan cried as the sounds died away. She gripped Derwin's hand so fiercely that her knuckles popped.

He huskily replied, "I don't know, but we'd better find out. I wish I'd brought a sword with me." After unhitching the horses to let them freely graze, Derwin led Meghan into the forest.

Inside the wood, a mellow twilight reigned. Golden sunbeams slanted through the treetops to gild ferns and flowers, mosses and mushrooms. Most of the gold-headed trees resembled torsils. Unlike their chatty northern cousins, however, these passage trees were watchful and aloof, adding to Meghan's uneasiness. For the first time in her life, she felt out of place in the forest.

She picked up a fallen leaf, which had the heft and feel of a usual green one. "This leaf isn't real gold at all," she said to herself. "Those men are going to be very disappointed."

With twitching fingers, Derwin took the leaf from her. "Of all things," he murmured. "It's just a shiny old leaf." Crumpling it, he ruefully remarked, "We came all this way for nothing."

No, we didn't, Meghan thought. *Not if my family is here.*

Hurrying through gloom-gathering colonnades of trees whose leaves hung high out of reach, Meghan and Derwin came at length to an opening where the trees' boughs hung lower. Beneath them lay scattered bodies, as if they had fallen where they stood. Clutching a fistful of golden leaves, Asper was among them, his eyes wide open.

With a groan, Derwin knelt beside his brother. "Andil told him not to touch the leaves. Why wouldn't he listen?"

Meghan put her hand to her mouth. "Is he . . . dead?"

Feeling Asper's face, the woodcutter replied, "He's still warm and breathing. Let's see to th' others." They found the rest of the men also locked in wide-eyed slumber, leaves in hand. No amount of poking, prodding or shouting would awaken them.

Derwin plopped down on a log and rubbed his stubbly face. "This smells of sorcery, or my name's not Derwin son of Stolland. I don't suppose ye know any waking-up spells—?"

Giving him a "you-should-know-better-than-to-ask-that" look, Meghan sat down beside him. "Maybe they will all wake up in the morning," she suggested.

"I hope ye're right," sighed Derwin. "In th' meantime, we'd best leave these woods. I don't want to be bumping around in here after dark. No tellin' what might come out at night."

However, outside the glade, nothing looked familiar. Fog pooled in dells and hollows like curdled milk and groped into the treetops with long, gray fingers, pearling the light of a rising full moon. Thrice the pair set out for the forest's edge, and thrice they stumbled back. "It looks like we're stuck here for th' night," Derwin grumbled dejectedly as he settled down again on the log.

"I'm not afraid of the lurky-murkies," Meghan declared.

"Of th' what?" Derwin nervously peered into the bushes, as if a pack of savage wild animals were lying there in wait.

Meghan giggled. "That's what I call these foggy, creepy places. Whenever I'm out in the woods after dark, I ask Gaelathane to keep me safe, and He does."

"Oh, He does, does He?" grunted Derwin. "Well, I hope He knows we're in this wood. I don't like this place; I'm afeared that if'n we sleep here with the others, we'll never wake up again."

"Then let's pray," said Meghan. She bowed her head and folded her hands as her parents had taught her to do. "Dear Gaelathane," she began, "You know that we're lost in this big forest, and we can't help these sleeping men. Please protect us all tonight, and show us the way back home. Thank you. The Tree lives!"

"The Tree lives," sighed Derwin, patting Meghan's hand. "Now, let's move off a ways and find us a spot to sleep." Leaving the glade, the two piled up some golden leaves at the foot of a mossy tree and snuggled into them like hibernating squirrels.

"We're all alone now, Missy," Derwin whispered hoarsely.

"No, we're not," Meghan answered. "Gaelathane is with us." Yawning, she wriggled deeper into the warm, crackly leaves.

Soft, silvery moonbeams were caressing the trees when Meghan dimly sensed someone stepping over her. Other figures were moving through the moonlit forest with rustling whispers. Then all was quiet again, except for the hooting owls.

Meghan awakened the next morning with stiff limbs and a terrible itch from sleeping in the dry leaves. Floundering around, she sat up to discover Derwin's side of the leaf pile was empty.

She trembled. Had Derwin gone off with the others and left her behind? Having found the Golden Wood, surely they didn't need her help any longer. Dashing through the trees, she burst into the clearing. At first glance, her worst fears were confirmed: The sleeping men had disappeared. Then she saw Derwin sitting with head bowed and a hangdog, bewildered look on his face.

"What's the matter?" she asked the woodcutter.

"They've vanished without a trace," he said in a strangled voice. "My brother and all of his men—gone."

CHAPTER 31
Catch Coney, Cross Open Plain

M y spasel isn't working!" Resting after another dank, dreary tunnel march, Timothy was just coaxing his spasel to life when its "stars" winked out.

Looking up, he realized that gray light seeping into the burrow was washing out the spasel's mysterious scene. The air smelled fresher, too. Wafting over the mustiness of moldering stone came the sweet scent of sun-drenched greenery. Laughing for joy, Timothy raced past his friends into a blinding, green-and-gold world of billowing grasses and boundless sky.

"Sunlight, honest-to-goodness Lucambrian sunlight!" Gemmio shouted. With cries of delight, the sorcs shot out of the tunnel to frolic and roll in the grass, all their dignity forgotten.

"We can't strike out across this prairie without some sense of the proper heading," practical Opio reminded the others. Again Timothy consulted his spasel. This time, it yielded only a muddy mosaic of sun-bleached greens and browns.

Now the griffins joined the discussion. Some held that the Golden Wood lay southwest, while others insisted the proper course was southeast. The argument was going nowhere when Keeneye froze in a big cat's hunting pose. "Something's out there; I can smell it!" he chirred. His beak twitched as the grasses parted with a *swish-swish*. Thirteen other eagle's heads swiveled south.

"Woodchuck," said Sharpclaw, his paws poised to strike.

"No, it's just a killdeer," sniffed Flamefeather, a sorc with bright yellow wings. "It must have a nest nearby."

"I say it's a ground squirrel," Grayneck offered. "This whole place is riddled with their burrows. They do make mighty fine eating."

"Those are badger burrows, birdbrain!" Sharptongue said.

Just then, two tan ears poked above the grass. "Coney!" howled the griffins as they pounced on it. The hapless rabbit's glazed eyes bulged with terror as it struggled under the sorcs' claws.

"Let it go, brothers," said Runt. "It's just skin and bones. We'll find plenty of antelope and deer on these plains."

"You keep your runty beak out of this!" the other sorcs snarled. They were about to tear the coney to pieces when Bembor and Elwyn rushed in and snatched it out of their clutches. The sorcs lashed their tails in fury and gnashed their beaks.

"Not fair!" protested Starwind. "If you two-legs want a coney, get one of your own. By all rights, this one is ours."

"The riddle tells us to *catch* the coney, not eat it!" Bembor retorted, handing the hare to Timothy. The rabbit's heart hammered against his chest, as if the animal would die of fright.

"Oh, you poor thing," crooned Gwynneth, stroking the rabbit's fur. "You wouldn't make a mouthful for all those sorcs, would you?" The coney's ears lay back and its nose twitched.

"Maybe it would calm down inside the stoneworm burrow," said Timothy. He and Gwynneth retreated with the rabbit into the tunnel. Even there, a pair of sorcs still paced hungrily outside. Amplified, their voices carried down the passage.

"After they've talked with it awhile, perhaps they'll let us eat it," said a hopeful Blacktail to his cousin Longtail.

"Hardly," said Longtail glumly. "Most two-legs dote on small wild things. They'll make a pet of this one before you know it."

"We could offer to protect it from the others and then carry it off and eat it," Blacktail suggested. "No one would miss it. By Whitewing's crown, I haven't tasted fresh coney in months!"

"Hush up out there, you two!" Timothy yelled at them.

"Don't let them eat me!" the coney squealed. When Timothy and Gwynneth wheedled some sense out of the rattled animal, they learned its name was Longears, and that it was on an errand for "the Lady."

"What sort of errand?" Gwynneth asked.

"It was about some two-legs," Longears replied, collecting his few wits about him. "Just give me a moment. Bless me, those flying lions out there badly befiddled and befuddled me. I've near to forgot my own name. Imagine that! My own name. Now, where was I?"

Tiring of the coney's rambling chatter, Timothy asked, "And pray tell, who is 'the Lady'?"

Longears hopped out of Timothy's arms to sit on a boulder. "You haven't heard of her? She's queen of all the Sunwood. Goodness! I thought everybody knew that."

"Well, we didn't," said Timothy. He and Gwynneth exchanged glances. Was the coney speaking of the Golden Wood? "What does she want with two-legs?" he asked, thinking, *and why would she send such a scatterbrained hare on an important errand?*

Longears chewed on a whisker. "There's a mystery for you! What would anybody want with such rude, short-tempered folk? Always tromping about and spoiling everything, they are."

"If you hadn't noticed, we're two-legs," Timothy said dryly.

Longears sat back on his haunches and blinked. "Why, so you are! Mortals you must be, too, since the Yellow Eye is in the sky. And here I've gone and ruffled your fur, after you saved my life. Now what was it she said about mortals?"

Gwynneth rubbed the coney's back, and he relaxed and closed his eyes. "Mmm. You'll put me to sleep, you will. Oh, yes—I remember now. 'Longears,' she told me, 'bring me back any two-legs you find wandering in the light of day. Don't dilly-dally along the way, either.' She didn't tell me I'd nearly be et by those big brutes of yours. 'Never leave the woods,' my pappy used to say. 'If you do, there's always hawks and owls, coyotes and foxes ready to make a meal of you.' I haven't dilly-dallied, either."

"There's a faithful coney you've been," said Gwynneth with a fetching smile. "Now, could you take us to your Lady?"

The rabbit thought for a minute. "Yes, but only if you swear by your ears that you won't let anyone eat me afterwards." At the coney's insistence, Timothy and Gwynneth grasped their ears and promised to keep him out of harm's way. Then they took Longears outside and set him loose in the grass.

He hopped off a few yards and looked back at the Seekers of the Wood. "Are you all coming or not?"

"I'd as soon eat the little furball as follow him," hissed Spearwind. "If the other sorcs back home in their dens hear about this, we'll be the laughingstocks of all sorcdom. Oh, to have my wings again!"

By spurts and dashes, Longears led the Seekers southward. Day upon blazing day, the sun poured relentless waves of shimmering heat over their heads, while vultures circled above. Driven by thirst, the travelers at last found a boggy stream, where they refilled their few remaining water skins. Later, the griffins broke ranks to chase ground squirrels, which they devoured on the spot.

One sultry evening, thick, black clouds began shouldering their way over the Willowahs. Mumbling and grumbling, the thunder-thumpers leapfrogged across the sky, feeding on the sun's dying rays. The fitful breeze faltered. Harsh, dry heat-lightning flashed from cloud to cloud, splitting the air with thunderclaps. The sorcs' scabby tails bristled with alarm.

As the first lightning bolts flickered earthward, Gwynneth scooped up Longears and held the quaking rabbit close. Under leaden skies, the ragtag company forged onward.

All at once, the griffins all raised their heads and stared around uneasily. "What's that smell?" they murmured.

"Smoke! I see smoke, and it's coming our way!" cried Keeneye. He gazed north and east, where a dark cloud shot through with yellow streaks smudged the horizon.

"Nothing can outrun a prairie fire!" moaned Spearwind.

"We must try!" Rolin told him.

Now the Seekers ran alongside their mounts. Soot and scorching embers rained on them and a hot, airless wind stole their breath away. Orange fire-fountains spouted skyward like a thousand rampaging dragons. The long, ragged wall of roaring flames cut a black swath across the prairie, driving before it swarms of fleeing groundhogs, prairie dogs, deer and other creatures. Once, a herd of antelope bounded by, leaping high over the griffins' heads. Not even Garth's tales of the burning of Beechtown had prepared Timothy for this.

All at once, the earth swallowed up the stampeding animals. A gaping, rock-rimmed gorge lay directly across their path, stretching as far as sight could reckon. Hundreds of fear-crazed creatures were hurling themselves over its brink.

To all appearances, Longears was bent on joining them. Squealing, he sprang out of Gwynneth's arms and scuttled toward the ravine. At the last moment, he popped down a hole.

"Hey! Don't leave us out here!" called the Lucambrians.

Longears' nose reappeared at the hole. "DIG!" he snapped.

"With what?" Mycena wailed, wringing her hands. The sorcs stared at one another in dismay. Though their kind lived in tunnels, stoneworms had done all the excavation work. Then Runt attacked the burrow. Dirt flew as his claws ripped into the ground. In moments, his wiggling hindquarters had vanished inside the hole. Dirt and stones continued spraying out as the sorc flailed away with all four paws.

The flames were fewer than a hundred yards away when Runt's head popped out of the enlarged burrow. "Come!" he commanded. Then he disappeared again.

"Womenfolk first!" Rolin shouted. Gwynneth, Marlis and Mycena wriggled down the hole, followed by Emmer, Sigarth and Skoglund. Elwyn and Timothy entered next, while the others waited their turn. After a wild ride down the corkscrewing shaft and a mouthful of dirt, Timothy flew out the other end at the foot of the precipice and landed on Elwyn. Above them, sheets of flame crackled near the cliff edge.

"It's the Golden Wood!" gasped Elwyn. He pointed at a dense, golden-canopied forest waving in the valley below.

"Fresh air!" wheezed Bembor as his soot-flecked head appeared at the tunnel's gaping mouth. He crawled out and collapsed, coughing and gasping. Then came Gemmio. After that, thirteen sorcs popped out one after another like furry peas squeezed out of a pod. Finally, Opio rolled out head-over-heels.

"Where is Papa?" cried Gwynneth.

"I'm here." Rolin's grimy head and shoulders emerged from the burrow. Kicking off his smoking shoes, he glared at Opio. "When we return home, I'm going to lock you in a hollow tree until you can fit through a knothole sideways. If it weren't for your short rations lately, my feet would still be toasting in the fire!"

"Is it my fault that I got stuck?" Opio came back in an injured tone. "Anyway, I'll wager I broke a rib falling down that blasted burrow. You needn't have pushed me so hard, Gannon's son!"

Miraculously, all twenty-seven Seekers of the Wood had escaped the blaze with only minor scrapes and some singed hair. After giving thanks to Gaelathane for sparing their lives, they praised the small but courageous Runt and Longears, who both beamed with pride.

"I couldn't have done it without Timothy's gold dust," Runt said modestly. Longears boasted, "Dug that burrow myself, I did. Took me three days. Wait till I tell my relatives about this!"

Exhausted from their harrowing ordeal, the travelers straggled down from the cliffs and made camp near the forest beside a limpid, rushing river. "So the Golden Wood wasn't a legend after all," Bembor remarked, peering into the silent, leafy shadows.

Emmer studied the ground by the trees. "We are not the first to visit this place," he said. "Several days ago, a number of riders entered the forest on foot. They did not return this way."

"Riders on foot?" asked King Rolin, confused.

"Yes. Their horses' hoof prints are all around here. Yet, only two-legged tracks lead into the woods. *Thalmosian* tracks."

Later, Timothy threw down his borrowed bedroll under a spiny hawthorn, curled up and tried to ignore his growling stomach. He would have traded all the leaves in the Golden Wood for just one bite of his mother's savory fish-and-potato stew. He was drifting off to sleep when Gwynneth appeared. Her flushed face shone with a grace and comeliness to put gogoniants to shame.

"During the fire," she began, "I was afraid that if something were to happen to one of us . . ." The blush spread over her cheekbones. "Anyway, I thought you might like this." With a shy, sidelong look, she drew an amber ball from her cloak pocket.

"What's that?" Timothy asked, sitting up.

"It's a *spallith*—a 'sharing spasel,'" Gwynneth said. She sat down beside Timothy. "When I was about Meghan's age, I made this from a torsil that Father planted by the seashore." She scooted closer.

Feeling giddy, Timothy wiped his sweating palms on his tunic. "Uh, what can you see in it?"

"It shows a secret place I call my 'butterfly world,' because so many butterflies live there," said Gwynneth. "They sip nectar from the red flowers of the butterfly trees. You'll have lots of fun looking into this. Meghan and I always did." A tear trembled in her eye as she pressed the ball into Timothy's hand.

"You're giving it to me?" he asked in astonishment.

"That's what a sharing spasel is for, silly. You give it to someone to whom you wish to show your special torsil world."

Timothy's heart swelled in his chest. "Thank you! But now you can't visit your butterfly world any longer, can you?"

"That's all right. I'll make another spasel. I—I can't look into this one because it reminds me of Meghan, and I thought you might like to have it as a keepsake instead."

Timothy's muscles went weak. Not for the first time, he reminded himself that he was the son of a common Thalmosian tinker, and Gwynneth, the daughter of Lucambrian royalty.

"I'd better go now before my parents come looking for me," Gwynneth said. With a flip of her silky hair, she was gone.

While a bloated, bleary sun sank world-weary below the valley's smoking rim, Timothy sat staring at the spallith, marveling that he held Gwynneth's heart in his hand.

CHAPTER 32
Golden Forest Gain

Timothy awoke to a golden world. Glinting in the morning sun as if freshly minted from the lustrous metal, the forest's foliage tinted the very air with gold.

"If these leaves are truly gold," Skoglund marveled, "there is more wealth here than in all of Gaelathane's worlds combined." Picking up a fallen leaf, he rubbed it between his fingers and ruefully remarked, "I fear the only gold in this leaf is its color."

"I'm not surprised," said Marlis. "If those leaves were made of the real thing, their weight would break down all the branches!"

Elwyn was just reaching up to pluck a leaf when Rolin grabbed his arm. "Don't you remember what Elmar told the sorcs? 'Pick no leaf from any tree in the Golden Wood.'"

"Picking a few leaves won't hurt anything," Elwyn grumbled.

"Maybe not," his father said. "However, if this wood belongs to the Guardian of whom Elmar warned Winona, we ought to tread lightly. We can't risk provoking the locals when we are so few."

"And so hungry," grumped Grayneck. He drooled longingly at Longears until the rabbit took refuge behind Gwynneth.

"Hungry, did you say?" croaked a harsh voice from overhead. With a flip-flap of its coal-black wings, an enormous vulture settled on a dead snag by the Seekers of the Wood.

"Shoo, buzzard!" shouted the Lucambrians. "Go find your carrion elsewhere!" Some picked up stones to fling at the creature.

The scavenger cocked its naked pink head at them. "I have already eaten my fill from yesterday's burning," it said smugly. "Between drought and fire, I have no lack of food. It's a shame you two-legs find ripened meat so distasteful. There's plenty to go around." The vulture let out a sniggering squawk.

Timothy and his companions needed no reminder that the foul carrion-eater's larder was well stocked. The sickly stench of death was already thickening in and around the valley.

"If it is not food you seek, then begone, vile creature, before we wring your scrawny neck!" growled Gemmio.

"I would peck out your eyes first, two-legs," hissed the bird. It drove its beak into the snag, gouging out a chunk of wood, and a shiver of recognition crawled up Timothy's spine. Some three years earlier, just such a buzzard had tried to open the latch on a certain leather satchel. A buzzard that was not a buzzard.

"What do you want with us, then?" Rolin asked.

The bird lowered its head in a disarming gesture. "If only you will listen, I can offer you some useful advice."

"What sort of advice?"

"Just this. You and your companions are lost and hungry, and your mangy eagle-lions are sick and cannot fly." The vulture threw a venomous glance at the griffins, who snarled back. "You are clever enough to recognize that these leaves contain no gold, but you do not realize their true worth. As food, they are sweeter than honey, more nourishing than the finest meats. Not only will they make you wise beyond all reckoning, but also immortal."

The thunderstruck Lucambrians stared at one another. "We have been warned not to pick those leaves," said Sigarth.

"Of course you have," the vulture crooned. "Why do you suppose Gaelathane guards this forest so jealously? Its leaves are the very source of His own wisdom and immortality! Eat them, and you will live forever! Just touch one and see there is no harm in it."

Hesitantly, Sigarth raised his arm and brushed his hand across a low-hanging spray of golden torsil leaves. Timothy held his breath, but nothing happened.

The vulture hopped up and down on its branch with glee. "What did I tell you? You have been deceived by those who would hoard this great treasure for themselves. If only you could freely eat of these leaves and enjoy their benefits forever!"

The Greencloaks' faces darkened. "Why can't we?" said Opio.

The buzzard crooked its long, ruff-ringed neck. "Alas, a cruel and crafty sorceress rules this wood, and if you so much as pluck a single golden leaf, she will learn of it and cast a sleeping spell upon you. Only by destroying her can you break the spell."

Now Longears began running in circles, yammering, "Liar! Liar! Don't listen to him. She's not a sorceress. She's a—!" The vulture glared him into whimpering silence.

Raising her lightstaff, Marlis declared, "The power of Gaelathane is far greater than any spell or sorcery."

Fear flickered in the bird's eyes. "This one is the equal of your Gaelathane for enchantments. If you would undo her spells, pay heed! She lives in a certain tree deep in the woods and comes out only on moonlit nights to work her wizardry. Do not approach her then. Mark well her tree, and when dawn comes, chop it down and burn it. After that, you may pick and eat as many leaves as you like. Immortality shall be your reward."

Something like the sweet scent of water lily blossoms benumbed Timothy's brain. His friends stood still, rooted in place. Mouth agape, Marlis let the staff fall from her limp fingers. As if in a dream, Timothy picked it up. In its light, the buzzard appeared as a horrid, loathsome creature, full of a deadly, brooding malice.

Timothy pointed the staff at the vulture. "Be off, trickster bird!" he cried. "You are that starglass peddler I have read about!"

The lightstaff's blinding ray went wide as the vulture shrieked and flew at Timothy, its claws poised to rake his eyes. At the last moment, Gemmio struck the bird a glancing blow with his bow, and the foul buzzard flew away. The Lucambrians' faces paled.

"I should have known," said Rolin, scowling. "Twice I have spoken with the fiend face-to-face in his human form, and twice my blood ran cold in my veins. Whoever or whatever that thing is, it serves the lord of Gundul, and no other."

"We all should have known," said Marlis. "We were not warned against *touching* the leaves, but against *picking* them. That carrion-bird twisted Sigarth's words into a knotty lie."

"I suggest we leave this place at once," said Rolin. "If the peddler-bird returns, it may go the worse for us." The Seekers of the Wood faced the forest, more mysterious and menacing than ever. Timothy wondered whether the Guardian really had cast her influence like a net over the wood, and how she would treat uninvited guests.

Bembor recited, "'A grove of trees with golden leaves awaits for those who persevere.' We have persevered; we've caught our coney, crossed the open plain and the Golden Forest gained, but how loth am I to set foot inside it! I fear the enemy's enchantments and Elmar's madness more than any mortal foe."

"Let's not forget Winona's 'Ballad of the Ball,'" said Mycena. "It says that we're to 'Seek the queen amidst the green of vacant trees and tall.' Since all the trees here appear to have golden leaves, maybe we've come to the wrong place."

Sigarth mumbled, "How are we supposed to know a 'vacant' tree from a full one? Knock on its trunk?"

"Wrong place or not, into this forest we must go if we wish to obey Gaelathane and help our sorcs," said King Rolin.

"Alas, we griffins cannot join you," said Broadwing. "Our king bade us bring you to the verge of this wood, and so we have. Now we will return to our eyries in the mountains."

"Not all of us," growled Ironwing. "Windsong and I will remain here. Someone has to keep these blundering two-legs out of trouble, and it might as well be us."

"I, too, will stay," said Runt, standing on his paw-tips to appear taller. With many well-wishes for a safe journey, the exiles sent their sorc friends back along the river flowing into the valley. Afterwards, the remaining Seekers of the Wood plunged into the forest, following the course of the clear, bounding river. Overhead, waving torsils roofed the sky with their golden crowns.

"I wonder if any golden squirrels live here," Ironwing said with a hopeful gleam in his eye. He glanced thoughtfully at Longears, who bit the sorc's tail and was kicked into the brush for his trouble. After that, the coney stayed at the back of the line.

Before long, the scouts found some wild strawberries growing atop a heathered hill that overlooked the forest's billowing sea of gold. While the two-legs feasted, the sorcs sulked.

"Berries make poor sorc-food," Windsong moaned, burying his head under his paws.

Marlis stroked his neck. "I'm sure we'll find something here to your liking." Even as she spoke, a deer trotted partway up the hill and began grazing. The griffins pounced. Before you could say, "Hair and hooves," little else was left of the unwary animal. Marlis shuddered and turned away.

After the sorcs had napped, the company pushed on through groves of sky-stretching, thick-boled trees of passage. From time to time, rain showers, sweet flower scents and flocks of colorful birds burst from the rustling, golden canopy.

"Truly this place is enchanted!" Gemmio exclaimed.

"Not enchanted, just unusual," Bembor told him. "When so many torsils grow together in pure stands that lead to the same land, breakouts are more likely to occur."

"Breakouts?" asked Timothy. He hoped Bembor wasn't speaking of jails. He'd seen quite enough of Beechtown's already.

Bembor said, "That's when one world bulges rather like a bubble into another. If the bubble weakens or bursts, you have a breakout. Small breakouts or 'spillouts' like these aren't uncommon, but large ones are quite rare and are extremely dangerous."

At length they came to a part of the wood where the ancient trees of passage were green leafed instead of gold. "Now we've found some real torsils," said Scanlon. "Let's set up camp right here."

Finally feeling more at home, the exiled Lucambrians whiled away the afternoon resting and exploring. Runt, Windsong and Ironwing caught salmon in the river, while Timothy, Elwyn and Gwynneth climbed rocks and skipped flat stones across the water.

When the soft cooing of mourning doves signaled the approach of nightfall, the Seekers gathered around a crackling fire at the campsite. Before long, Timothy and his friends were enjoying baked salmon.

Afterwards, they all sat around the fire chatting with Longears. Though the coney still maintained "the Lady" had sent him, he was much less clear about how to find her.

"She and her people live in this wood," he said, munching on some long-stemmed river grass. "My, this is sweet. You all ought to try some. And stop staring at me like that, Ironwing. I can't help it if you don't like vegetables." Timothy suspected Ironwing's interest in the coney had nothing to do with vegetables.

"We sorcs eat grass only when we're too ill to stomach anything else," Ironwing disdainfully replied. Resting his head on his paws, he closed his eyes and sighed.

"About the Lady," said Marlis, feeding Longears more grass. "Does she live in a manor or palace somewhere near here?"

Longears stopped chewing. "Manor? Palace? What are those?"

"They're big hills of wood and stone, full of runways and dens," Opio explained. "Rich, important two-legs live inside."

"Oh, no. She's not a two-legs like you. She's a *moonsinger*."

"A moonsinger?" Marlis asked the rabbit. "What is that?"

"You'll see," Longears replied with a whiskery smirk. Nobody learned anything further of interest from the coney. Between green mouthfuls, he would only comment that a diet of river grass would restore the griffins to perfect health.

Heads were nodding and the fire was dying down when a branch snapped in the woods. Clutching their swords, bows and blowpipes, the scouts leapt up just as a big man staggered out of the bushes and collapsed with a groan by the fire. Dressed in a woodcutter's rough garb, the intruder was covered with scratches and welts.

Opio and Gemmio were helping the stranger to his feet when a tattered waif with straggly blond hair appeared at the firelight's edge. "Mama? Papa?" she whimpered.

"Meghan!" With a shriek, Queen Marlis threw herself on the weeping girl. Soon, everyone was laughing and crying and hugging Meghan and each other for joy. Even the griffins perked up and took turns licking the dirt off the princess's face. While his hungry daughter devoured a roast fish, Rolin turned to the stranger, who was eyeing the three sunsorcs with guarded amazement.

"Sir, you are welcome in our camp. May I ask your name and how you and my daughter found us here in this wood?"

Derwin brightened. "Ye're Missy's father? She takes after you." Noticing Rolin's perplexed look, the Thalmosian explained, "Eh, that's just my pet name for her. I'm Derwin son of Stolland. Right glad to meet ye." He stuck out his hand, which Rolin shook.

"Yer Highness," Derwin went on, "I might as well tell ye right off that I'm the man who kidnapped yer daughter."

Blue veins bulged in Rolin's neck as he backed the woodcutter against a tree. "You're . . . the one . . . who . . . ?!" Iron rang as the chiseled-faced Greencloaks drew their swords.

Meghan looked up from her fish. "It's all right, Father," she said. "Derwin is my friend, even though he's not one of us."

Still glowering, Rolin said stiffly, "Very well. For Meghan's sake, you may speak, Stolland's son. But if you stray so much as a gnat's eyelash from the truth, so help me, I'll see you hanged from the tallest tree in this wood at dawn!"

Derwin retold his and Meghan's misadventures, including finding the flattened spasel that had led them to the Golden Wood. His hosts listened attentively, nodding whenever a detail fell into place. The woodcutter wound up his tale with the disappearance of Asper and his men. "After that," he said, "Missy and I tried to find our way out of this blasted forest. We ended up more lost than ever. If we hadn't come across yer fire, we would've starved out there, and no one would have been th' wiser. Thank ye fer helping us!"

Marlis gently touched his arm. "On the contrary, Derwin son of Stolland, we have badly misjudged you. You have our heartfelt thanks for looking after our daughter." Derwin blushed.

"What about General Gorn and the rest of his army?" asked Rolin. "Do you think they have followed you here? We are too few and in no condition to repulse such a battle-hardened horde."

Upending Bembor's water skin, Derwin drank deeply and wiped his mouth with the back of his hand. Then he shared the water with Meghan. "Gorn's a bloodhound," he answered. "He knows if he fails to bring any gold back, Mardoc will have his head. That's why he'll march his men to th' ends of the world to find some."

"Then we will pray he marches around our wood and not through it," said Rolin softly. "That is enough for now. We will talk more of these things in the morning." Thanking Derwin again for his help, the king and queen bade everyone good-night.

Timothy tried to make himself comfortable on some dry leaves he had mounded up beneath a golden torsil. Then he gazed again into his spasel. In the darkness, the starflowers blazed up like bright sparks. Next, he took out the spallith Gwynneth had given him. Though night was falling in that world as well, he could dimly make out clouds of gaily-colored butterflies flitting above the trees. Closing his eyes, he dreamt of flying with them back to Beechtown.

THE GOLDEN WOOD
PART IV
GWLÂN GORGE, WORT HAVEN

CHAPTER 33
The Guardian of the Wood

"Wake up, everybody! *Wake up!*"

For a groggy instant, Timothy was back by the lily pond, trying to rouse his companions before the rising water made an end to them all. This time, however, it was Scanlon who was rushing about and shaking the others.

"What is it?" yawned King Rolin. "Has Gorn found us already?"

"This had better be worth losing my sleep over," Opio muttered. "I was dreaming that we'd discovered a cave chock full of chestnut cakes. They were tasty ones, too."

"I don't want to hear about your dratted chestnut cakes," Gemmio grumped. "All you ever think about is food."

A feverish light burned in Scanlon's eyes as he exclaimed, "I met someone else in the forest!"

"Someone else?" asked Bembor, rubbing his eyes. "Do you mean a two-legged or a four-legged someone?"

"Two-legged. And she's the most beautiful creature I've ever seen!" Scanlon described how the sound of singing had awakened him. Creeping through the forest, he had come upon a young woman sitting on a stone under the bright full moon, singing as she combed her long, dark hair. When he stepped into view, she fled.

Scanlon lamented, "When I tried to follow her, she ran like a deer and disappeared among the trees." He sighed heavily. "I will not rest until I have found her again."

Bembor stroked his beard. "This is news indeed. Since all our womenfolk were asleep, we can only assume that you saw someone who lives here. But who could she be?"

"A trick of the moonlight?" Sigarth suggested with a sly grin.

Scanlon snorted. "Moonbeams don't sing."

"Maybe she was Longears' Lady," Timothy said.

"Look!" Elwyn pointed into the night. Gliding among the trees as silently as a summer's fog, a tall, pallid form was approaching.

"Is this your mysterious maid, Scanlon?" Marlis teased.

"I think not," he replied. "She was wearing brown, not white."

"Wh—who are you?" asked Mycena breathlessly as the phantom floated up to a tree just outside the circle of firelight.

"I am she whom you seek," replied the fair-skinned woman, whose silver hair flowed down her back like spun moonbeams. "Please come with me. Time is short; the night is growing old."

Throwing together their bags and bundles, the Seekers followed their visitor, who strode so swiftly through the moon-shadowed woods they could hardly keep up with her. The woman stopped in a grove of high-branching golden torsils and gestured toward a fallen log. "Please be seated."

Timothy found a spot between Gwynneth and Elwyn, and the sorcs stretched out in front of them. The Lucambrians thrust their lightstaffs into the ground to use as lanterns to drive off the gloom.

When everyone was settled, the pale woman smiled and said, "Welcome to the Goldwood of Maedlandia—'the Midlands,' in your tongue. I am the Lady Llanwyn, Queen of the Torsils and Guardian of this wood by the grace and bidding of Gaelathane the Leaf Lord, Who has bade me assist you in your quest." Whatever else she may have been, with her fine, fair features, high forehead and graceful limbs, Llanwyn looked every inch a queen to Timothy.

"Then you must know why we are here," said Skoglund.

The Lady Llanwyn shook her head. "That I do not. Who are you and what do you seek in the Goldwood?"

King Rolin stood and bowed. "We are indeed honored to make your acquaintance, Lady Llanwyn. I am Rolin son of Gannon, king of Lucambra. My companions and I have come from afar in search of you and your splendid golden forest. Surely there is none like it in all the land. I must confess, though, that I had not imagined the Guardian to be a woman of such beauty. Twice now we have been forewarned against you and your charms."

The Lady threw back her head and laughed like the chiming of bells in a cloistered garden. "Have you, now? By whom?"

"By one of our own, Elmar son of Selwyn, who came here long ago. He lost his reason and all his men in the bargain. 'Beware the Guardian of the Golden Wood!' he told our queen just before dying. Now I can perceive his peril, for the sight of you must have broken his heart. Alas for those who glimpse the Guardian in her Goldwood and return to the green forests of the north!"

A cloud passed over Llanwyn's moon-silvered face. "I remember poor Elmar and his foolish companions. In love there is oft great peril, but in greed, a greater peril still, as those men learned to their regret."

"My pardon, Lady," said Emmer. "On the fringe of this forest, we met a foul carrion bird who accused you of sorcery and worse. He has a reputation as a liar and a troublemaker."

Llanwyn sighed. "Broggnag the Boncath will not rest until he and Gundul's other minions have enslaved or destroyed the Leaf Lord's servants. What he cannot attain by force he will attempt to gain by deceit. Still, his most insidious lies oft contain a germ of truth. Now tell me, who are these with you?"

As King Rolin introduced the other Seekers of the Wood, the Lady nodded to each in turn. Last of all, Timothy's name was called. He stood and awkwardly bowed, clutching the flattened spasel in both hands. Llanwyn regarded him with a troubled look. "So you have come at last," she said softly.

When lad appears with frozen tears
That show the starlit blooms,
My hand will grant the Tree to plant
Ere bitter curse consumes.

For mortals come with beating drum,
First sending forth their spies;
They'll hunt the gold within the wold
With madness in their eyes.

Though men should maim and bring to shame,
And forest fair defile;
The Leaf Lord's love, brought from above,
Shall tree-foes reconcile.

"This ancient *pos,* or riddle from the Leaf Lord presages the arrival of one bearing a 'sap-window' such as yours, Timothy. In our tongue, we call these things *coedagrau,* or 'tree-tears.' We know our mutual foe has followed you here in search of gold, 'sending forth' his spies; his horses' drumming hoofbeats are running through the earth. I am curious, though, as to what 'starlit blooms' you see in your tree-tears."

"I think it shows a patch of starflowers," Timothy replied.

Breaking in, King Rolin said, "Like Elmar, we come here seeking the starworts' last haven. Our sorc friends are sickening for want of starberries. Can you tell us where to find some?"

"Perhaps," Llanwyn said. "In seasons of old, flowers-of-the-stars grew so thickly that the winged lions flew here in droves to harvest them. However, their numbers have dwindled over the years. Now they hide in deep canyons near waterfalls, for they love fogs and mists. Speaking of hiding," she said to Timothy, "I believe a friend of mine is lying near you. Come over here, Longears!" The rabbit scampered out from between Timothy's feet to stop before the Guardian.

"My brave coney, you have done well in bringing the two-legs here," said Llanwyn. "Your reward will be great. Now go and spread the word among your kin that our guests have arrived." His stubby tail wriggling with joy, Longears bounded away.

"We care not only for the trees here, but also for all other wild creatures," Llanwyn added. "Longears has been my faithful helper for several years now, though sometimes he forgets what he is about."

"Pardon me," said Bembor. "You have said 'we' twice now. I see only one of you. Have you any relatives here?"

Llanwyn laughed again, her eyes flashing in the moonlight like twin opals. "The Wood Folk are many, although we are not nearly so numerous as we were before men multiplied in the land. This forest is one of our last havens in the Land of Light."

"But who *are* the Wood Folk?" Timothy asked. The Greencloaks put their fingers to their lips, but the Lady only smiled at him and touched his cheek. Her hand was colder than river stones.

"We are who we are," she said. Lifting her head, she called, "Come out, friends and kinsmen!" At her cry, shadows stirred among the trees. Voices murmured like the rustling of leaves in an evening breeze. One after another, tall, erect figures glided into the glade.

Bembor chuckled. "I should have known. The 'Wood Folk' are tree spirits—nymphs or dryads—are they not?"

"We do go by those ancient names," said Llanwyn. "Nymphs are tree-maidens and dryads are tree-men. However, we call ourselves '*memerren*,' or '*moonsingers*,' for we love gathering under the light of the moon to sing Gaelathane's praises."

Timothy's heart leapt. Even in Thalmos, he had heard of nymphs and dryads, sylphs and wood-sprites. Never had he dreamed, though, that tree spirits actually existed!

Bembor bowed. "We are honored you have revealed yourselves to us. I last saw one of your favored race when I was a lad, before Felgor had so despoiled our land."

Llanwyn's eyes darkened with an ageless sorrow. "In these evil days, we dare not oft show ourselves. Bitter experience has taught us how treacherous mortals can be."

As Llanwyn introduced her companions, they stepped into the staff light. There were Birchbind and Llewellyn, Ashmead and Byrta, Anweth, Calymon and Cledwyn; Bledwyn, Marsina and Merrowyn, Glaspeth and Glonnyll. Many other Wood Folk came forth, all clad in light, loosely fitting gowns. While the nymphs spoke in hushed tones, the dryads stood silently by with watchful eyes.

"Where is she?" the nymphs murmured, looking this way and that. A strained silence was settling over the group when a dark-haired nymph with doe eyes and slender limbs darted up.

"And let us not forget my daughter, Medwyn," the Lady sighed. "Though flighty for her age, she sings like a nightingale."

Scanlon bleated, "It's her! It's her!" Then he fell backwards off the log. Emmer and Rolin tried to hush him up, but he babbled on all the more, clamoring to see Medwyn.

"You must forgive my grandson," Bembor said. "I don't know what has come over him. He's not inclined to such outbursts."

"There is no need to apologize," replied Llanwyn with a twinkle in her eye. "I understand. We are no strangers to love-smitten mortals, although we try to discourage them."

Eyes downcast, Derwin muttered, "Beware of this witchery, Scanlon son of Emmer! I've heard that if a nymph snares ye with her gaze, she'll make ye her slave for life!"

"You are greatly misinformed," Llanwyn bristled. "It is we who are enslaved by you mortals! Men in every world have hunted us with their hounds and snared us in their cruel traps. They make us out to be monsters, witches and wizards; enchantresses and kidnappers; hags and hobgoblins. Yet we are not unlike you. Can we not speak? Do we not bleed when you cut us and grieve as you do over the loss of our loved ones? Do we not worship the same Creator, Who loves us all and made us to help each other?"

Derwin hung his head. "Forgive me, Lady. I did not know."

Llanwyn gestured at her guests. "Look at yourselves. You can walk, skip, and run; sing and shout; create works of beauty; touch and hold one another. As trees, we can do none of these things. Day after day, year after year, we are rooted to the selfsame spot. Thankfully, by the Leaf Lord's grace, we can 'moonslip.' When the moon shines upon us, we may leave our leafy prisons for a time and walk the fallen world as mortals do. However, if we fail to return to our trees by dawn, we will become as mortal as you are."

"Does that mean that most memerren never die?" asked Gwynneth, her eyes wide with wonderment.

"Of course not. Since we live so much longer than you two-legs, we regard you as mortals. Yet, when our trees sicken or perish, so do we. When men hack down our homes, they murder us in droves. If we have already moonslipped and our tree dies before dawn, however, we return to the wood whence we came."

"So that's why the vulture told us to cut down your tree after dawn!" Marlis said. "He didn't want you to moonslip first."

Derwin squirmed. "I had no idea. I'll never fell another tree as long as I live, even if I have to heat my hut with straw!"

"What happens if a nymph moonslips and a woodsman cuts down her tree after sunrise?" Elwyn asked.

"Once she is mortal, her fate is no longer bound to the tree's," Llanwyn replied. "Of course, most of us will not moonslip whilst any mortals are about. It simply isn't safe for us or for you."

She glanced at Scanlon. "Suppose a mortal lad chances upon a nymph singing in the forest. At his approach, she flees. He follows, moon-smitten, as we memerren would say. If he catches and holds her until daybreak, she is cursed with mortality. If she escapes, he combs the woods for her day and night. Heartbroken, he wastes away or even contemplates taking his own life.

"Then again, touched by her suitor's plight, the object of his love may willingly embrace the joys and pains of mortality, just as the Leaf Lord gave up His eternal splendor for the love of us all. Taking on mortal flesh, He suffered death in His Tree that we might become His bride. As Moonsinger of moonsingers, He alone may walk in the light of day without suffering mortality, for He is immortal."

Gwynneth asked, "If dawn does catch one of you outside and makes you mortal, what happens to your tree? Does it die?"

"Abandoned trees usually remain empty," Llanwyn explained. "Soulless, they will eventually wither away unless cared for."

King Rolin's face lit up. "We were told to 'seek the queen amidst the green of vacant trees and tall,'" he said. "We have found you, the queen, but do such trees still grow in this wood?"

"Alas, they do," Llanwyn replied. "In our forest, most of the green trees are *gwag*—vacant. The Leaf Lord has entrusted them to my care, although I also look after the other trees here."

"And what of the trees with leaves of gold?" Emmer asked. "How did they come by their color?"

The Lady caressed some of the golden leaves hanging down within her long-armed reach. "To recount the history of this wood could take us to the very brink of dawn. However, if you wish, I will tell you what I can while the sun sleeps."

"Please do!" chorused her guests.

"Long ago, the Leaf Lord planted a great forest here, far from the axes of men. In it He placed for safekeeping at least one *torsyl* for each of His created worlds. Those were the days when our wood lapped against the foothills of the Willowahs in the north and east and reached as far south as the Drylands.

"Green was that forest, and its trees fairer than those in any world before or since. For years, we memerren walked freely beneath its moonlit leaves without fear of man or beast. Then came the Tree-Slayer, requesting passage to any world he wished.

"'In whose name do you come?' we asked him.

"As slyly as the vile serpent he was, he answered, 'In the name of Finegold, King of Fineland and of all the Vacant Lands.'

"'We acknowledge no king but the Leaf Lord Who put us here,' we said. 'In His name only may we grant you passage.'

"'Then no one will ever climb you again,' he snarled. Departing in great wrath, he set fire to the woodland's northern reaches. On that hot, dry summer's day, the flames spread rapidly, consuming vast tracts of trees. Unable to moonslip, many brave tree-lads and tree-lasses perished in the blaze. Once night fell, others fled their trees in terror, hoping that morning's light would find them before the flames found their tree homes.

"At the blaze's height, Gaelathane sent a drenching rain to quench the fire, saving better than a third of the forest. By then, however, the sun had risen on thousands of moonsingers."

"Leaving them mortals," said Bembor sadly.

"These became the 'worldwalkers,'" Llanwyn went on. "Doomed to mortal lives of fear and loneliness, they wandered wooded hills and valleys, climbing up and down torsils to avoid the prying eyes of men. Their furtive ways spawned many of the old tales of 'elves' and 'sprites,' though they possessed no magic of their own. Beneath the dying moon, we still sing of the exiles' sorrows:

The sun was burning high and bright,
When fire flickered in the wood;
The hearts of trees grew cold with fright
As flames devoured the green and good.

No passage had they given him,
Whose tongue did drip with dragon's guile;
His heart with Gundul's greed a-brim
Was set to ravage and revile.

Forsaking glen and forest fair,
Moonsingers took on mortal ills
To walk the world in dread despair
And haunt the lonely, hallowed hills.

"My own tree barely escaped the flames," Llanwyn continued. "When it was safe again for me to moonslip, I found myriads of vacant trees, silent, stricken and hollow-hearted. North of them lay a lifeless waste of charred stumps and smoking snags that in time became the Plain of Gaelathane."

"Tens of thousands of torsil worlds would have been lost to us, were it not for the Lady Llanwyn's foresight," put in the sunny-haired nymph named Llewellyn. "She scoured the smoldering ashes for ripe nuts. These she planted to perpetuate the burned trees of passage. We also watered the stump sprouts that came up the next spring, a custom all moonsingers still practice."

"We must ensure that every corner of Gaelathane's realm remains open to the word of His love," Llanwyn explained. "If our labors bear fruit, a golden forest as grand as the green one that burned long ago will someday wave where now only grasses grow."

"You still haven't told us how the trees got their golden leaves," Meghan said, fidgeting on the log next to her mother.

"Patience, child! After the fire, the Leaf Lord came to console us. Then He plucked some hairs from His head, breathed on them and scattered them about the wood, giving rise to the mangles.

"Next, He raised His hand, and the ground sank down to form this canyon that we call *Calydon*, protecting us from fire and other foes. 'Today,' He said, 'this wood is twice Mine. First I planted it, and now I have preserved it with My body. As for you, from this day forth, your leaves shall reflect the purity of your hearts.' Then every green tree (save the vacant ones) flashed golden."

"Let's get back to the mangles," said Sigarth uneasily. "What are they, and have we anything to fear from them?"

By way of answer, the torsil queen plucked a single golden leaf from an overhanging branch. The forest held its breath. With rustling sounds, slithery shapes fell from the treetops. Timothy's scalp crawled.

"Snakes!" screamed Mycena. "Help! Get them away from us!"

The Lady Llanwyn held up her hand. "Do not move, friends, or the mangles will bite you."

CHAPTER 34
The Weeping Trees

Faces blanched as hundreds of scaly green snakes glided over the ground, their forked tongues flicking at the visitors' feet and legs. The tips of the sorcs' tails twitched.

"Begone!" cried Llanwyn, and the snakes slithered back up the trees. "The Leaf Lord granted me this authority over the mangles, to protect the innocent. The snakes drop down only when men ignore the King's warnings against leaf-picking in His wood."

She raised her arms beseechingly. "Why must mortals spend their short lives striving for riches they cannot eat or wear? Haven't you sorrow enough without chasing after emptiness? If your people must grasp, let them grasp for Gaelathane."

The torsil queen seemed to notice Derwin for the first time. "Not many days ago, we came upon some mangle-bitten men. One of them strongly favored you, son of Stolland."

Derwin jumped up and shouted, "What have you done with my brother? If he has been harmed in any way, I'll—"

"Peace," said Llanwyn. "Your brother and his feckless followers are alive and unhurt. You may even see them. However, mangle venom brings a greed-sleep from which there is no awakening."

Marlis's hand went to her mouth. "So that's what Gaelathane meant in His riddle, 'When mangles' fangs have bitten deep, and men shall fall from bitter sleep.' It also says that Winona's diary is to 'lead to wealth indeed, where greedy hearts will not awake.'"

"Winona, did you say?" In two strides, Llanwyn was towering over Lucambra's queen. "What became of her? Is she still living?"

Bembor broke the brittle silence. "King Elgathel's bride she was before he perished while defending the Hallowfast. Exiled in Thalmos, Winona fled this life long ago. Why do you ask?"

Llanwyn said, "You may know, Brenthor's son, that Winona was one of us. She took on mortality for the love of your king. During our darkest days, she visited me here in the Goldwood."

"So the legends were true after all," said Rolin. "My grandmother really was the spirit of Elgathel's amenthil."

"Your grandmother?" Llanwyn took Rolin's hand and looked into his eyes. "I thought I sensed in you something of her sweet and selfless nature. Blessed are you, Rolin son of Gannon!"

"Blessed are those who obey Gaelathane!" Rolin returned.

"Alas, Elmar's starberries arrived too late to save the kingdom in Winona's day," Bembor said. "Now the fate of Lucambra and its dying griffins once more hangs in the balance. Do you know where Elmar found his starworts, Lady Llanwyn?"

The torsil queen replied, "As I recall, his band traipsed south along our River Rondolyn into the Graylands. Days later, a ragtag remnant returned with bags full of berries. That night, despite our warnings, those men went on a leaf-picking spree. Their captain tried to stop them, but by then it was too late."

"The mangles got them, eh?" Skoglund declared.

Llanwyn gazed into the moon-shadowed forest. "No," she sighed. "Follow me, and I will show you what became of those men."

Their lightstaffs bobbing along like a procession of lamps, the Seekers of the Wood followed Llanwyn and the other moonsingers through the trees. Trailing at the rear, Timothy was surprised to see Medwyn drop back in the line to talk with Scanlon.

Presently, a suffocating pall of deep, woodsy shadows wove about them. Brooding, sinister shapes loomed out of the gloom. Hollow, hound-dog eyes drooped in moss-bearded trunks with gnomish noses and jowly mouths. Warty twig-fingers tangled hair and poked eyes, while slack, dry leaves stirred mournfully.

"What horrid trees!" Gwynneth said, taking Timothy's hand.

"A dismal place, is it not?" said Llanwyn with a half-smile. "Here dwell twelve members of Elmar's ill-fated expedition."

Bembor protested, "That can't be! Not even Lucambrians live that long, especially when separated from their life trees."

"Oh, they're alive, all right," Llanwyn assured him. "They cannot die while the sap of life still flows in their host trees."

"Where are they, then?" snickered Sigarth. "Hiding in the treetops? Sleeping in some stumps? Swinging from limbs?"

"Nothing of the sort!" said Llanwyn severely. "In order to escape the mangles, Elmar's men foolishly climbed these vacant torsils. Ever since that day, they have lived in the 'weeping trees,' which have grown to mirror their misery."

"Do you mean the trees are hollow?" asked Opio.

Now Medwyn spoke up. "You do not understand. Anyone who climbs to the top of a *gwag* tree becomes its new tenant. Your greedy countrymen will remain trapped inside their hosts until the trees die, when they will likewise perish. I am very sorry."

The Lucambrians gaped. "Why can't they come out after the moon rises, as you do?" asked Mycena.

"Even we cannot escape a vacant tree," sighed the moonsingers.

Timothy winced to think of being cooped up inside a wooden cage, unable to move or speak, languishing day after day, season after season in lonely solitude, with only birds for company.

The Lady Llanwyn said, "To release someone from a *gwag* tree, you must carefully climb it—only partway, mind you—so as to avoid becoming imprisoned yourself. It is a rather risky act.

He who would the captive free,
Must ascend the weeping tree,
Then descend, but not too deep,
Or he'll become the next to weep.

"That doesn't sound too difficult," said Marlis. "Surely the men in these 'weeping trees' could have been let out before now!"

"If it were possible, we would have done so years ago," replied the Lady. "Unfortunately, we discovered that only mortals may release mortals, and moonsingers moonsingers. Since you are the first of your kind to speak with us since Elmar's visit, his companions are still trapped inside these trees."

"What a horrible fate!" murmured Mycena. "It's little wonder Elmar went mad, losing his men like that. How sad that he blamed the Guardian of the Golden Wood for his plight. Let's leave this place at once. It reminds me too much of Felgor's dungeons."

As Timothy lingered in the weeping grove, the trees seemed to say, *Please don't leave us like this.* Then Timothy recalled Winona's ballad:

So count the cost to save the lost,
The twelve who still survive;
Release from gloom of leafy tomb
And wooden eyes revive.

197

A short tree-climb is a small price to pay for setting loose a lonely old man, he decided as he clambered over the nearest torsil's deep-set eyes and sunken cheeks. Halfway up the trunk, he stopped to rest. Only a few fluttering moths disturbed the still night air. He fancied the tree spirit stirring beneath him, awakening from an ageless slumber. *He who would the captive free, must ascend the weeping tree.*

Upon reaching the top, Timothy looked down, half-expecting a little man to pop out of the trunk. However, neither man nor mangle emerged. *Then descend, but not too deep.*

Ever so slowly, he started climbing down. Still nothing. Maybe the tree wasn't vacant after all. *Snap!* The branch beneath him broke and he dropped several dizzying feet. Catching himself, he was trying to climb up again when a peculiar sinking sensation came over him. *Or he'll become the next to weep.*

Timothy was settling into the tree as if it were quicksand. As he sank, his limbs began to stretch. Legs, feet and toes divided into tree roots, while arms, hands and fingers splayed into limbs, twigs and leaves. His torso thickened to fill the torsil's trunk.

"Help!" he cried soundlessly as his body knitted and knotted into wood. He tried to take a breath, but his chest felt bound with iron bands. As panic welled up within him, he realized that fresh air was effortlessly flowing through his leaf pores, which also served as tiny eyes. Each pinhole displayed a different view of his shadowy, moonlit world, creating a confusing jigsaw puzzle of images.

When he pieced together the mosaic, he saw a hunchbacked, two-legged figure standing below him. Trying to walk, the stranger kept tripping over his long white beard. It was such a comical sight that Timothy laughed, a sensation that started in his root-toes, tingled up his trunk and quivered through his limbs. "I didn't know trees could laugh!" he said to himself, pleased he had managed it on his first try.

When the stooped old man turned his face upward, Timothy shuddered. That same gnomish visage was stamped on the torsil's trunk. He had released one of Elmar's men "from gloom of leafy tomb," but at the cost of his own freedom.

CHAPTER 35
The Measure of a Tree

The torsil's former occupant tottered off, leaving Timothy alone with his thoughts. How would his friends find him now, much less release him? Before him lay long, lonely years of waiting in vain for rescue. The stubby limb that was once his nose began to itch unbearably. Unable to scratch it, he groaned and rattled his leaves. He longed for a familiar face—even Baglot's.

Just then, he felt a heavy, measured tread on the soil over his roots. Someone was approaching! A tall, white-clad figure was striding past with firm, decisive steps. Timothy sensed that if only this One would glance at him, all would be well. *Help me. Please.*

The Man looked up with burning eyes that pierced him to the core. "You've gotten yourself into a bind this time, haven't you, Timothy."

Timothy shook from the tips of his roots to the top of his crown. How could this Man know his name?

"Who are You?" His question came out as a wordless sigh.

"I am the Immortal and Everlasting One Who left eternity to take on the form of men and memerren. Before any torsil world was, I breathed the stars into being and wrapped them in a symphony of song. Where I am, there My Tree is also."

"Gaelathane!" Timothy gasped, his leaves fluttering.

With a smile, Gaelathane began singing. His melodious words pierced the prisoner's soul like the fragrance of amenthil blossoms. The King sang of the world's beginning, of its torments and of the love that bade Him sacrifice His life for all creation.

"I am very proud of you, dear boy," the Singer said. "Few lads your age would lay down their lives for a friend. Yet, you have risked all to help someone you have never even met. You took his place, just as I took yours before you knew Me."

You took my place? How?

"In My Tree," Gaelathane replied. "Not long ago, My enemies did their worst to Waganupa while I was inside, just as you are inside this tree." The Man held out His scarred hands and arms.

Timothy-the-tree shivered. *You couldn't get out, either?*

Gaelathane tenderly smiled. "I could have left at any time, but I chose to stay out of love for you. It was the only way to save you. In dying the death of memer and mortal, I now can give My life to both. But we have little time. Men with axes are coming to raze this golden forest, and they will chop you down, too."

Chop me down?! Timothy shook until his limbs clattered. He could already feel the sharp steel biting into his belly. Never before had he felt so helpless. *Please get me out of here!*

"All in good time," He said. "First, I must take your measure."

Timothy looked down on all sides of his trunk at once with his tree eyes. "I must be over ten feet around!" he marveled.

The King shook His white-maned head. "The measure of a tree is not its girth, but the soundness of its wood." Gently, He began probing Timothy's trunk. At first it tickled. Then it really hurt.

Stop that! he cried. But Gaelathane only prodded all the more. Finding a soft place, His fingers burrowed in until Timothy was sure he would faint on the spot—if trees could faint. As the King dug deeper, vivid images from Timothy's painful past flashed before him, starting and ending with the taunts of Baglot and his bullying friends. "Tim-mie boy, the tin-ker's son, watch him run, O what fun . . ." As Timothy relived each bitter memory, Gaelathane healed the hurt and shame with a touch of His fingers.

Finally, recalling all the lies he had ever told and all the mean things he had ever done, Timothy wept great, sweet tree-tears that dripped off his leaves and trickled down his trunk. Still Gaelathane worked, deftly gouging the rotten spots out of Timothy's heartwood, trimming away his deadwood and shedding light on all his dark places. A healing warmth spread up and down his wounded trunk. When it was over, Timothy-the-tree was as weak as a slender, sun-starved sapling but cleaner inside than a new leaf. He even felt ready to forgive Baglot, if given the chance.

"Are You . . . done?" he asked the King.

"Yes, I am. And don't you feel better?" asked Gaelathane. "Before, you knew about Me, but now you have really begun to know Me and My ways. Now let's see about getting you out of there."

With that, Gaelathane swiftly climbed into the torsil's top. The next thing Timothy knew, a great weight was steadily pressing him deeper and deeper into the trunk. His tree-stomach turned over.

Crack!—he shot out of the torsil and sprawled on the ground. He was free! Laughing, he rolled over and over in the fallen leaves, waving his arms and legs for the sheer joy of it. Then he wiggled his fingers and counted them, just to be sure he hadn't left any behind. "Thank you, Gaelathane!" he shouted.

Looking up at the tree, he was shocked to see bright, beaming eyes instead of sad, baggy ones, while the moping mouth was upturned in a radiant smile. Then it dawned on him: He was looking into the King's face! *Gaelathane really did take my place.*

Suddenly, a hand roughly hauled him to his feet. "Where have you been?" Skoglund scolded him. "We've searched the woods for you all night. It's nearly dawn, and the moonsingers must soon return to their trees." Then Windsong, Ironwing and Runt bounded up. Sniffing Timothy, Ironwing growled suspiciously, "You don't smell the same."

"I don't feel the same, either," Timothy confessed. "Gaelathane has changed me!" As he spoke, the other Seekers came along.

"Where were you?" King Rolin demanded. "We thought we'd lost you for sure this time." When Timothy told of his experience in the vacant tree, the others goggled at him in disbelief.

"Why not tell us what ye really were up to?" Derwin said.

"That's right," said Sigarth. "If you lost your way, just say so. It could happen to anyone at night in a dark wood."

"How can you be certain he is not telling the truth?" the Lady Llanwyn said. "His heart seems sound to me." The men hemmed and hawed, but nobody could come up with a ready answer.

Bembor peered at Timothy. "You do have the look of someone whom the King has touched, as if a lamp's been lit behind your eyes. Still, if your story is true, then . . ."

"If his story is true," Skoglund filled in, "where's the leaf-picker he booted out of the tree?" Timothy couldn't answer that question, since he hadn't watched where the "leaf-picker" had gone.

"I believe you, even if the others don't," Gwynneth declared, giving Timothy another of her heart-stopping smiles.

"So do I," said Elwyn. Though everyone else but the sons of Sigwyn also sided with him, Timothy felt miserable. He'd just had the most amazing adventure of his life, and he couldn't prove it!

Opio was fussing over the impending dawn when a shaggy old man clothed in green rags stumbled out of the bushes. "Who are you people?" croaked the haggard stranger. It was Timothy's torsil-mate.

After a flurry of introductions, Lyle son of somebody-or-another admitted to being trapped in the torsil but couldn't recall how he had gotten out. When he was told of Timothy's selfless rescue attempt, he fell down before him and kissed his feet.

"Thank you, young sir!" he wept. "I have been bound up in that tree for eons. Truly you are worthy to wear Winona's ring."

"Winona's ring!" Rolin exclaimed. Everyone turned to Timothy, who backed away from their frank, searching stares.

"Don't look at me!" he said. "I don't have any rings."

"Then what's that?" asked Gwynneth. She pointed to Timothy's chest. Suspended from his neck, a silver chain was dangling inside his tunic. He lifted the chain, and up came a gold ring set with a great, glowing gem. The Greencloaks gasped.

"The tenth gogoniant—the lost Glory Stone!" cried Windsong, flapping his wings. "None of Whitewing's nine can rival it. Truly this is a ring fit for royalty!" The sorc was so beside himself with joy that Timothy had to explain to the others what a "gogoniant" was.

Lyle said, "Elmar gave me the ring for safekeeping when we reached this cursed wood—begging your pardon, m'lady." He bowed sheepishly to Llanwyn. "It must have remained behind in the tree when Timothy bumped me out."

"And it caught on my neck when Gaelathane freed me," Timothy finished. "But why did the queen lend it to Elmar in the first place?"

Meanwhile, Gwynneth was examining the ring. As she angled the gold circlet in the moonlight, some fine silver lines engraved on its inner surface sprang to life. Squinting, she read:

Os am griffwn i'ch arwain chi
Y fodrwy hon a'n geilw ni.

Lyle translated:

If you should need a griffin guide,
This ring will draw us to your side.

"I wonder what that means," said Elwyn with a huge yawn.

Windsong explained, "For us sorcs, gogoniants symbolize power and authority. During times of distress, griffins always rally 'round the Glory Stones, for where the Stones are, there also is our king. The sight of this one shining in the night would bring sorcs from miles around to the wearer's assistance."

Rolin nodded. "That's why Winona couldn't escape to Luralin. This ring represented her last and best hope for summoning a sorc that could fly her there. Gwynneth, as her great-granddaughter, you should have the honor of wearing it."

As Timothy handed the ring and chain to the princess, the Lady Llanwyn cried, "Dawn comes swiftly over the world's edge; memerren, to your trees!" Timothy caught a glimpse of lithe figures melting into tree trunks like a vanishing mist. Seconds later, the sun's burning disk climbed above the canyon's rim, smiting the Golden Wood with its blood-red rays.

Lyle shaded his eyes. "It's a bad sign, that. 'Red at night, no storm's in sight; red in the morning, trouble's aborning.'"

"That grass fire is still smoking up the sun," said Emmer.

"Not smoke. Dust," Bembor said. Yellow clouds of the fine stuff were sifting through the trees like rain.

"Prairie dirt, if color is any clue," said Opio, brushing some out of his sandy hair. The scouts exchanged uneasy glances.

"Medwyn says she smells iron in the air," Scanlon offered.

"Wood nymphs are very keen to sense such things," Bembor said. "Bring an axe or hatchet anywhere near their homes, and they will know it. Judging by the wind, General Gorn has come calling with his army, or my name isn't Bembor son of Brenthor."

CHAPTER 36
Trouble's Aborning

Timothy swayed near the top of a tall torsil, wishing someone else would volunteer for tree-climbing, tunnel-crawling and spasel-packing. At least this time the torsil had golden leaves. Though occupying a vacant tree had been a curious experience, it wasn't one he wished to repeat.

Where the Canyon Calydon ended and the prairie began, the earth was crawling with men, horses and wagons. Dust drifted thickly over the enemy camp on a dying evening breeze. Sliding down the tree, Timothy warned his friends of their peril.

"We must keep them from entering this wood at all costs," said King Rolin. "They don't know the danger that awaits them. I would not wish the mangles' greed-sleep on anyone, even Gorn."

"They won't easily be turned back after coming all this way to find gold," Derwin cautioned him.

"If only we sorcs still had our wings, we could drive them off," muttered Ironwing. "Even without our wings, we'll make them wish they'd never invaded Lucambra in the first place."

"Nay, good sorc," said Emmer. "They are too many for us."

Gemmio rubbed his bloodshot eyes. "I say, let the Thalms blunder around in this forest. When they finally realize there's nothing of value here, they'll leave the way they came."

"In the meantime, they will wreak havoc among these trees," Rolin said. "I cannot allow that, especially since we're partly to blame for Gorn's army being here." Ignoring the pleas of his family and friends, the king set out to parley with the enemy. The other Seekers of the Wood reluctantly followed. Although Timothy had already tasted enough adventure to last him a lifetime, he wanted to see if King Rolin could face down a pack of gold-thirsty Thalmosians!

They had reached the forest's eaves near the northern tip of the canyon when Meghan cried out, "It's Midge and Maggie!"

Sure enough, the stable boy was leading his horse down to the River Rondolyn for a drink. Above and beyond them, General Gorn's army had entrenched itself on the plain.

Derwin trotted out of the woods to greet Midge. The two spoke briefly. Then the stable boy galloped back to the sprawling enemy camp, only to return minutes later to speak with Derwin again. The woodcutter rejoined his companions with grim tidings.

"Gorn was expecting us to put up a stiff fight, so he's about to mount a frontal assault on this wood," he said. "Since we have asked to parley, the general's willing to meet with us. He's a sly fox, that one. We can't let our guard down fer a second with him."

"I fear this day will not end without bloodshed," said Emmer. He pointed skyward, where hundreds of batwolves flapped in the mellow evening light. "Even they can sense a battle is in the offing. They're waiting to scavenge the dead and wounded." He raised his glowing lightstaff, but Rolin gently pushed it aside.

"Not now," he said. "Unless it comes to a pitched battle, we don't want yeg statues dropping on the Thalmosians' heads."

His face set like flint, Rolin led the Seekers up to the scorched plain. Timothy sucked in his breath as a magnificent black charger pranced up to meet them. On its back sat the mail-clad Thalmosian general, armed with spear and sword. Midge, Maggie and some fifty mounted men followed at a respectful distance.

Throwing back his head, Gorn bellowed, "Where is that peasant who styles himself a king? Show yourself, if you are a man!"

On impulse, Timothy pressed his wormsticker spine into Rolin's palm. "You might need this," he whispered. The king gave him a quick smile before approaching Gorn's horse.

"I am the one you seek," he said. "What do you want with me, and why do you bring armed men to this place of peace?"

Gorn glared at him. "You know very well why. You tree-rats sneaked out of your tower without paying the three million gilders you still owe the crown." He waved his arm at the wood below. "We will take what is due us in golden leaves from this forest, which we claim in the name of King Mardoc."

"In other words," said King Rolin dryly, "you intend to take by force what does not rightfully belong to you."

"I see we understand each other," sneered General Gorn.

Rolin's eyes turned to cold steel. "The Golden Wood belongs to the One Who created it—Gaelathane, the King of the Trees. If you attempt to despoil it, we will defend it to the last man."

Gorn roared with laughter. "I would crush you like so many puny cockroaches. We both know you are no match for my army."

"What you do not know, General, is that these leaves are gold in color only, and that they bring a deadly curse upon those who pick them. You will find no costly treasures here! Return to your master before you and your army perish."

Gorn snarled, "Do you take me for a fool? Any dolt can plainly see these trees are as gold as King Mardoc's crown. When I have stripped them of their leaves, I will take great pleasure in burning this rebellious forest to the ground!" Something like a mask slipped partway off his face. Behind it, a pair of murderous red eyes burned in a sea of black. Then the mask righted itself.

"'Rebellious forest'?" said Rolin coolly. "Having failed the first time to destroy it, have you returned to finish the job, *Felgor*? How very clever of you to cloak yourself in mortal flesh, and how craven. May your foul sorceries burn in Gundul's fires!"

Gorn stiffened, his eyes flaring. "I don't know what you're talking about, *vassal*. If I hadn't promised the king to impale you on a pole in his presence, I would run you through right now for your insolence."

Rolin removed his cloak. "Then I propose a wager. Let us meet on this field in mortal combat. If you slay me, then this forest and all it contains is yours. If I defeat you, then your army must leave Lucambra and never return. Agreed?"

Grinning slyly, General Gorn dismounted and hefted his spear, his ring-mail hauberk clinking. "I should have slain you in your mother's womb when I had the chance," he hissed. "You were correct about 'finishing the job.' After striking you down, I shall make this accursed wood your funeral pyre. Prepare to die, river-scum!" With that, the Thalmosian general lunged.

"The Tree lives!" cried the king, fending off Gorn's spear thrust with the sword of Elgathel. While both sides egged them on, the two combatants circled on the burnt grass, each testing the other's mettle with deliberate weapon strokes.

Whack! Crack! Wood and iron clashed and rang as the dueling warriors exchanged blows. Throwing dirt into his opponent's eyes, the general followed up with a two-handed spear jab. Rolin threw out his arm to deflect the lance, which he then neatly chopped in half with his sword. Blood dripped from his gashed arm.

"A more even match now, don't you think?" panted the king as Gorn drew his own sword. Barely parrying a flurry of furious sword strokes, Rolin was beaten to his knees. Gorn was about to pierce him through when Rolin slipped under his sword arm and slashed his thigh. Bellowing like a wounded bull, the general charged, disarming Rolin with a vicious backhand swing.

"I like these odds better, tree-filth!" Gorn taunted him.

While Rolin tried to retrieve his weapon, the gloating general forced him backward with short jabs, kicking the fallen sword out of his reach. The Seekers of the Wood groaned as their enemy's sword poised for a killing thrust. Their dismay was short-lived. Something tan and furry darted between Gorn's legs, throwing him off balance. Before he could recover, Rolin feinted with his right hand, then ducked inside Gorn's guard and with his left, drove Timothy's sharp wormsticker spine into the Thalmosian's throat.

With a gurgling shriek, General Gorn collapsed in the dust. "You forgot to watch my left hand," Rolin told him. "And you should never underestimate a rabbit! Now go and trouble us no more, Felgor."

"My . . . men will . . . tear you to . . . pieces," Gorn gasped. Then his head fell back and his face went slack. A wailing cry poured from his sagging mouth and carried over the plain as the servant of Gundul returned to his own place.

Silence struck the stunned onlookers. Then a confused murmur rose from the Thalmosians' restless ranks.

"We are still in grave danger," Rolin told his companions. "With Felgor-Gorn out of the picture, his men may not honor the terms of our wager. I suggest we withdraw into the forest."

Sigarth scowled. "My lord, I am loth to retreat, especially after your victory. For one who rarely handles a sword in combat, you gave a good account of yourself."

"Thanks to Longears' bravery and Timothy's wormsticker spine!" Rolin replied. Removing the spike from Gorn's neck, he wiped it off and returned it to Timothy. "Something tells me you'll be needing this again," he said with a grim smile.

Even as the king spoke, the restive Thalmosians broke into a deep, full-throated roar. "Gold! Gold! GOLD!" Like floodwaters breaching an earthen dam, they swept toward the Canyon Calydon.

"Run!" cried Rolin. Keeping to the Rondolyn's left bank, Timothy and his companions raced back to the forest and plunged into its dusky depths. Behind them, the fanatical gold-hunters were recklessly throwing themselves down the canyon's steep slopes. Then they tore into the trees, ripping loose all the leaves they could grab. In turn, squirming mangle-clusters dropped onto them, biting everything in sight. With terrified screams, scores of soldiers fell stricken under the weight of an eternal slumber.

More howling waves of Thalmosians followed the first, each one surging deeper into the forest than the last. Fleeing on foot and on sorc-back, the Seekers barely outran the onslaught.

Now Mardoc's army came to hushed groves of high-branching trees whose leaves hung well out of reach. Enraged, they hacked at the hapless torsils with swords and axes, felling large and small alike to get at their leaves. Trees crashed, mangles slithered, men shouted and cursed. Trying to escape the snakes, many of the tree-slayers climbed their would-be victims. Some of those trees were golden leafed, while others were green.

Finally the moon awakened the forest, releasing its memerren. As their trees toppled under the soldiers' bitter axe strokes, moonsingers collapsed with shrieks and groans, turning to wood where they lay. Timothy ran to one of the stricken nymphs.

"Help me, Mortal!" she wailed, her feet and legs stiffening into wood before his eyes. "Pray—!" The moonsinger's face furrowed into bark, choking off her last cry. It was the Lady Llanwyn.

"Please help us, Gaelathane," Timothy whispered earnestly. As yegs swooped down to prey upon the mangle-bitten, the King's voice burned in Timothy's heart. *Plant the staff.*

What staff? Timothy was looking about when a batwolf dove on Scanlon, striking him a glancing blow. Timothy knelt beside the fallen

Lucambrian, who was bleeding from a nasty gash in his temple. His lightstaff lay beside him, glowing in the dusk.

Ducking to avoid another yeg, Timothy snatched up the lightstaff and pounded it into the ground with a flat rock, as Emmer had done near Mt. Golgunthor. Suddenly, a sharp pain speared his leg. The stone fell from his hand and his arms dropped limply to his sides. Wobbling on his knees, he fell over.

"Timothy! What's wrong?" cried Gwynneth, hurrying to him. She prodded his leg, which felt as numb as an old log.

"Never mind . . . me," he murmured. "Scanlon . . . hurt."

At Gwynneth's shout, Marlis came to her brother's aid. Then Elwyn joined his sister. "What happened here?" he asked.

"A mangle's bitten Timothy!" Gwynneth groaned. Even as the other Lucambrians came running, Timothy felt the ground tremble. Forcing his head up, he saw that the lightstaff was rapidly becoming a mighty tree. Shining shoots were breaking out of it on all sides. *My hand will grant the Tree to plant, ere bitter curse consumes.*

As the yegs fled and the golden trees joyfully clattered their limbs, Timothy's friends gathered around the sprouting staff. "What in the name of Elgathel is this?" exclaimed Gemmio.

Timothy stifled a yawn. "I'm afraid it's Scanlon's lightstaff." As he gazed into the dazzling light, feeling slowly returned to his fingertips, spreading to his hands and arms, feet and legs.

When sleep-snakes strike, keep your eyes on the light, Gaelathane whispered to him.

Emmer gaped at the swelling staff. "What did you do to it?"

"Nothing at all," said Timothy, propping himself up on one elbow. "Gaelathane told me to plant it, and so I did."

"I don't understand," Rolin said. "Why is this staff sprouting like a willow-wand in May, when Emmer's didn't?"

"The King's touch must have made it grow," said Marlis with tears in her eyes. As she spoke, Scanlon's eyelids fluttered open.

"Amazing. Simply amazing," he said, staring up at the staff. "It looks just like the original Tree after it returned to life on Luralin!"

"Please hold still; you're badly hurt," Marlis warned her brother. Ignoring her, Scanlon sat up and touched his head.

"I do believe I'm much better now," he declared.

Feeling his strength returning, Timothy jumped up and shouted, "I'm well!" Then he waved at the bitten Thalmosians. "Hey, fellows; just look at this Tree and you'll be healed!"

Unable to move, one fallen soldier gazed up at the towering Staff-Tree. "I'm cured!" he cried. "Five o' them snakes bit me, but I'm cured!" Whooping, the man cavorted about the trunk. Soon, many of his snake-bitten comrades had joined him.

When mangles' fangs have bitten deep,
And men shall fall from bitter sleep,
Who would be free, behold the Tree,
For in its light the lost will leap.

"One look at the Tree and they're healed," King Rolin marveled. "We'd better spread the word before we have a whole army of sleeping soldiers on our hands."

"You'll just be wasting your time," said Sigarth sourly. "Thalms never look up. They're sky-blind and tree-blind, too."

Still, they all scattered throughout the wood to proclaim the good news. "Look up! Look up at the Tree and you'll be healed! Gaelathane will help you!" they told their enemies. Though many of the bitten men had already fallen asleep, Gaelathane's name brought them around. Weakened with venom, some of the leaf-pickers could only lift their heads in obedience, while others crawled toward the Tree. A few spat in the messengers' faces.

"Tree? What Tree?" the doubters sneered. "It's only the moon, ye daft rapscallions. Now leave us to our dreams of gold."

By now, Scanlon's staff had reached a truly colossal size. Black, grumbling storm clouds billowed above it, while lightning flashed from horizon to horizon. Several bolts struck the Staff-Tree, which only glowed all the more fiercely. Then the rains came.

"We'll never save them all," groaned Elwyn as water plastered down his red hair and dripped off his nose. "For every Thalmosian who turns to the Tree, the mangles bite five more. And how can we help these poor moonsingers?"

Just then, the Tree brightened as a glowing figure emerged from its trunk. Standing between the mangles and their victims, the Ancient of Days let the snakes strike His own body. Hundreds of the hissing serpents twined about His legs, arms and neck, biting Him. When the mangles had spent their venom, the King dismissed them to their trees with a wave of His hand.

Lightning slashed the sky as Timothy and his friends bowed to their King, Who gazed sadly at the moonsingers lying stiff and wooden upon the ground. "If I revive My children, they will become mortal," He told Timothy. "Do you understand that?"

With a gulp, Timothy nodded. Surely Llanwyn and her people would prefer mortality to rotting away like logs on the forest floor! Squaring his jaw, he led Gaelathane to the block of wood that was once the torsil queen. Weeping, the Leaf Lord laid His hands on the Lady Llanwyn's frozen features.

"To restore a life requires a life," He said, holding out His hand. "Please give Me the Sting of Death."

Timothy fumbled in his pockets for his knife.

"Not your knife, precious child, but that which brought you to death's doorstep." The King touched Timothy's back, and his wounds' lingering ache melted away. Then he understood. Hesitantly, he handed Gaelathane the wormsticker spine.

Taking the spike, Gaelathane plunged it into His hand. Crimson blood spattered upon the Guardian's motionless figure.

"Awake, sleeper, and rise from your wooden death," the King commanded the torsil queen.

Wherever the blood fell, wood gave way to soft pink flesh. Like ripples widening in a pool, the transformation spread across Llanwyn's grainy features. As the woodenness retreated from her head, her solid brown locks melted into glistening strands that lay rain-limp along her whitening brow. When she was wholly flesh again, the Guardian opened her eyes.

"Thank You for rescuing me, Leaf Lord. But why did You not come in time to save those who perished in their trees? They have left this world, never to look upon Your face again!"

"Your people are already with Me in Gaelessa," said Gaelathane tenderly. "Their suffering has not been in vain." He gestured toward the Tree, where thousands of Thalmosians were climbing into the dripping night sky. "See how many of these mortals I have healed and reconciled to Myself! When they return home through My Tree, they will spread the word of My love among their countrymen."

Sigarth grumbled, "After what those potato eaters did, I just can't understand why You revived them, much less let them go."

"Do not forget that I gave My life for those men as surely as I did for you. You must forgive them, for they knew not what they were doing. Give Me your grudges and let Me heal them."

Sigarth's head sagged, and tears streamed down his cheeks. "Help me to forgive, for my hatred is strong!" he groaned.

"My love is stronger!" said Gaelathane. "However, to receive that love, you must first be reconciled to your foes. Here is Derwin son of Stolland, one of the despoilers' race; will you not offer him your hand in friendship?" Sigarth gripped the woodcutter's callused hand and the two shook like long-lost brothers.

"And what of you, Derwin?" said Gaelathane. "Little Meghan has already told you much about Me. Whom will you serve now, King Mardoc or the King of the Trees?"

The woodcutter knelt before his Creator. "Ye will be my Master for as long as I live, and thereafter," he said humbly.

Gaelathane embraced him. "I am pleased to welcome you into My family and My kingdom," He said. "Now come with Me; more of My children are awaiting deliverance."

Sprinkling His blood upon the other wooden memerren, the King restored them to mortal life. Less fortunate were the many brave nymphs and dryads who had perished in their trees when they were cut before moonrise. Calymon, Cledwyn, Glaspeth and Glonnyll were among those who had entered life eternal in Gaelessa.

Gaelathane finished awakening the last nymph just as the Tree faded away with the break of day. Dawn's first light fell upon the exiled moonsingers, who covered their eyes and wept for the lives they had lost. Scanlon moved among them calling Medwyn's name, but she was not with her sun-stricken companions.

"It's just like her to disappear," said Birchbind crossly. "She's never around when you need her. Let's go find her tree. If it's still standing, she might be inside it by now, with any luck."

Medwyn's torsil grew some distance away on a wooded hill. As the searchers approached the knoll, sharp-eyed Bledwyn gave a shout.

"There it is! It's still—oh, no." Everyone hurried up the hill to find Medwyn's once-comely torsil lying broken on the ground, stripped nearly bare of its golden leaves.

"We can only hope that she moonslipped before the Thalmosians felled her tree," blonde Anweth murmured.

Scanlon's face turned pastier than a moonlit nymph's. "If she did," he said huskily, "she should be somewhere nearby."

"She is," said Gaelathane. "Come, and you will see." Following the King down the back side of the hill, the searchers came upon a statue of wood lying on a cushiony bed of sword ferns. Scanlon knelt beside the figure. Stroking its stiff, wooden hair, he said with trembling voice, "It's her, all right."

"Medwyn lies here because she gave herself for others," said Gaelathane. "When the gold frenzy had seized the Thalmosians, she moonslipped and lured some of them to her tree with promises of easy pickings. In so doing, she saved the lives of many memerren who else would have lost their own trees."

Llanwyn's mortal tears dripped on Medwyn's sightless, staring face. "'From wood she came, and to wood she has returned,'" the queen murmured, reciting age-old words of ritual mourning.

"We never knew how brave she was," sobbed Marsina.

"She was no braver than the rest of you," said the King quietly. "Her love simply overcame her instincts. Courage, you see, is doing the right thing despite your fears. Timothy also showed that kind of courage when he climbed Lyle's torsil to release him."

Scanlon looked up at Gaelathane expectantly. "Could You please revive Medwyn now, even at the cost of Your own blood?"

The King of the Trees gazed sorrowfully back at him. "My son, it is too late. Even I cannot bring her back the way she was."

"Too late? What are You saying?" Scanlon cried. "You have just restored all these others; why not Medwyn?"

Gaelathane laid His hand on Scanlon's shoulder. "I may raise a wood-bound memer to mortal life only while the moon still hangs in the sky. Once the sun rises on her, I can still revive her, but she will look even as she does now, a creature of wood and not of flesh and blood. Let Me release her spirit from this wooden prison, and I will take her to Gaelessa to live with Me forever."

Scanlon groaned in anguish. "Is there no other way? I thought nothing was impossible for the King of the Trees!"

"All things are possible for him who believes. Do you believe, Scanlon son of Emmer?"

"Yes, Lord, You know that I do. But what You are telling me is too difficult to bear. I have lost Medwyn forever."

"Nothing of Mine is ever lost, either now or in eternity. In earthly terms, however, what Llanwyn has told you is true: Only mortals may release mortals, and moonsingers moonsingers. Still, a mortal's tears of love may awaken Medwyn to the form she once knew, for mortal she is and mortal she must be."

Scanlon kissed the nymph's cold-barked cheek. Still she did not respond. Weeping bitterly, he crumpled up a handful of her wilted, golden leaves. "What love is strong enough to change a beam of wood back into flesh and bone?" he cried.

"Mine is," said the King gently. "Love her with My love."

With an agonized sob, Scanlon bowed his head and sang,

You walked the woods by light of moon;
Your voice would put the lark to shame;
Your beauty made the stars to swoon,
Though daylight never knew your name.

Medwyn of the melting eyes,
Do not now my love despise!
Waken from your wooden sleep,
Your mortal covenants to keep!

With feet more swift than swallow's wings,
You once escaped my longing arms;
But now you've fled with fallen kings
Beyond the reach of earthly harms.

Medwyn of the melting eyes,
Do not now my love despise!
Waken from your wooden sleep,
Your mortal covenants to keep!

Alas, you've wandered past the pale
Of mortal grief and broken song;
Against the night though I should rail,
To death's decay you now belong.

Medwyn of the melting eyes,
Do not now my love despise!
Waken from your wooden sleep,
Your mortal covenants to keep!

Where Scanlon's tears spattered onto Medwyn's wooden body, small white specks appeared. The specks rapidly ran together, forming patches of skin. Those patches expanded and merged like puddles in a rainstorm, until the last traces of wood had melted into flesh.

Though restored, Medwyn lay pale and still, her eyes closed as if in death. Scanlon lifted her arm and let it limply fall back. "There is no life in her," he moaned.

Then Gaelathane touched her face, saying, "O death, where is your sting? O grave, where is your victory?"

Medwyn's wan cheeks flushed pink, she took a long, shuddering breath, and her eyes fluttered open. "Thank You, my Lord," she said to Gaelathane. "I heard Your voice in the darkness!"

She took Scanlon's hand, and he raised her to her feet. "Bless you for calling me back, my love!" she told him. Weeping for joy, Scanlon kissed and embraced her, as did her mother. The other nymphs blushed and giggled.

Ironwing muttered, "I suppose I'll have to carry the both of them from now on, scorbies or no."

"It could be worse," Windsong said. "If poor Medwyn had not awakened, you might be bearing a wooden statue on your back!"

Then everyone laughed, even Ironwing, in his peevish way.

CHAPTER 37
The Gwlân Gorge

Timothy and company were feasting on some quail the sorcs had caught when Midge and Maggie trotted up in a cloud of tiny flies. *So that's how Midge got his name,* Timothy thought.

"Hullo!" said the long-haired stable boy with a freckled grin.

"Where have you been?" asked Rolin, somewhat taken aback.

"I heard what you told General Gorn about these golden trees, and I steered clear of 'em. After the ruckus died down, Maggie and I thought we'd better see what had happened. You're the first people I've come across. Where are the rest, anyway?"

As Midge picked through the leftovers, Derwin described the gold-crazed Thalmosians' fate. "Serves 'em right," the stable boy said between mouthfuls of quail. "Even if there was any gold out here in the first place, it warn't Gorn's to take. I'm just glad I didn't pick any o' them leaves."

"Well spoken, lad," said Bembor. "When you're done there, I'd like you to join me on a little errand." Having eaten his fill of quail, Midge set off with Bembor on Maggie. When they returned, Llanwyn was riding Maggie sidesaddle, expressions of delight flitting over her face like clouds scudding across the moon.

"Perhaps mortality won't be so unpleasant after all," she mused as Scanlon helped her dismount. When he spoke in her ear, she smiled impishly and said aloud, "You needn't ask anyone's consent. Indeed, I give you my blessing." Scanlon reddened.

"Thank you for seeing us, dear Llanwyn," said Rolin. "I wish to take up the matter of the starworts with you again. Our friend Lyle disappeared yesterday, so we can't ask him where to find the plants. Our only clue is that a 'Gwlan Gorge' is the 'Wort Haven.' Do you know of such a place?"

Llanwyn frowned. "I may. Beyond the southern boundary of our wood, where the Graylands begin, the Rondolyn flows through a deep, narrow canyon. Moonsingers rarely go there; for safety's sake, we stay close to our trees." A shadow crossed her face. "As a mortal now, I am free to take you there by day or by night."

Greatly encouraged, the starwort-seekers packed up their meager provisions and set off for the River Rondolyn. Timothy and Elwyn, Meghan and Gwynneth took turns riding Maggie in pairs, while Midge walked in front holding the reins. Medwyn tagged along as well, sticking very closely to Scanlon and the sorcs.

On their way to the river, they passed through tracts of butchered torsils, whose leaves were already crisping in the sun. Llanwyn pointed out one of the splintered wrecks. "There lies Fairleaf." Farther on, the travelers came across a snapped-off torsil whose shattered limbs were partially bare of leaves. Five or six Thalmosians lay crushed beneath its checkered trunk.

"Not Tallslip, too!" Medwyn gasped. "She must have broken from the climbers' weight." Sobbing, she caressed the stump.

Llanwyn explained, "Tallslip was Medwyn's closest friend. Now they will never meet again under light of moon or sun."

"Won't the torsil just resprout?" asked Gwynneth.

"Even if it did, the tree would still be empty," said Llanwyn sadly. "Tallslip has left our world for Gaelessa." The grieving company moved on until the Guardian knelt beside another fallen torsil, tall and straight of trunk. "This was mine," she said, her hands fluttering over the hewn form like aspen leaves trembling in the wind.

Saddened by the sight of so much wanton carnage, the Seekers continued their journey, guided by the glad sound of the Rondolyn's rushing waters. On reaching the river, they turned south, tramping through untouched stands of golden torsils. Even here, a deathlike heaviness clung to the forest.

Presently, they found themselves back in the gnome-tree grove, whose gnarled torsils looked even more morose than before. "We have yet to 'release from gloom of leafy tomb' 'the twelve who still survive,'" Bembor reminded Rolin.

"Make that eleven," Marlis said. "Lyle is out now. I wonder where he is; we could use his help in freeing his friends."

"You're too late!" boomed a cheery voice behind them. It was Lyle, accompanied by a bevy of boisterous old men. Like Lyle, they were shabbily dressed; their hair and nails badly wanted cutting, and they had thrown their long, tangled beards over their shoulders to avoid tripping on them.

"You're it!" one cried, thumping his companion on the head. The "thumpee" tromped on the thumper's beard.

"No, I'm not. Erwin's it!"

The sight of Maggie and her riders brought them up short. "What have we here?" they cried. "Two-legs on a four-legs! The more legs the merrier. And sorcs to boot! You'll join us in a game of tag, won't you? We can't run as fast as you young 'uns, but we're still past masters at hiding. Come on now; who will start?"

When King Rolin declined their offer, Lyle shrugged and began jogging from one foot to the other. "Suit yourselves. You're missing out on some real fun. Anyway, after all these years of 'playing tree,' we don't like standing in one spot too long. We might sprout roots." He waved his companions on. "Hey, boys! Let's off to the river for some rock-hopping."

"Hold on," Opio growled, blocking Lyle's way. "First, we want to know where these friends of yours came from."

"Why, they're the rest of our party—the ones that got trapped in these trees, like me. Count 'em. They're all here." He proudly stuck out his chest. "Since I'm the eldest of the bunch, that makes me the oldest living Lucambrian, doesn't it?"

"At least the longest bearded and the quickest tongued," muttered Opio as Lyle's companions lined up beside him.

"Ten . . . eleven . . . and Lyle makes twelve," Marlis counted. "He's right. That's all of them."

Bembor's eyebrows climbed his furrowed face. "How did these others escape their trees? Did you release them?"

"Not personally," said Lyle. "When those men came charging through the woods, I figured they were after gold, so I told them these trees were loaded with it." He chuckled. "A mean trick, I'll admit, but it worked. In the dark, they couldn't tell green leaves from gold. Up they went, and out tumbled my mates. We've had a jolly time since then becoming reacquainted."

"If you don't mind," Rolin said, "we'd like you to acquaint us with the spot where you found your starberries."

"That is, if you still remember," added Mycena.

"Oh, we remember, all right," said Lyle. "How could we forget? We will take you to the place. It's the least we can do after all your help, and it will keep the moss from growing under our feet." With that, he began snooping through Maggie's baggage.

"Where's the rope?" he demanded.

"Rope?" returned King Rolin. "What for?"

"Why, for climbing cliffs, of course!" said Lyle. "The starworts grow only in the Gwlân Gorge, where the rocks are perilously slick. We lost several men from falls as it was."

Gwlân. So that was how the name was pronounced. Timothy didn't like the ominous sound of it or the feel of it, either. A place of death, it seemed. And how were they to climb into it without any rope?

"First things first!" said Lyle. "'Play before work;' that's my motto." With that, the twelve longbeards hobbled off to the River Rondolyn. Bringing up the rear, Timothy and his companions found their new friends gleefully shouting as they bounded among the river boulders. Several of them fell into the water and had to be dragged out when their heavy beards pulled them under.

"A fine expedition this has turned out to be," grumped Sigarth, sulkily crossing his arms. "Here we are playing nursemaids to twelve half-cracked codgers acting like schoolboys on a lark."

King Rolin laughed. "But isn't it fun watching those old fellows have such a good time? Maybe we should join them."

And so they did. Afterwards, the waders climbed out and dried themselves on the sun-warmed rocks. It was late afternoon when they set out again for the southlands, following a faint, broken path that snaked along the forested riverbank. Lyle and his friends rode long-suffering Maggie by turns, much to her annoyance.

Now the swiftly flowing river chewed into the earth, carving an ever-deeper channel between beetling bluffs bristling with pines and golden torsils. Far below those wooded rimrocks, the murmuring Rondolyn gleamed dully amidst sullen, cliff-spun shadows. Soon, the hikers had grown so hot and thirsty that they had to stop to drink from the river's icy water.

The setting sun was slanting through the trees when a growing thunder shook the cool, pine-sweet air. Then the trail abruptly ended where the Rondolyn's frothing waters cascaded over a cliff and dropped into a midnight, misty chasm like a silver spear.

Shouting to be heard above the waterfall's roar, the Lady Llanwyn said, "This is the Liggion, the 'Dagger Falls,' whose plunging waters reach the bottom of this abyss only as a mist, or so our legends tell. Farther south, these bluffs fall away into the Drylands, where no river gladdens the parched ground."

Timothy peered into the mist. "This gorge looks bottomless!" he told Elwyn. The two flung rocks into the chasm, which swallowed them up in shimmering rainbows of spray.

"Don't stray too near the edge," Scanlon warned them. "As Lyle said, the rocks are very slippery there. We wouldn't want to lose you to the Gwlân Gorge, where 'none can scale the wall.'"

"Where did it get its name?" asked Elwyn.

Lyle said, "It all started with Gwilym son of Gallion, a shepherd who lived on the plain. One day, some yegs chased his flock into this canyon. Following the sheep, he found the gorge, which he called Ceunant Gwlân, the 'Wool Gorge,' for its fleecy clouds of mist."

"The starflowers grow down there?" asked Meghan.

"Probably, but much may have changed since I was last here. Even with climbing ropes, our original party could not plumb the gorge. Instead, most of us backtracked up to the plain and trekked miles downriver to where the gorge shallows out. Entering from that end, we found a few starworts, but yegs harried us all the way."

"The Lady Llanwyn told us that your company returned with many bags full of starberries," Bembor pointed out.

"That is true," said Lyle. "Elmar gathered most of those. Where he found them he would not say, but he took no rope with him. By now, I fear, those starworts may have completely died out."

"Some of them must still grow in the gorge, because they appear in Timothy's spasel," declared Gemmio.

The spasel! Timothy had forgotten all about the sap-platter. While the others gathered around, he warmed it with his faltering breath. Unfortunately, the evening sun washed out all but the brightest of the starflowers' sprinkled, firefly lights.

"This still may mean nothing," said Llanwyn gently. "Even after a tree of passage perishes, its *coedagrau* will continue showing the dying tree's last vistas. Judging from this spasel's condition, its *torsyl* most likely rotted away many seasons ago."

Since there was little else to see in the shadow-shrouded canyon, the starwort seekers settled beside the rumbling Rondolyn, where they hung on Lyle's tales of old Lucambra. Impatiently waiting for nightfall to bring out the starflowers in his spasel, Timothy listened with only half an ear. His stomach rumbled.

Rolin handed him a roasted, sorc-snagged trout. "You must be hungry," the king said as Timothy tore into the fish. "I was hoping to have another look at your spasel before bed. If it shows starflowers, then a torsil must have grown somewhere down in that gorge. Even if the tree is gone now, the old spasel-images might still help us locate the starberries."

"What about my spasel?" said Meghan, hopping onto her father's lap. "Don't you want to look at it, too? It's very pretty."

Rolin reared back and blinked at his daughter. "Your spasel? I'd forgotten about that one. I'm surprised you still have it."

"I saved it just for you, Papa," she said, solemn-eyed.

Seeing Meghan's spasel, the others drifted over with curious looks. "We never would have found th' Golden Wood without that funny glass pancake," said Derwin. "Missy had her eyes glued to it the whole trip. Kept us on the right course, she did."

"Let me see those for a moment," said Rolin. He pressed the two "sap pancakes" back-to-back, flat sides together, and their images blazed up sharply. "I thought so!" he exclaimed. "These spasels must have come from a pair of tara-torsils, one at the top of the gorge and the other at the bottom. Timothy's spasel was made from the upper tree, since it shows the view from the lower tara-torsil."

"So my spasel is from the bottom one, 'cuz it shows the golden trees at the top," said Meghan, clapping her hands.

"Precisely," her father replied with a kindly smile.

"Then who originally planted those tara-torsils here?" puzzled Marlis. "They don't grow that way in nature, after all. Elmar couldn't have done it, since he could only have molded these spasels from the sap of full-grown trees."

"I agree," Bembor said. "Torsils generally don't produce enough sap for a decent spasel until at least their twentieth year. After that, the sap oozes out of their bark naturally. To increase the sap's flow, you can score the bark with a knife." As Llanwyn's face froze in a look of horror, Bembor quickly added, "Of course, no true lover of trees—or of Gaelathane—would ever do such a thing."

Scanlon sighed. "But we still have no idea where the tara-torsils themselves might stand, much less who planted them."

"I believe I can answer both your questions," said the Lady Llanwyn with an embarrassed smile. "I planted those trees."

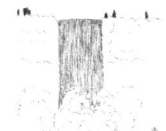

CHAPTER 38
The Ceremony of the Seeds

Y ou planted them?" Marlis exclaimed. "Whatever for?"
"Let me explain," said Llanwyn. "As a young nymph just learning to moonslip, I fell in love with a dryad named Burlion. One night, we decided to visit this canyon. Straying so far from our trees was foolish, but I was fleet of foot, and Burlion was even swifter. After dancing in the Liggion's mists and sealing our love with the Ceremony of the Seeds, we ran all the way back and entered our trees just before dawn."

"Ceremony of the Seeds? What's that?" Timothy asked. He loved pomp and ceremony, though he had seen few spectacles worthy of the name until King Mardoc's arrival in Beechtown.

"Just as you mortals exchange rings in betrothal, so, too, we moonsingers give and receive the fruits of our trees. I presented Burlion with one of my *torsyl* nuts, and he gave me one of his. Then on a whim, we made 'traveling torsyls' of them. Splitting both nuts in twain, we planted two of the halves near the River Rondolyn. The other two sections we threw into the canyon.

"'May these seeds fare wherever they may,' said Burlion. 'Let us hope they come at last to the Isle of Light and take root there, that together we may visit that wondrous place where the Leaf Lord reigns in glory.'" A tear trickled down Llanwyn's cheek.

"What happened to Burlion?" asked Gwynneth.

"Alas, after Medwyn's birth, he perished in the Burning of the Wood," Llanwyn replied. "I have avoided this place since."

"At least one pair of tara-torsils must have survived," mused Rolin. "However, we have no way of knowing where the half-nuts you threw into the gorge ended up. They may have floated far before fetching up on dry land."

"It doesn't matter, so long as we can reach the spot by torsil travel," said Windsong, who had been keeping an eye and an ear partway open during the discussion.

Since it was already too dark for further exploration, the starwort seekers agreed to search out Llanwyn and Burlion's tara-torsils first thing in the morning. Before bed, Timothy was taking a last drink from the river when something brushed against his back and he caught the sweet scent of Gwynneth's hair.

"Hello, Timothy," she said coyly. "I loved the Lady Llanwyn's story, didn't you?" Her head leaned perilously close to his.

"Uh, I guess so," he replied. Why was Gwynneth bringing up Llanwyn's tale now? His palms began to sweat again.

Dreamy-eyed, Gwynneth said, "Just the two of them, dancing in the moonlight. I think their betrothal was simply lovely, too."

"I suppose," Timothy said offhandedly. "If those two hadn't traded torsil nuts, we wouldn't have our spasels, and there'd be no chance of getting to the starworts, either."

Gwynneth's green eyes narrowed. "That's not what I meant. I thought it was sweet how they gave each other their most precious possessions. Moonsingers don't own much, you know. They can only share what grows on their trees—fruits, nuts, and the like."

Timothy felt dizzy. Then he realized he had been holding his breath. "Yes, that was nice," he exhaled. "Leastwise, if you're a nymph or a dryad."

"I think the Ceremony of the Seeds would be perfect for anyone, not just moonsingers." Gwynneth touched Timothy's hand. "Since it's still early in the evening, why don't we perform our own ceremony?"

Timothy tried to swallow the lump lodged in his throat. It wouldn't budge. "You mean, exchange something? Don't you think the sharing spasel you gave me was enough?"

"But you didn't give *me* anything."

Timothy sighed. Ever since meeting Gwynneth, he'd dreamed of spending more time with her. "All right," he croaked.

Together, they edged away from the riverbank and into the woods. Moon-spun mist-pearls rose in shimmering clouds from the rumbling waterfall nearby, filtering through the torsils. Though Timothy saw no memerren moving about, the dark forest seemed watchfully awake.

Gwynneth bent down. "Here's a torsil nut." She held up the tan, roundish object and shook it. "It's empty."

"Here's another!" Timothy pounced on a seed hiding among the leaves on the forest floor. Warming to the game, he soon learned that the freshest nuts shone with a fine, silvery sheen. When he and Gwynneth had filled their pockets with nuts, they each selected the largest and soundest one and discarded the rest.

By now, their wandering feet had taken them into a white-boled poplar grove whose rustling leaves and graceful branches shadow-dappled the ground with lacy patterns. Gwynneth held up her torsil nut for Timothy to see. His own seemed dingy by comparison. With a sigh, he offered the nut to her, stammering, "This is f-for you."

As she accepted the seed, Gwynneth's comely face lit up as if the nut were a flawless diamond. "Thank you!" she said. "This is my pledge-gift for you, in Gaelathane's name." Solemnly, she laid her nut in Timothy's hand, sending a shiver up his arm.

"Now what should we do with these nuts?" he asked her.

"Why, make four tara-torsils out of them, of course," replied Gwynneth. She carefully cracked hers with a rock and removed the meat. Marveling at how the princess could dignify a simple gesture with such grace, Timothy did the same.

"Now we have to split each one exactly in half," Gwynneth said. Following her direction, Timothy sliced both nuts lengthwise through the center with his knife.

"Perfect," she breathed. "Now let's plant one half of yours and one half of mine here in this glade."

"What about the other two halves?" Timothy asked.

Moonlight pooled beneath Gwynneth's eyes as she smiled at him. "Let's save them until we find a spot worth visiting."

After dropping one of his nut halves into his pocket, Timothy pressed the other into the moist earth. Gwynneth had just finished planting her half-nut when the leaves stirred and a feathered head emerged from the shadows. "You've been missed," murmured Runt as he stalked up to the pair.

As he and Gwynneth followed the sorc back to the river, Timothy couldn't help thinking that there was much more to the Ceremony of the Seeds than exchanging a couple of torsil nuts.

CHAPTER 39
Spasel Dust

We'll never find those starworts now," Opio declared. He picked up a stone and flung it into the Rondolyn.

"I, too, wish things had turned out differently," sighed King Rolin. He stroked Windsong's head. "I am sorry, dear friend. We've done our best." The griffin settled deeply into the river sand, as if to drown his misery in it.

Gathered in a grove of dead trees, the gloomy company stared at two stark tree-skeletons that stood apart from the others. Their sun-bleached limbs gleamed bone-white in morning's light.

"The river must have flooded and killed this part of the forest," said Bembor. "Are you certain this is the place?"

Llanwyn inclined her head. "Quite certain. I could never forget this spot. Burlion planted his *torsyl* nut on the left, and mine was on the right. How fair these trees must have been in life!"

Marlis said, "Now they live only in Meghan's spasel."

"We're sunk for sure," said Skoglund. "No ropes, no torsils, no starberries, and with sick sorcs, no way home except on foot."

"I'm going fishing," Ironwing said and slunk off. Windsong curled up and fell into a twitching sleep. Runt chased squirrels.

"Cheer up, everyone!" said Rolin. "With Gaelathane, things are never as bleak as they might seem. After all, thanks to His help, the Thalmosian army is no longer a threat. Let's ask Him what to do next." Then the king knelt and all his subjects with him.

"Thank You, Gaelathane, for bringing us this far," Rolin began. "You know how desperately our sorcs need more starberries, but we have no way to reach them—if they still exist. Please show us where to find some. Thank You. *Mae'r Goeden yn fyw!*"

"*Mae'r Goeden yn fyw!*" everyone echoed.

After a subdued breakfast of dewberries and pine nuts, the grownups chatted with Lyle and his men, while the young people built sandcastles on the riverbank. The first resembled the Hallowfast, only with a high wall around it. "The better to keep out the Thalmosians," Elwyn explained very seriously.

The second castle was even grander, boasting so many towers and turrets that Timothy had to prop them up with twigs. Meghan dug out little doors and windows. After congratulating each other on a job well done, the builders knocked down their handiwork. One thing led to another, and before you could say, 'Tower of the Tree,' a spirited sand war had broken out. Some of the castle ended up in Gwynneth's hair, courtesy of Timothy.

"You beast! You'll pay for that!" she cried. Her eyes flashing with delicious anger, she chased Timothy along the riverbank, driving him into a field of wet boulders. Before he could stop himself, Timothy slipped on a slime-slick rock and pitched backward into the sand. *Crrack!* Something gave way beneath him.

Gwynneth and Elwyn picked him up and brushed him off, finding all his bones intact. After feeling through his pockets, Timothy pulled out the flattened spasel in pieces. It was ruined.

Rolin wrapped an arm around his shoulders. "That's all right," he said. "It was an accident. Anyway, now that we've found the Golden Wood and Gwlân Gorge, we won't be needing the spasels any longer. In fact, we'll be leaving for home tomorrow."

"Not before you have picked your sorcs some starberries," said the Lady Llanwyn with a mischievous smile.

Ironwing ambled up, his beak full of wriggling fish. "Did someone say 'starberries'?" he asked. Curious-eyed, Windsong raised his sleep-rumpled head and yawned.

Bembor stared at Llanwyn. "What are you saying? We still cannot 'scale the wall,' as the Ballad of the Ball foretold."

The Guardian replied, "I am hoping you will not have to." Placing the pieces of Timothy's shattered spasel on a flat river rock, she began grinding them up with another stone.

"What is she doing?" Gwynneth whispered to Timothy.

"I don't know," he whispered back. "Maybe she's going to make a new spasel out of the old one."

Soon, the sap-pancake was reduced to a mound of amber powder. Briskly rubbing her hands together, Llanwyn brushed the last few grains of spasel dust onto the pile, which she scooped into a small bag from her gown. "Now I will need Meghan's *coedagrau* also."

Meghan clutched the spasel to her chest. "What for?" she asked.

The tall worldwalker knelt beside the princess. "Please trust me, dear girl," she said. Reluctantly, Meghan handed over the spasel.

In turn, Llanwyn laid it on a different flat rock and likewise pounded the solid sap to a fine powder. Meghan loudly wept all the while. "Now I can't see the golden trees anymore!" she wailed.

"Why are you destroying our spasels?" Rolin sternly demanded.

Dusting off her hands again, the Guardian replied, "It is necessary for your quest. Does anyone have another sack I could use?"

"I have one," said Timothy, offering her his gold-dust bag. Llanwyn promptly scraped Meghan's spasel-dust into it.

"There!" she said, holding up the two bags. "Now they are ready."

"Ready for what?" asked Timothy, perplexed.

"Ready for you," Llanwyn said, blinking her eyes in the sunlight. "I believe such a large amount might do for two."

King Rolin looked doubtful. "Two of what?"

"Why, two mortals, of course. I'll have to be extra careful with the sprinkling to divide the amounts evenly."

"Sprinkling?" repeated the young people.

"Sprinkling?" asked the grownups.

"Sprinkling?" growled the griffins.

"Let me show you what I mean," said the Guardian. She laid one of Ironwing's fish on a third river rock and dribbled several specks of the ground sap onto it from her pouch. The fish disappeared.

CHAPTER 40
Wort Haven

Magic!" cried Derwin hoarsely. He aimed a quivering finger at the Lady. "I knew it; she's a sorceress!"

"Nonsense," Bembor snorted. All the same, Lucambra's chancellor also appeared shaken by the vanishing fish.

Laughing merrily, the Lady Llanwyn hiked up her long skirts and capered around the grinding stone, her face flushed with triumph. "It worked! I was afraid the sap was too old. I had forgotten about this little trick." Seeing the others' shocked looks, she said, "I've always wanted to dance in the daylight. Now at last I've done it!"

"And may your lovely feet never falter," said Bembor gravely. "Tell us, though: What happened to the fish?"

Llanwyn replied, "In a pinch, if we Wood Folk cannot find a *torsyl*, we bring the *torsyl* to us, so to speak. A sprinkling of powdered sap is as good as climbing the tree itself, and much faster. We always carry some of it with us, just in case."

"What a clever idea!" Skoglund exclaimed. "Here we have been climbing torsils for years and never knew we could use spasel dust!"

Rolin chuckled softly. "So there's nothing magical about that dust at all. It's just another way of making passage!"

"Will this spasel powder work on anything?" asked Mycena.

"When applied to the uppermost parts, yes," said Llanwyn. "That's why I could safely handle the dust with my hands. Also, the larger the object, the more powder is required. We should have enough to send two small mortals into the canyon and back."

"Why not just send one person?" Lyle asked.

"Many things may go awry on such a venture," said Llanwyn darkly. "Besides, two can gather more starberries than one."

"How would they return afterwards?" asked Marlis.

Llanwyn answered, "The powder in my sack will take them down, and the bag with Meghan's dust will bring them back again. They only need to shake the 'used' dust out of their hair to prevent mixing. You do not wish to be in two places at the same time!"

Timothy squirmed under his friends' pointed looks. If his slight build held any advantages, he hadn't found them yet. Still, he wanted to see what might lie at the bottom of the gorge—if it had any bottom. The same curiosity burned in Elwyn's eyes.

"Timothy may go, but Elwyn's red hair would mask the spasel dust," said Llanwyn, as if reading their minds. Elwyn pouted as the Lady's gaze fell upon Meghan. "Too young." Then she nodded at Gwynneth. "She will do." Timothy's heart skipped a beat.

Fear-lines etched Marlis's face. "Not my daughter!" she cried in anguish. "I have just been reunited with Meghan; must I now lose Gwynneth also? Let another go in her stead!"

"Don't worry, Mother," Gwynneth declared. "I'll be all right. Gaelathane will be with me." Under her breath, she added, "First sand and now spasel dust. I'll never get my hair clean!"

"What about you, Timothy?" asked Rolin. "Are you willing?"

Timothy took a deep breath. "For the sorcs' sake, I will go." Lyle and his graybeards bobbed their heads in approval.

Everyone scrounged up some bags for collecting starberries and divided them between the two. Next, Llanwyn gave Timothy back his gold-dust bag to take with him and Gwynneth for the trip back. "When you are ready to return, you must not forget to sprinkle your heads—and the starberry bags—with the Meghan-dust *at the same time.* If you don't, one of you may be left behind.

"Now please stand back-to-back like twin trunks sprung from a single seed," she advised the pair. Then she emptied half her sack into her cradling palm and raised her long-fingered hands over their heads. "Keep your eyes closed, or the powder will get into them."

"Bring me back my fish!" Ironwing told Timothy.

Windsong snorted. "You can always catch more fish. What we need now is starberries, and lots of them!"

"We commit you to the Leaf Lord's watch-care," Llanwyn said. "May He speed your journey and bless you with success." Spasel dust poured from her fingers and pouch onto Timothy and Gwynneth.

As the sandy powder showered Timothy's head, he gripped Gwynneth's hand. Then his stomach lurched and he went falling into thunderous, leafy shadows. Gwynneth shrieked as the tree they landed in toppled over and they tumbled out. As he tried to steady himself, Timothy planted his hand on something slimy. It was Ironwing's fish.

"Agh!" he gargled. Reflecting that at least he wouldn't be returning empty handed, he stuffed the fish in his pocket. He was about to brush himself off when Gwynneth reminded him they needed to shake the spasel dust out of their hair to prevent mixing with Meghan's precious powder. Fortunately, most of those grains had already fallen out in the couple's topsy-turvy tumble.

They shivered, and not only from the damp chilliness. They were hemmed in by sheer cliff walls that soared to unguessable heights, blocking all but the dimmest daylight. Nearby flowed a river fed by a pool at the Liggion's base. Mist swirled in the air, beading moss and ferns with dewy droplets and coating the stones with an oily sheen.

Timothy groaned. "Now that our torsil has fallen over, nobody else can reach this spot, since we'll need all our spasel dust just to get back!" Weakened from years of poor light, the tree's spindly trunk had given way under Timothy and Gwynneth's combined weight.

"Then we'd better find those starworts," Gwynneth declared.

However, the spasel had given no clues as to where the plants grew. In vain, Gwynneth and Timothy poked about the cliff base. It was only when the shadows deepened that they noticed clouds of cross-shaped, luminescent blossoms floating on a carpet of whorl-leafed herbs.

"These must be the ones! We've found them!" cried Gwynneth. She jumped up and down and hugged Timothy for joy.

Reluctantly breaking away from the princess, Timothy knelt to smell the blossoms, savoring their sweet fragrance. Then he picked and ate one of the red berries.

"How does it taste?" asked Gwynneth anxiously.

"Sort of sour and sweet at the same time." Glancing up, Timothy noticed faint stars winking in the darkening strip of sky overhead, though the lands above still basked in the sun. "We'd better get to work before the daylight fails," he said.

Picking mainly by starflower light, the two filled their sacks with handfuls of firm, tart fruits. "I wish we had brought more sacks," said

Gwynneth as she tied off the last bag. "I'm afraid these few berries won't last long among so many sorcs."

"I've picked quite enough of them already, thank you very much," said Timothy as he rubbed his aching back. Why didn't starworts grow higher off the ground? "Besides, we may not have enough spasel dust to go around as it is." Lying on a springy starflower-bed, he gazed up at the pinprick stars. Would he and Gwynneth have to choose between saving themselves and sending the starberry sacks back? Shaking off his dread, he softly sang,

Starflower, starflower, starflowers sweet,
How fragrant your blooms beneath my feet;
Starflower, starflower, starflowers grow
Where waterfalls tumble and mist-rivers flow.

So long have we sought you o'er mountain and plain,
And how in this world shall we find you again?
Starflower, starflower, starflowers glow,
When shadows are gath'ring and sunlight is low.

Then your flowers shall fly to their place in the sky,
Where I'll watch them unfold when the twilight is nigh;
Starflower, starflower, starflowers blow,
Till your petals shall drop like the new-fallen snow.

"That was lovely!" said Gwynneth. "I didn't know you could sing." Her eyes were like deep pools ringed with starflowers.

"Neither did I. There's just something about this place that makes my heart dance and sing all at the same time."

"Mine, too," Gwynneth said, edging closer to him.

Timothy nervously cleared his throat. "I suppose we'd better get back before the others start worrying about us."

"Yes, I suppose so," sighed Gwynneth, not moving. "I hope there's enough spasel dust in that bag of yours, or we'll be stuck down here." Despite the darkness, Timothy caught her shy, sidelong glance. He patted his chest and felt his bag's reassuring bulge beneath his tunic.

"Eww, you smell like fish!" Gwynneth said, pinching her nose.

Timothy inwardly groaned. "Bother the fish!" he growled, digging it out of his pocket. He was about to fling it aside when he noticed the other half of his torsil nut clinging to its skin.

Fully formed, an idea leapt to his mind. "We never did finish the Ceremony of the Seeds, did we?" he said.

"Are you thinking what I'm thinking?" said Gwynneth, her voice breaking with excitement.

"Yes! Let's plant both half-nuts down here so we can come back again someday. The sorcs will need more starberries sooner or later." Dragging their bags with them, they worked their way downriver to a sheltered alcove where the starflowers grew thickly, lighting up the sloping sward as brightly as lilies under the moon.

"This would be a good spot, don't you think?" Gwynneth said.

Timothy nodded. "The light here is better than where we were, and the torsils will be close to these starflowers, too."

Together, they cleared a patch of sandy earth where they lovingly planted the pair of half-nuts. "At least one of these should grow," Gwynneth whispered.

"I hope so," said Timothy. He was tamping the dirt over the nuts when a giant, moth-like shape silently swooped down and landed among the starflowers. As the thing raised its dish-faced, horned head, Gwynneth shrieked. It was a moonsorc.

CHAPTER 41
The Valley of No Return

*H*oo! *Hoo!* Whooo are you?" hooted the sorc. "Begone, two-legs! These berries belong to us."

Timothy quailed before the griffin's huge yellow eyes and wicked beak. Collecting his courage, he said, "We're not picking for ourselves. Our friends need them."

"Whooo friends? What friends? Do you mean the sunsorcs? All the more reason to drive you off!" With a warbling cry, the sorc called down other silent, winged shapes. Tails lashing and beaks gnashing, they stalked toward Timothy and Gwynneth.

"Shoo, sorcs, shoo!" shouted Timothy, flapping his hands. The creatures kept coming. Grabbing Gwynneth's arm, he ran.

As the two raced along the river, Gwynneth panted, "The spasel . . . dust . . . sprinkle . . . now!"

With the moonsorcs bounding close behind, Timothy ripped the bag off his neck and was about to open it when a griffin knocked him to the ground. The sack went flying into the river.

"Oh, no!" wailed Gwynneth as the pouch floated away into the darkness. Snatching up a stick, she began beating the moonsorc with it. "Now look what you've done! Thanks to you, we can't go home!" She was still thrashing the griffin when it broke away and slunk back to rejoin its companions. Chattering in their own tongue, the owlish moonsorcs stared at Gwynneth.

"Now what's the matter?" she said. "You ought to be ashamed of yourselves, picking on us like that!" As she punctuated each word with a finger-stab, the sorcs focused on her hand.

"It's your ring, Gwyn," Timothy said softly. "They must like your ring." Gwynneth glanced down at her hand. Queen Winona's ring was glowing more fiercely than a thousand starflowers.

"*Hoo*—where did you get that?" the largest sorc demanded.

"It was my great-grandmother Winona's, Queen of Lucambra," Gwynneth stiffly replied. "Now it is mine. Why? Would you claim this also as your own?" The moonsorcs conferred again.

"Nay, good lady," replied the griffin. "My name is Moonwing. *Hoo!* On behalf of my comrades, I apologize for our most unseemly behavior. We did not know you were the Ringmaiden."

Puzzled, Timothy and Gwynneth looked at each other and then back at the sorc. "Ringmaiden?" asked Gwynneth.

Moonwing bowed his head. "Forgive me; I see you are not familiar with our *hoostory*. When our kind broke faith with your King Elgathel, we were banished from the Willowahs to live in the Dyggorech—the frigid Moooon Mountains. Ever since that dreadful day, we have fought to reclaim our ancestral home."

"What does this have to do with Gwynneth?" Timothy asked.

"Patience, small one!" keened Moonwing. "After our exile, the One you two-legs call 'Gaelathane' appeared to us with a message of—*hoo!*—hope. 'You shall return to your beloved birthplace after the passing of many years,' He said. 'Here are the signs:

When red the maw and cruel the claw attacking kith and kin,
No warring might nor bitter fight shall win your home again;
For first you must submit to her who wears the hallowed ring;
Who from of old bears with the gold the blessed, shining thing.

Now all the moonsorcs bowed as one. "*Hoo!* We now await your commands, Ringmaiden, that we may obey them."

Flummoxed, Gwynneth looked down at her hand and then back at the moonsorcs. "As the ah, Ringmaiden, I must ask you to fly us out of this canyon. We have lost our spasel dust, you see."

Blinking his round eyes owlishly, Moonwing answered, "We would gladly carry you wherever you wished, but—*hoo!*—not from this place. Treacherous wind currents pass between these narrow cliff walls, and you would risk death to ride us hence."

"Then can you at least take a few of our berry bags up to the top?" asked Gwynneth. "Our friends the sunsorcs await us there. Please do them no harm, for they are very ill."

"As you wish," said Moonwing, hooding his eyes.

Several moonsorcs trotted back to pick up some of the sacks of starberries. As they flew off into the dark mists, Timothy turned to the princess. "You know what this means, don't you?" he said.

A tear rolled down her cheek. "Yes. We cannot leave."

"Perhaps I may be of some—*hoo!*—assistance," cooed one of the moonsorcs. "My name is Shortneck." *An apt name*, Timothy thought. "What does this—*hoo!*—'spasel dust' look like?"

Timothy described the powder and the fate of his neck-pouch. "It's gone for good now," he said morosely as he sat down by the river.

Shortneck's head comically swiveled. "You are most probably right. The *Garwafon*, 'River of No Return,' does not willingly give up its boooty. Eventually it plunges into another chasm even deeper than this one, I'm told." Then the moonsorc flew off.

"No matter," Gwynneth remarked. She joined Timothy on the riverbank. "We have done what we came here for, haven't we, *cariad*? That's all that really counts. Gaelathane will take care of us."

The two sat in silence for a long while. "I just hope we don't have to live on starberries," Timothy finally said. "They have tiny seeds that lodge between my teeth. And I think we ought to call this place 'the Valley of No Return.'"

A moonsorc fluttered to the ground beside them and shook some water out of his fur. "I should think 'Starberry Valley' would make a more—*hoo!*—suitable name, don't you?" said Shortneck. He dropped a soggy brown sack on the sand.

"The spasel dust!" Gwynneth cried. "Where did you find it?"

"Snagged on a branch in the river, it was," said the sorc with a modest blink. "A two-legs pointed it out to me. *Hoo!* I never would have seen it otherwise."

"Thank you, Shortneck!" Gwynneth told him. "But *another* two-legs? Could someone else have climbed down from above?"

"Who knows?" said Timothy. Squeezing the water out of the bag, he knelt on the riverbank and opened it. "Why, it's brim full of spasel dust!" he exclaimed. "How did that happen?"

Gwynneth laughed and cried by turns, taking Timothy aback. "It was Gaelathane, of course!" She held out her hand and Timothy shook half the spasel dust into it, saving the rest for himself.

"Oh, no!" Clutching her fistful of powder, Gwynneth stared at Timothy with raw fear in her eyes.

"What's wrong?" Timothy asked her.

"I just realized that we could travel down here because the torsil was still alive. But how can we return if both torsils up there are dead?"

Timothy's heart went cold. *How indeed?*

"I suppose we'll just have to try using the spasel dust anyway," he croaked. "If it works, it works. If not…." He didn't relish the prospect of being trapped in the Gwlân Gorge for the rest of his life, even if he was with Gwynneth. Raw fish and starberries made poor fare.

Gwynneth's face brightened. "Meghan's spasel still showed the golden torsils, even though its tree was long dead. Maybe that means the powder can take us back to the same spot."

With a shiver, Timothy replied, "Let's hope so! But don't forget about the starberry bags. We'll need to sprinkle dust on them, too."

He and Gwynneth formed the remaining sacks into a tight circle. Then Gwynneth pulled Timothy into the ring's center.

"We'll need to stand close together, so the dust can fall on the bags as well as on us," she reminded him.

Timothy happily obliged, this time coming face-to-face with the Lucambrian princess. He gazed into her sea-green eyes, twin spasels that drew him into their limpid depths. His head spun and his heart thudded. With trembling fingers, he caressed Gwynneth's soft, smooth cheek. Then while the starflowers shone round their feet like fallen stars, they embraced and their lips met and clung.

In the midst of the murmuring river stood a shining Man, a faint smile creasing His face. In each hand He held a bright star. Cupping His palms, He made the two stars into one, which soared into the heavens. As He raised His arms in blessing, Timothy and Gwynneth also raised their powder-filled fists over each other's heads, releasing twin clouds of glittering spasel dust that also rained down on the bags.

CHAPTER 42
Reconciliation

I'd say those two found more than just starberries down there!" Emmer observed with a chuckle.

Meghan made rude smooching sounds with her pursed lips. "How long can they hold their breath?" she teased.

Timothy's eyes flew open. The other Seekers grinned back at him in the thickening dusk.

"They make a fine couple," Bembor remarked with a sentimental look in his rheumy eyes.

"Indeed they do," murmured the king, his own eyes watering. "Timothy already looks the part of a prince."

"A Thalmosian prince," Sigarth told him with a wry smile.

"And look—they brought us more sacks of starberries!" Windsong exclaimed. He trotted over to stick his head into a bag.

Still embracing Gwynneth, Timothy roguishly whispered, "Are you really a tree-spirit, Gwyn?"

"Of course not, silly boy! If I were, what would it matter?"

"I'd have to hold you until the sunrise made you mortal!"

"Then I suppose we'll just be standing here all night, *cariad*," she replied with mock resignation and snuggled closer.

"What about my fish?" Ironwing broke in.

Timothy turned to point at one of the sacks. "It's right on top there, and welcome to it," he said, wrinkling his nose.

"Don't make yegs of yourselves," Moonwing told the sunsorcs. "Just a cupful of berries will do." Windsong, Ironwing and Runt looked up from the bags, their beaks dripping red with starberry juice.

The other moonsorcs sat by, silently watching. Tearing herself away from Timothy, Gwynneth doled out a few berries to each. Then she and Timothy made them a gift of a full bag.

"*Hoo!* Such a quantity would take us weeks to gather, for our beaks are not nearly so nimble as your fingers," said Moonwing. "I shall share these with our—*hoo!*—kin as a token of our renewed allegiance to Elgathel's heir and to the Ringmaiden."

Rolin smiled. "Your noble deed this day has washed away the shame of your former faithlessness. Lift up your heads and rejoice! At the behest of the Ringmaiden, we have one more request of you." He raised his arm, and Windsong, Ironwing and Runt trotted over to their cousins. Hackle feathers raised on sorc-necks, while eagle's and owl's eyes met in murderous glares.

"You are all griffins," the king told them. "Though some of you prefer the night and others the day, you share much in common. Now put aside your ancient differences and be reconciled!"

"The thing you are asking is very *hoo!*—hard," said Moonwing. "Bitterness runs deep within our hearts. How can we forgive the wrongs these mangy fur-bags have done us?"

"Don't forget theirs against us!" snarled Ironwing.

"Much blood has been shed on both sides," Rolin admitted. "Yet, I say to you that if your house remains divided, your race shall decline and pass away from this fair land. Fell beasts will inhabit your holes and dens, and your memory shall linger only in children's tales and dim legend. However, if you should consent to live again in harmony, then you shall prosper, and your descendants will inherit the high places and mountain strongholds. Do this not for me, but for the love of Gaelathane and for the Ringmaiden whom you also now serve."

The moonsorcs hooted and screeched among themselves. Then Moonwing spoke again. "If we did sheath our claws, what assurance have we that our enemies would do the same? We have little to gain and everything to lose by such a bargain."

Rolin turned to his own griffins. "What say you, dear friends? Will you lay down your old hatreds?"

"To what end?" Ironwing said. "These 'owl-heads' will multiply in our dens and tunnels and drive us out! They have homes of their own; let them live there."

Just then, Meghan pattered up to her father. "What's all the fuss about?" she asked. Before Rolin could answer, one of the moonsorcs bounded over and knocked her down, licking her face.

"Stop it!" she giggled. "You're tickling me!"

"What is the meaning of this?" Rolin loudly demanded.

The moonsorc reluctantly let Meghan up. "I most humbly beg your—*hoo!*—pardon," he said with a heavy-lidded blink. "My name is Sleepyeye." The griffin went on to describe his earlier encounter with Meghan. "So you see, friends, I owe my—*hoo!*—life to her."

He bowed to Meghan. "Upon the wood of the Tree, I pledge my faith and service to you until death parts us."

Rolin took Meghan's hand. "Seeing how matters stand, will your people bury their grudges not only for the Ringmaiden's sake, but also for her sister's—and Gaelathane's?"

Sleepyeye hesitated. Then he padded over to Runt and nuzzled him. Runt returned the gesture. Soon, Sleepyeye was gabbing with all three sunsorcs as if they had been litter-mates.

The other moonsorcs hastily put their heads together. Then Moonwing came forward again. "We will reconcile with our brothers, but only if we are allowed to return to the Willowahs."

The sunsorcs conferred. At last, Windsong spoke. "I will carry these terms of peace back to our king," he said. "We three cannot speak for him. However, if you will pledge fealty to Whitewing and abide by the Code of Threeclaws, you may find more hearts among us open than not. Perhaps it is time to heal old wounds and reforge our old alliance. For my part, I am weary of these petty wars between us."

Moonwing bowed. "As are we, good Windsong. Having lived so many generations without a true—*hoo!*—king of our own, we would gladly acknowledge Whitewing as our sovereign and follow the Code of Threeclaws. How then shall we seal our pact?"

"Will you swear upon the Maiden's ring?" asked Rolin. Clacking their beaks, the griffins consented. As Gwynneth stretched out her left hand, Winona's ring shone like a small moon fallen from the heavens. Moonwing and Windsong laid their left paws upon it.

"On behalf of your races, do you, Moonwing of the moon and Windsong of the sun, solemnly swear to abide in peace, unity and brotherly love, so long as you both shall live?"

"We do, as Gaelathane is our witness," they replied. Then the two sorcs reared on their hind legs and pressed front paws together in the ancient griffanic ritual of goodwill.

So it was that the rival sorc races took their first small steps toward becoming one again. Ironwing, Windsong and Runt spent the next few days sampling starberries and talking with their cousins. The three sorcs' recovery was little short of miraculous. After two days of berry-munching, their neck feathers began sprouting back, thick and brown, followed on the third day by crisp new wing feathers.

On the morning of the fifth day, they tested their wings and found them "fresher than a griffling's," as Ironwing put it. The next day, Midge and Derwin left for the Goldwood on Maggie, while the other two-legs flew there on sorc-back. Long beards streaming behind them, Lyle and his friends whooped and shouted the whole way. After moonrise, Llanwyn assembled everyone on Medwyn's torsil knoll, where many worldwalkers and moonsingers were already waiting.

The Lady explained, "I have brought you here because Derwin son of Stolland has asked to see his brother's resting place. It is close by."

Then she led the solemn throng through the woods to a massive granite mound. A dark opening yawned in one side.

Entering the portal, Scanlon and Emmer shone their staffs into the cave's dark corners. "There's nobody in here," they said.

Then Llanwyn pointed out a narrow passage concealed at the back of the cavern. Squeezing through it, the Seekers discovered a hidden chamber filled with hundreds of men laid out on stone benches. All were wrapped in open-eyed greed-sleep.

"Here's my poor brother," said Derwin in a choking voice. "He may as well be dead." Asper lay motionless with hands folded across his chest, his eyes blankly staring into space.

"We bring the mangle-bitten ones here to protect them from the weather and wild beasts," Medwyn said. "So shall they sleep until the Leaf Lord restores all things at the end of days."

"Then farewell, dear brother," Derwin wept. "May yer sleep be deep and yer dreams sweet." Sadly, the company filed out of the cave and into the moonlight. They found an old man in a hooded white cloak waiting for them.

"Why, it's Andil of the Wood!" exclaimed Derwin.

"That is how you first knew Me, yes," said the King. He extended His arms toward the cave and cried, "Come forth, you wandering, weary sheep who lie in silent, deathlike sleep!"

A sigh escaped the cave. Then Thalmosian men-at-arms began tumbling out, blinking in the bright moonlight with befuddled looks. "Snakes! Where did them snakes get to? Three of them bit me!" one said, staring wildly about.

"What happened to my gold leaves?" said another. "I had a whole fistful just a minute ago. I'm about to become a rich man!"

"It's Andil of the Wood!" a third cried. The sleepers fell back as Gaelathane shed His disguise and raised His arms again.

"The man who would be truly free, come out to Me from empty tree!" He called in ringing tones. Shadows oozed out of torsil trunks, taking on human form and feature as they gathered about Gaelathane. Others retreated back into their trees.

The former captives bowed before Him. "Thank You for rescuing us," they said. "Who are You, and what must we do now?"

"I am called Gaelathane, the King of the Trees," He said, and He showed them His scars. "In My love I sought you, and with My blood I bought you for My kingdom. I ask only that you follow Me."

When the men promised to obey Him all their days, Gaelathane told them, "I advise you to buy from Me imperishable gold seven times refined that will not crumble or pass away like these leaves. Then you shall be truly rich in Me."

Gaelathane pointed to the Tree of trees, which had reappeared where Timothy had "planted" it. "My Tree is your only way home now. You'll find no gold or diamonds among its limbs, but in climbing it, you may catch a glimpse of Gaelessa's greater wealth."

As the leaf-pickers streamed toward the Tree, one man fell on his knees before Derwin. "I have treated you shamefully these many years," said Asper. "Please pardon this black and bitter heart of mine!" Tearfully, the two embraced.

"All is forgiven," Derwin told his brother. "I think ye owe Missy here an apology, too. Ye can thank her for introducing us both to Gaelathane. He's a true gentleman amongst us poor ruffians."

"Derwin is right, Meghan," Asper confessed. "I had no excuse for hurting you as I did. Fear and greed can twist a man's mind and make him a beast. Can you find it in your heart to forgive me?"

Meghan solemnly nodded and shook the captain's proffered hand. "I do forgive you," she said. "Don't forget Gaelathane loves you!"

"I won't!" Asper promised with a joyful laugh. "I'm going to tell the whole world about Andil of the Wood, that is, Gaelathane, the King of the Trees! I am also leaving Mardoc's army."

"That's better!" said Derwin. "When you and I meet again, Brother, I dare say we'll have some real tales to swap."

Asper's face fell. "You won't be joining me and my men?"

Derwin shook his head. "I'm staying here until winter to help build cottages for the worldwalkers with some of the fallen timber. It's what I do best, and one way I can make amends for their loss. We'll see where Gaelathane leads me after that."

The two parted with many expressions of affection. Swarming up the Tree, Asper and his men sang in deep, lusty voices,

We have seen Him in His glory,
He Who made the moon and stars;
We shall live to tell the story
Of the love that left His scars.

When He speaks to us in thunder,
We'll obey His sweet commands;
Precious souls our peaceful plunder;
Highest joy to bear His brands.

Gold and silver lose their luster
When we look upon His face;
Pride and power all but bluster
In the presence of His grace.

Onward, men, to higher calling,
Climb the Tree to seize the prize;
Help the sick, the weak, the falling,
Heed their hurting, helpless cries.

By His death we are forgiven,
By His life we all shall gain;
By the gifts He's freely given
One day with Him we will reign.

As the men ascended the Tree, golden angels appeared among its bright branches, singing in aching harmony as they flew.

Glory, glory, glory to the mighty, risen King,
Let creation worship Him and highest praises sing;
All His ways are just and true to them that love His name;
Those whom He has called to life shall never be the same!

See the men who once despised the Leaf Lord and His love;
Now in faith they climb the one Limb leading to Above;
Who can fully fathom such a sacrifice He made,
So that all the living might no longer be afraid?

Glory, glory, glory to the mighty, risen King,
From Whose heart at the very start sprang every living thing;
Let all the trees of all His worlds in worship wave their hands;
The number of His wondrous works is countless as the sands.

Let the gold and silver seekers leave their selfish ways,
To yield their lives in service to the Leaf Lord all their days;
Who of them can help but fall in homage at His feet,
Knowing that in Gaelathane their hearts are made complete?

Glory, glory, glory to the Tree for two-legs slain;
Suffering the axe that men from evil should refrain;
Taking on mortality and every worldly woe;
In spilling out its lifeblood, it has vanquished every foe.

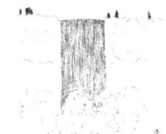

CHAPTER 43
Love is Lord and Death is Dead

I t's your turn, Meghan," whispered Gwynneth. "Walk slowly; don't be afraid and for pity's sake, don't trip in the dark! I'll be right behind you, but don't look back. Everything will be fine."

Clutching a bouquet of white moonflowers, Meghan strolled down twin ranks of whispering moonsingers to join her father at the head of the receiving lines. Beside Rolin stood Gaelathane, Scanlon and the Lady Llanwyn. Gwynneth followed, bearing a folded green cloak that cushioned two rings of gold, which the memerren had taken from enemies of old.

Last of all came Medwyn, her simple white gown shimmering in the moonlight, a shining Tree-bough circlet in her hair. Wading through the piling flowers that her sisters tossed in her path, the nymph beamed with joy.

It was the first wedding between any mortal and worldwalker that Lucambra had seen in many a year, and all the moonsingers in the Goldwood had come out to watch. Many wore flowers in their hair for the occasion. Even Longears the rabbit brought his kin, who nibbled on the bouquets and generally got in everyone's way.

Though nervous as a hare in a sorc's den, Scanlon remembered what to say and when to say it (with Rolin's help). Rings, vows and kisses were exchanged before Gaelathane bestowed His marriage blessing on the couple. Afterwards, Scanlon turned to his best man. "If you can get along without me for a few months, I'd like to remain here with Medwyn," he said. "Her friends will need my help to prepare food and shelter for the winter."

Rolin slapped him on the back and winked at Timothy. "I give you my leave and my blessing. Just don't be surprised if you return home to find that Timothy has taken over your post!"

Towards dawn, Timothy was attempting to nap beneath a tree when someone touched him. It was the Lady Llanwyn. "Please come with me," she whispered and led him to the foot of the Tree. She laid her hand upon its glowing trunk.

"What are we doing here?" Timothy asked.

Llanwyn patted his cheek. "I am going to live in Gaelathane's land, and I wanted you to know it, Relic-Bearer."

Timothy staggered backward. "What?! But why? There is still so much to do, and you haven't yet seen the Tower of the Tree, or the Sea of El-marin, or Thalmos, or—"

The Guardian of the Golden Wood smiled at him and shook her head. "Dear boy, the world is changing, and my treeless people need your race's wisdom more than mine. I have fulfilled my life's purpose here. Besides, I am weary of this mortal body, and the sun burns my eyes and skin. It is time to move higher."

Tears welled in Timothy's eyes as he knelt and took Llanwyn's hand. "Please don't go! Your people do still need you—now more than ever—and so do we. Anyway, I had wanted to ask you more about moonsingers. If you leave, I'll never have the chance."

"Of course you will, when you join me in Gaelessa one day. In the meantime, your weeping willow can tell you all you wish to know about the hidden lives of trees and memerren."

"My willow? How did you know I live near a willow tree?"

Llanwyn laughed musically. "Word travels swiftly among our folk." She looked Timothy in the eye. "My work in this world is done. However, yours has just begun. I am appointing you to take up where I left off by helping tend this forest. Having lived as a tree, even briefly, you know our needs better than most mortals do." Timothy started to object, but Llanwyn forged on.

"I would not leave you without some reward for your labors. While the Tree still stands here, you may pick all the golden leaves you wish. Do not take a few, mind you!"

"But—the mangles!"

"They will not disturb you," said the Lady as she climbed into the Tree. "Farewell, young Timothy son of Garth, until we meet again!" Her gossamer cloak floated down on the words, "For Gwynneth!" Timothy was picking up the cloak when he heard voices.

"I'm hurrying as fast as I can," someone grumbled.

"Then hurry faster," retorted another. "We don't know how much longer it will remain here." Then all twelve of Elmar's men straggled out of the woods. Seeing Timothy, they stopped in their tracks with the guilty looks of small boys skipping school.

"What are you doing here?" they demanded.

"I should ask you the same thing," Timothy coolly replied.

Hemming and hawing, Lyle finally confessed, "My mates and I want to get away from this wood and its treacherous torsils. That's why we're going up the Tree to see what we can see."

"Then may your travels be pleasant," said Timothy. Standing aside, he watched the stooped, bearded men clamber up the Tree's shining trunk and into its spiraling branches. "Good-bye!" he called up to them. "Don't climb any more empty trees!"

"We won't," Lyle called back. "Thank you again for freeing me!"

As the men climbed out of sight, Timothy slumped against the Tree. How many more of his companions would desert him? He idly wondered whether he should return home by climbing the Tree, too. Just then, Gwynneth appeared, her face pale in morning's first light.

Timothy's heart sank. "Are you going away, too?"

Gwynneth laughed. "Of course not. Lyle and his little band of friends were acting a bit strangely, so I thought I'd better tag along. Were you also following them?"

In a cracking voice, Timothy told her about Llanwyn. "Why did she have to leave?" he cried. "She was so good and kind and noble. What will the world be without her?"

"Alas, the poorer," Gwynneth agreed. "For now, though, let's pick some of these golden leaves before Waganupa disappears. We can save them as mementos of our journey." With that, she reached up and plucked a leaf from the nearest tree.

"Look out!" Timothy cried. But as Llanwyn had promised, no green snakes slithered out of the treetops. Taking heart, the two picked handfuls of leaves and stuffed them in their pockets.

Minutes later, the Tree faded away, leaving Scanlon's staff still standing in the ground. After plucking up the rod, Timothy wrapped Llanwyn's cloak around Gwynneth and walked hand-in-hand with her back through the moonlit trees, singing,

---

Lady Llanwyn, Queen of trees,
Her hair of silver starlight spun;
She loved the moon; she shunned the sun,
And left me weeping on my knees.

Lady Llanwyn—Gaelessa's gain!
No one could find a finer friend
When Golden Wood she did defend,
As guardian of His domain.

The Keeper of the Wood has fled,
To meet the Maker of all things;
With angels chorusing she sings
Where love is lord and death is dead.

Why weep we now? The Lady lives;
For we shall go to her in time,
The day when we are called to climb
The Tree of trees that glory gives.

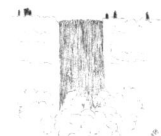

CHAPTER 44
Whitewing's Final Flight

S omber were the farewells the next day as the Seekers took their leave of Midge, Maggie, Scanlon and Medwyn, who would be helping Derwin build the worldwalkers winter cottages.

"Good-bye, Missy!" Derwin told Meghan, hoisting her high. "I shall miss ye. Do not forget me when ye grow up!"

Meghan threw her arms around the woodcutter's neck and kissed him. "I won't, Uncle Derwin. Don't forget me, either!"

Derwin was wiping his eyes when Rolin told him, "You will always be welcome in Lucambra and in our home. Next time you visit, though, I hope you'll leave Mardoc's army behind!"

Having sent the three sunsorcs ahead with sacks of starberries, the Seekers mounted some moonsorcs and flew northward. Riding on Moonwing, Timothy looked back at the golden slash in the earth. "Farewell, blessed Goldwood," he cried, grieving for all the axe-hewn moonsingers who would never see another spring. He vowed that if Gaelathane willed it, he would return to carry on Llanwyn's work.

On their arrival at the griffins' lair, the visitors were escorted to the royal hall, where Keeneye, Runt, Windsong and Ironwing greeted them. A lone white feather lay on the ominously empty throne.

"Greetings, friends," croaked the bedraggled king's courier. "For bringing us starberries, you have earned our everlasting gratitude and praise. I wish King Whitewing could thank you personally." Then Keeneye noticed the moonsorcs. His beak fell open and his feathers bristled with fear. "Who are—? Why are—?"

Moonwing bowed. "Forgive this—*hoo!*—untimely intrusion, O noble Keeneye," he gravely began. "My companions and I have come seeking reconciliation with the servants of King Whitewing, whom we also hope to serve. May we see him now?"

Keeneye's head and tail drooped. "Woe is us! You are all too late. Our king has flown into the arms of Gaelathane. This very morning we found him lying lifeless in his den."

"Alas!" cried Rolin, covering his face. "He was such a great-hearted griffin and true. The world will never see his like again. Were it not for him, Scanlon and I could not have fulfilled Gaelathane's Prophecy."

Sagging on his lightstaff, Bembor murmured, "May the king find an abundance of fat conies to chase in Gaelessa."

"I beg your pardon!" huffed Longears, who had hitched a ride on Moonwing with Timothy and was hiding behind Marlis.

Timothy wept. "Who will become king now?" he asked.

"Ai! Ai! Ai!" cried Keeneye. "Whitewing's heirs have all perished of the scorbies, and his throne grows cold. Worse yet, we are too weak to perform the Ceremony of Final Flight for him."

Before Timothy could ask what Keeneye meant, a fluttering sound signaled the moonsorcs' abrupt departure. "Our moon-brothers have returned to their own place," Windsong wailed.

"Good riddance to the owl-heads, I say," grunted Ironwing.

"Come, dear friends," said Keeneye. "You must be weary from your many ordeals. Brave deeds are done, and it is time to rest." Too worn out to argue, Timothy and his friends trailed the sorc to an empty cavern, where they found straw mats already laid out.

"This will do nicely," yawned Opio as he collapsed onto a mat and began to snore. Before Keeneye could quietly back out of the chamber, most of the Lucambrians were already asleep.

Awakening early, the travelers had just finished a filling breakfast of pine nuts when Keeneye returned. "I have just conferred with our council," he told them. "We all agree that the time has come to show you the resting place of our departed king."

Following Keeneye through dim tunnels and up a treacherous trail, the Seekers came to a lofty peak where snow still lurked in the shadows. "What a marvelous view!" Marlis said. "You can see west to the El-marin and north all the way to the Forlorn Fens."

Mycena cried, "That nub must be the Hallowfast! How I wish we were home again, safe and sound." A tear etched her cheek.

"I'm sure the sorcs will be happy to oblige, once they recover their wings," Bembor said with a kindly wink.

"Until Whitewing's death," said Keeneye, "neither commonsorc nor any two-legs (save Rolin son of Gannon) had ever set foot on this sacred spot." He nodded toward a dark wound in the earth. "Down there lies a secret cave where we will entomb the king's body with the hallowed Wilith of Luralin. Fearing the cave's secrets would die with him, Whitewing left us a map revealing its location. From this day forth, the King's Cave will be open for all to view."

As he spoke, a thrumming cloud rose in the northeast, eclipsing the sun. With the thunder of a million beating wings, a host of griffins converged on the peak. The moonsorcs had returned.

"Block the tunnels! Bar the gates!" the sentries screeched.

"Our enemies have come!" wailed Keeneye. "They are attacking us before we can partake of the starberries. Alas! We are undone!"

Breaking away from the circling moonsorcs, a lone figure alit nearby. "Friends and brothers," cried Moonwing. "Be not alarmed. My people and I come not in war, as you might suppose, but to share your sorrow and—*hoo!*—your joy. Since we could not swear allegiance to Whitewing during his life, we shall do so in his death. Please, let us now perform the Ceremony of Final Flight for him."

Keeneye's beak fell open in his astonishment. "Thank you!" he managed to reply. Then he warbled piercingly, and four sunsorcs—Sharptongue, Broadwing, Spearwind and Flamefeather—emerged from the cave bearing a blue-wrapped burden, which they gently laid on the ground. Unfolding the sheet, they revealed King Whitewing's body, his sightless, milky eyes set like pearls in his serene features.

"The king will now fly over his beloved mountains for the last time," Keeneye told his guests. "Mind your heads!"

After securing the blue sheet's edges with heavy stones, the four griffins returned to the cave. Meanwhile, Moonwing's relatives had packed themselves into a spinning column of blurring bodies that towered into the thin blue sky. Increasing its speed, the sorc-cyclone kicked up clouds of rocks and sand.

Anchored by the stones, the sheet billowed and snapped like a ship's sail. Then Whitewing stirred and rose into the air. Caught in the tornado's dusty updraft, he shot up through the center of the whirling sorcs, his wings flapping as they had in life. Emerging at the top, he floated weightlessly high above the mountains.

"May King Whitewing soar on wings of light!" Keeneye keened. Multitudes of sunsorcs and moonsorcs took up the plaintive cry, which echoed hauntingly among the frowning rocks.

As the vortex widened and slowed, Whitewing spiraled back down the middle until he returned to earth. The living tornado dispersed, its moonsorcs settling on crags and ridges.

"That was beautiful!" breathed Gwynneth.

"Now we will lay our king to rest," said Keeneye, his eyes moist. Beneath the sun-slanting sky, Whitewing's pallbearers rewrapped him in his blue shroud. Then with slow, stately steps, they bore his body down the mountainside and into the King's Cave.

CHAPTER 45
Redwing Son of Whitewing

That evening, the Seekers feasted in the Riders' Room, a cavern where sorcs of old hosted griffin-riders. From its wide window, the sun's dying rays fell upon the painted rock walls, illumining lifelike scenes of the sorc-riders' aerial battles with the dragon.

"What will you do now without a king?" Timothy asked Keeneye, who was looking quite dejected.

"The sorcathon will reconvene later tonight to discuss that very matter. Since Whitewing was the last of Threeclaws' line, choosing a new king will be difficult. For time out of mind, all of our monarchs have arisen from the lineage of Threeclaws."

The next morning, the visitors were escorted to the royal chamber, which fairly bristled with sorcs of both varieties. The king's courier and twenty-three other elders flanked Whitewing's throne, vacant but for his soros and jeweled crown lying upon it.

When his guests were properly seated, Keeneye reared on his hind legs and announced, "In the name of the One Tree and before the Maker of all things, this sorcathon is now in session. Let all that is said and done here bring honor to the King of the Trees and peace and prosperity to sorca everywhere!"

"May the Name be ever blessed," chorused the other elders.

"We are met this day to welcome back our exiled Brothers of the Moon," Keeneye went on. "May their owls' beaks be strong and their feathers long!" Deafening click-clacks erupted in the room.

When the racket had died down, Keeneye nodded at the empty throne. "On this solemn occasion, we must also crown a king in place of Whitewing—may his wings never wither! After careful search and in accordance with the laws of this realm, this council has determined that the heir-apparent is . . . *Runt son of Broadbeak*. Is he present?"

A shocked silence fell over the gathering. Then every tongue wagged and beak clicked with astonishment. Propelled forward by his companions' legs and wings, Runt skidded to a stop before the throne and huddled there, nervously preening himself.

With a stern glint in his eye, Keeneye asked, "Are you in fact the sorc known as Runt son of Broadbeak?"

"You know very well I am," retorted Runt. "You all ought to be ashamed for putting on this *carlomon*, this charade, in front of our honored guests. Have your fun at my expense if you will, but not in this hallowed hall nor on such a high occasion."

His feathers bristling at Runt's rebuke, Keeneye snapped, "This is no charade; I will explain all in good time. Now, are you willing to serve as our sovereign, or must we seek another?"

After composing himself, Runt answered, "I am willing—but why me? Am I not the least in my father's den?"

Keeneye replied, "We have just learned that Broadbeak—may his wings never falter—is not your actual father. While yet a griffling, you were removed from the last royal litter and placed under Broadbeak's care, should anything untoward befall Whitewing's other offspring. Now you are his sole surviving heir."

More startled outcries interrupted Keeneye. Motioning for silence, he addressed Runt again. "Henceforth, as befits your royal rank, you shall be known as 'King Redwing son of Whitewing.' In honor of the griffin-friend King Elgathel, I will now ask Bembor son of Brenthor to administer the Coronation Oaths."

As a stunned Redwing raised his trembling left paw, Bembor raised his left hand and began, "Redwing son of Whitewing, in the presence of Gaelathane and these witnesses, do you solemnly swear to serve your King with a whole heart and to uphold His laws; to promote peaceful relations between our races; to aid our mutual friends and oppose our mutual enemies; to lift up the weak and helpless; and to place your subjects' welfare above your own?"

Redwing swallowed nervously. "I do."

"Then repeat after me: 'In the name of Gaelathane, I, Redwing son of Whitewing, being of sound mind and sober spirit, do hereby accept my forefathers' crown, which I swear to wear and cherish in all truth and humility until the end of my days.'" When Redwing had finished repeating the oath, Bembor reverently placed the gogoniant-studded crown on his eagle's head. Then Rolin picked up the soros from the throne and solemnly looped it over the new king's neck.

"As I once gifted this to your father, so I also do now for his son," Lucambra's king told Redwing, who beamed with delight.

"King Redwing, you may now ascend your throne," Bembor told him. No longer a cowed runt but a dignified monarch, the sorc settled on the golden chair, his chest swelling with pride.

"Long live King Redwing!" screeched the sunsorcs. "Long live King Redwing!" hooted the moonsorcs. When Keeneye had restored order, Redwing said, "I wish to thank my friends for their kindness, especially Timothy son of Garth, who always made me feel full sized, though his feet dragged when he rode me!"

Sorcs and two-legs were still chuckling when Keeneye brought in a slender, cloth-covered bundle. Then he and the new king held a whispered consultation.

"Timothy son of Garth, please come forward," said Redwing with a sly glint in his eagle's eyes. As Timothy approached the throne, the king deftly unwrapped the bundle. Inside was a short sword sheathed in a jeweled scabbard.

"Keeneye tells me this is a *breggiath*, a 'rider's knife,' once used for fighting at close quarters from griffin-back," said Redwing. "It once belonged to a Greencloak named Gillion. He lost it—and his life—in defending us from the dragon. In gratitude for your service to our race, and as a token of the personal friendship between us, I hereby present you with Gillion's breggiath. May it strike fear in the hearts of your enemies and hope in the hearts of your friends." Then Redwing laid the weapon in Timothy's outstretched hands.

Timothy's heart overflowed with joy. His own sword! "I will wield it well in memory of our friendship and of our trials together," he said, bowing deeply.

The king spread his wings. "I also name you 'Griffin Friend.' This title may be passed down to your children and to their children after them. You will be welcome in these halls whenever your travels take you under the shadow of our mountains."

Keeneye looped a silver tube on a gold chain around Timothy's neck. "As you know," he said, "we sorcs are a proud lot, quick to pick a fight and quicker still to finish it. We are also fiercely loyal to our friends. In time of need, blow upon this whistle, and every sorc within hearing will speed to your aid."

Timothy thanked the two griffins for their gifts. Digging through his pockets, he said, "I, too, have something for you, King Redwing." Taking out one of the golden leaves he had picked at Llanwyn's behest, he was about to say, "This is just a dried-up leaf, but—" The words died in his throat, for the leaf had turned to solid gold.

"Not even our finest metalsmiths are capable of such exquisite craftsmanship," said Redwing gravely. "However, they can fashion a chain for this leaf, which I will wear around my neck with the soros. I could not have asked for a finer memento of our shared adventures."

"And misadventures!" Timothy replied with a smile.

The Seekers stayed on with their hosts several months, resting from their journeys, mourning the old king's death and celebrating the new king's crowning. Meanwhile, autumn was stealthily ascending summer's mountain throne, whitening the heights with its icy scepter. One day, as Timothy was flying on Redwing, the frozen sky began shaking out snow-crumbs from its gray skirts.

"I fear you must leave us soon," Redwing said. "Otherwise, an early winter might make you our guests longer than you had planned. Sorcs do not care to travel in snowy weather."

Timothy affectionately scratched Redwing's head. "I would love to stay here forever," he said. In truth, he was also homesick. So many months had passed since the jail incident that he feared his parents had given him up for lost. Before he returned to Thalmos, however, he had at least one more world to visit.

Two days later, the Seekers of the Wood bade Redwing farewell, thanking him for his hospitality. Opio grumbled under his breath, "It's about time we're leaving. I couldn't stomach another pine nut." The Lucambrians wished the new king a long and blessed reign, and many offspring to fill his den with joy.

"May evil never again darken your own dens," Redwing returned. He winked at Timothy. "Since I cannot accompany you on your homeward journey, dear friend, I am sending someone in my stead." The king whistled softly, and a brown-feathered moonsorc the size of a small dog trotted into the room.

"This is Smallpaw son of Broadface," said Redwing. "His size belies his bravery. Though he is too young to bear your weight, I think you will find him a faithful friend and companion." Smallpaw sidled up to Timothy and nuzzled against him.

After provisions were brought for the two-legs' trip back to the Hallowfast, the Greencloaks climbed onto their mounts. They glanced quizzically at Timothy and Gwynneth, who stood to one side holding hands. "Aren't you coming?" Rolin asked them.

"Gwynneth and I wish to return home from another torsil world—with your permission, of course," Timothy replied.

King Rolin's mouth dropped open. "From another world? You and Gwynneth?" He glowered thunderclouds at his daughter.

"We won't be gone long. Please, Father?" Gwynneth put in.

Marlis argued, "No torsils grow this high in the Willowahs."

Grinning all over, Timothy patted his pocket. "I have a fresh batch of spasel dust!" He had hated to grind up the sap ball, seeing that it was a gift, but Gwynneth could always make another.

The king and queen exchanged worried looks. "I suppose it couldn't hurt," Marlis said. "It would save the sorcs having to send extra mounts. What is this place you wish to visit?"

"It's only a torsil's climb away from our tower," said Gwynneth with bright eyes that pleaded, *Please let us go!*

"I take it there's only enough of that spasel dust for the two of you," said Rolin dryly. When Timothy shyly nodded, the king told him, "Just be careful, then, and don't dilly-dally!"

"We will—and we won't," the pair promised. With Smallpaw perched on his shoulder, Timothy sifted half the spasel powder into Gwynneth's hand, saving the rest for himself. Then they held their fists above each other's heads, as in the Gwlân Gorge.

"Good-bye, dear ones!" said the couple.

"Until we meet again!" said the Greencloaks.

"May your wings never fail you!" cried the sorcs. Then Gwynneth and Timothy released their spasel dust. The next thing they knew, they were standing next to Gaelathane in a meadow splashed with colorful wildflowers and flitting butterflies.

"Let's see who can catch the biggest one!" Gaelathane said.

And they did.

CHAPTER 46
A Message for Baglot

On returning to the Hallowfast, Timothy and Gwynneth found the tower swept clean and most of its furnishings restored to their proper places, thanks to the faithful Lucambrians who had remained behind in the Valley of Liriassa.

After Mardoc's army had departed, Larkin and a handful of picked scouts retook the tower. Entering through Winona's tunnel and secret room, they had surprised a small garrison of men-at-arms that Gorn had left in charge of the place. After handily disarming the shiftless squatters, the Greencloaks had exiled them to a particularly desolate world and posted a guard at the torsil.

In searching the Hallowfast, Larkin and his men had also come upon Bart and Wiggin still locked in the wine cellar. Most of the oaken barrels, kegs and casks had been drained to the dregs—including some not smelling of wine that were marked with a "G."

Larkin sent the two drunken deserters back up Scarlimb with dire warnings never to return. Oddly enough, they didn't. Instead, the pair settled down in Beechtown to become solid, sober citizens, never knowing that "G" stood for "Glymmerin."

One evening, Timothy stood atop the Hallowfast admiring the fine display of autumn colors. Amidst the buttery yellows of beeches and birches, torsils flaunted their flaming reds. A sea-haze hung over the scene, smelling sharply of salt and sweet old leaves. Reminded of Beechtown's gray alders, Timothy felt a sudden pang as he sang,

In distant dreams, I walk the riverbank,
Where swaying rushes rustle, rank on rank,
Still sweetly singing 'midst the floating foam,
Of harp and hearth in hallowed, humble home.

Then he heard soft footfalls, and Gwynneth threw her arms around him from behind. "What lovely words!" she said. "I didn't know you were feeling homesick." Tears glistened in her green eyes. "If you are to return home, it must be soon. See how swiftly the torsil leaves are falling? Tarry longer, and tree-sleep will either shut you out of Thalmos or strand you there till spring. I could not bear to spend the winter here without you."

"I know," Timothy sighed. Though Baglot's taunting voice still haunted him, his heart ached for his riverside shanty. Bully or no, he had to set things right at home. Scrounging up some old clothes and a tattered cloak as a disguise, he bade Gwynneth and her family farewell and set off to climb Lightleaf.

To his great surprise and relief, Timothy found that Beechtown had all but forgotten him and the daring jail breakout. When King Mardoc had finally left in disgrace without his army or a single gilder of tribute, he had also left Mayor Bigglesworth deeply in debt. Now the fine house beside the square was for sale, and men muttered in their ale that it was high time to find another mayor.

All this Timothy learned from his mother and father, who were weak with joy at seeing him again. Timothy told them only that he had been sojourning in the land of the Greencloaks, where the king had taken him under his wing. "I've taken someone under mine, too," he added, throwing back his cloak. There sat Smallpaw on his shoulder, blinking sleepily in the lamplight.

Timothy left his speechless parents with a solemn promise that he would return in the spring. He also gave them enough golden leaves to keep them well off for a hundred springs to come.

As Timothy stepped outside, the weeping willow's dangling branches stirred with a musical sigh. However, when he pulled back the swaying green curtain, he found no one inside. "The moonlight's playing tricks on my eyes," he told himself. Still, moonbeams couldn't sing, as Scanlon had once observed.

Following the old, familiar paths back to town, he was cutting through an alley when a hulking form blocked his way. "I knew you'd come back some day, you sniveling weasel," snarled Baglot. "You nearly got me hanged! Nobody double-crosses me. Nobody!" The bully grabbed Timothy and aimed a fist at his face.

Timothy didn't flinch. Drawing himself up, he looked Baglot straight in the eye and said evenly, "The king of the Greencloaks sent me with a message for you."

Taken aback, Baglot lowered his fist. "A message? For me?"

"Yes. He thanks you for your clothes. Disguised as you, I drew Mardoc's men away so Opio and Gemmio could escape."

Baglot's face purpled and he drew back his ham-fist again. "Then you give him this message from me!" Before Baglot could deliver the blow, however, a spitting ball of talons, fur and feathers dove from the sky and exploded in the bully's face.

"Get it off me! Get it off me!" he yelled, batting at the sorc.

Timothy whistled, and Smallpaw flew into the night. Leveling his sword at Baglot's neck, Timothy growled, "Your days of bullying me are over, *churl*. Though I have forgiven you, you'd better mend your ways in this town, or I shall cleanly separate your miserable head from your miserable body. Now begone!" A stinging slap with the flat of the blade sent Baglot howling down the alley and across the square.

As Timothy sat in Lightleaf's top preparing to make passage back into Lucambra, sadness filled his heart. Both he and Beechtown had changed, and his former home no longer knew him. Though he sensed his future lay in the Land of Light, the Foamwater's call still tugged at his heart. Climbing down, he recalled his adventures in a simple song:

Looking back across the days,
I see His hand in all my ways;
From river hut to Hallowfast,
I've learned to trust His love at last.

Pursued by men with wicked swords,
I've counseled with Lucambra's lords;
I've braved the knotted hangman's noose
To set the guiltless captives loose.

Beneath the hills my paths have led,
To regions where the rocks are bred;
I've smelled a perfume sickly sweet
That lulls into a deadly sleep.

I've walked the waving prairie grass
Beneath a burnished sky of brass;
Through flames I gained the gilded wood,
And in the deepest gorge I've stood.

I've been a tree with twig and leaf,
To bring me to a sound belief
In Him Who bore the dragon's breath
To save me from a living death.

Sweet stars I trod beneath my feet—
Fair flowers burning without heat—
Bright berries rare I gathered there
When sorcs were sick beyond despair.

And in the midst I met my love,
A mortal maiden from above;
Who follows in His footsteps, too;
A kindred spirit, kind and true.

So many things I've seen and done;
Against all odds the battle won;
And all because He walks beside,
My life to lead and paths to guide.

EPILOGUE

After burying Elmar's remains beside the Hallowfast, King Rolin stashed a cache of weapons and provisions in Winona's secret chamber, in case of another siege. Otherwise, the room was rarely disturbed. Timothy shivered whenever he trod the stairs above it, and he always skipped the fourth step from the bottom.

Drawing on the entries contained in Winona's diary, Bembor son of Brenthor finished his history of Lucambra, which he titled, *The Complete Chronicles of Lucambra from its Discovery to the Present*. To the end of his days, he remained Lucambra's high chancellor.

True to his word, Derwin never again raised his axe against a living tree. After returning home by torsil, he brought his entire family to Beechtown and with Gannon's help, took up beekeeping. Midge stayed in Lucambra with Maggie, who was always delighted to give children a ride around the Hallowfast. Free at long last, Gert and the Thalmosians' other horses still roam wild over Gaelathane's Plain.

Tenderleaf the torsil survived being split in half and continued life as two tara-torsils on either side of the ravine. Longears the rabbit lived to a ripe old age in the Golden Wood with his mate and their many offspring. To his dying day, he made out that he had saved the Seekers of the Wood all by himself.

Spasel dust became such a popular means of torsil-travel that for a time, most of the spasels in Lucambra were ground up to make it. The powder eventually spawned many myths and legends about "fairy dust." In torsil-less regions, canny Greencloaks still often appear and disappear with a sprinkling of the precious powder.

Redwing became a wise and beloved king, fond of inventing such pithy sayings as, "Speak softly but sharpen your beak," "A starberry a day keeps the scorbies away," and the like. Despite a steady diet of starberries, though, he never grew another inch.

During his reign, both the moonsorcs and sunsorcs put aside their ancient feud to forge the mightiest alliance since King Threeclaws' day. Together, they rid Lucambra of its growing batwolf scourge and established new sorc colonies in the Brynnmors.

As Scanlon's assistant and the Royal Sorc-Master, Timothy daily groomed the sorcs and fed them enough starberries to keep them in sleek, sassy form. He also planted some starworts beside a secluded waterfall, where they flourished. When his duties permitted, he and Gwynneth visited their worldwalker friends in the Golden Wood. There they planted more torsils and tended the *gwag* trees, including those still occupied by greedy Thalmosians.

Best of all, a new branch of the Glymmerin sprang up where Scanlon's staff had stood, flowing into the Rondolyn and staining it crimson. Now free of the mangles, the Golden Wood and its healing waters became a haven for the heartsick and ailing.

Nowadays, the shy Wood Folk are rarely seen. However, their bolder cousins, the water nymphs and water dryads are known as "*mer*-maids" and "*mer*-men"—from the word, "memerren."

Whether in the end Timothy received a "great reward," I will leave for you to decide. To his own way of thinking, meeting Gaelathane was reward enough and more than made up for his wormsticker scars. Timothy, Gwynneth, and their relatives and friends enjoyed further adventures in other tales of the King. For as long as the earth makes its rounds of the heavens and the seasons pass over it, the King's love will continue changing lives and giving us reason to put pen to paper.

THE GOLDEN WOOD

GLOSSARY/PRONUNCIATION GUIDE

Adel'ka (pr. uh-del´-kuh). Queen Winona's Thalmosian name.

a´menthil (pr. aw´-men-thil). Tree of understanding.

Andil of the Wood. One of Gaelathane's guises.

Asper son of Stolland. Thalmosian captain who kidnaps Meghan.

Bag'lot son of Baldwyn. The brash bully of Beechtown.

Bart and Wiggin. Thalmosian deserters.

bat´tlements. Notched wall (rampart) encircling tower's top.

batwolf. Creature with wolf's body; wings and head of a bat.

Beechtown. Nearest town to King Rolin's birthplace.

Bembor son of Brenthor*. High chancellor to King Rolin.

breg´giath (pr. bray´-ghee-oth). Short sword used in aerial battles.

Broggnag the Boncath. Vulture form of starglass peddler.

Bryn´nmor Mts. (pr. brinn´-more). Lucambrian coastal range.

Canyon Cal´ydon (pr. kal´-uh-don). Home of the Golden Wood.

car´iad (pr. kar´-ee-odd). Lucambrian term of endearment. ("Dear.")

coeda´grau (pr. ko-ed-daw´-grai). Dryadic term for spasel, meaning "tree-tears."

common tongue. Trade language spoken in Thalmos.

Cottonwood Creek. Stream near Rolin's former home in Thalmos.

dais (pr. day´-us). Raised platform.

Derwin son of Stolland. Thalmosian woodcutter who originally found and befriended Meghan.

dry´ad. Tree-spirit (male). Plural: dryadin. (see Nymph.)

Dyg´gorech (pr. dig´-gor-ech). Moonsorcs' name for the Mountains of the Moon.

El´gathel (pr. el´-guh-thel). Rolin's grandfather and the former king of Lucambra.

El´mar son of Selwyn. Leader of patrol sent to help sick sorcs.

El´wyn son of Rolin*. King Rolin and Queen Marlis's son.

Emmer son of Fandol*. Father of Marlis, Scanlon and Mycena.

Fel´gor. Sorcerer (formerly "Finegold").

Flamefeather, Spearwind, Sharpclaw, Keeneye, Grayneck, Sharp-tongue, Brighteye, Starwind, Longtail, Broadwing, Blacktail, Runt. Sorcs who accompany the Seekers of the Wood on their desperate quest beyond the Willowahs.

Foamwater. Beechtown's river (Thalmos).

Forest of Fellglade. Uncharted forest northeast of Beechtown.

Forlorn Fens. Peat bogs occupying Lucambra's northern reaches.

gaol (pr. "jail."). Jail.

Gae'lathane (pr. gay'-luh-thane). King of the Trees.

Gaeles'sa (pr. gay-less'-uh). Gaelathane's home, reached only through the Tree.

Gannon son of Hemmett. Rolin's father.

Garth. Timothy's father.

Gar'wafon (pr. gar'-wuh-von). Sorc name for Gwlân Gorge river.

gil'der. Thalmosian coin, equivalent to a penny.

Glenna daughter of Girta. Rolin's aunt. (Father's sister.)

glo (pr. glow). Lucambrian word for coal.

Glym'merin (pr. glim'-mer-in). River flowing from Luralin.

gogo'niant (pr. go-go'-nee-awnt). Glory stone, a priceless gem found beneath the Willowahs.

gorks. Felgor's foot soldiers (pl. also gorku; adj. gorkin).

Gorn. General of King Mardoc's army.

Green Sea. Thalmosian body of water.

Greencloak. Thalmosian name for Lucambrian scouts.

griffling. Young griffin.

Gun'dul. Underworld; a place of darkness and death.

Gwilym son of Gallion (pr. gwi'-lum). Discoverer of the Gwlân Gorge.

Gwlân Gorge (pr. goo-lawn'). Canyon in the Golden Wood. Also "Gwilym's Gorge."

Gwyn'neth*. Rolin and Marlis's eldest daughter.

Hal'lowfast. Tower of the Tree (near the Sea of El-Marin).

hau'berk (pr. haw'-berk). A long suit or tunic of chain mail armor.

Ironwing. Griffin character (Scanlon's mount).

Janna daughter of Adelka. Rolin's mother (deceased).

Keeneye. King Whitewing's courier; member of sorcathon.

Leaf Lord. Dryadic name for Gaelathane.

Lightleaf. Torsil between Thalmos and Lucambra.

Liriassa (pr. leer-ee-oss´-suh). Hidden Lucambrian valley north of the Hallowfast.

Llan´wyn (pr. hlan´-win). Guardian of the Golden Wood.

Llwcym´raeg (pr. hloo-kum´-reig). The Lucambrian language.

Longears. Lucambrian coney who helps Seekers of the Wood.

Longlimb. Tara-torsil to vicinity of Mt. Golgunthor.

Lucam´bra (pr. loo-kam´-bruh). "Land of Light." (In Lucambrian: *Llwcymru.*)

Luralin (pr. lure´-uh-linn). Lucambrians' original (island) home.

Lyle. Torsil occupant whom Timothy frees.

Maedlan´dia (pr. med-lawn´-dee-ya). Ancient dryadic name for "the Midlands."

mangles. Tree snakes that guard the Golden Wood.

Mar´lis daughter of Emmer*. Scanlon and Mycena's sister; queen of Lucambra and wife of Rolin son of Gannon.

Med´wyn. Llanwyn's daughter.

Meghan daughter of Marlis. Rolin and Marlis's younger daughter.

mem´erren. Dryadic name for "moonsingers." (sing. "memer.")

Midge. Thalmosian stable boy.

Midlands. Region of Lucambra south of the Willowahs.

Misty River. River that flows through the Valley of Liriassa.

moonsingers. What the memerren call themselves.

moonslip. When a nymph leaves her tree by moonlight.

moonsorcs. Owlish griffins that live in the Mts. of the Moon.

moonwood. Luminescent wood infected with lunicep mushrooms.

Mountains of the Moon. Second highest Lucambrian mountain range.

Mt. Golgun´thor. The dragon's mountain.

Myce´na daughter of Emmer*. Scanlon and Marlis's sister, once carried off by yegs.

Nora. Timothy's mother.

nymph. Female memer.

Opio and Gemmio, sons of Nolan*. Advisors to King Rolin.

par´apet. Notched wall (rampart) encircling tower's top.

People of the Tree. Ancient name for Lucambrians.

pos. Dryadic term for "riddle."

Ringmaiden. Prophesied bearer of Winona's ring.

River Ron´dolyn. River that runs through the Golden Wood.

Rolin son of Gannon*. King of Lucambra.

Scanlon son of Emmer*. Rolin's chief deputy; Bembor's grandson.

Scarlimb. Torsil between Thalmos and Lucambra.

scor´bies (pr. skor´-bees). Chronic illness that afflicts griffins.

Sea of El´-marin. Lucambrian sea; location of Isle of Luralin.

Seekers of the Wood (*). Those who searched for the Golden Wood.

ser´enblod. Griffanic term for "starworts."

Sig´arth and Skog´lund, sons of Sig´wyn*. Brothers who serve as royal huntsmen in Lucambra.

Sleepyeye. Moonsorc whom Meghan helps and befriends.

sorc. Ancient name for griffin (plural: sorcs or sorca).

sorc´athel. Courtyard at top of Hallowfast.

sorc´athon. Griffin council, inc. the king and twenty-four elders.

spal´lith. A "sharing-spasel."

spasel (pr. spass´-uhl). Torsil sap ball (plural: spasels or spasla).

starberry. Fruit of the starwort plant; used medicinally.

starwort. Rare plant that bears starflowers and starberries.

sunsorc. Moonsorc term for eagle-headed griffin.

sythan-ar (pr. sigh´-thun-ar). Lucambrian word for "life tree."

tara-torsils. Trees of intra-world passage.

Tartel´lans. Mountains above Beechtown.

Tenderleaf. Torsil split in half near Mt. Golgunthor.

Thalm. Short for "Thalmosian."

Thalmos (pr. thall´-mose). Timothy's home world.

Timothy son of Garth*. Thalmosian friend of the Greencloaks.

tor´sils. Trees of passage.

Waganupa (pr. wog-un-oop´-a). Tree of Life that grew on Luralin.

White´wing. King of the griffins.

wil´ith. Griffanic word for spasel.

Wil´lowahs. Highest Lucambrian mountain range; home of sorcs.

Wind´song. Royal scribe and King Rolin's personal mount.

Wino´na. Rolin's grandmother and Elgathel's queen.

Wood Folk. The dryadin; also known as nymphs or memerren.

worldwalker. A nymph or dryad that has become mortal.

yeg. Batwolf (plural: yegs or yeggoroth; adj. yeggish).

THE GOLDEN WOOD
ORDERING INFORMATION

Readers may purchase autographed copies of *The Golden Wood* in paperback format directly from the author at:

https://www.greencloaks.com

This title is available on Amazon in softcover and Kindle formats. *The Golden Wood* is also available for other electronic devices.

OTHER TITLES BY WILLIAM D. BURT

Titles in the "King of the Trees" series (listed in order):

The King of the Trees (1), *Torsils in Time* (2)
The Golden Wood (3), *The Greenstones* (4)
The Downs (5), *Kyleah's Mirrors* (6)
The Birthing Tree (7)

Titles in the "Creation Seekers" series (listed in order):

The Lake Lights (1), *The Vikings of Loch Morar* (2)
